Planet Can I Blame This On?

Ellie Pilcher

First published in Great Britain in 2021 by Hodder Studio
An imprint of Hodder & Stoughton
An Hachette UK company

1

Copyright © Ellie Pilcher 2021

The right of Ellie Pilcher to be identified as the Author
of the Work has been asserted by her in accordance with
the Copyright, Designs and Patents Act 1988.

Interior Art: Shutterstock

A CIP catalogue record for this title is available from the British Library

Paperback ISBN 978 1 529 36372 2
eBook ISBN 978 1 529 36370 8

Typeset in Plantin Light by Hewer Text UK Ltd, Edinburgh
Printed and bound in Great Britain by Clays Ltd, Elcograf S.p.A.

Hodder & Stoughton policy is to use papers that are natural, renewable
and recyclable products and made from wood grown in sustainable
forests. The logging and manufacturing processes are expected to
conform to the environmental regulations of the country of origin.

Hodder & Stoughton Ltd
Carmelite House
50 Victoria Embankment
London EC4Y 0DZ

www.hodder-studio.com

For my Grandad. Don't worry, be happy.
I miss you. Love, Ellie Roo (Ada) x

I

Leo: Tension may help you get things done . . . Venus is in retrograde.

'Although we've come to the end of the road, still I can't let go . . .'
This really was the worst birthday playlist I had ever made. 'Please Don't Go' by KWS, 'Stay' by Shakespears Sister and 'Would I Lie to You' by Charles & Eddie. All Number Ones from the year I was born, 1992, and all the things I didn't want subliminally playing in the background while I kicked my boyfriend out of the flat.

Nearly 29 years after these songs were released, they mock me as they play through Bluetooth speakers in the kitchen. I'm not sure why it's the playlist I chose to leave on during a break-up, but I was still reeling from the revelation that my entire relationship was a sham, so I'll forgive myself.

'Apparently every relationship is an open relationship?!' I quickly added to my best friends' WhatsApp group – 'The Chamber of Secrets' – feeding them the latest from my dramatic life. They replied almost immediately.

Paige: *Seriously?!?!*
Tina: *What a douche.*
Tina: *Do you want me to set him alight.*

I snickered as the thought crossed my mind – too dark? – but I didn't reply. Instead, I turned up the volume of my birthday playlist so that it was loud enough to cover David's voice as he continued to tell me about his philosophy on open relationships – and that, apparently, we'd been in one for the last six years.

And that the photo I found on his phone is not one of a vagina but is actually a picture of a badly creased pink t-shirt.

Firstly, this would be the only pink t-shirt with a landing strip in existence. And secondly, the vagina was attached to a woman whose Tinder profile was helpfully screenshotted along with his messages below.

Ahh you look so hot!! 💦💦💦
Can't wait to see you tonight. Your place again??
Can't we go to yours? We're always going to mine.
No. My housemate's at home and doesn't like me bringing
*   back dates.* 🙄

Funny that. *I* was his housemate, and his girlfriend – nay, fiancée as of last night.

After six years of dating, he'd proposed a week before my birthday – to avoid the inevitable public proposal at my upcoming party – over a Chinese takeaway and re-runs of *The Great British Bake Off.*

Out of pure excitement, I took endless selfies of us to commemorate the moment, using his phone because it was closest to me at the time. It was a full-on photoshoot, and David humoured me by going all out with the poses and various angles, encouraging me to take more shots even after I thought we must have got a good one.

And so, the next morning before work, while he was in the toilet, I excitedly scrolled through what felt like hundreds of photos of my squinty-faced smile and triple chins, searching for the cutest image to share on Instagram to announce our #BigNews.

On and on, my search went through countless selfies from different angles in different rooms; bad lighting, acne scars, he's blinking, I'm blinking – wait – vagina was not on the photocall as far as I remembered.

He was cheating on me. And not even well. He hadn't tried to hide the screenshot of the Tinder profile and infamous vagina pic in an unimaginatively named folder like *work stuff* or *selfies*, not even after we took countless photos together which he knew I would want to search through at some point.

And I didn't need to ask for his password to his phone, it was 1-1-1-1 for Christ's sake. Anyone who spent more than five minutes with him knew that because that was about as long as he could last without opening his lock screen and aimlessly checking his phone.

Who even saves a photo of a vagina anyway? Do people actually get off on that? And who sent the photo? It must have taken a lot of effort. I couldn't get the angle right on my engagement picture, let alone manage to shoot my fanny in a flattering manner.

The group chat pinged:

Paige: *What's he saying now?*
Kris: *That Monogamy is for baby boomers.*
Paige: *Ahh …*
Paige: *Ahh that motherfucker!*
Tina: *Well …*
Paige: *Tina! Don't you dare.*
Tina: *He's a bastard for doing it without permission! But …*
Paige: *TINA!*
Tina: *Each to their own.*
Paige: *But not to Kris! And not after SIX years!*
Tina: *KICK THAT TRASH TO THE KERB WHERE IT BELONGS*

Rubbing the space between my eyes, I put the phone face-down on the sofa and thought back to when, upon seeing

David's photos, I thought it must have been a first-time mistake; innocently assuming that his nerves at finally deciding to propose had gotten the better of him in the worst way.

But no! The revelations kept coming from that moment on.

How had I not noticed he was cheating on me?

Had he *wanted* me to find out?

I was always at home, working as a freelance journalist for most of our relationship. I cooked us breakfast – badly – and made us dinner – even worse – like I was a 1950s' housewife in training; he was rarely late and never missed one without a reasonable excuse. He was out two nights a week at most, and I just assumed that that was the regular amount of *me* time he needed, and that he had planned to meet with friends – I had no idea that it was *fuck* friends he was meeting.

How could I not have suspected anything? How much had I ignored?

'I don't care, David,' I told him, as he realised I couldn't hear his excuses over the warbling sounds of Whitney Houston screaming 'I Will Always Love You'. Well no, he fucking won't, Whitney!

'And not everyone's in an open relationship!' I chastised, turning to glare at him from the sofa, as my phone buzzed frantically with new messages from the girls. 'I'm pretty sure *both parties* have to be involved for it to be classed as an *open* relationship! Otherwise, it's just . . . ajar.'

He laughed at that.

'This is not funny!' I said, in my best attempt at my mother's haughty disciplinary tone. She was never any good at it either, so I had no idea why I thought I would be.

David continued to laugh, but this time he had enough of a self-preservation instinct to try and stop himself.

'Kris, I'm sorry,' he said, for the first time. Typically, he wasn't apologising for his affairs with Tinderellas, but for laughing at my poor attempt at light humour.

'Sorry doesn't cut it,' I said definitively.

'I know.'

Did he, though? He was treating all of this like some light-hearted mistake, as if none of it mattered and it would all blow over within a few days.

This wasn't just some minor argument though.

I turned back and picked up my phone as I considered my feelings for a minute. David grew silent in the background.

As I sensed, there was a storm of messages between Paige and Tina waiting on my lock screen. I ignored them and just wrote:

Kris: *Six years of my life wasted on this shit.*

Paige: *Oh babe! They've not been wasted – you found us. We love you.*

Tina: *But not monogamously.*

Paige: *TINA?!*

Tina: *Sorry? Too soon?*

Tina: *Do you want me to make him into a meme?*

Paige: *Cancel culture is not healthy, Tina!*

Tina: *It's basically a 21st century rite of passage.*

Paige: *How would that help?!*

I shook my head, not even finding the energy to laugh at my friends' awkward attempts to humour me.

This was not how I had expected my week to go down; the proposal after years of waiting, the unexpected fanny pic and the even more unexpected confession of David not believing in monogamy!

Why did he even propose in the first place?

People who are cheating on their partners should not propose marriage. You propose at the height of your relationship, when you realise you can't live without the other person. That's why I kept bringing it up in not-so-subtle-hints for the last three years. I thought we were perfect for each other, and utterly in love. We finished each other's sentences, gave each other foot rubs and knew what to order from the takeaway whenever one of us had had a bad day. Our toothbrushes matched, and we had purchased personalised posters showcasing the day we met – it started with a swipe! – to adorn our new living room, as if it wasn't already clear how much we adored one another.

And yet, during all that time, he never got down on one knee to ask me to spend the rest of my life with him.

And when he finally did, it was under the guise of an early birthday present. He hadn't even got me anything else to commemorate my 29th birthday, just a ring.

Admittedly, a ring was all I wanted (I know, #BadFeminist, but after six years who can blame me?). I felt lucky to have David, and comfortable in our life. After spending almost a quarter of our lives together, I thought we were ready to be more than just juvenile-sounding boyfriend and girlfriend. I wanted to be husband and wife, or partners at the very least. Something more concrete and dependable.

But now a ring was up there with the worst presents I'd ever received, in between a copy of Donald Trump's book on making a deal and the butt plug David bought me for our anniversary, which he thought was a wine stopper.

> Tina: *If you kill him I'll happily get the Central Line to help you hide the body.*
> Tina: *And I wouldn't do that for just anybody.*
> Tina: *And I know how to get blood stains out of everything! Cold water and salt – who knew?!*
> Paige: *Let your inner Uma Thurman out and go crazy bitch. And if that involves an axe/an assault rifle/a poison dart/a*

> *vat of acid/starving pigs/frozen toast I'm here for you!*
> *Whatever you need.*

Kris: *Thanks. You're both real pals.*

Tina: *I'm sorry, frozen toast?!*

Paige: *That shit's real deadly when cut on the diagonal. Then cover it in Nutella, it's delicious! And the murder weapon is gone!*

Paige: *No weapon. No crime. No more cheating scum. Tasty brunch.*

Tina: *But frozen TOAST?*

Paige: *Oh don't be pedantic!*

'So . . .' David began, and I turned in my seat to look at him as he awkwardly swayed on his feet behind the sofa. 'What are we going to do?'

I swallowed and closed my eyes, surprisingly still too angry – even after Paige and Tina's Morecambe and Wise act – to so much as look at him, and also distracted by the fact that Madness' 'It Must Be Love' had just come on over the speakers. This was seriously the worst playlist I'd ever made.

I tried to channel my inner Greta Gerwig and not let it bother me, to continue appearing to be the composed and reasonable one in this scenario. While internally wanting to scream about the stupidity of the patriarchy and how unfair it was that my life was ruined, not his. I opened my eyes.

'You're going to move out.'

I looked into the open-plan kitchen in my dream London flat – which I knew I wouldn't be able to afford to rent without him.

We had only just moved in a few weeks beforehand. I'd spent the better part of July on my hands and knees building furniture until I had blisters and callouses on every part of my skin. David had built the bed – his priority of course

– and then left me to do the rest, claiming that work was particularly busy at the moment. I now knew better.

The kitchen was the last room we completed, going on a special shopping trip to TK Maxx to spend the remainder of our joint account on showy Le Creuset kitchenware and overpriced utensils.

Now, I had no savings to my name, a dream flat that I knew I would likely have to leave and no boyfriend, after six years of never being alone.

'Okay,' David said now, nodding as if my telling him to move out was just a suggestion. 'Whatever you need.'

'Whatever *I* need?' I burst out and stood up from the sofa, because even Greta Gerwig would throw her hands up at that statement! 'You're the one who's been cheating, but you're acting like I'm the one that's overreacting.'

'Well,' he began, as if to suggest that I was overreacting. I held my hand up to stop him instantly.

'No!' I shouted. 'Don't you dare put this on me like I'm the one that's done something wrong. I've only ever loved you and been there for you, and you've just completely shit on that!'

His lips curled over one another as he stifled a laugh.

'Seriously!' I yelled. 'How is this *funny?*'

'I'm sorry,' he said, a little laugh escaping him. 'I've just never seen you so angry before. It's actually quite a turn-on.'

Without thinking, I began throwing the sofa cushions at him, it was the only thing that was near at hand. They bounced off his arms, which were protecting his face and chest, and fell to the floor. Well, that was pointless. Throwing cushions is a recommended course of action during a shitty break-up, but I expected it to feel more satisfying, quite frankly.

'Get out!' I shouted, pointing to the front door. 'Leave!'

'Oh Kris, come on,' David said, stepping towards me, still struggling to suppress his laughter.

'Don't you dare.'

'Babe, I've got to at least pack.'

'Fine. Then pack.'

He looked around the room. 'I can't pack all my things tonight.'

'You don't need to! Just pack some fucking clothes and go.'

'Well, what about . . .' he looked at the kitchen and pointed to the appliances. Some of them were still in their boxes, waiting for an excuse to be used. Like I was ever going to use a pressure cooker or a bloody steamer; I could barely cook a Pot Noodle without burning it.

'You want to pack the kitchen sink?' I asked, dramatically. 'Seriously?'

'No, not the sink. The blender?'

'The blender? *I* bought the blender.'

'No,' David said, his brow creasing in surprise. 'I did. We got it from Tesco.'

'*No,*' I said, unbelievably. 'We got it from Asda, and I paid for it!'

'Oh, come on,' David slapped his hands down. 'You don't even use it.'

'I might!' I said, instantly recalling the hours I had spent scrolling Pinterest for smoothie recipes and how to make homemade soups. I had also created boards for dream wedding inspiration, my eyes glazed over with white dresses, themed cakes and pro/con lists for having photo booths at receptions.

'Really? *You* use the kitchen?'

I reached down for another sofa cushion, but there weren't any left. We should have spent the money on throw cushions, not bloody appliances.

'Oh, fuck off David! Just get out. Get out!' I reached for the next best thing to throw, a vase, and threw that at his head. My aim was so bad it completely missed him and, as the vase was made of cheap plastic, it just landed and bounced along the laminate floor noisily. The downstairs neighbour we had yet to meet began bashing on their ceiling and shouting incomprehensible profanities.

'Sorry!' David and I both shouted, looking at the floor like we had just awoken hell.

Appropriate, as that's where I felt like I was.

My anger was starting to subside to a place of deep discomfort. I so badly wanted him to just leave so that I could cry and eat copious amounts of chocolate and call the girls to bitch about what an absolute bastard he was. Or, in their case, plan his brutal murder.

But at the same time, I also wanted him to hug me and tell me how much he loved me and what a mistake he had made cheating on the best thing in his life. Not that he would ever say that.

He was never good at romance and I accepted that – I was ready to live a whole life without romance if it just had him in it. I just assumed he hadn't got around to realising how much I wanted us to be married, and to be each other's family.

But I knew that wasn't true anymore. I was just a habit he couldn't kick, an annoying clinger-on who was always planning outings to bizarre London museums – the Vagina museum was a personal favourite – and holidays to Greece. Never questioning him about his work life or why we never hung out with his mates as a couple, or why he never came up with ideas for a weekend that expanded past take-out or going to the gym.

I went to the gym for this man! That's how dedicated I was. I wore uncomfortable leggings and sweated in public, desperately holding in farts as I squatted and lifted stupid kettlebells off the floor as if it was fun.

Paige always told me that a man who thought the gym was a couples' activity was a patriarchal sadist. But Tina, the ever-polar opposite of Paige, seemed to think that it would bond us and lead to inevitable sweaty, beach body sex. It may have led to that for David, but not with me.

'Every time I look at you, all I can think about is you with another woman. It's like every memory I have of us being together has another person in it, because I don't know what you were doing before or after you were with me. I used to trust you,' I told him, not looking at him as I scrunched my eyes together, desperately hoping to hold in the tears that were seriously burning my irises. 'I can't trust you anymore.'

'Babe,' he said softly, and I felt his hands on my shoulders. I immediately shoved them off.

'Please get out,' I repeated, unable to hold in the angry tears any longer. A painful lump rose in my throat and threatened to choke me.

For once, though, it appeared as if David had listened. I heard him walk slowly to the bedroom and pull down the suitcase from the top of the wardrobe. Technically, it was also *my* suitcase, as we only owned the one. He was going to leave me with *our* suitcase.

Kris: *He's finally leaving.*
Tina: *Oh babe.*
Paige: *Do you want us to come round?*
Tina: *I've got Pimm's!*
Paige: *And I've got grown-up alcohol.*

Did I want them round, though? I knew it was pathetic to drink alone and gorge on chocolate, but in all honestly, I couldn't face another few hours of dissecting disgusting Tinder messages and David's infidelity.

I let the tears spill now, turning my energy towards keeping my lips together to avoid sobbing overzealously. Once I had been told I cried like Elle Woods in *Legally Blonde*, all fat tears and noisy gasps; a completely pathetic spectacle. It wasn't exactly the last image I wanted David to see of me after hours of trying to hold it together.

We had spent all morning in the flat talking about this, or rather him talking about it, while I sat texting the girls on the sofa, barely able to keep up with his nonsensical ramblings on natural urges that aren't fulfillable in a monogamous relationship.

I didn't even interrupt to point out that open relationships literally depend on open communication, and secretly cheating on me is not what an open relationship is.

It was only after he rambled on for over an hour that I asked him why he had never told me any of this before; a question he danced around like an oily politician, never giving an answer but acting as if he had.

I had called in sick to my new job in order to deal with the revelations of his extra-curricular sex life, unable to face going into the office without confronting David first.

The editor at *Craze*, the magazine I had just started working at, likely thought I was the flakiest employee he had ever hired. I had gone from passionate – or slightly annoying – in my first week, to a no-show in my second. But I knew that there was no way I would be able to go into work and act as if everything was fine.

I couldn't be the woman who cried at the office because her fiancée was playing away in my *second week!* That was at least a two-month privilege; a bit like doing a shit in the toilet or coming in fifteen minutes late in order to have got a seat on the tube.

Kris: *I'm good.*

I texted the girls quickly.

Kris: *Just want to get into bed and sleep the rest of the day away. I'll deal with it all tomorrow.*

Paige: *Are you sure?*

Kris: *Let's meet up tomorrow instead. Just can't tonight.*

Paige: *Okay lovey.*

Tina: *No worries. I'll send you a surprise Deliveroo tonight though.*

Paige: *It's hardly a surprise if you just told her about it . . .*

Tina: *What I order will be the surprise.*

Paige: *Still not a surprise.*

I put my phone down on the coffee table and put it on silent, leaving the girls to have their petty discussions on their lonesome. A surprise Deliveroo, however not much of a surprise, would still be nice. Particularly as it was unlikely I would be able to afford take-out for a while.

'Do you want me to leave the hangers?' David shouted from the bedroom.

I sighed loudly. For fuck's sake, no wonder he kept stringing me along for years – the bastard couldn't even pack on his own.

'I'll do it,' I said, shaking my head and walking zombie-like to the bedroom to take his clothes and pack them for him. He wouldn't remember to pack pyjamas or socks otherwise, and the last thing I needed was for him to come knocking unannounced in the next few days just to fetch a manky t-shirt that he'd had since university or a pair of thermals for the gym.

I shoved him out of the way with my hip, still refusing to look at him as I focused my attention solely on getting his plain black and white tees off the hangers and all of his ripped jeans into the open suitcase on the bed.

For a moment there was nothing but the sound of sliding hangers to fill the silence between us, much like forks on ceramic plates. We had reached the awkward stand-off in a break-up, where if either one of us were to say something, it would end with either instantly regrettable break-up sex or – more likely – a screaming match.

Knowing my luck, I would get pregnant during the break-up sex, á la my mum and dad. So that was a definite *must-not-happen* on my list.

Silence broken up by the sound of sliding hangers was all that I could allow at that moment. For the first time, and also the last, David respected that choice and said nothing.

That was the true end of the relationship right there. David had finally shown me respect.

Everything had changed, and as Felix's 'Don't You Want Me' played from the kitchen, I accepted that he had never truly wanted me at all.

2

I woke up, alone, at 7.48 am. This was 48 minutes after I would usually wake up since I had left my phone and consequently my alarm on the coffee table overnight. I could hear it faintly beeping from the other room, sat beside two pizza boxes filled with leftover crusts and pineapple chunks. Tina knew me well but had clearly forgotten that when I'm eating my feelings, I don't want to eat anything even vaguely healthy. And that includes pineapple chunks on pizza.

'Oh shit!' I shouted to no one, as I rolled out of the safety of my duvet cocoon to get dressed.

So much for taking another personal day off work. It was only my second week at *Craze* and David had done enough to screw up my life as it was. He wasn't going to cause me to screw up my dream job as well.

I raced to squeeze into yesterday's cigarette trousers, still lying on the floor, not even bothering to change my underwear. Fuck it, no one would know, it's not like anyone would be getting into them anytime soon. I hooked on a bra that I had flung over a radiator and found a stripy Breton top that was always fashionable in an office setting.

My blitz to the bathroom was just that. I crouched over the toilet seat peeing away yesterday's alcohol content – you can't have a surprise takeaway without a bottle of Merlot to wash it down with – at the same time as brushing my teeth and spitting out the foaming toothpaste into the sink. My non-existent skincare routine would have to wait until I got my life back in order, and my make-up set was portable, thankfully, so I could deal with that on the train.

Grabbing my phone, which was still screeching like a toddler in the background of a Zoom call, I ran for the door, pulling my summer coat and handbag with me.

'I'll see you toni—' I stopped myself in my tracks. Who exactly was I shouting goodbye to? I was alone.

Shutting my eyes for half a second, I released a breath I didn't know I was holding in and slammed my thumb on the 'STOP' button on my phone to silence the alarm.

My instincts were telling me to drop everything in my overloaded hands and curl up on the floor. But I was a stubborn bitch when I wanted to be, and a break-up was not going to trigger a melodramatic breakdown.

I opened my eyes and quickly shuffled the items around in my hands; at this rate I would leave the flat looking like a shambolic version of Villanelle from *Killing Eve*. I twisted the lock and left.

But not before catching my coat in the lock and having to re-open the door to release it.

It was going to be one of those days, I just knew it.

★ ★ ★

There is a special art to putting on your make-up on the tube. One I have not yet mastered.

By the time I reached Bank station, my eyeliner on my left eye was winged, even though it was not my initial intention. I had no choice but to match the other eye in precisely the same manner, as I'd forgotten the sacred rule of always bring-ing portable make-up wipes.

Using only the crowded window opposite me as a mirror I dangerously attempted to draw on a perfectly shaped wing.

Faces turned in my direction from all along the carriage, as the train jolted from side to side. Women winced on my behalf, while men tried not to laugh at my pointless concentration.

This was it, I realised. This was the city's rock bottom.

Not only was I hungover, newly single and broke, I was also the pitiful commuter of London fables we're all told about by the commuting elite. If any poets were on that train they would be sure to write a depressing verse inspired by that moment, probably entitled something obnoxious like 'The End' or 'A Testament to Failed Feminism'.

I gave up on the winged eyeliner with a 'fuck it' huff, after I began to draw over my eyebrow and started to resemble a badger. I'm a proud Hufflepuff but there are limits.

Shoving my make-up pouch to the bottom of my bucket bag, I theorised that it was only two more stops until I needed to get off, and then I could pop into a Pret A Manger and grab an over-priced but much needed pastry and coffee in order to qualify for the code to their customer toilets so that I could put myself together.

I knew I wasn't looking great, but I didn't realise quite how bad the situation was until the over-smiley Pret server gave me my coffee on the house. They're only allowed to do that once a day, and this guy had decided that I was the most-in-need-customer just two hours after the café had opened. Nevertheless, I was thankful for it. I used the last of my change on the pain au chocolat and ate it depressingly while sat atop the closed toilet seat of the bathroom.

Upon wiping off the winged eyeliner with water-clogged toilet roll I took a few deep breaths and tried to centre myself before I walked into work and absolutely killed it, just as I had promised my boss that I would on my first day.

I was definitely not in 'killing it' mode, or even any kind of mode besides pretty depressed. But work was nothing but habit and muscle memory, and the distraction would help me get through the day a lot better than binging on chocolate and horror movies.

The *Craze* office was only a few buildings down from Pret (though this is not exactly an anomaly in London since every office building is a few seconds away from a Pret). The magazine sub-let a floor in a 16-tiered building along with other press and advertising firms.

Feeling a little more in control now that I was in the clean and professional setting of the lobby, I asked the lift coordinator – a genuine job in the city – to call for a lift to floor 15.

'Lift C.' She told me, smiling and disinfecting her hands in between each button press.

I returned her smile and walked obediently to my lift.

Glancing at my watch I realised I had made good time, despite over-sleeping. The managers and superior staff would have been flocking in from their morning meetings and impressive, pretentious spin classes, leaving me plenty of time to blend in with the other assistants without anyone noticing I was late.

'Krystal,' a clipped voice said behind me. I turned and froze at the sight of my boss, the Editorial Director.

'Andy,' I said, forcing an embarrassed smile, and really hoping the dodgy lighting in the Pret toilet hadn't stopped me from getting all of the eyeliner off of my face. 'Going up?'

Of course he was, we were on the ground floor.

He nodded and stared ahead at the reflective lift doors. 'I hope you're feeling better?'

I said yes, and smiled again, feeling the blush of my cheeks as I wondered whether or not to fake a cough orconjure up a sneeze.

'Would you mind dropping into my office when you get upstairs?' he asked. I opened my mouth to say yes again, but nothing came out.

He didn't believe I was sick. He knew I was a pathetic liar. I was going to have to explain to my boss that I had taken a random sick day on a Thursday to have it out with my fiancée of 12 hours about his theory on monogamy.

Andy tilted his head slightly, waiting for my response, but still nothing came out.

'Give it ten minutes,' he said. 'See you up there.' He swiftly stepped into Lift C, along with a few other workers who had been waiting behind us. One held his hand against the door to keep it open for me.

'You getting in love?' he asked after a moment's pause.

'I forgot something.' I said, not moving as he retracted his hand slowly, unsure if he should or not. The doors began to close and I didn't move. Andy, pushed against the mirrored back wall of the lift, glanced at his phone, which I could see wasn't even turned on since there was no light reflection in the mirror.

'Fuck,' I whispered to myself, as the door finally closed. Only for it to immediately re-open mid 'uck'. The lift co-ordinator had called the same floor for me.

'Lift C for floor 15,' she called out from her station, gesturing her ridiculously clean hands for me to get in.

'Oh, right,' I said, awkwardly hopping in and pressing myself against the hoard of men who looked across at each other as if to ask: 'is this woman losing the plot?'

Yes, gentlemen, I was.

The next ten minutes of my life passed by ridiculously slowly. The office was much quieter than I was expecting, but then again, it was Friday. I assumed most assistants and execs had taken the day off for a long weekend to enjoy the height of summer in the city.

No one was hanging out in the kitchen, idly flipping through last month's edition of the magazine or topping up their espresso cups with the battery acid the office machine poured out. Even the ever-bustling production department was quiet, with only a few people sitting at their desks, knee-deep in a design hole or on a call to the local distribution centre about the latest timetable screw-up.

As I was walking past the editorial section to my cubicle, I noticed the dwindling numbers of staff were staring at me. I rubbed my face subconsciously, worried that I had a giant mark of foundation on my neck or that I was still parading the black-eye effect. But I couldn't tell what it was exactly that kept their eyes glued on me.

I casually sat down at my cubicle, exhaling as I convinced myself that the glances were purely my imagination playing tricks on me. Instead, I focused on turning on my computer and going about my regular routine of gently spraying water on my bonsai plant – his name was Keith – and opening my fancy leather notebook to write my to-do list for the day.

But I couldn't log on to the server. Just my luck, another typical unlucky post-break up omen.

I blew out my lips and decided to wait until after my meeting with Andy before calling IT and asking them to sort it. The last thing I needed was to be late chatting with the Editorial Director as I was being put through to Kelsey in IT, who was notoriously slow at doing anything – including answering her phone.

Kris: *Well today is going shit so far.*

I texted the girls on WhatsApp; not that I was expecting a reply from either of them at 9 am.

Tina was a primary school teacher, and while on her summer holiday at that point, she was doing summer school teaching at an all-girls private school in Richmond for a little extra cash on the side. As she put it, living in London is expensive generally, but particularly during the summer when you have nothing to do but spend money you don't have.

Paige, on the other hand, was the literal mic drop of the female workforce. She was a legal representative for the London Chanel office. She was the badass woman you went to when you had to check to see if it was okay to hire an actress for a TV commercial who once had a drug problem or call the next Chanel product *Bibliothèque* or some other fancy French word.

Not only did she get to go to A-list meetings and decide whether or not these people were hired, she would also get tickets to Paris Fashion Week and access to clothing lines months in advance.

How we were all friends when none of us moved in the same circles was a shock to everyone.

Tina kind of inherited me after we went to university together and I ended up shit-faced at her dorm room during Freshers' Week. I legitimately don't remember how we met, but the next morning she made a good breakfast and started to mother me, so I knew I'd found a good thing.

I discovered Paige when writing a freelance profile piece on her for *Vanity Fair* and fangirled about her so much in the article that she phoned me up to ask me out for a drink. I didn't realise at the time that she had asked me out on a date, but as soon as I did, I overreacted so much in her presence – there was a definite spit-take of surprise – that she said:

'Darling, darling. Calm down. We can just be friends.'

I was so enamoured with her confidence and waspish kindness that there was no awkwardness about the moment at all. We ended up getting so drunk on cocktails – regaling each other with anecdotes about our lives – that we found ourselves sat in Kings Cross station with kebabs until security kicked us out at 2 am. The rest is history.

Tina and Paige were not compatible as friends, but they were mine, and as such they were each other's. They accepted it happily enough, although not without competitive sarcasm.

Got a meeting with the big boss now. Wish me luck. I wrote to them, hoping that by sending the message into the void I would receive a helping hand from the universe. I needed all the luck I could get.

Andy's door was slightly ajar when I knocked. He immediately called out.

'Come in.'

Andy was sat behind his desk with his chair turned towards the wall, and was just closing his laptop when I realised a woman was standing next to him. I'd only met her once, when I'd gone up to HR to hand in my signed contract.

'Krystal, you remember Keira?'

I nodded and gulped audibly.

'Keira will be sitting in with us for this meeting.'

'Okay,' I said, my mouth going dry as I fell into the nearest seat.

'You okay?' Andy asked, seeming genuinely concerned. I nodded, a little too hard and my neck twinged painfully. 'Right, well I won't beat about the bush. This isn't going to be the best meeting, I'm afraid.'

The universe hated me.

'You would have found this out yesterday, but of course you were off sick. I really do hope you're feeling better?'

I 'mm-hmm'd and prayed that he would just cut to the chase.

'So, yesterday we announced that *Craze* is shutting its doors.'

'What?' I asked suddenly, leaning forwards in shock.

It wasn't just me being fired, it was everyone.

'Yes, it's a surprise to all. What's not a surprise is the declining print sales across the entire industry. We're certainly not alone in this sort of situation. However, *Craze* is being absorbed by another magazine within the global company, but sadly *Craze* is no longer . . . well, *Craze*. And, as such, we have to make some tough decisions regarding staffing.'

Suddenly the staggeringly low numbers of staff and all the staring made sense.

'Oh,' was all I managed before Keira jumped in.

'The magazine that *Craze* is being absorbed by already has a full editorial staff, so I'm afraid your role is now moot. As such, we have to renege on our contract with you and let you go.'

Let me go. What a nice way of saying you're unemployed.

On top of being single and broke I was *really* broke, and completely unemployed.

Keira was still talking, talking me through pay in lieu of notice and my probationary period. I got the basic gist: I was to pack up Keith the bonsai and leave the office before lunch, I would be paid one month's salary, and that was it.

I hadn't even finished training yet and I was gone, and there was nothing I could do about it.

*   *   *

Kris: *I just got made redundant.*

Kris: *I'm sat on the pavement with a bonsai and there's chewing gum on my arse.*

Kris: *Could this day get any worse?*

Kris: . . .

Kris: *Someone just dropped their falafel box on me.*

Kris: *There is hummus on my trousers where one should never have hummus.*

Kris: *Who has falafel this early in the morning??*

Kris: *I think I might walk into traffic.*

Paige: *I've booked an uber and table at your nearest pub. Go inside, there will be two Bloody Mary's waiting. Drink both and order two more. I'll be 20 minutes.*

3

'Is it even legal to be made redundant after two weeks?' Tina asked, pouring me a glass of red wine only to hand me the bottle upon looking up at my tear-stained face.

'Technically yes, but it's a fucking shitty situation.' Paige counselled calmly from the other side of the sofa. She felt it best to call in reinforcements in the shape of Tina and expensive wine, after finding me slumped over the sticky pub table unable to control my loud racking sobs at 10 am. Paige had called her assistant and told her to cancel all of her meetings – she was powerful enough to do that – and then shoved me into a taxi and took me home.

I had spent the best part of the day half-sleeping, half-wailing in my bed.

'I never thought I'd be *this* person.' I said croakily, my throat overused from sobbing. The wine was helping sooth it, though. 'I haven't cried this much since Heath Ledger died.'

Tina placed her hand on her heart and took a moment for this.

'Well,' Paige said, 'luckily for you, you have a kickass lawyer for a best friend who can counsel you on the legal shit in this shitty situation.'

'*And ...*' Tina pointed out, not wanting to be left out of the love fest. 'A wonderfully kind best friend who gives good cuddles and understands the qualities of a good Cabernet.' She chinked her glass against my bottle.

'Thanks guys,' I mumbled, tears still streaming down my face. I had no self-control anymore and I was past the point of caring to wipe my face. Tina wrapped her arm around my shoulders and pulled me into her fuzzy warmth. Her bright pink poncho was shedding fake feathers all over my new sofa, but it was worth it for the softness of the hug.

Both Tina and Paige were being extra sweet and less snarky with each other to make me feel better, but even with all their kindness and excellent alcoholic beverage choices I couldn't stop acting the 'woe is me' part and complaining about having to start over again and again.

'Well, you're nearly 29, it's bound to happen,' Tina said sagely.

'You can start over at any age,' Paige pointed out, not that she had ever had to. I should know, I wrote her perfectly linear profile piece.

'But specifically at 29, it's in the stars,' Tina retorted, getting excited at the prospect of knowing something that Paige didn't. 'It's called the Saturn Return.'

'The Saturn what?' Paige asked, exchanging a blank look with me.

'When Saturn returns to the position it was in when you were born,' Tina said, as if this was obvious. 'It takes 29 years, give or take. And it marks the beginning of the next stage of your life. In most cases adulthood, and then middle age and finally as an elder,' she explained Saturn's power as if we should all have been taught this in Year Six along with basic fractions and compound sentences.

'I've never heard of a Saturn Return before,' I told her, interested but not convinced by her starry-eyed concept of life.

'Honestly, it explains *everything*.' She reached into her pocket and pulled out her phone. 'Look, I have this horoscope app and it's really specific.'

'Oh God, here we go,' Paige muttered and I elbowed her gently in the ribs as she reached for her glass of wine.

'I know it's a bit hocus pocus and shit, but honestly, half the time it's right!'

'A broken clock is right two times a day,' Paige pointed out in a sing-song voice to tease Tina who merely rolled her eyes at her.

'Oh, come on, you've got to admit that this seems a lot like a Saturn Return moment.'

'I still don't really get it,' I told Tina, who had started to flick through the pages on her app to show me something.

'Look, read this.' She pointed to a brief paragraph in her 'star chart' that read:

Saturn is the last planet we can see with the naked eye. Before telescopes were invented, it was once believed to be the final planet. Therefore, Saturn was thought to be the holder of our system – the slowest, furthest planet away from the earth – and dictated the full completion of a period of life. It takes roughly 29.5 years – dependent on your birth chart – to return to its position at your birth, marking a transition period in life and often a rude awakening.

'See! It fits,' Tina shouted excitedly. You would have thought that she had just solved the entire world's problems with an app.

'It's also a load of mumbo jumbo. How can planets and stars affect our everyday lives? It's nonsense,' Paige argued. 'Every newspaper and magazine has a horoscope or some sort of astrology thing in it, and each one of them is different, so which one is right? The fact that there are so many different horoscopes proves that it's a load of shit.'

'That's because you're closed-minded. Everything is open to interpretation,' Tina argued, forgetting that I was in the middle of them, the ever-unfortunate piggy in the playground.

'Okay, *Mystic Meg*.' Paige held up her hands to Tina's face and I felt before I saw the frustration begin to rise in Tina.

I stood up to bring the attention back to me.

'Before we start blaming the stars for everything and deciding whether or not I'm a good Leo, or whatever, I really need your help dealing with all of this.' I motioned to the flat and empty bottles of wine in wide arm gestures.

Tina softened immediately and slinked back to her corner of the sofa, while Paige's sympathetic smile returned as she carefully placed her glass back on its coaster. You can tell a lot from a person instinctively using a coaster without being asked.

'Good plan. Well, to start off with, have you heard anything from—'

'He-who-must-not-be-named!' Tina shouted, refusing to allow David's energy to permeate our girls' night in. I laughed softly at her insistence, and both of them brightened to see me pull an expression other than dramatic woe. It only lasted a second before the tears began to flow again.

'I don't even miss him right now,' I told them honestly.

'Good,' Paige said. 'He's not worth missing. We just need to figure out how to get his stuff over to him without you ever having to see his pig of a face again. I can organise it so that his things gets put into storage, and then I'll send him the bill so you don't even have to pay a penny.'

'What about all of the things we bought together?'

'Oh no, don't worry about that. You tell me what you want to keep, and I'll make sure you keep it. Let him try and mess with me.' I loved that Paige was a lawyer.

'I definitely want to keep the blender,' I told her. 'The bastard is convinced he bought it, and he didn't. I did. I refuse to let him have it.'

'That's it!' Tina said, 'Get angry. Show him who's boss. You should also keep the sofa. Sofas are really expensive.'

I nodded. 'He can have the bed. I don't want anything I shared intimately with him. And God knows who else he shared it with. Oh no – what if he shared the sofa with someone too?!'

Tina and Paige both rose up immediately, as another racking, high-pitched sob came out of my throat before I could stop it. Soon their arms were around me, and therefore each other, and the comforting smell of Tina's sandalwood perfume and Paige's Clinique – because Chanel didn't own her – brought me back to the safety of feeling loved.

I was loved and I was still capable of love, too. I just needed to get through a crappy day and all would be well again. Even if it was technically a start-over of my whole life.

Paige brushed a piece of my greasy hair off my face and handed me the last clean tissue in the living room.

'Here, we got you,' she reassured me.

'I can help you find an affordable sofa,' Tina promised me, before hesitating a little. 'How do you feel about seventies' fabrics?' I snorted into her shoulder and she gripped me a little closer.

'One of your hopeful upcycle projects?' I asked. This time she snorted.

'Ha! Like I've upcycled anything in my life. I just like the idea of it, I'm too busy to actually do it. And besides, three housemates and a fourth-floor flat makes it kinda hard to bring in new furniture.'

'Well, if you want my sofa,' I told her, now unable to think of it as coming with me. Not to mention the likelihood that I would have to move into a flatshare, therefore making my own sofa less of a requirement.

'You could sell it,' Tina suggested.

'Be sure not to get any wine on it then,' Paige snarked.

'Please, like I would waste a drop of this,' Tina scoffed.

'We don't have to think about all of that today,' Paige pointed out, releasing me from our hug to fetch the bottle of wine again, like I was a baby in need of comfort food. 'Just a few bits and bobs.'

'Like your party!' Tina gasped, looking at Paige who she had been working with begrudgingly to plan the event. 'You can't cancel your party.'

'Yes, we can,' Paige reminded her, stressing that it was the two of them who had organised the small get together of my old friends so they could therefore unorganise it.

'Fine,' Tina grunted. 'But you're not staying here on your birthday. Even if we're not going to do the full-on Gatsby party and bring the house down at Rosé the Bar, we are still going out.'

'I don't know—' I began.

'Nope, Mystic Meg's right.' Paige shrugged. 'We're still going out. You can't stay in on your birthday. Not like this. That's just depressing.'

'Wow!' Tina shouted gleefully, causing Paige to roll her eyes this time. 'I just can't believe she agreed with me.'

'Don't get used to it.' Paige smirked, chinking her empty glass against Tina's.

'Fine, but make it something small,' I told them. 'And I can't afford drinks out in a club so let's make sure to pre-drink.'

'I'll bring the brie, you bring the prosecco,' Tina suggested to Paige, who nodded. 'When did pre-drinks get so civilised?' Tina teased, releasing me from her death grip of a bear hug and heading for the mint green turntable I had treated myself to as a birthday present the year before. It's true what they say, music sounds so much better on vinyl.

'Remember at uni when we used to play *Whores vs Sluts?* And we had to do drinking challenges against the other dorms before we could even leave campus to get to the nightclub.'

'Oh Christ!' I gagged at the thought. 'That spitting game we had to do. When we had to dribble the drink into other people's mouths . . .' I gagged again.

'Urgh! And then the losing team captain had to drink the other team's spit-drink.' Tina put the needle on the well-loved Spice Girls' *Greatest Hits*.

'Spice Up Your Life' began to blare throughout the tiny turntable speakers. Tina turned up the volume so that it was impossible to hear Paige's berating of our old university habits over the music. Apparently, the University of St Andrews had been much more civilised. (They had once had royalty in residence, so that was a given, really).

I topped up the girls' drinks from my wine bottle as the 'La la la's ramped up from the speakers and the three of us began reciting the famous lyrics to each other.

'Ahhhh . . .' The jumping and 'rou-ou-ound' dance moves kicked in and suddenly we were jumping and screaming 'La la la' at the top of our lungs, competing with one another as well as the turntable to be the loudest in the room. We were spilling red wine over the Wayfair rug I was yet to pay off, and the sofa I had definitely rejected despite Tina's prom-ises. But I didn't care. There's something about screaming Spice Girls' lyrics when drunk and emotionally wrung out that is better than therapy.

For a moment everything was okay again. Sure, I was single, drunk, practically penniless and more than a little stressed, but I had two amazing friends and some auton-omy over my life still. I just needed to get through the next few days and I would bounce back. I knew I could do that. I smiled and danced on the spot.

'Ahhhh . . .' all of three us screamed into each other's faces before we slammed our hips together and jumped in unison – only for a pipe to burst above us and the emergency sprinkler system to go off throughout the entire apartment.

4

Leo: You may be in a frenzy trying to figure out where to move next ...Venus conjoins with Pluto.

'I don't know what happened ...' I told my landlady, as we stood, shoes ruined, in an inch of water in my now sodden living room, equipped with umbrellas. While my neighbour and apparent handyman tried to switch off the sprinkler system.

'It's on a different line!' he shouted over the noise of the rushing water like a mechanic on the *Titanic*.

'And the pipe just fell through?' The landlady ignored him and shouted to me. I held up my hands to make it clear that I had no idea. One minute the girls and I were dancing – or, as far as my landlady knew, I was eating dinner alone – and the next the pipe had suddenly collapsed through the ceiling, spilling its contents all over the kitchen and living room furniture just moments before the sprinklers kicked in.

'No warning, nothing. Not even a groan or a–a–a *bang*.' The alcohol was definitely going to my head right now. It's a lot to harder to have a serious conversation with your landlady when you've got a buzz and so feel like everything's fine – you'll just swim to your bedroom tonight rather than walk. That clearly wasn't going to happen, though.

'Hugo!' she suddenly said, pushing back her grey fringe from her forehead.

'Who who–go?' I slurred.

'Hugo. My stupid idiot of a cousin. He talked me into letting him do the plumbing when I was renovating. I should have listened to Julie Andrews: nepotism belongs in the arts not in plumbing.' I was impressed that my somewhat elderly and stodgy landlady had seen *The Princess Diaries 2* in order to make that reference, but before I could comment she was wading through my living room to speak to the handyman who had just about got the sprinkler system to subside to a dribble rather than a spray.

Something inside me told me not to start re-enacting the scene with Gene Kelly in 'Singin' in the Rain' but I was mighty tempted I've got to admit.

'Well?' my landlady asked the handyman, who was wearing a pair of mucky overalls over pyjamas with Marvel characters on. He was no a spring chicken either.

'Completely rusted through,' he said. 'Must have been a used pipe. Not soldered properly and definitely not union-approved. Problem is, it's unlikely to be the only one he used. I can't tell but I'd say you'd have to take the whole lot down and replace the entire system.'

The landlady sighed and groaned into her hands.

'And how much is that gonna cost me?'

The handyman shrugged. 'I just do sinks and boilers. You'll need to get a proper quote for the work. But in terms of time, it will take a good few weeks to get the work done. Not to mention the drying and clearing out of all this mess.'

He referred to my lovingly decorated flat and for a moment I was insulted. But then I remembered that what was once aesthetically pleasing decor was now just a selection of bath toys.

'Jesus,' my landlady said, her head in one hand.

'So, what am *I* meant to do?' I asked, peering over the sodden sofa to remind her of my presence.

'Erm ... well,' she began, and released a large exhalation as she looked around. 'I have building insurance so I can pay for the damages and reimburse you on the costs of your furniture, if you can send across that information. And, of course, your tenancy agreement is defunct so long as this place is inhabitable.'

'So I'm homeless.'

She didn't say anything to that, but she didn't need too.

'I have a spare room at my place if you need it tonight?' the handyman, whose name I had yet to ascertain, offered. But it wasn't necessary as I knew I could I crash at one of the girls. Unbeknownst to my landlady and neighbour, Paige and Tina were upstairs on the garden roof still drinking and wringing themselves out while I dealt with this. Paige, ever the lawyer even when drunk, thought it would make me look at fault if it the three of us appeared drunk when a pipe burst, so she and Tina had decided to hide instead.

I brushed off my neighbour's offer and completed the last of what handover I could with my landlady before I took to my damp bedroom in order to pack a suitcase of whatever undamaged goods I could find. Only to remember that David had taken my suitcase. At which point I left and headed to the roof to confer with the girls.

I was still too buzzed to really take in that I was, as of that moment, completely homeless, unemployed and still newly single. After the day I'd had, it now just seemed like another inevitable disaster, and I moved straight from 'freak out' to vague acceptance.

* * *

Upon finding my way up to the roof I stopped in the doorway at the top of the staircase, mostly because I was out of breath from climbing – I really should have made more of an effort at the gym. I stared out of the small wire-framed window in the fire door.

Paige and Tina were sitting on a concrete block, which

seemed to lack any purpose up here, laughing . I smiled at the picture, not having seen them enjoy each other's company before when they were alone together. More often than not they bickered and barked. Sometimes I thought that they only got on for my sake, and that made me incredibly grateful to the both of them. I didn't have the aptitude to manage two close separate friendships. I was like a musketeer, all for one and one for all.

I kicked open the door and laughed as the two of them jumped and split apart as if lightening had struck.

'What's the verdict?' Paige asked immediately, and I explained everything.

'At least one good thing has come out of this,' Tina said a few minutes later, as we sat together on the block and she passed me the bottle of wine she had managed to rescue from the wreckage of the flat.

'Oh yeah, what's that?' I asked, guzzling the last of its contents.

'His shit's been destroyed as well.'

'Hear hear!' Paige proffered, giggling to herself. Drunk Paige was always very giggly.

I sat in the middle of the two of them and Paige rested her head on my shoulder. Tina leant forwards to look over the side of the building to the deserted street below.

I had no idea what time it was, but it had got dark, and the distant city was lit up like a Christmas scene. The restless noises of sirens and car horns were melodic to the three of us as we sat and ignored all of my problems for a minute. We were just three women in London, drunk on a Friday night. Nothing more and nothing less.

I inhaled deeply and looked up at the stars, suddenly remembering what Tina had said about Saturn returning.

'Which one is Saturn?' I asked, squinting to see if what I thought were stars twinkling in the sky were actually stars or just a few planes.

Tina looked up as well, only to immediately flop forwards again, as the blood rushed to her head and she had to put her head between her knees to steady herself. Paige snorted in amusement but kept her head firmly on my shoulder.

'You can come and stay at mine,' she offered, with a small yawn.

I was glad that she suggested it, rather than making me ask. I was never very good at asking for things. I had theorised in my head that either I would have to ask to stay at Paige's one-bedroom flat in Dalston for a few days or return to St Albans and move back in with my mum and grandad, ten years after I'd moved out. I loved my mum and grandad, but three generations under one roof was difficult at the best of times. Add on my monthly PMS, Grandad's arthritis and mum's menopause and it would become a house of horrors within a matter of weeks.

'Would you mind?' I asked.

'Of course not. It'll be fun,' Paige said, snuggling into my neck as the tired portion of her drunken state set in. 'I'll sort out a service that can come and collect your things from here as well. David can sort out his own.'

'The prick,' Tina added darkly, her head still between her knees. I stroked her back. The least I could do was show them both some appreciation after the girls had come to my aid on what had to be the shittiest day of my life.

The alcohol was definitely helping me stay calm in the current situation. Not my typical reaction to a Friday night drink, but my emotions were all over the place and I had no idea what I needed to feel right now. I could imagine the characters of *Inside Out* in my head pressing countless buttons in panic mode as I went through grief, anger, sadness, panic, happiness, relief and love in a matter of seconds throughout the night.

'Could my life get any worse right now?' I laughed wryly.

'I'm telling you,' Tina said, slowly. 'It's all down to your Saturn Return. You need to appease the planets.'

Paige sighed heavily. 'Oh, what a load of bollocks. You can't *please* a planet. It's like trying to please my Korean mother. Impossible.'

'Oh, baby,' Tina said, sitting up and leaning over to pat Paige on the leg. Paige only ever got self-conscious about her family's opinion of her when she was drunk. The rest of the time she refused to give two shits, as she shouldn't.

'How does one *appease* a planet?' I asked.

'Recycle your plastics,' Paige mumbled sardonically.

'And when would it kick in?' I asked over her. 'After a cycle of the Sun? After my next period? After my next disastrous life choice?'

'It's not your life choices that have made this disaster,' Tina said ethereally. 'Our lives are laid out in the stars from the moment we're born. Honestly, I've looked at my birth chart. I'm practically a shaman.'

'So the stars are to blame for my shithole of a life right now.'

'Pretty much,' Tina nodded; Paige groaned. 'And planets are just stars. Just not blown up yet.'

'If we keep talking about this shit, I might turn this planet into a star,' Paige mumbled before breaking out into giggles again. Tina started laughing with her, leaning over me to take Paige's hand. All the while, I continued to look up at the pitch black sky and distant lights, staring at the planets that were supposedly responsible for ruining my life purely because I hadn't realised that there was already a plan in place.

Well, if that's the way the game was to be played, I was taking up my mantle as Player 1.

'Appease the planets,' I repeated. All I had to do was take a leaf out of their book and follow their rules. Maybe that wasn't such a bad idea. I mean, what else did I have to lose?

5

Paige had definitely chosen her sofa for style reasons over lumber support. While it was gorgeous and expensive-looking, with its blue velvet cover and designer throw cushions, it did not make the most comfortable of beds.

After three nights of sleeping on it, I was pretty sure I was going to need a chiropractor.

I had spent the better part of three days cycling through the six stages of grief – despair, denial, chocolate, shouting at romance movies, staring at the ceiling and, finally, deleting social media.

What was the point of having profiles online if I had nothing boastful to share; and I didn't need obnoxious 'on this day' reminders of the times that David and I spent on holiday or 'how well do you know your partner' quizzes online. Besides, what did it matter that I knew that his favourite Power Ranger was Yellow or that he used to have a bearded dragon called Phil. These quizzes would only be useful when they started to ask important questions like '*monogamy, thoughts?*'

Every time Paige left me in the flat she said goodbye like she was leaving the side of my deathbed. I couldn't believe I was suddenly so fragile.

Feeling as deflated as ever, I stared at the ceiling. It was popcorn-textured and white; about the only thing remaining in Paige's otherwise modern flat to indicate there had been previous tenants.

The popcorn bubbles looked a bit like constellations in their random spacing on the ceiling. I spotted an Orion's belt and a Cassiopeia crown in the time I stared at it.

'Saturn,' I said aloud, remembering what Tina had said about my Saturn Return.

There was no harm in looking it up, I thought, reaching for my phone to Google the term.

'Add in your birth date, time of birth and location,' I read aloud, as I found an online programme that could create your astrological birth chart for free and tell you more about your personality and Saturn Return date.

With nothing to lose I added in the information. I knew my birth story well enough, as my mother was keen on telling it to me as a child. I didn't get fairy tales and happy endings at bedtime, my mum much preferred honest, real-life (to the point of scarring) stories to *Cinderella*.

'24th July 1992,' I said aloud, as I typed it into the required boxes. 'St Albans, at noon.' I swear my mother's greatest pride wasn't in giving birth to *me*, it was the fact that I fell out of her – she was standing up at the time, as she had just decided to leave the hospital since she no longer wanted to give birth – at precisely 12 pm. The bells of St Alban's Cathedral could be heard tolling as I gave my first cry. It's a very memorable entrance to the world.

Immediately, my Saturn Return date appeared before me: 6th February 2022.

That gave me roughly seven months before the next period of my life began.

I scrolled down the page to read more about my birth chart and my Saturn Return.

'*Your Saturn Return is, in its essence, a test to prove that you have learned from the challenges over the last 29 years of your life.'* Well, great.

Not only do we get put through SATs, GCSEs, A Levels, apprenticeships, bachelor's degrees and God knows what else, we also get tested by the stars about our accomplishments in life.

Well, the stars picked the wrong person to give a pop quiz.

I continued to scroll down the page, reading more about astrological birth charts, houses and my Sun, Moon and rising signs. The page was incredibly detailed and went on for an age, so much so I realised that my phone battery was beginning to die before I had even completed reading about the effects of different planets in different houses.

It was hard to take in all of the information, but I just wanted to understand why this was happening to me and why the planets supposedly had an effect on my life.

As I scrolled nearer the bottom of a page there was an ad:

Local course on astrological charting.Want to learn more about your star signs and what the future holds for you? Join today. £59.99 for a twelve-week course at Dalston Community Centre.

Aha! The planets had devised a new test for me. Well, the planets should have done their research because I was a class queen. A boffin of epic proportions at school, I loved nothing more than doing research and learning new things. Although I really wish I had done my research in more detail before dating David for so long, as the learnings there were a bit more than your standard, 'I've never seen *Pulp Fiction* and I don't like watching box sets.'

I hovered over the button, momentarily concerned that it might be a spam bot about to infect my phone with a virus, but I quickly pushed that thought aside as I had something to prove to the planets that were fucking around with my life.

Clicking through, I came to the Dalston Community Centre website. Right at the top, under Astrology, was the class that the ad was talking about. Every Thursday at 6 pm, run by Aoife McQueen, all ages welcome regardless of experience or knowledge. A one-hour weekly course on astrology, for 12 weeks. At £59.99 in total, that was only £5 per class, and that's cheap by London standards.

Before I could truly consider it properly, I added the class to my basket and selected the date I would join – the following Thursday – and clicked on the PayPal icon. I was about to use up the last of my overdraft funds, but I couldn't supress the thought that, somehow, this ad was fate.

And fuck it, the refund on my sofa would cover this class ten times over when it came through, even though it was water damaged and had a red wine stain on it when I left.

Of course, the moment I processed the payment and got the confirmation email in my inbox, a little voice of regret sounded in my head, reminding me that it wasn't fate that led me to that ad; it was targeted advertising that had tracked my phone to Dalston and seen that I was on an astrological website. Technically, it was Big Brother stealing the little remains of my overdraft, not fate, intervening with my life choices.

I silenced the voice in my mind, put my phone on charge and headed to the bathroom, avoiding all mirrors as I entered lest I gave myself a face-to-face telling off for being fiscally reckless. Who knew if I would even be in London in 12 weeks' time? Or if I'd even *enjoy* the class?

I jumped in the shower, washed off all the tears, alcohol-induced sweat and body odour that came with cocooning and got dressed for the day ahead. It may not have been the day that Paige had planned for me – she had left a list of phone calls I needed to make and insurance documents I needed to fill out – but I had a plan, and for once I was going to listen to my gut and go for it.

★ ★ ★

'What's all this?' Paige asked upon returning home from work with two take-out bags of sushi and a six-pack of beer. Paige was not one for cooking, ever.

'All what?' I asked, without looking up from where I was sat – cross-legged on the floor of her living room surrounded by books about astrology and planetary movements that I'd borrowed from the library.

'Are you studying?' she asked, dropping the bags in the kitchen and taking the beer to the fridge.

'Sort of. I'm trying to learn more about this Saturn Return thing that Tina told us about.'

'Saturn Return? You're taking that seriously?' she asked, unable to hide the scepticism in her voice.

'Yeah. Turns out my astrological birth chart is spookily accurate.'

'Birth chart?' she repeated. 'I'm confused. What?'

I reached for the reporter's notepad I was using to make notes on everything.

'So, my *Sun* sign is in Leo – which is what people often call your *star* sign.' I held up my fingers in air quotes to point out that *star* sign is a misnomer. 'Technically, there are actually three signs that are really important. The Sun sign is most commonly known, as it's the sign your Sun was in during the month you were born. In my case, late-July to late-August, so my Sun sign is a Leo. Then, there's your Moon sign, and this is the position of the Moon on the day and place of your birth. So, for me, my Moon sign is Taurus. And finally, there's your ascendant sign, or your rising sign, which you discover by looking at the time of your birth. For me, I was born at noon, and that means my ascendant sign is in Libra.'

Paige had frozen entirely. A 100% confused-looking statue.

'It's easier when you write it down,' I told her, pointing to the little diagram I'd doodled on my reporter's notepad.

'Why are you researching this?' Paige asked, smiling awkwardly at me.

'It was just something that Tina said, about how I need to appease the planets.'

'That's just a load of starry-eyed bollocks,' Paige laughed. 'It's not real.'

I think she was hoping that I would laugh along and explain that this was all a practical joke made up to freak her out. But it wasn't. The more I learned about my birth chart and the positions of the planets when I was born, the more it all seemed to be plausible.

'Just look at this.'

I cleared my throat and turned over the page of my notepad to read the description of my personality based on my birth chart.

'As a Leo, I'm outgoing, loyal, genial and determined. I have an active social calendar, I live life to the full, love to entertain and be the centre of attention. I have a strong sense of humour, vivid opinions and I appreciate luxury. I respect hard work and I'm willing to shoulder responsibility. But I'm also afraid of people knowing how hard I try. I'm a people pleaser; I tell people what I think they want to hear and I can be controlling, demanding and a bit of drama queen. Plus, I often struggle to admit my mistakes.'

I laughed and dropped the pad in my lap.

'Tell me that doesn't sound like me.' In my opinion it was basically my biography.

'It sounds like a lot of people I know,' Paige said, still sceptical as she began to fetch some plates and bamboo chopsticks for us to eat dinner.

'Oh, come on, I couldn't have written a better description of my personality. It even has details about my love life, my working life and health. Like, I'm a bit high maintenance when it comes to love, but I'm really loyal and tender. And with work, it says I'm resourceful and organised, opportunistic and a solo practitioner.'

'Speaking of jobs, did you have a look at any of those websites I suggested?' Paige asked coolly as she shovelled sashimi and nigirizushi onto our plates.

I rolled my eyes at my her with a smile. 'Thanks for the reminder, *Mum*,' I said.

'I'm only saying. You're going to have to replenish your bank balance at some point. Insurance on your flat can take ages to come in. You'll have to do something in the meantime.'

'And I will. I'll drop my contacts a note about freelancing again tomorrow. But this is something that I need to distract me right now,' I said, gesturing enthusiastically to the wide selection of books and notes that I had organised around me.

'Aha,' Paige said, reaching into her pocket to get out her phone. She began to dial someone.

'Who are you calling?' I asked, wondering if she thought I had snapped completely and was calling the men in white jackets to take me away.

'Hey!' A familiar happy and bright voice came from the other end of the line. Paige smiled warmly at her phone screen and turned to face me. I saw Tina smiling back from the video call.

'What does this look like to you?' Paige asked her, pointing the phone towards me with one hand and using the chopsticks to pick up a piece of sashimi with the other.

'Oh God. Is that *study* Krystal?'

'What?' I asked in a slightly affronted tone, surprised to hear that Tina had a name for this persona of mine.

'Oh God,' she grimaced. 'It's worse than we thought. We need to get you out love. Sooner rather than later.'

'Right?' Paige interjected with her mouth full.

'We're already going out for my birthday on Saturday.' I reminded the both of them. 'Pre-drinks then a bar.'

'Nope, this calls for something bigger than that,' Tina said, slightly recoiling from the sight of me sitting cross-legged with a load of books around me. I couldn't have looked that bad – at least I'd showered and changed into a rescued stripy tennis dress. I looked passably human for the first time in days.

'Club night?' Paige suggested. 'I can get us into that new club in Soho.'

'Ooh!' Tina shouted gleefully down the line. Paige smiled again.

'Fine!' I shouted, holding up my hands in defeat. We'll go clubbing, but I don't know how you expect me to pay—'

'Oh, for god's sake, it's your birthday. We'll treat you,' Paige said defiantly, as if this wasn't already obvious. I felt bad for just accepting this generosity, just as I had the rent-free flat and the food she was constantly bringing in.

'You guys spoil me,' I told them, blushing slightly.

'Well, with the way your life is falling to bits, you need it,' Tina said candidly. Both Paige and I pulled the same 'really' expression at her. 'What? Too soon?' she said.

After hanging up, Paige gestured for me to come and get some food before she ate it all.

'Seriously though, thanks for covering me at the minute,' I told her, awkwardly stabbing my nigirizushi with the chopsticks. Paige shrugged.

'No worries. But you do need to get a job,' she poked me with the clean end of her chopstick teasingly.

'I know,' I grumbled. 'I'll look into it tonight.'

'Either that or you'll have to ask the cards for help,' she sniggered, before heading to the fridge to get each of us a beer.

'Sure, because *cards* are going to hold the answers to life's problems,' I scoffed, catching the relieved look Paige was giving me.

6

Leo: You may feel a great deal of nervous energy today ...
The Moon trines Uranus.

On Thursday evening I headed out to my first astrology charting class at the local community centre. As far as Paige knew, I was going to work in a café on some freelance pitches while she did her regular Thursday night flat clean. I was beginning to learn that Paige was a stickler for routine, and though I had thrown a spanner in the works by moving in and dumping what little of my belongings I still had in her living room, she still needed to stick to a semblance of her regular at-home-life to function.

I had spent the better part of the week sitting at her breakfast bar on my (thankfully) undamaged laptop, sending out pitches and alerts to editors I'd previously worked for to tell them that I was available for freelance pieces. Some replied straight away asking me what had happened at *Craze*, while others already knew about its absorption and offered their condolences. But no one offered me any work.

There were hardly any in-house roles going in the industry as far as I could tell. I saw a job alert for a copywriter at a landscape magazine (my only knowledge of landscaping came from trimming my lady garden) and another for a part-time social coordinator for a cruise ship company (I was terrified of the ocean, paranoid that everything in it wanted to kill me, so this didn't seem the best fit, either). And, as desperate as I was, I wasn't *that* desperate ... yet.

I decided to focus on pitching ideas to magazines I loved and knew well, so as to have the best chance of actually getting commissioned. As much as I knew I could write articles on CBD oil, or how *Buffy the Vampire Slayer* content hasn't aged well, I would much prefer to write op-eds on the true expense of living in London, both the metaphorical and fiscal, or insightful pieces on the importance of web design for multi-hyphenate entrepreneurs. I was a serious journalist, goddamit!

Although it was July, I knew print magazines would be dying for some upcoming Christmas content, and so I began to look up gift ideas. I put together pitches for gift guides and eco-friendly activities that fit with the zeitgeist of the millennial mood. The other topic I surprisingly started to pitch about was astrology. After all, if I managed to get an article published based on my research so far, then everything I was doing counted as work, and that meant Paige could stop rolling her eyes at every mention of my Saturn Return.

As soon as Paige went to work and left me to my own devices, I was back to researching my birth chart and the different houses that planets can move into. I was still wrapping my head around all of it, but I hoped that the class at the community centre would straighten it all out for me.

Unanticipated excitement was bubbling over, and I was shaking as I packed up my notes full of astrological queries, and even my favourite astrology book from the library, *All in the Stars* by Zolar, as a classroom reference point. My behaviour was reminiscent of days at school when I rushed to get homework finished early, just to have the pleasure of handing it in at the beginning of class so that I could receive a look of delight on my teacher's face. I was the epitome of a teacher's pet, and in *all* of my classes. A somewhat dumb pet (a Boxer dog over a Golden Retriever, but still).

According to my research on the workshop leader, there was nothing newsworthy about Aoife McQueen. She had no book credits to her name, or a website. On the Dalston Community Centre site it simply said she was a long-term believer and professional astrologer with various educational credits to her name. If you can get a degree in Beckhamology – the study of David Beckham and his family – then you can also get one in astrology it seemed. This was good to know, as I was just reaching the point where I started to wonder whether I should re-enrol in university to get another useless degree; it appeared that my BA in Communications wasn't the best at preparing me for a secure career (or communicating in general, if my relationship with David was anything to go by).

I followed my Google Maps app religiously as I went in search of the community centre; turning left onto Englefield Road and then up De Beauvoir Road, past Beavertown park – as it was known by locals – and finally onto the street where the centre was meant to be. But, as far as I could tell, it didn't appear to be there.

'Oh, come on.' I said, staring up and down the near empty street in search of an old, greying building with water stains dripping down its sides – my interpretation of a community centre – or at least for some sort of sign indicating a nearby local hub. But there was nothing.

I returned to my phone, ignoring Google's irritating automated voice telling me that I had *reached my destination*. Unless the community centre was hovering above me like the Tardis, it didn't seem to exist.

With a large sigh, I decided to walk a little further up the road in case the app was premature in announcing my arrival, staring intently at the little arrow like it might suddenly realise its error and jump to another place entirely.

'Oomph!' My head collided with a man's chin.

'Ow!' He exclaimed, as I stumbled backwards, almost keeling over.

'Oh my God. I'm so sorry,' I said, throwing my hand out to balance myself and almost toppling off the side of the pavement. The man, with one hand rubbing his stubbly chin, grabbed me with his other hand and pulled me back onto the side.

'Shit!' I shouted in his face.

'Steady,' he said, still gripping my cardigan sleeve as I worked to catch my balance as any normal human could (and not act like a drunk penguin).

'Oh Christ. I'm so sorry,' I repeated, closing my eyes as I felt the burning sensation of my cheeks flooding with colour. 'I wasn't looking where I was going.'

'That much was obvious,' the guy said, although not rudely. He sounded amused, and Irish. My ears instinctively pricked up when I heard the Irish lilt. It practically became a rule of nature after *Normal People* aired on BBC that an Irish accent will turn you on – man or woman alike.

'Sorry.' Was that all I could say? 'I was looking for the community centre, but the map . . .' I thrust my phone up into his face, almost bashing him again. 'Sorry!' I repeated. 'And sorry for saying sorry so much. I can't seem to stop.'

He was laughing, but didn't say anything. Wasn't that just great. I had lost the ability to converse properly with men on top of everything else.

'I guess I'll go this way,' I pointed to the road behind him. 'And stop having a stupidity fit in front of you. Bye!' I sidestepped him, too embarrassed to try to apologise further or attempt a lame joke about how I was geographically awkward at the best of times, and not just because of his Irish accent. Or his very cute face, which I only registered was cute after I began to move away.

'Wait!' he called, and I stopped to face him immediately. Yep, I wasn't wrong, he was cute. Short stubble, well-managed brown hair, cheek bones you could grate cheese on. Exactly my type. Although I would have to verify his opinion on monogamy before deciding that for certain. 'The community centre is this way.' He pointed in the opposite direction. 'I'm heading there now if you want me to show you.'

'Great,' I said, not moving. He smiled briefly, and began to walk. I followed him, like an aged dog, two steps behind him, all the while giving myself strict messages not to look at his butt.

We do not objectify men, Krystal. I told myself. I glanced up at his jeans. *Okay, maybe a little bit is okay.*

He stopped suddenly.

'Do you want to walk along with me me? I feel a little odd being followed! I'm not a murderer, if that's what you're worried about.'

'That's exactly what a murderer would say.' I pointed out, although it didn't stop me from hopping forwards like a child to join him. Could I *get* any more awkward? I was nearly 30! Surely I should be able to walk up a street with a complete stranger and make small talk. But I hadn't had to for years – that was one of the pleasures of nearly always going out with either a friend or a boyfriend. I was out of practice when it came to instinctive socialising.

That's no excuse, I heard my irritating inner voice tell me – she had the voice of Dame Mary Berry and was very hard to ignore sometimes – *it's basic communication, and you have a degree in it for god's sake. Girl up!*

'So why are you headed to the community centre?' I found myself asking him.

'Art class. You?'

'Are you sure we're heading in the right direction?' I asked, ignoring his question as I checked my Google Maps again.

He scoffed lightly. 'Yes. I've been there lots of times.'

'It's just that it says that it's back there.' I pointed behind us.

'There used to be a hall there, about 20 years ago. Maybe it's still tracking to that one.'

'Is Google Maps even 20 years old?' I asked.

'Nope,' he said, his voice a little sharp but still with that edge of amusement. I had enough sense to pocket my phone then. 'Why are you headed to the centre?' he asked again.

And I replied. 'I'm joining an astrology class.'

Immediately he began to laugh – lightly, but still, he was laughing at me.

'What? Why is that funny?'

'Did you lose a bet or something?'

'No,' I said sternly, not taking my eyes off his face as he continued to smile. 'Why, is there something *wrong* with astrology?'

'Besides the fact that it's a bunch of hooey?'

'That's your opinion,' I returned, looking away from his symmetrically handsome face towards the end of the road. There did seem to be a large white building appearing out of nowhere after all. So, he wasn't lying about the community centre, at least, which probably meant he wasn't lying about being a murderer either. But he *was* a bit of an arse for laughing at a stranger's desire to take an astrology class.

'Maybe ask the stars next time you need to get somewhere. Might work better than Google Maps.'

'Oh wow. Do you laugh at everyone you give directions to?' I snapped, my temper still on edge what with everything going on in my life.

'Pretty much.'

God, he was an infuriating stranger. What is it with men?! And yes, *all* men. I had reached the stage of my break-up where all men truly seemed to suck, regardless of what Nora

Ephron and Phoebe Waller-Bridge communicated via their various movies and TV shows. Men are arseholes. Irish accents or not.

'Well, good to know. I think I can find my way well enough from here.'

'Enjoy your class,' he said, as I headed off, picking up my pace and rushing for the large double doors with *Dalston Community Centre* written above them in Comic Sans. I denied the urge to give the guy the finger as I opened them.

What an absolute arse. First, I bump into him – and *he* didn't see me either so it could very well have been just as much his fault as it was mine – and then he has a go at me for not walking beside him, only to laugh at my choice of class?! Where did he get off behaving like such a righteous prick?

I was fuming audibly as I made my way through the maze of corridors inside the building, following sellotaped paper signs that read *Astrology Class 6 pm* until I reached another set of double doors with an *Astrology Class in session* sign, and knocked.

'Come in!' a voice rang out.

I was feeling so irritated that I didn't even have a chance to get nervy about going into a class that had already begun to introduce myself. Heading inside, there wasn't actually much to be nervous about. There were only four others in the large hall and all of them were ladies above a certain age.

'Hello,' a smiling woman with long grey hair in a pair of linen dungarees said from her seat. She was leaning forwards on a jet-black walking stick, and from her position at the front of the room, I guessed she was Aoife.

'Hi,' I said, exhaling softly. Already this felt like a safe place, even if the hall did smell a bit like a PE class. 'I'm Krystal – I've signed up for the astrology class.'

'Welcome Krystal,' Aoife said, rising from her chair with difficulty. Clearly, she needed to use her walking stick to manoeuvre herself, but she still walked over to me incredibly quickly once she stood up and offered me her hand. 'Come and join us. We've only just started, and we never stick to much of a schedule anyway.'

'We were just discussing our ascendant signs,' one of the older women said, pulling out a chair for me to sit beside her.

All three of the women were very well-made up with perfectly coiffed hair, and each of them wore a similar shade of pink lipstick and an almost matching M&S outfit. Kind of like a bridge club gathering in an American movie. Aoife stuck out a little bit with her youthful clothing and clear, cosmetic-free face, but she had an ethereal glow about her that reminded me a lot of Helen Mirren. Or maybe I was just projecting.

'The ascendant sign is one of three core signs that make up our person,' Aoife said, helpfully.

'The others being your Sun and Moon sign,' the woman on the end of the table said, quickly followed by the last woman who sat in the middle who added: 'But it can also be referred to as a rising sign.'

'There,' Aoife said with a smile. She returned to her seat with a groan and what looked like a painful set of movements. 'You're all caught up on what you've missed so far,' she said.

I laughed lightly, grateful for being so quickly accepted without even having to do a 'hi, my name is' routine.

'Thanks,' I breathed out, dropping my bag onto the floor and placing my notepad and pen on the table. 'I've been reading up on the signs already.'

'Fabulous, so you'll already know what each of your signs are?' Aoife said softly.

'Yes,' I paused to find the page in my notebook where I had written it down. 'My Sun sign is Leo, my Moon sign is Taurus and my ascendant sign is in Libra.'

'Quite a mix.' Aoife smiled at me. 'I would say that you must be a determined and confident young lady, but you're prone to insecurity and need balance.' Aoife described me as if it were a question, but the way her voice lilted – another Irish descendent in the vicinity it seemed – it sounded more like a confident appraisal.

'Pretty much,' I agreed, smiling towards the three other women who seemed incredibly impressed by Aoife and her knowledge of star signs.

'I'm a Libra,' the woman in the middle offered. 'I'm Millie.' She didn't offer her hand to me, mostly because she was too busy leaning across the table to a plate of digestive biscuits and helping herself.

'I'm Zelda,' the woman next to me said shaking my hand this time. 'Aries.'

'And I'm Jane. Sagittarius,' the smallest woman from the end of the table waved at me.

'And Aoife is a Taurus,' Millie said, her jaw nearly concreted together with the amount of biscuits she was chewing at once.

'Oh Millie,' Zelda said, rolling her eyes affectionately. 'Can't take her anywhere,' she whispered playfully. I smiled at them all.

Already I could tell that this was going to be a fun evening out, if a little musty. There was something about learning a new skill in the presence of strangers – particularly older strangers – that was comforting after so much unsteady change.

The lesson was great! Aoife wasn't preachy or stringent about paying attention and taking notes. Mostly, we all conversed about our various Sun signs and what each of them meant, using some print-outs that Aoife laid out on the table in front of us.

Mine pretty much spouted off the information that I had already surmised from my days of Googling and note-taking, but it was comforting to hear about the traits I recognised so well in myself narrated by a woman who didn't once question whether or not astrology was a load of 'hooey', as the Irishman had so narrow-mindedly described, or a waste of time, as Paige seemed to think. It made sense to me and reassured me that maybe I wasn't the culprit behind every bad thing happening in my life. It wasn't just me who had a part to play – the planets and stars did, too.

After everything that had happened over the last few weeks, it felt like a weight had been lifted discovering that maybe I wasn't 100% to blame for my disastrous life right now. As much as I felt the cynic in me try to remind my conscious self that I had no idea about the condition of the pipes in my flat or the financial state of *Craze*, something in my core refused to let me lay the blame anywhere but myself. I should have done due diligence on my job before taking the role, and I should have looked at the pipes myself before signing the contract.

It wasn't until I discovered that the stars had a plan for me all along, and that these events were all in the cards due to my Saturn Return, that suddenly I felt a little less responsible. And it was a relief.

I couldn't say that I was 100% sure all of the information that Aoife spoke about resonated with me; the ability to predict the future from the stars, or how many babies or marriages a person would have depending on the position of the planets at their birth. If that were true, then surely everyone would be following their birth charts. But I couldn't fight the thought that the stars' placement in the sky at the time of your birth had to have some sort of power over your personality. Or at least the random things that occur throughout our lifetimes. There had to be *some* sort of order in the universe, right? It couldn't all be down to chance.

This was the idea that I couldn't get out of my head as I returned to Paige's that evening. When I got in, she was already in her bedroom seemingly getting an early night (really she was probably working on one last email while simultaneously using a vibrator to help her relax after a long day's work). She had had no qualms in telling me that this was her favourite way of winding down from the day. Fair dos to her.

I, however, chose to immediately plug into my evening Spotify playlist and start working on a new project – a blog.

If I couldn't get paid to write for someone at the moment, I was going to work on my profile-building, starting with a new portfolio of posts on astrology and my Saturn Return. I thought I couldn't be the only person living through Saturn's chaos at this stage in my life – maybe this blog could be a lifeline to those like me. I could be the Dalai Lama of Saturn Returns, a mystic guide to help others (without the desire for hefty library loans) navigate life's complexities.

Also, I wanted to document this journey and see if what Tina and Aoife had said about my Saturn Return was true. As much as I wanted to believe that by appeasing the stars and following their rules I could live a happier life, with fewer David-sized mistakes, I needed evidence in the form of a highly documented journey to confirm it.

Since all of my research into astrology was all I wanted to talk about right now, but no one was picking up on my pitches since I didn't have a professional background in it, it seemed prudent to prove that I did know what I was on about. I wanted to show that there was a commercial space in journalism for more astrological stories, and I was the perfect journalist to be commissioned to write insightful pieces for the masses.

This was going to be a win-win-win situation, I decided. I would beat the planets at their own ethereal plan, sort out my life *and* kick-start my career all in one.

I christened the website ZodiActually and found myself writing until 3 am.

I am a writer, albeit a writer without a job. I write about things I want to know more about. And right now, that's the stars and their power over my life. Do exploding gases billions of miles away really get a say in my life and how I live it? If I follow their rules, will they make all my dreams come true? Is this what it truly means to make a wish upon a star? I don't know yet. But I'm going to find out.

7

*Leo: Intense emotions are apt to dominate the scene today . . .
Pluto resides in Aries.*

'The mirror can't help you anymore!' Paige shouted, banging on the door of the bathroom. Tina was getting ready for our night out, but she'd been in there nearly an hour. 'How much time does it take to shower off a day of work?'

'We were gluing macaroni and glitter all day!' Tina shouted back, already slightly tipsy on the bottle of wine she had pretty much downed when she arrived at Paige's flat.

She had wished me a happy birthday with a hug that was more like a wrestling move, since she'd practically fallen on top of me under the weight of her giant rucksack (which held not only her laptop and eveningwear, but also every school-book a child had ever written in, it seemed).

Thank God it's Friday didn't apply to teachers, even during summer school, since they appeared to take their work – and maybe a few of the kids, based on the weight of Tina's bag – home with them.

'I hate children. They hike up my water bill,' Paige muttered as she returned to answering emails on her ever-present laptop on the breakfast bar.

She had spent the day working from home to be with me, treating me to birthday pancakes – the only thing she could cook like a professional – in the morning, and then the pleasure of her company for the rest of the day. She had bought me a whole new outfit as a gift (and by bought, I quickly realised she meant stole from the various closets in her office building). It was an extremely flattering gift; it made me feel stellar hot on my first night out since the break-up.

I was in the process of lacing up the over-complicated, gorgeous boots she had given me from the safety of the sofa when I asked her, 'Don't you ever want kids?'

She scoffed so loudly at my question that I jumped and almost undid all of the lattice work around my calf.

'Uh, no. I'd think I'd rather shit in my hands and clap.'

I laughed, as she carried on explaining: 'They're all alien little bastards with no tact and no taste. They just want to talk about poo and constantly ask *why* like it makes them more interesting.' She crumpled her face and thought for a moment. 'Basically, a tinier version of Tina.'

'Oi!' Tina banged the bathroom door. 'I heard that.'

Paige smiled slyly and winked at me.

'They're much taller than her anyway,' I pointed out; Tina's nickname was unimaginatively Tiny Tina as she was barely five foot two in heels.

'I heard that too!' Tina bellowed.

'If you can listen into our conversation from in there, you can bloody well get out here,' Paige returned, and almost at once the bathroom door opened with a wannabe-dramatic slam, and Tina appeared in her 'out-out' outfit. School-teacher Tina was gone, and 'I-can't-wait-to-get-wasted-Tina' emerged. The difference was startling and involved a heavy amount of Jean Paul Gautier perfume and Claudia Winkleman eyeliner.

'Come on then. Chop-chop. Aren't you guys ready yet?' she asked, picking up her clutch from the table and heading for the door.

Paige and I exchanged looks and rolled our eyes as we began to gather the last of our going out gear.

While Paige and Tina sniped lightly at one another from the front door, I went to pick up my phone. Remembering the promise to myself, and the three readers that had so far discovered ZodiActually online, I opened my horoscope app. It was the same one that Tina used and had shown me on my birthday, therefore the one I chose to adopt as my chosen horoscope to follow.

It held a lot of useful information for the day, from do and don'ts to quotes to live by. There was also an indication of the kinds of people I'd work best with on that day – today I would work well with those who were born under water signs i.e. Cancer, Scorpio or Pisces – but best of all, it had a one-line daily horoscope to live by:

Simple pleasures hold the greatest satisfaction for you today. Keep close to home and enjoy some quiet time in self-reflection.

Not quite conducive to going out on the town with the girls for a night of pure drunken rioting. But it's not every day a girl turns 29, and I would be lying if I said I wasn't looking forward to the small break in the monotony of pitching, writing and moaning about life.

I turned off my phone and dropped it into the matching clutch Tina had kindly contributed to my ensemble and headed out with an energetic *whoop whoop*.

* * *

Paige had got us into the hottest new club in Soho called The Bronze. Inside, it was immaculately clean, and decorated like we were in the Opéra district of Paris. Nothing like the Slug and Lettuce I was used to in St Albans. There was an ornate chandelier above a circular, never-ending bar in the centre of the room, which was already crowded.

'Bloody hell,' Tina exclaimed, gaping open-mouthed at the extravagant iridescent decor and ambience of the place.

'Is this a club, or are we here to see *Phantom of the Opera*?'

'Don't be silly,' Paige said, as she opened a tab at the bar with a simple swipe of her card at the bartender. 'We would be here to see *The Marriage of Figaro* at the very least.'

Tina and I silently exclaimed, *Oh my God*, to each other as Paige continued to boss the bartender about like her own personal pageboy.

'What have you ordered?' I asked her, the noise of the club beginning to rise as more and more people entered. They weren't playing typical club music or anything that we recognised. Instead, the invisible DJ had selected a type of energetic lift music. It felt less like being in a nightclub and more like being at a mini rave in Selfridges.

'The house special. Supposedly it rehydrates you as you get drunk, or some shit.'

'Is that even possible?' Tina asked, leaning onto the bar as a group of men in suits barged past her without request or apology. '*Charmant!*' she screamed at them, then to us: 'I gave a French class today.'

'Oh, *tres bien.*' I replied.

'*Merci.*'

'*Et voila!*' Paige exclaimed, with an elaborate display of hand gestures at the drinks she had just been served. 'The house special.' They each had a carrot stick in them.

I twirled the stick aroundmy green, smoothie-consistency drink to be sure, but it was definitely a carrot.

'I've had a celery stick in a drink before, and an olive, even an onion,' Tina said. 'But not a carrot.' She lifted the stick out of the goop and stared at it suspiciously. She didn't try to lick the green concoction dripping off it, and I agreed with that decision.

Paige shrugged off our disdain, ever the calm one. 'It's probably just a point of difference. They're trying to be unique.'

'It's not very appetising,' I told her, still a little unsure as to whether I was supposed to drink the green stuff or spoon it into a toddler's mouth.

'Well, here goes nothing. Happy birthday Krystal!' Paige sung to me.

'Happy birthday Krystal!' Tina joined in enthusiastically, and we all gathered our glasses in front of us to cheers.

In mutual support, we each took a gulp of the drink. Instantly, Tina turned the colour of the drink and I was about a nanosecond away from spitting it out on the nearest patron's fishtail plait.

'Oh my God, that's awful.' Paige muttered, eyes wide in horror. 'I can't think what could be worse than that.'

'Trump?' I offered, still gagging on my pitiful mouthful.

'Worse.'

'Thrush?' Tina joined in.

'Worse.'

'Trump giving you thrush?'

'Oh God.' Paige put her glass back on the bar with a heaviness that seemed to reverberate around the entire surface. 'Bartender!' she screeched.

'Wow,' I didn't know what else to say, but I had to keep air flowing into my mouth to keep the rancid taste at bay. 'Whatever vegetables they used were definitely off.'

'It's like putrefied tequila vomit and rotten avocados mixed into a glass,' Tina said, still scowling. 'With a hint of cinnamon.'

Like Paige, we returned our glasses to the bar. If that was the house special, we were pretty sure we were not going to get any other decent cocktails to our taste out of The Bronze that night. Paige closed the tab as quickly as she opened it and refused to pay for the alcohol ,but she did leave the bartender a flirtatious tip to let us go quietly.

'World of Pop?' Tina suggested, calling us an Uber.

'God yes.' Paige said. 'I hate poncy places.'

Tina and I exchanged brief sarcastic glances. Neither of us wanted to remind Paige that she had selected the venue; she would ultimately turn the argument around so that we all ended up agreeing that it was in fact our fault entirely.

'World of Pop it is,' I agreed.

*   *   *

If The Bronze was poncy, then World of Pop was classically cheap.

Everything *smelled* cheap, from the bathroom soap to the alcohol they served, and everything *looked* cheap, from the 90s' neon decor to the too-tight dresses the clientele wore to accentuate their curves. It was perfect.

'Hallelujah, I've found my tribe,' I said, dancing into the club as a remix to 'Reach' by S Club 7 deafened us.

Almost at once we found ourselves on the dance floor, although it only took a minute until Paige declared she *had* to get a drink. If she was going to dance in four-inch high heels, she was going to need pain relief first. Tina and I were content enough to boogie on down together while she went to open her standard tab. We had perfected the routine to Steps' '5, 6, 7, 8' in second year at uni, and that was a life lesson that I never begrudge spending thousands of pounds to learn.

Sweat was streaming down our faces as shoulders, boobs and chests bumped, glided and accidentally motorboated us on the dance floor. Paige returned with four bottles of beer and handed one each to Tina and me, while she balanced out her life with one bottle in each hand.

We re-did our birthday 'Cheers!' and practically downed the bubbly concoctions in one, screaming in delight at having found a drink that didn't induce vomiting so early on in the night.

Within minutes we found ourselves back at the bar, trying to return our pre-drinks buzz by downing shot after shot. The club only served the worst of our teenage drink choices, from WKD and Sour Apple shots, so that soon, we were not only buzzed, but high on sugar.

We returned to the dance floor with fresh zest, as 'Movin' on Up' by Five was the next classic to play. Paige and Tina were quick to serenade each other, since they apparently knew all of the words, but I was never much of a Five fan. I contented myself to bopping and drinking my WKD, shoving other dancers out of the way so that my friends could have their nostalgic moment together.

I shoved one too many dancers aside though.

Clearing the way for the three of us to get closer to the DJ's turntable to make our requests – mostly more Spice Girls and a bit of Boyzone – I saw a sight that made me crave the opportunity to down The Bronze house special and throw up.

It was David.

And some other girl.

David with some other girl's tongue in his mouth.

David with some other's girl's tongue in his mouth, with his hands wrapped firmly around said girl's butt which was practically hanging out of her camel-toe-style playsuit.

The club was ridiculously packed and the music overly loud, but I still heard Tina's almighty exclamation of 'Fuck!' from behind me.

And then I did vomit. Right down the back of the clubber in front of me. His white vest top got an unwanted multicoloured tie-dye special.

8

'I've never met a person as unlucky as you.' Paige said, rather unhelpfully, from the back of the Uber.

Of course, the moment I vomited, Tina and Paige ushered me out of the club with the efficiency of two air stewardesses evacuating plane passengers. I vomited again the moment the cold air hit me, although there was barely enough alcohol in me yet to issue a proper chunder.

The queue of fellow clubbers outside all cheered and 'urghed' at me, while Tina and Paige both held their fingers up at them in unison.

'It's not even 11 pm yet?' The bouncer exclaimed in disgust.

Tina, once again, arranged for a taxi, this time agreeing that my initial plan that consisted of a cheese board and Prosecco at the flat would have been a better way of celebrating my birth.

'I shouldn't have gone out,' I said, wiping mascara tracks from beneath my eyes.

The Uber driver, when he turned up, was very kind, offering me a box of tissues the moment the three of us piled into the car, me squashed in the middle enveloped by the girls hugging me. He also had the good sense to put in his earphones and turn off the radio so that the three of us could talk.

'That good for nothing shit-stain. I should cut out his tongue. I should have pissed on his shoes. I should have . . .'

'Not taken four paracetamols in an attempt to avoid a hangover.' I finished for Tina, who was fuming, but also desperate to wake up fresh as a daisy, as she needed to mark a load of schoolwork this weekend.

'I'm not high,' she said, although both Paige and I had a sneaking suspicion that she was lying when she said she had *just* taken paracetamol. Tina was always carrying around slightly dodgy sounding energy pills that she got from some backstreet chemist, and we were 90% sure that some of them contained marijuana.

'I'm furious! That raggedy bitch. That gangrenous toe!'

'One day, someone will study her brain,' Paige whispered to me, in an attempt to make me laugh, which almost worked. I was angry and confused, and still feeling very nauseous (although we weren't telling the driver that).

'How many days has it been?' I asked, already knowing the answer. Eight days.

Eight days since I discovered he was cheating on me and kicked him out. Seven days since the flat flooded and literally washed away our entire lives. And yet he had already found himself *another* date and started snogging her on the dance floor at *World of Pop*.

'He doesn't even like clubbing!' I shouted, slamming my hands against my exposed thighs and leaving thick red marks.

'Oi, don't hurt yourself,' Tina said, claiming one of my hands for herself while Paige took the other.

Why, out of all the nightclubs on all of the nights of the week, would he come to my *favourite* club on my birthday? Did he expect me to wallow at home instead of living my life after I kicked him out? Had he planned this? Was he trying to make me feel bad, hoping for me to catch him to feel like I was missing out on his snogging technique?

'I wanna kill him,' I said. 'Excuse me,' I leant forwards to ask the driver to turn around.

'Ignore her,' Paige instructed. 'No, we're going back to mine. We're going to keep drinking and order in takeaway—'

'Multiple takeaways,' Tina interjected.

'And we're going to bitch and moan about our lives and men and discuss Demi Moore still being in love with Bruce Willis and the shocking ageing of Brad Pitt.'

'What is it with Hollywood men reaching fifty and then trying to be all hipster and surfer-dude-esque? It just ages them,' Tina exclaimed. 'Johnny Depp did it, George Clooney.'

'And now Brad!' Paige agreed, giving Tina a high-five. 'He just looks dirty. Not a turn on at all.'

'Maybe that's what I should do,' I suggested.

'What?' Tina laughed.

'I should become a surfer-chick hipster and not wash. Become a walking man-repellent. Honestly, I never want to see another man in my life again.' I fell back against the headrest of the car and spotted the driver looking at me apologetically in the rear-view mirror. 'Not taxi drivers, though, I like taxi drivers,' I said.

'Oh, poor baby,' Tina said, leaning over to give me another sideways hug. 'It's not all men, just David. He was M&S-priced and Poundland quality.'

'I'm pretty sure it's all men,' I repeated.

'No, no, we're not doing this,' Paige said sullenly, gently slapping Tina's shoulder to get her off me and leaning forwards so that she had a better view of my face. 'We're not going back to the pity-Krystal stage, we've already done that, and if David can move on as quickly as he has—'

'The lettuce-eating wanker,' Tina added. She had been very affronted when she discovered he was vegetarian when she cooked us dinner one night.

'Then *you* can get on with your life as well. So, no moping.'

'What am I supposed to do instead?' I asked, denying the urge to cry again. 'Nothing's working.'

'That's because you haven't got a real plan in place. Without direction you're not going to reach the destination.'

'No!' I exclaimed suddenly. 'No *rejection is redirection* bullshit, no corporate crap. Give it to me honestly.'

'Fine,' Paige smiled brutally. 'It's time to get a grip and stop acting like you're 13 years old and going through your first heartbreak. David's a dick, we're moving on. Your flat is ruined, you need a new one. You no longer have a job, it's time to be proactive.'

'Ooh, I love a bucket list,' Tina added, her arms shaking from whatever 'pill' she took.

They were both holding my hands still; I was shackled to them and I had never felt safer.

'It's not a bucket list, it's a to-do list. So come on, what needs to go on it? You're the writer, write this down.'

'With what?' I asked – we were in an Uber, not a Paperchase. The taxi driver, who had evidently not been listening to any music through his earphones, offered a pen to us from between the front seats.

'You're an angel,' Tina told him extravagantly, as Paige took the pen and aimed it at my arm.

'Number one,' she said, and began to write on my skin. 'Find a new affordable flat.'

'In London,' Tina pressed. 'You're not leaving me in this city,' she said; I rested my head on her shoulder to reassure her that I didn't want to leave London either.

'Number two,' Paige continued to narrate. 'Get a new and *secure* job.'

'I'll do my research on the company's finances and structural history next time,' I promised.

'Number three – and this is the most important of all,' Paige explained, 'Let go of David.'

'With a ceremonial burning of all of his possessions,' Tina added furiously. I sometimes wondered if she was a descendent of Boudicca or Cleopatra with all her passionate, borderline man-hating (okay not *borderline*) enthusiasm for destroying the patriarchy.

'*Or,*' Paige added, 'By getting back out there. And by *there*, I mean the wider London dating scene, not back in David's laundry basket, doing his chores and organising his life.'

'You mean there are men left in this city that Tina hasn't shagged?' I fake gasped.

'That's unfair,' Tina said. 'I've shagged the women too.'

'And besides,' I continued. 'I'm not sure I should be taking dating advice from the woman who was blocked from Tinder *twice.*'

Paige rolled her eyes and growled. 'So sending dick pics is fine, but screenshotting doodling ratings on them and sending them back is a block-worthy offence. I mean, come on!'

Paige and Tina giggled lightly as I took a deep breath, reviewing the promises that Paige had literally just etched into my skin. It seemed like a pretty binding to-do list from the back of that cab, with my two best friends as witnesses and even an eavesdropping spectator.

'Fine,' I said, exhaling heavily. 'It's time to get a grip.'

'Atta girl,' Paige said warmly, if a little patronisingly.

'We can still burn David's things if you like,' Tina whispered into my hair and I laughed.

We were nearly back at Paige's flat now, where there was plenty of alcohol I could drink to touch up the buzz I had thrown up at the sight of David on that dance floor. It was also a bit closer to midnight, the time that my next horoscope would go live and I could see what the following day held for me.

I really should have listened to its advice earlier and stayed in for a night of quiet self-reflection. Going out hadn't done anything for me (except remind me that I had two amazing friends) and that I really should take my horoscope more seriously if I wanted to truly appease the stars.

My Saturn Return was only six months away and time was ticking. I decided, without voicing it to either of the girls on our drive home, to add a number four to my list of to-dos: be emotionally and mentally ready for my Saturn Return in February.

9

Leo: There's a great deal of air to fuel your fire today ... a Leo Moon resides in your sixth house.

Having a to-do list did wonders for my energy and proactivity over the next few weeks.

I transcribed the list written on my arm into a Word document on my computer (I didn't want a shower to wipe away my goals for the next six months of my life). To act on them and get them all completed within the timeframe I had set myself, I needed to think of them as more solid than just ink. They were my lifeline to success, and the directions I needed to get back on the right path. Or at least, according to Paige they were.

I did everything I was supposed to do to get myself back on the straight and narrow. I applied for the two jobs I had previously found but thought I was too 'good' for, and I got nice rejections from both parties. I sent double the number of pitches I had been sending up until now and upped my posting on ZodiActually from three times a week to once a day.

In the last few weeks I had managed to secure a few proofreading jobs for a B2B company and even a chance to write an article on hemp – it does wonders for anxiety – for a mental health magazine. The latter gave me enough money to start paying off some of my overdraft and contribute to buying a few takeaways for Paige and I.

My hunt for a flat was not going so well.

The flat shares I found were barely affordable, and the ones in my price range were surely the crappiest of the entire city. A Zone 6 flat share with five other girls sharing one bathroom. A studio flat in someone's garage that had a porta-loo instead of an indoor toilet. Or, my personal favourite, a single bed in a warehouse with no walls to share with sixteen others in the middle of Tottenham. And those were my best options. Even Paige agreed that none of them were actual choices.

The dating scene was something I categorically wasn't ready for yet.

I had let Tina download Hinge onto my phone during the recovery of my birthday night out, but she was the first and last person who had gone through the app and actually matched with anyone. Mostly because she spent way too much time dissecting the quotes they used, picking apart the photos – 'That's definitely not candid' – and falling to bits every time someone included a photo of a dog.

The only part of my to-do list that I felt I was really making any headway with was the part about listening to my horo-scope more often. Initially, it was harder than I thought it would be.

Sometimes my horoscopes were really specific:

If a contract or other type of legal document comes across your desk today, don't sign on the dotted line until you've explored every possible downfall.

And other times they were as vague as IKEA furniture instructions:

There is a growing imbalance between your heart and your head, and it's necessary for you to deal with it.

Well, no shit Sherlock. But *how* did I deal with it? That was the real question.

For the most part, I dealt with everything by sticking to a routine; Paige was clearly rubbing off on me. She still didn't know about my astrology classes on Thursday nights. She thought I was going out for a solo dinner to get out of the flat or simply to roam around the city looking for article inspiration. Being who she was, Paige never really understood 'creativity' and how to get the journalistic juices flowing, but she never questioned it either.

Some of the astrology classes had been cancelled at the last minute, usually because Aoife was unwell, but whenever they did go ahead, the girls – Millie, Jane and Zelda and I – were all there.

Thankfully, there had been no return of the rude Irish man on my trips to the community centre. I was sure that if I were to see him again in the course of trying to get my life back on track I would give him a piece of my mind just as an excuse to vent all of my frustrations.

As focused on moving on, and maybe finding myself again, I discovered a little of my old confidence and no-shit-taking personality come back into the fray. It was only after a few days of feeling happier and more confident in my choices, that I realised it had been a long time since I had felt this good about myself. And I realised I hadn't felt fully *happy* for a long time, not until I started my astrological journey.

Aoife was so patient with the four of us when we gathered together. We all made a mess of our birth charts the first time we tried to plot them on the print-outs she brought along with her. All we had to do was look up which houses and signs the planets were in the day we were born in a book she provided, and add our names to the corresponding triangles outlined on the sheets. But none of us managed to do it properly the first time around.

'I keep getting confused between which one's a house and which one's a sign,' Zelda sighed dramatically, pulling the plate of biscuits away from Millie's grasp, since Millie was like a Pac-Man and seemed to munch through the whole lot before any of us could get to them.

'Can you have more than one sign in a house?' Jane asked, pushing her tinted glasses up her nose.

'What do each of the houses mean?' I asked, after Aoife sorted out the other two ladies. She was definitely a lot wobblier on her feet since the last time we'd had class two weeks beforehand. She was gripping onto her cane so tightly that her knuckles were white. With that in mind, I went to her.

Pulling my chair up alongside her, I showed her my chart. She didn't say anything but smiled softly in thanks.

'This is grand,' she told me, her faint Irish accent coming through. 'A lot of your planets are under the same sign.'

I nodded. 'Capricorn, Leo and Taurus all appear at least twice.'

'Well, Leo appears three times. That's definitely your dominant sign.'

'But what do each of the houses mean? I keep thinking that if they've got the same astrological sign then they must be the same?'

Aoife shook her head. 'No, each house means something different, similar to how your Sun, Moon and rising sign depict a different part of your personality.' I waited for her to continue, and she took a long breath.

'The first house depicts your appearance and the impression you give others. The second house is about money and things you value. The third house is all about communication, including your relationships with siblings and neighbours. Each focuses on a different area in life, but there are multiple things in each house, too. For example, the fifth house is about your romantic life, but also your children and things like recreation and creativity. Do you see how they're slightly connected?'

'Sort of,' I said, repeating what she said in my head to memorise what each house represented, and how each of them focused on a multitude of areas in my life.

'So, what does it mean to have . . .' I looked at my birth chart and pointed to Neptune. 'Neptune in Capricorn in the fourth house?'

Aoife took the sheet from me, her hands noticeably shaking, and laid it on her lap.

'Are you okay?' I asked quietly as she rubbed her finger joints. She shook out her hands, ignoring my question and smiled up at me.

'Could you grab the book?' she asked, to which I did. The other three women were still chattering together, piecing together their birth charts bit by bit and giggling like schoolgirls over the positioning of Uranus. That joke never gets old.

Aoife expertly flicked to a chapter in the book, looking up Neptune in Capricorn, all the while still speaking to me.

'So, off the top of my head, Neptune stays in each sign for around 14 to 15 years, so it rules a generation more than a singular person. It rules dreams, imagination and the general unconscious. But when Neptune is in Capricorn—' She tapped the paragraph of the book she was looking for and showed it to me.

'—Neptune in Capricorn means that your entire generation finds inspiration through hard work, seriousness, responsibility and ambition.'

'If only the media would realise this and stop calling millennials lazy snowflakes,' I suggested.

Aoife laughed and took the book back from my hands. 'And you said it's in the fourth house?'

I nodded.

'If Neptune is in Capricorn in the fourth house then you have to add the qualities of Neptune to Capricorn and then to the meaning of the house and you get a result. So, if

Neptune rules dreams and the unconscious, you add in hard work and ambition from Capricorn to the fourth house, which focuses on home, roots and security, then you tend to get a person with a manifestation of the ideal, particularly with regards to home and family.'

'Manifestation of the ideal?' I repeated, having lost her at that point.

Aoife nodded but her expression had changed somewhat, almost sympathetically.

'Because of the placement of the planet, you're likely to have an ideal vision of what home and family life should be, usually one that is unrealistic or impractical.'

'Oh,' I said, a little taken aback by the fact that according to my birth chart my idea of my life, basically, was a false and unachievable goal.

At first it felt like someone was stomping on my dreams, and then I realised that that had already happened. I thought of David as my family, that was why I had been so desperate to get engaged to him. But it turned out he wasn't even interested in monogamy, let alone family. It was an impractical belief that I had tried to force upon him. 'Woah, that's spooky,' I said aloud.

'Does it fit?' Aoife asked, screwing up her face a little as if afraid to insult me.

'Boy, does it,' I said, smiling at her in reassurance. 'I thought my last boyfriend was *the one*, but it turns out he didn't even believe in one – he believed in multiples. Many, *many* multiples. Of course,' I quickly added, feeling that in this open space I didn't want to appear prejudiced to people's choices. 'There's nothing wrong with believing in multiples if you communicate that, but men – or all the men I've been with – suck at communication.'

'Urgh,' I heard Zelda proclaim loudly from her table. 'Don't they just!'

Jane and Millie nodded, although Millie was unable to join in with the conversation that followed since her jaw was, once again, welded shut with malt milk biscuits.

'I'm always surprised by how spot-on my birth chart is,' I told Aoife, sitting back in my chair as I processed that latest revelation and thought about how I would translate that into a blog post on ZodiActually tonight. She nodded and attempted to shrug but winced a little as her shoulders rose. I winced as well, feeling my shoulders ache in solidarity with her private pain.

'A lot of people often are. Not many people actively realise that there is a whole astrology guide just waiting to be pieced together to explain their choices and desires. I think that if we were all given a chart at the time of our birth, we'd have a better sense of judgement as we got older. Not much better, mind,' she laughed wryly. 'Everything astrological is open to interpretation, but it would give us a better sense nonetheless.'

'If only they could tell us what was coming around the corner. That would help me tons.'

But the planets really did love a laugh, particularly when it came to me, I quickly rediscovered, when the door to the hall opened suddenly and in walked the infuriating Irish man.

'Hey Auntie,' he said, not once pausing to see if it was okay to come in or register who else was in the room. It was hard to miss me, though, since I was sitting next to the woman he so casually called *Auntie*.

'Hey lad,' Aoife said, quickly reaching for her cane to push herself up from her seat. She was clearly struggling with pain, and when she involuntarily released a large groan I instinctively stood to help her up. The Irishman came rushing forwards at the same time, and our hands briefly touched as we both gripped Aoife's arm in the same place. It was only then that he recognised me.

'Found the class then?' he asked, smirking over Aoife's

shoulder. I wanted to say, *Pay attention to her*, but Aoife had already recovered and with the aid of her cane was walking towards a nearby table that stood with a handbag and Sainsbury's tote bag placed on top of it.

'I'll just be one minute,' she called to her, I suppose, *nephew* from over her shoulder.

'Yes, I did find my way. Though not entirely thanks to you.' I said hastily.

I picked up my chair and began to walk it over to my place at the table next to Zelda. All three of the ladies had gone quiet at the Irishman's entrance, but that didn't mean they weren't watching our exchange as eagerly as the viewers on Gogglebox watch TV.

'I think you'll find I directed you.'

'You turned me around, that's all you did.'

'After you bumped into me.'

'You could have looked where you were going as well, you know.'

'I wasn't the one walking around a corner with my face in my phone.'

'You also weren't the one who stopped and checked if anyone was coming, either!'

'I'm a pedestrian, not a car.'

'Doesn't make any difference. You walked into me.' I pronounced each word of the last sentence very precisely, sending a little spittle across the wooden laminate top of the table, which I was quick to wipe away with the edge of my sleeve in the hopes that no one would notice.

Without another word, I placed my birth chart down on the table and began to make non-descript scribbles across it in the hopes that the Irishman would think I was very busy and leave me alone. But alas, men don't understand signals.

'Well then, I guess we both owe each other an apology. I'm

very sorry for catching you as you ran into me. I promise not to do it again in the future.'

I looked up to glare at him, but the ever-present amused smile was on his face, and I just wanted to slap it away.

'Don't you have an art class to go to?' I asked.

'Yes, but I'm not going now 'til I get an apology.'

'Well, you're going to be very late then,' I told him, returning to my chart.

Within a second he had placed a hand on the chart and pulled it out from underneath me. He was lucky that I had raised my biro in the air so that when he pulled it from under me I didn't draw a great big line through the middle of it. If he ruined a whole evening's worth of charting, I'd do more than run into him – I'd find a car and run over him.

'Oi!' I shouted (un-ladylike but hey, he wasn't exactly a gentleman). I kicked back the chair and raced around the table to grab the paper from him. He wasn't that much taller than me, but his arms were much longer than mine.

'This is a very interesting chart,' he told me, although I hoped to high heaven that he couldn't understand any of it. There was something indecently personal about a practical stranger reading my entire personality from a page. It may not even be correct – this was only my second attempt at charting. I may have put Saturn in Aquarius when really it was in Cancer.

'Give it back!' I shouted, swinging my arms around and jumping for the chart.

'You're a Leo, are you? I'm an Aries.'

'I said, give it back.'

'Ryan. What are you doing?' Aoife piped up suddenly, her voice sharp and markedly more Irish than before. Clearly, she hadn't lived in Ireland for a while, but as soon as she was around a family member (or specifically, telling that family member off) the accent went full tilt, kind of like Graham Norton around the O'Donovan brothers.

Ryan smiled cheekily, but had clearly been taught to respect his elders – even if not his betters – and returned the birth chart to me. I couldn't believe he had made me jump in the air like some rookie at Barry's boot camp, all to get a piece of paper back. I was 29 years old. God, I would have loved to have shoved him away then and there, but I was not a child and this was not a playground, however much he treated it like one.

'Just teasing Auntie.' He held up his hands and turned from her to face me. 'I apologise if I invaded your personal space. And your, well, *space.*' He pointed to the ceiling.

'That doesn't even make sense.' I told him.

'You know *space*. Like planets and stars. They're all in space. You map them and position them. No?' He looked to the older ladies for help, all three of them shook their heads. I could have high-fived them. Instead, I chose to gloat in the form of a pretentious smile at Ryan.

He scoffed, clearly finding the whole situation funny, but not for long. Aoife had approached us and tapped him on the shoulder.

'Here's the paperwork you need to complete. I need to give it to the lawyers by the end of the month.'

'By next year, got it.'

'Ryan . . .' Aoife said, clearly wanting her non-funny joker of a nephew to listen to her seriously. He simply smiled and leant down to kiss her forehead.

'End of the month, I promise.'

'Go on with yer,' she said, slapping his arm gently as she prepared to lower herself back into her seat. I returned to mine as well, smoothing out my birth chart that Ryan had creased in his childishness. What was it with men and sucking, lately?

'Ladies,' Ryan said, folding whatever paperwork Aoife had given him into his back pocket. 'Pleasure to meet you.'

The three old ladies made a few tittering sounds that sort of sounded like 'nice to meet you too' and 'until next time'. All the while I stayed silent.

'See you later, Leo.'

I rolled my eyes, refusing to look at him as he headed for the doors. I sighed and let my shoulders drop when I heard the door slam shut behind him on his way out.

'Well,' Zelda began, reaching over to tap me on the arm. 'No need to look to the stars to find out if he's interested in you missy.'

'What?' I practically shouted.

'Oh, that was some definite flanter going on,' Millie added. She had been so engrossed in the interaction between me and Ryan that she hadn't even attempted to reach for the last biscuit on the plate.

'Flanter?' I repeated.

'Flirty banter,' Jane explained, deadpan.

'What?!' I shouted again, looking to Aoife who said nothing and simply attempted to give a short shrug. Clearly she was not the sort of auntie who got involved in the minutiae of her relatives' love lives. What a rarity.

'Mm-hm,' Zelda hummed, before leaning over to the girls and speaking quietly. 'And that accent. *Oh*. I practically creamed my knickers.'

Oh my God.

IO

'She did not!' My mum was cackling down the speakers of my laptop over Zoom as I told her all about my new acquaintances from my latest hobby.

'She did!' I shuddered. 'God, I didn't know whether to throw up or offer her a tissue.'

Mum continued to laugh loudly, tears welling up in her eyes.

I thought it was safe to call her when I got home as Paige had texted to say that she would be out late. She didn't say what she was doing, but I assumed it was work so I left her to it. I needed someone to talk to after such an experience, and I really did owe mum a proper chat.

She was aware that David and I had split up, and had even sent me a condolence pay-out of £100, either as an incentive to pay for a train ticket home *or* as a reward for finally splitting up with him. She never liked him, but then Mum had never really liked anyone. The only man in her (and I guessed now my) life was Grandad Harold.

He and Mum lived together in St Albans and had done since I was a little girl. He was the only real male presence in my childhood since my dad, who was nice enough and always remembered to send Christmas cards, lived in Cornwall with his new wife, and I hadn't been to visit him since I was 16. I'd never been bothered about being raised by a single parent, though; my mum was a Gemini, which I had recently discovered meant she basically had two personalities inside her. It must have naturally balanced out her parenting in some way.

If Mum wasn't being 'fatherly' enough for me, though, there was always Grandad Harold to fall back on. He would join the call in a bit, my mum said; he was currently putting the finishing touches on his latest craft project in the dining room: a hand-stitched, silk brocade waistcoat.

My grandad was my favourite person in the whole world, positioned slightly in front of Paige and Tina, if only by a moustache hair. He was pushing 90 but looked 70, and every season he seemed to undertake a new hobby. Ever since my grandmother died, when I was too young to remember her, he spent his time trying new things.

He'd taken piano lessons, learned to line dance, joined a Sherlock Holmes appreciation society and even volunteered at the local heritage railway as a signalman. But over the last five years his hobbies had become even more unique. First, there was the sky-diving classes to become an instructor, which he qualified to do at the sprightly age of 86. Then, he undertook plaster-cast body art – a hobby neither Mum nor I mentioned during his undertaking of it. In the spring he had made a profile on TikTok and by this point had over 15,000 followers! And his latest hobby was antiquarian needlework.

He was working with a retired costume designer on making his own Regency-era clothing and had nearly finished a whole look. He was one a cravataway from being the next King George III impersonator at parties.

'Good on her,' my Mum said, finally able to catch her breath as she wiped a comical tear from her eye. 'Oh, that did me good to laugh.'

'I don't think any of us did more work on our charts after that. Mostly because Aoife couldn't look any of us in the eye after Zelda said *that* about her nephew. It was hard enough to concentrate after *Ryan's* rude interruption, but then when Zelda said that . . . it was game over.'

'Oh, I'm glad to see you looking so animated, baby.'

Baby. Here it comes. The typical 'I'm-worried-about-you' Mum comments.

'It's been such a long time since you were happy.'

'*Mum*,' I groaned, elongating the word. 'I'm fine, I've always been fine. Well, I wasn't so fine when the whole David thing kicked off the world's worse course of bad luck, but I promise I'm much better now. I feel good.'

'You look it. You look brighter. Getting in touch with your spiritual side will do that to you though. Have you tried crystals yet?'

I shook my head. 'I'm just experimenting with horoscopes and birth charts right now. I don't want to put too much stock into it just yet since I only want to learn about it.'

'Oh, I know baby, but if you're going to learn, why not find about all forms of astrology? I used to love doing meditation and yoga when I was your age; it really helped to realign my chakras when you were a toddler.'

'You mean when I was making you want to pull your hair out,' I teased.

'No, you were the one pulling it out. I was the one sitting cross-legged on the floor willing you to go away.'

'You shouldn't have let yourself be such an open target then, should you,' I stuck my tongue out at her playfully.

Our family was notorious for teasing, and it often led to us getting into trouble. Neighbours and friends often thought that we all hated each other whenever they heard us talking, by the way we called each other names and shouted things like, 'You useless piece of poo!' at the top of our lungs whenever someone forgot to throw down their darks or put on the dishwasher overnight. But that's just family for you. At least, *our* family for you.

I hadn't been the easiest of children, by all accounts. I was your typical loud and clingy child one minute and then grumpily sullen and independent the next. Mum said that every morning I woke up like Drew Barrymore in *50 First Dates*, with a different personality each time, but acting as if nothing had ever changed. Personally, I think I was just trying to find my best self.

'What did your horoscope tell you today then? Did it not say *you will meet a handsome stranger*?'

'No,' I grumbled, still infuriated by Ryan the Irishman. 'He was so childish.'

'Childish or child-like, there is a difference.'

'Whichever one is negative,' I told her definitively, opening the horoscope app on my phone to share my horoscope for the day.

'It says: *Feed yourself well in every sense of the word.*'

'Ooh, so it's telling you to eat vegetables for once.' What a typical motherly answer.

'Possibly. It's open to interpretation.' I pocketed my phone again. 'I took it to mean 'feed your mind', so I read an article on climate change and a few chapters of a book by Jay Shetty on behaving like a monk.'

'How interesting,' Mum said, her tone of voice implying that she thought nothing could sound worse. 'Well, fingers crossed you have a *romance is coming* one soon.'

'I'm not really interested in romance right now, Mum. I've barely been single a month yet.'

'One word: "rebound", darling. They're always so much more fun than relationships.'

'Are they, though?' I questioned. My idea of fun and my Mum's were clearly very different. She found working at the local garden centre fun, whereas I had found it boring as hell when I took a summer job there before university. Who in my generation ever needed to know the difference between a hoe and a rake? They're basically the same bloody thing!

To my mother, an evening out involved a leisurely dinner at Pizza Express and a long walk back to the car. Not going to a board game café with your besties and getting drunk on cheap Merlot and The Game of Life.

'Is that my little Krissy?' a sing-song voice called out from Mum's background. I instantly smiled. My grandad's voice was so warm and inviting; every time he spoke it was like getting a hug.

'Hello!' he sang over the screen. Mum had already told him that I was on Zoom 20 minutes ago, yet he still acted like it was all a big surprise.

'Hey Grandad, you alright?' I asked.

'Dandy, my darling. Did your mother tell you that Rita is coming over to teach me embroidery tomorrow?' He looked to Mum who plastered a *here-we-go-again* smile on her face.

'No, that's cool. Is Rita the costume designer?'

Grandad nodded, and I spotted the flirty look pass across his eyes, as his grey and wild moustache twitched above his smile. He was a free agent and loved a good flirt, and the ladies loved him for it. There was no woman for him but my nan, or so he said, but just because he had already ordered it didn't mean he couldn't look at the menu.

'And what are you up to? Your mother said something about stars. Are you going star-gazing at the Royal Observatory? I've heard it's something I must try one day.'

'I've not started star-gazing, but whenever you want to give it a try, let me know. You know I love a day trip.'

'Well, it'll have to be an overnight trip, actually,' Mum pointed out.

'I've been learning about astrology, Grandad,' I said, in answer to his initial question, ignoring my mother and her facetiousness. 'Star signs and such.'

'Oh,' his faced screwed up like a lemon sherbet had just burst on his tongue. 'Why would you want to learn about that?'

'Why? It's just a new thing to learn about. You love to try new things,' I pointed out, a little surprised by his lack of enthusiasm. He was the sort of grandad who would jump for joy if I told him I got a discount on maxi pads in the chemist – yes, we over-share in this family – but not when it came to a new past-time in astrology, it seemed.

He shook his head. 'I'm not that interested in what the stars supposedly have to say about my life. Not when I've lived through most of it; I think that makes me a much better judge.'

'It's not like that,' I forced a laugh. 'I'm not trying to predict my future or read my palm. It's more about what position the planets were in when I was born and how that may have led to a certain personality trait I have. I'm writing about it on my new website.'

'Have you got a new job?' he asked, more excited about the prospect of a new job over my new hobby.

'No, it's not a job per se but I'm using it as a chance to grow my portfolio. I've been writing about some astrology classes I've been taking and all the things I'm learning about. Like what it means to have been born under a planet in retrograde and what each house in a birth chart symbolises. It's actually quite interesting when you break it all down.' Not to mention a helpful way to appease the planets before a Saturn Return so that your thirties don't absolutely suck!

Mum was nodding along with me, but Grandad still looked confused – even with the filtered look of confusion that the grainy pixilation of Zoom gives people automatically.

'I've told her she should try crystals,' Mum said, pointing to the screen as if Grandad wouldn't know who she meant.

'Not just because of the link to her name – I just liked the name, it wasn't anything to do with physical crystals at the time – but wouldn't it be funny if she were called Krystal and used crystals?'

'Sure,' I said, rolling my eyes a little.

A reader on my website had commented on my post about the phases of the Moon, saying that crystals were supposed to have some sort of tie to energy and planets. And that she charged her crystals in an upside-down plant pot outside her shed on the full Moon. She had lost me at that point. But who knows where the future might lead? If it came up as a 'do' in my daily dos and don'ts chart then maybe I'd give crystals a whirl.

'Well,' Grandad began, still smiling but huffing a little as if he had given up on something. 'I say don't waste your money. Speaking of which, how are you doing on that end? Do you need me to send you any? I can give you your inheritance early if you need it?'

'Oh, really!' Mum said, turning to face him. 'She can have hers, but I can't have mine? I'm the one paying the rent here, mister.'

'Well, you've got half a life left, she has her whole one. She needs it more than you do.'

'Half a life,' Mum repeated, shaking her head playfully. She was too much like Grandad to be offended; it was part of his DNA to be cheeky and that's what we all loved about him.

Mum was just the same. Growing up, Mum never referred to Grandad as 'Dad', she always called him 'Old Man', and he always referred to her as 'Pee-Pee' as that was what she used to say whenever she wet herself as a child (which was quite a lot according to my grandad).

The love in our family was immeasurable.

'I'll tell you what,' Mum began, shoving her father slightly out of the frame to talk to me. I could already tell by the way my grandad was wiping his hands with a piece of cloth, which was perpetually in his pocket for such a moment as this – in order to make him look busy as he was itching to get back to his needlepoint. 'I had my cards read once, at the Christmas fair down at the cathedral.'

'How very pagan,' I interrupted.

'Listen!' Mum whinged.

'I'll speak to you later my darling,' Grandad said, deciding he had heard enough already.

'Okay, bye Grandad.'

'Don't worry,' he sang, blowing me a kiss as he jauntily headed for his study and his work with a little two-step dance.

'Be happy,' I finished for him. It was our little thing, to say 'Don't worry be happy' after every phone call, visit and night time Ovaltine. We had never finished a conversation without it, no matter how old either of us were.

'Anyway . . .' Mum interrupted, 'I'm trying to tell you a story here.'

'Sorry Mum, go on,' I said, leaning my face in my palm to get comfortable. This could take a while, knowing my mum.

'I got my card read at the Christmas fair. Tarot cards I mean. This was years ago – I was still dating your father, *that's* how long ago it was.' So before I was born is what she is basically trying to say. 'This lady beckoned me over, she was German, I think. Or maybe Armenian? She sounded like she was off Eurovision.'

'Well, that narrows it down,' I said sarcastically, but she carried on.

'She was desperate to read my cards, and said she wouldn't even charge me. So I let her. I got The Empress, The Five of Cups and The Tower.' Mum paused as if this was all very dramatic, but in all honesty I had no idea what any of it meant and waited for her to explain. She exhaled loudly, disappointed in my reaction.

'She explained that I was an extremely fertile young lady with good survival instincts, but that a change was coming, a loss of some kind, and that the loss would be very heavy and lead to heartache. The Tower is supposedly one of the most feared cards in a deck, you know, because change brings about the biggest upheaval and stress in a person's life.'

'Sounds great – or, not so great,' I stammered. 'But what did it actually mean?'

'Well, that's the thing – she told me point blank that I was going to get pregnant.'

'Huh?' That didn't seem like the kind of thing you'd expect from a hand that was as depressing as she made it seem.

'Yep. She told me that I would get pregnant, which would save me from the innumerable loss and heartache.'

'Oh, so she was basically warning you that you and Dad were going to split up only to get it on in the back of Dad's escort, and I would come about as a result?'

'Exactly!' Mum clicked her fingers and grinned, clearly very impressed. 'Isn't that amazing.'

'I'm not sure if it's amazing. Did she actually say you're going to get pregnant?'

'She said I was a fertile Myrtle, because of the Empress card. And that the man I was with was a waste of space.'

I closed my eyes and sighed. 'She was telling you to use a condom Mum.'

'Good job I didn't listen, aye,' Mum winked. 'You should get your cards done, too. There must be tons of places in London.'

'Maybe,' I shrugged, as I tried to wipe the image of my parents' break-up sex from my mind. It was impossible, though, as Mum had gone into a lot of detail to me before about that moment in time. She said it was the most defini- tive moment in her life – not because I was conceived, but because it was the evening she discovered her G-spot.

That's the sort of detail a daughter just doesn't forget.

'Do you think a card reading could forewarn me of conversations like this?' I teased, but Mum was on the tarot card train and she was determined to get me onboard.

'Oh, go on. What's the worst that could happen? You said yourself you weren't even sure if any of this stuff was worth listening to or not. Why not just go and try it?'

She had a point, and I was really enjoying my astrology classes. It would be something more that I could bring to the table to discuss with Aoife next time I saw her. Maybe she would have some opinions on it and whether or not it was worthwhile. Also, a little pre-warning about life would be pretty decent right about now. Particularly since I didn't know where the next pay cheque was coming from or whether or not I would turn 30 as a miserable, unemployed sofa-surfer unable to get into World of Pop because I once threw up on a fellow customer. What's the harm in asking for a little sneak peek of what's to come? Particularly with the cataclysmic Saturn Return on the horizon. If it signalled towards an upheaval in my life I wanted an idea of how I was to deal with it.

II

Leo: Important connections can be made today if you keep all the lines of communication open ... the Moon is waning in Leo.

I decided, for once, to take my mother's advice, and so the next day I booked an appointment for a tarot card reading in a bookshop on Cecil Street. I took it as a good sign to have found a bookshop doing a reading there, as Cecil Street was supposedly the street that inspired J.K. Rowling to create Diagon Alley in Harry Potter. Since astrology was all about signs, I decided to take it as a good one.

I booked an appointment for the following week, and was determined to ask Aoife her opinion at our next class, but there wasn't a chance. Yet another class was cancelled due to her ill health, and my mind was distracted by what was going on with and if there was anything I could do to help her.

None of the ladies had discussed Aoife's struggle with her mobility before; the constant wincing and flinching at every little movement she made. There was never an opportune time for us all to talk about it, and besides, it was her business, and she had never offered a reason for it, so why should we pry?

Aoife was clearly much older than she looked, even if her complexion was as youthful as Prue Leith (how that woman looked as good as she did in her eighties, I would never know). Maybe Victoria Sponge was good for the complexion? That would be a skincare routine I'd gladly follow.

To decide whether I should attend the tarot card reading, I referred to my horoscope app on the day, instead: *Coasting through life today will help you greatly tomorrow.*

Well, that was positive at least. Why not coast?

I had already booked my session for noon and I had plenty of time to kill in the meantime.

I closed the app, picked up my handbag and grabbed what I needed for the day; my phone, Paige's spare keys, a notepad, pen and a bottle of water, and headed out.

Cecil Street was just off Charing Cross Road, one of my favourite streets in all of London. The amount of second-hand and antiquarian bookshops, as well as the joys of nearby Chinatown and the National Portrait Gallery, would keep me entertained for the whole morning.

I couldn't remember the last time I had just headed out and spent the day to myself without having a real plan.

With David, everything was coordinated – by me – to suit him. I would be home at a certain time in order to get dinner sorted. On weekends when we had long lie-ins and went to the gym together, he'd sometimes go out afterwards for a run, or should I say '*run*', and I'd head home to do the chores and get some writing done in private. He'd come home and maybe, *maybe* strip the bed or do some DIY project that I had asked for his help with likely six weeks beforehand. But mostly, we stayed in and watched telly or went out to the local high street for a little retail therapy.

We were just your average boring couple with a sub-standard lifestyle routine. We never did anything spontaneously after he started a full-time job in the city, and I hardly ever had a moment spare as a freelancer where I felt I had the time to go out and just enjoy life on my lonesome. I was always too frazzled about getting more work in and making sure I had enough money to pay my portion of the rent that month.

But today, I was a tourist in my own city.

The overground was quiet as the Friday rush hour had slowed to a minimum flow; only a few passengers passed me by as I changed at Highbury & Islington for the Victoria line. I had my earphones in and closed my eyes, listening to a calming Spotify playlist of piano covers from movie soundtracks, and felt at one with my surroundings.

The tube carriage on the Victoria line was practically empty, so much so that I didn't even care if anyone heard me humming the melody of 'Shallow' from *A Star is Born*.

But then, not even a minute after the train had begun to move, or the rousing chorus in my earphones came on, the train stopped. There was no way that we were at Kings Cross St Pancras yet, so I opened my eyes and removed an ear-pod to listen to the overhead tannoy.

'. . . due to a broken down train ahead. We'll be held here for a few minutes until we get a green signal. I apologise for the delay this may cause you and will update you as soon as I can.' Okay, so nothing serious then. That was a typical tannoy announcements for the Victoria line, which was forever breaking down it seemed.

Rather than get all huffy and anxious that I was going to miss my appointment, I simply relaxed. I had plenty of time. My card reading wasn't for another two hours and not all that that far away. Even if I had to get off the underground at Kings Cross and walk, I'd still make it with minutes to spare; in fact, that sounded like a great idea. I could go outside and walk through the city, watching as it shed its summer colours for autumnal shades.

I pressed play on my phone to resume the piano cover, but as I looked up from the screen, I spotted something that gave me pause. A woman in a bright red trench coat with a giant rucksack wedged between her legs was fanning herself alarmingly fast. Her face was at red as her coat and she seemed to be unable to catch her breath. The tell-tale signs of a panic attack; something I had experienced a great deal at university.

Whether it was the upheaval of leaving the safety of home for the first time in my life, or that fact that I was generally not very good at coping with large quantities of stress – which tended to happen when you mixed exam season with hangovers and a propensity to end up in bed with guys who you were pretty sure had once tested positive for chlamydia – panic attacks were something I had experienced on the regular.

Tina was my saving grace in those days. She used to get pulled out of lectures by my personal tutor who would ask her to come and calm me down. And bless her, she never complained about it. She truly did have the patience of a saint, did Tina, and the speaking power of a narcotic, as she always calmed me down within a minute of turning up just by cracking some terrible joke.

Feeling that I couldn't just leave the woman to hyperventilate on the train, although the Londoner in me was telling me not to engage, I stood up and moved to the seat across from her. She was so panicked, she hardly seemed to register that I was there until I pulled out my bottle of water and offered it to her.

'Here,' I said, gently touching her hand and holding the bottle beneath her gaze. 'This will help. It can get really hot down here.'

She didn't speak at first. I doubt she had the air in her lungs to do so, but she smiled and took the water gratefully. It was a miracle she didn't drown herself judging by the speed at which she drank it down. When she came up for air she was gasping, but at least she was taking full breaths.

'Thank you,' she said, smiling and breathing heavily.

I smiled back. 'No problem.' She offered the bottle back to me but I shook my head. 'Oh no, you keep it.'

'I completely forgot to bring a drink with me,' she said, pulling at her collar and laughing, clearly embarrassed. 'I hate the underground.'

'You're not from here,' I smiled already guessing where she was from, from her heavy and cheerful accent.

'No, Liverpool. Can't you tell?' She gestured to her flaming red coat.

'Ah, so not an Everton fan.'

'I should wash your mouth out,' she said, in fake horror, as she finished the last drop of water from the bottle. 'Thanks again. I'm all over the place today.' She began forcing the bottle into her over-filled rucksack.

'First, my train was delayed, now this blinkin' tube. I hate confined spaces as well,' she shuddered. I got the sense that this was a woman who could talk for England and never stop for breath. Not my usual type of person, but since my horoscope said to go with the flow I did just that.

'How my granny survived all those years here, I'll never know.'

Clearly my face asked the question of 'Granny?' for me, as she went on to explain.

'My grandmother lives – lived – in London. She passed away recently.'

'I'm sorry,' I began to say, but already the woman had begun to talk over me with an infectious laugh and smile that made me grin. 'Oh God, she was ancient! Nearly 102 when she passed.'

'Really?'

'Really. I'm convinced the old bird preserved herself with whiskey and wine, but good genes run in our family. Even my ma is still around, but she's much too old to go traipsing down to the big smoke to sort out her mother's belongings. That unbridled joy has fallen to me.' She swung her arm in front of her in an 'oh well' panto manner.

'I'm Clare, by the way,' She said, leaning forwards excitedly.

'I'm Krystal.'

'Krystal,' she repeated, her smile widening – if that was even possible. 'Gorgeous name!'

'My mum chose it. She's a bit of a hippie.'

'I think it's lush,' Clare repeated, smiling earnestly.

'Everyone calls me Kris, though,' I told her. Only friends called me Kris, actually, but having her call me Krystal seemed extremely formal in that moment. 'And it's got a K, not a C.'

'Oh, even better. Very unique. I'm just stuck with boring old Clare with a C. You can't even shorten it, and the only thing that rhymes with it is *bear. Clare Bear* makes me think of those God-awful toys that smelled like bubble-gum.' She shuddered again.

I tried not to laugh but there was something energetic about Clare, even after she nearly had a full-on meltdown on a tube train.

We still weren't moving, and the driver announced over the tannoy that it would be a few more minutes yet.

'Are you okay?' I asked her, checking to make sure she wasn't going to require a paper bag or the recovery position at the latest announcement.

'Oh, yes love. I'll be fine now. I just bloody hate these tubes, there's no air.'

'Where are you headed?' I asked, thinking it best to change the subject quickly, as, despite her protests that she was fine, she had begun to fan herself again.

'Kentish Town. Although I'm pretty sure I'm lost. Honestly, I can't find my arse from my elbow in this city.' Her self-deprecating laughter reverberated around the carriage. 'My neighbour said to get on the Victoria line to Euston, but I went and missed it. Got all the way to Tottenham Hale before realising the maps were above me all along. Had to get off and turn around.'

'You haven't got far to go, actually, if you're trying to get to Kentish Town. You get off at Euston and change to the Northern line via Bank, and it's only two stops I think.'

'Oh, you're a darling.' She leant forwards to pat my knee. 'That's only the first journey, though. Once I get off the tube in Kentish Town, I've got to follow some directions that the lawyers gave me to the blinking flat. I've never been you see. Never had a chance to get down here before she passed away.' Her eyes drooped a little – clearly there was some familial guilt going on here, but she quickly shrugged it off.

'I'm only down here today to get the keys and sign the paperwork. Apparently, it's something you have to do in person, otherwise it could be fraudulent or some other nonsense. It's just a load of faff. And that's only the beginning.'

I leant back in my seat, denying the urge to look at my watch and will the train to start moving again. I was worried this was going to expand into a long-winded conversation about housing costs and the ridiculousness of renting; a topic that every 20-something avoided just as much as text messages from the gym asking where we've been.

'I don't know what the hell I'm gonna do with the place. My nan was a hoarder – has been for as long as I remembered. Lived in that tiny flat since the social workers forced her out of her old two-up-two-down place when my grandad died, yonks ago. She'd been buying up a storm ever since; got a little too fond of retail therapy, I think. Last time her carer FaceTimed with us she didn't have anywhere to sit, poor lamb, as there was no place to pull up a chair.'

Clare placed her head in her hands dramatically, all in a tizz again now. But thankfully the tube gods were listening to my prayers, and with a judder and a spine-tingling scream of mental on metal, the train began to move again.

'Oh, thank the Lord,' Clare said, beginning to laugh again in a deeply relieved way. 'I bet you were getting sick of me going on and on.'

I shook my head and tried to give her the broadest smile possible. Honestly, she wasn't bad company. I'd probably look back at this experience in an hour or so and giggle to myself about the fact that I had made a such friendly acquaintance on the tube. After eight years of living in London, that was a first.

'I hope the rest of your visit goes more smoothly for you,' I said.

'I hope so too. I don't suppose you know of a good flat clearing service, do you? Or someone who wants to live in a pigsty?' she laughed again, chortling at her own silly ideas. 'Honestly, if someone volunteered to move in and clear the place for me, I'd let them have the whole stinking flat rent-free. Or at least until it was habitable again – then I supposed I'd have to get it on the market to sell or such like.'

'Rent-free?' I repeated slowly. Was this what my horoscope meant when it said that coasting through life today would help me tomorrow? I didn't want to seem too eager at the prospect of her fly-away comment just in case it was, as I first suspected, a joke. But my heart skipped a beat at the idea that this might have been a connection the planets wanted me to make.

'Oh sure, sugar. It would cost me an arm and leg to hire a cleaning service, particularly in this city, and the faff of going back and forth and back and forth to sort out the tit from the tat would cost more than it's worth. Although, I know there'll be some things me mum wants to keep and, you know, it was my nan's home for her last good years.'

She sighed deeply and then looked up. There must have been a certain expression across my face that made her realise that I was doing more than just asking a question for the sake of asking.

We pulled into Kings Cross St Pancras, but I didn't leave my seat. Something inside me – maybe even the pull of Jupiter in the fourth House – told me to stay seated and talk to Clare for a little longer.

'Are you looking for a place to live?' she asked, leaning forward a little to shuffle her rucksack back between her legs as the passengers on our train carriage got off and a new addition of day commuters and tourists got on.

'Yes, actually. I've just broken up with my fiancé . . .' That was the first time I'd called David my fiancé in public, but something about splitting up with a fiancé sounded a lot more serious (despite the break-up element) than a boyfriend. 'Our flat was flooded, too, so I'm kind of couch-surfing at my friend's right now.'

'Oh, I'm sorry to hear that. He must have been an Everton supporter; no smart man would let go of a girl like you. Not for a million pounds.'

I chuckled at her overt friendliness, bearing in mind she had only known me a few minutes.

'I'll tell you what,' she began again. 'If you're truly looking for a place, I'm really in a tight spot and I'd be happy to swap numbers and maybe organise a chance for you to view it when I'm next in London. After you see it, though, you might go running for the hills.'

'Are you sure?' I asked, the little voice of Mary Berry in the back of my head questioning whether this was such a great idea. I'd only just met this woman. And on the tube! Isn't this where you met perverts and alcoholics – not potential landladies?

'Absolutely!' she said, her grin stretching further across

her face than ever before. How her cheeks didn't cause her agony, I'd never know.

'Great,' I said, ignoring the voice in my head and reaching for my phone. On the home screen there was a notification from my horoscope app with the quote for the day, as if to add support to my serendipitous meeting: *A friend may be waiting behind a stranger's smile – Maya Angelou.*

12

*Leo: If you meet opposition, stay strong ... Mars and Venus
enter a tense square.*

By the time I turned up for the reading in Cecil Street – after
deciding to walk from Euston to process my new-found
friendship with a Liverpudlian lady and a possible new housing situation – I was shaking with nerves.

Had I really just agreed to view a flat that I'd never seen
before, that had belonged to a hoarder and that I would need
to spend weeks clearing out? Or had I just found the dream
living situation in the city? Either that or I'd simply volunteered
to be an unpaid cleaner. These were things I was determined
to ask the tarot card reader about upon my arrival.

When I booked the appointment, I hadn't realised that the
reading was done in the window box of an antiquarian bookshop, with no privacy curtain between the window and the
reading. Any passer-by would be able to stop and peer into
my reading, potentially even see the cards that the reader had
pulled for me.

I stood outside said window and stared at the lady sitting
in the chair; she looked normal enough. Sure, she was wearing a tasselled headscarf that ran down her back and a chunky
set of beads around her neck, but apart from these clichéd
elements to her she was just a woman in a white t-shirt and
jeans. Nothing frightening or intimidating about her at all.

This was just first-time nerves; the same nerves that
appear the first time you get naked in a public dressing room

at a spa, or when you realise you have to poo when you stay over at a new boyfriend's house. A few deep breaths (and some strategically placed tissues in the case of a poo) would do the trick.

Without giving myself a chance to turn and run, I opened the door to the shop. My Sun sign was a Leo so I was meant to be determined, vivacious and daring. It was time to let the lion roar.

I registered giving myself this pep talk in my head and realised I was turning into my mother more and more with every day that passed. Was this another symptom of the Saturn Return?

★ ★ ★

The reader who 'serviced' me – the bookseller's term, not my own – was called Violet. She was very pleasant when I entered her little booth, sensing that I was both nervous and extremely claustrophobic from the way I awkwardly sat down.

I couldn't stop glancing out of the window and imagining seeing people I knew. The fear that someone would walk by and recognise me was not something I had considered. Before, I was just afraid that someone would see my future in the cards and realise that something terrible was headed my way.

'Don't worry, no one ever stops and stares here. They're far too civilised,' Violet said, shuffling a pack of pristine tarot cards effortlessly in her front of her.

She could have made a mint as a croupier in a casino if she were to take her shuffling skills to them. I could barely keep my eyes from looking at the expert – and pretty sexy – way she manoeuvred the cards smoothly between her fingers.

'Sitting here all day gives me plenty of time to practice,' she smiled, even though I hadn't complimented her aloud. Maybe she really was a psychic.

On that thought, I shook myself out of my stupor and reminded my consciousness that I was a cynic and therefore was only doing this reading *just in case,* not *because* I wanted to know the future. There was a difference.

'How does this work?' I asked, my voice shaking a little. I wanted to write a piece about my tarot experience on ZodiActually, but I didn't have the first clue how the process went and I didn't want to appear amateur. Although, that was precisely what I was.

Violet shrugged and quickly shuffled the cards into one solid, aesthetically pleasing deck.

'This is your first time?' she asked, and I nodded.

'Let me give you a little overview of tarot. At its simplest it's an ancient story system, and the story is told in a multitude of ways, depending on the placement of the cards. There are 78 cards in total, split across three groups: the Major Arcana and the Minor Arcana. The Major Arcana includes things like The Fool and The Empress cards, and the Minor Arcana includes the Wand, the Pentacles and the Swords, etcetera.

Now,' she placed the full deck in one hand and knocked on it seven times, 'I'm just activating the energy in the cards. In a moment, I'll ask you to select the ones that you're most drawn to.' She split the pile into three and took a brief pause to look at them, giving them a stare not uncommon for a headteacher during an interruption in morning assemblies.

She placed the three piles of cards one on top of the other until the deck was complete again, and with a quick swish of her wrist, placed all of the cards face down in a neat semi-circle in front of me.

'Wow,' I said, surprisingly impressed. She shrugged with a small smile, clearly happy with the praise I was lathering her with. I didn't need the cards to tell me that Violet had a little bit of an ego when it came to her card-reading abilities.

'Select the three cards that you're most drawn to,' she instructed.

'Any?' I asked, hovering my hands above the pack hoping for some sort of mystic guidance. But there was nothing. I was just selecting cards and hoping for the best – an activity I usually saved for Christmas day when Grandad would buy three £5 scratch cards as a festive treat for us, and ask mum and I to select one after we gorged on Christmas pudding.

'Any,' Violet answered assuredly.

I took a moment to really concentrate; see if there was anything calling me. None of the cards had particularly decorative designs on them to catch my eye. They were all blue and white with countless circles and cloudy edges.

Deciding to just go for it, I selected a card at the edge of the circle, one in the middle and one that I accidentally nudged with my little finger which I then assumed meant it was now one of my cards.

'Okay,' Violet said, pulling the three cards towards her and swishing the remaining cards to the side with elegance once more.

Dramatically, she flipped each card over in front of me.

'The Hermit,' she recited aloud, turning over the first card.

'The Three of Cups.'

And finally . . .

'Death.'

'Death?!' I repeated, my voice breaking in surprise. I heard the shuffling footsteps of nearby patrons in the bookshop stop, but Violet merely gazed at me beatifically beneath her long eyelashes.

'It's not what you might think,' she said, without any other explanation, moving her hands over to The Hermit card. I would have much preferred to have focused on the Death card first, but apparently we had to do it in order.

'The Hermit. It means you are alone.' Wonderful.

'Alone and loneliness are two very different things,' Violet pointed out. 'But you will experience both in between now and your next reading. Being alone can raise our insight and take us on a personal journey; it's a time for scholarliness and focus. It will alleviate your sense of FOMO but aggravate your sense of heartache.'

'Okay,' I said, not utterly thrilled by the results of this £50 reading so far.

'The Three of Cups. A potent love card – not in the sense of romance but friendship. Three maidens toasting each other. An achievement will be made, support will be given. But beware the Three of Cups and The Hermit, you may lose opportunities if you do not participate.'

'And Death?' I asked. In all honesty, I was only thinking about the Death card at that moment. It was an unwelcome flashback to my early teen years of listening to My Chemical Romance and reading about young A-listers who had unwittingly joined the 27 Club. At least they never had to worry about their Saturn Returns. Oh God, the Death card had me acting like an emo teenager again.

'Death does not mean death,' Violet laughed. Clearly this was a reaction she got often, because of course, silly me, why would Death mean death?! 'Death means change. A transition, either in progress or coming. A new era is ringing for you, which you must choose to accept or deny. But to deny it will only lead to difficulty.'

'So basically, what you're saying, when you add all of these together,' I said, pointing to the three cards that Violet's hand hovered over, her burgundy nails shining under the yellow wall sconce. 'Is that I'm going to experience a loss which leads to change, which I either need to embrace in order to celebrate with my friends or deny and suffer alone?' Why did my life suddenly sound like the plot of *P.S. I Love You?*

'No,' Violet said bluntly. 'All of this is subjective and

thematic; nothing in these cards is going to tell you defini-tively what is coming or has been.' Helpful, Violet. *Super* helpful. 'You need to interpret what they're telling you as a form of guidance on how to deal with either a prior, ongoing or future incident.'

I shook my head a little, still unsure what she wanted me to understand exactly, and if this was even true. Following your horoscope was one thing, but at least it was daily and usually gave some form of guidance, even if it was just: *Luck is not on your side today.* These cards – or rather, Violet's interpretation of them – weren't telling me anything.

Why couldn't she just say: '*Your cards have revealed you've had a shitty few weeks, but in a couple of days everything will be fine, and you'll find a new dream job via Indeed.com, and you'll get hired without an interview. You'll move into the perfect flat with a landlord who gives you a discount for being beautiful, which you'll initially refuse for feeling grossly objectified, only to accept it a few days later because it's a really good deal and you honestly don't care. You'll find romance in three years' time outside the gym (so you don't have to go in and sweat), have 2.5 children, head off to live in the Cotswolds where you'll discover Tom Hiddleston is your next-door-neighbour. And he likes to mow the lawn shirtless.*'

But that would just be too easy. And heavenly.

'I can break it down for you,' Violet said sharply.

I guessed that she wasn't particularly happy with my non-ethereal response and lack of gratitude towards her reading skills. For some reason, with cards, I didn't have the same pull as I did towards crystals or horoscopes. There was noth-ing in this reading that was making me sit up and think: 'Wow! You're good!' Neither was there anything to look forward to, by the sounds of it.

'I would say that the cards indicate a potential change in a relationship, a search for truth and community and an under-taking of a journey to find inner happiness.'

She could tell all of that from three cards about cups, death and a Gandalf-like drawing. Damn. I couldn't tell if I was pre-menstrual or just a grumpy bitch most of the time.

'Right then,' I said, thinking that maybe Paige wasn't all that wrong when she rolled her eyes at the idea of tarot card readings.

I would have continued to think along these lines and thank Violet politely, if sarcastically, for her time, if it wasn't for the fact that at that precise moment the universe decided to *once again* smack me around the head with a Thor-sized quantity of fate.

Ryan was running down Cecil Street in an ensemble of standard joggers and a t-shirt, equipped with airpods and a perfectly shaped V-line of sweat pressing his white shirt against his toned upper body.

'Oh fuck!' I shouted, double-taking at the sight of him and realising my mind wasn't playing tricks on me. It really was Ryan out for a jog.

I flung myself to the ground so hard in fear of him seeing me that I got tangled in the velvet curtain separating the alcove from the bookshop, ripping them down from the tabs that held them up.

How is it possible to run into the same person again and again? This is London, for Christ's sake. It would usually take me ten minutes just to find the girls in a pub. And now, everywhere I headed, Ryan was magically appear, like a zit or a period.

Was this what the cards were trying to say?

It certainly did feel like fate was shouting: *'Pay attention! I'm telling you things!'* in the form of a universe-sized bitch slap.

In tradition Krystal-cocoon style I found myself completely stuck, lying in the middle of the shop floor, with only my face visible underneath what felt like miles and miles of curtains.

A crowd of geriatric, fusty looking customers stopped their browsing for books to stare at me in disdain. Some giggling into copies of *Mind Reading for Beginners* and *Palmistry for Procrastinators*, while others closed their eyes in cringing embarassement.

The only benefit to being practically smothered beneath ten pounds worth of fabric was the fact that Ryan was not able to see me with a red-cheeked look of horror plastered across my face as I weakly asked: 'Can I get some help?'

13

Leo: Trust is the fuel to achieving your goals ... Venus and Pluto collaborate in your 8th house.

'You should create an accent wall in here,' Tina said to Paige, bundled up on my sofa-turned-bed in Paige's living room, multiple schoolbooks scattered across her lap.

'What accent, though? Australian? Russian? Liverpudlian?' Paige asked as she folded laundry in the bedroom nearby.

'Oh, har har,' Tina said, unenthusiastically.

I was standing at the hob in the kitchen, graciously stirring the packet carbonara sauce as part of a meal I had volunteered to make for our dinner after my hellish day in the city.

'Hey, speaking of Liverpudlian,' I began, thinking that this was a good a time as any to bring up my new acquaintance. 'I got to speaking to a woman on the tube today.'

Paige stuck her head out of the bedroom and Tina looked up from an eight-year-old's doodle-destroyed maths book.

'On the tube?' Paige repeated.

'I thought that was illegal?' Tina scowled.

'It should be,' Paige said.

I shrugged, ignoring their silliness as I drained the boiled tagliatelle at the sink.

'She was from Liverpool, that's why I'm bringing it up. She was really lovely.'

'I'm still confused about the whole tube element,' Paige asked, bringing the remaining laundry into the room and dropping it onto her neglected dining table.

'We were stuck in a tunnel, it's a long story. *But* the short story is that we got to talking and it turned out she was down from Liverpool to clear out her grandmother's flat. She needs someone to help her, kind of. And, well, she sort of offered to let me live there rent-free, so long as I cleared out her grandma's clutter.'

'What?' Tina said, her tone in utter bemusement.

'Like that actually happened!' Paige laughed.

It took her a good minute to realise I was, in fact, serious. 'You must be joking. She must have been a con-man or something.'

'Con-woman,' Tina corrected her.

'You know what I mean,' Paige snapped.

'I'm being serious,' I told them, carefully pouring the sauce over the pasta. 'We swapped numbers and everything.'

'Swapping numbers doesn't make a deal,' Paige pointed out.

'No, but we've already confirmed we are who we said we are.'

'How?!' Tina pressed.

'Funnily enough, she phoned me after I texted her. She sounded exactly the same as she had done on the tube.' Albeit less panicked than the first time. She had been on the train home and I was just approaching the flat after my disastrous reading. The relief in her voice when I answered and said that I was still interested was palpable. 'You'd think I'd done her a huge favour taking the flat off her plate.'

'Wait a minute,' Paige said, leaving the clothes and taking a seat on the sofa next to Tina. 'All of this sounds like dodge city, and I just want to make sure that you're not rushing into anything stupid.'

'You're the one who wrote the to-do list for my life on my arm, Paige,' I scoffed. 'And it sounds fine to me. Sure, a little Hallmark movie-ish, but after the last few weeks I've had I'll take whatever the universe gives me.' And since my horoscope was all about trust today, I felt like I was making the right decision.

'Oh shit,' Tina muttered, as I handed out the plates of pasta. Tina's face was flushed. 'You're really taking this horoscope thing seriously, aren't you?'

'I told you, you shouldn't have said anything,' Paige muttered to her, like it had been a grand plan between the two of them.

'It's nothing to do with Tina, Paige. I'm just taking life by the balls and going for it. Just because you feel like you need to plan everything out doesn't mean I can't be spontaneous.'

'It still sounds dodgy, though,' Tina said, sitting back from her marking in order to tuck into the carbonara. Paige, however, hadn't moved an inch, and was holding her bowl in one hand while staring at me.

'How are you so chill?' she asked. But I shrugged.

I knew that telling the girls about things like Clare and the flat was going to cause a conversation like this – my horoscope had said to expect conflict today as Mars was in the 11th house, the house of friendships and war.

'Eat up,' I said, stabbing a fork at my tagliatelle.

* * *

In the morning I woke up late. Paige had already gone out – to where, she hadn't said – and Tina had left, too, after she had decided to stay over at the last minute. It was a Saturday, so Paige wasn't working, but I theorised that she had just popped out, probably to stretch her legs or to get something from the bakery, when I spotted that her tatty old trainers were missing from the front door.

After helping myself to coffee and eating the last of the fancy bagels Paige had bought from a local French bakery, I opened my horoscope.

There are no restrictions on shopping or important decisions today. The stars are aligned to bag you a bargain.

Ooh! I thought. It had been a while since I had gone out and treated myself to a bit of retail therapy. Mostly because I didn't have any money to spare. But with my recent flurry of small projects there was at least enough in my account to go window shopping without fear.

Within an hour I was dressed and out the door heading for Brick Lane Market. Why bother going to a standard shopping centre to window-shop when you could go somewhere really appealing to the eye? My plan was twofold: shop until I got bored, since I didn't really have much money to risk, and to capture a few snaps for my newly reinstalled Instagram, to remind everyone (David) that I was a trendy, modern woman of the city who didn't need a partner to live a life worthy of Instagram shots.

It was packed. The market was in full force by the time I arrived. The smell of Vietnamese banh mi called to me as a perfect brunch choice, but when I remembered that in order to order one, I would have to tell the server to 'Duck Mi', I was swayed from the idea.

In the market, I waddled from side to side, pushing past people and crawling under outstretched arms to touch and fiddle with the variety of wares on display. Usually, I would spend a while browsing the vintage ring stalls or hunting for copies of my favourite classic books in yellowed Penguin varieties at the bookseller stalls but there was hardly enough room to expand my chest to breathe, let alone get close enough to see the merchandise.

I made a mental reminder never to come to the marketplace on a Saturday, even when my horoscope had suggested it. Maybe I should have stuck to the high street.

It was only as I was hoisting my bag above a woman's head

so that she could get past me that I realised there was some space in front of a nearby stall that would at least give me the chance to take in a full breath.

Without a moment's consideration I lunged for the space and landed with a thump against a table that was alive with tinkling glassware and stones.

'I'm so sorry,' I said to the stall owner who was readjusting and calming the wind chimes and rattling stones on his table.

I glanced apologetically downwards to see that they weren't stones but crystals. Rose quartz, tiger's eye, citrine and obsidian. Reflective moonstones the size of my palm and amethyst shards that sat eye-catchingly – or eye-stabbingly – close to the front of the table. If I had tripped and fallen forwards, rather than strategically lunged sideways, I would have likely been impaled by one. Now I could see why people were giving this stall such a wide berth.

'Wow,' I said, side-stepping the amethysts to run my fingers over some of the smaller stones.

'You like crystals?' the man asked with a slightly Slavic accent, and no smile.

I nodded cautiously. 'I don't really know much about them.'

'Ah,' he became animated. 'Which one draws your eye?' he queried rubbing his hands together.

I looked over the collection carefully and pointed to the glittering light green stone which was perfectly spherical. The stall holder picked it up and held it out for me to see.

'Jade,' he said. 'A pure stone. Lots of good energy, particularly for heart-healing.'

'Heart-healing?'

'It soothes the soul and removes negative thoughts in order to allow the good to flow through you. It will protect you from hurt.' He smiled and placed the stone to one side and motioned a hand towards the rest. 'What else?'

I picked up another stone and handed it to him. It was purple and yellow, and I had never seen its kind before.

'Ametrine,' he said, admiring the change of colours in the stone as he held it up to the light. He encouraged me to lean over the stall to properly see the colours change from within it.

'And what does ametrine mean?'

'It's good for astral projection. An out of body experience that one can have while dreaming or meditating. Good for the soul and to focus the mind.'

Sounded like a lot more like escaping the mind to me, but still I couldn't take my eyes off the stone.

'Choose again,' the stall owner said, repeating his previous actions of putting the ametrine to one side and wafting his hands over the stones. His eyes appeared to be glinting with growing excitement as I made my selections.

This time I selected the tiger's eye, a stone I recognised from *Practical Magic* – the go-to sleepover movie of my childhood. I held it up myself this time and admired the circles within the stone. It looked like a planet sitting in my palm.

'Aha, the Leo's stone,' he said, excitedly.

'Leo as in, the sign?' I asked, surprised to have selected my very own birth stone. The stall owner nodded.

'A passionate and creative gemstone. Good for endurance and self-confidence, but also to escape the evil eye.' He made some 'woo-woo' noises and lifted his hands into the air like a parent would do to scare young children on Halloween, before laughing and reaching out for the stone.

I handed it over, slightly less willingly than I expected, and he placed it with the others.

'Do you really believe crystals can do all you say they do? I asked him, genuinely curious. He nodded profusely, but then stopped and leant across the table with a serious expression carved onto his face.

'It's not whether they do, or whether you just believe

that they do. Crystals are conduits, they're aims and goals in rock formations. They're not drugs you take to cure an illness or a part you manoeuvre to fix a machine. The effect they have on your life depends on the strength of your belief that they will help. Mind power is their power,' he said, tapping his forehead while staring me straight in the eye.

Usually, this kind of one-on-one interaction would freak me out. But I was intrigued about what the man was saying. About crystals working as constant reminders of what you're working for; a way to focus yourself and your energy in order to manifest your goals. It made me feel like I was in the right place at the right time.

'How much are these three crystals?' I asked him.

'Well these are £2.50 each,' he said, referring to the stones on the table. I knew each of them couldn't be worth more than 50p, if that, but London prices were London prices. 'But you, you need something else.'

I looked up, surprised to see him throwing materials and fabrics into the air as he searched for something beneath his stall. He reappeared, holding a gilded box and made an 'aha' sound of success.

'You need something you can wear, something that travels with you throughout your journey.'

He opened the box behind the counter revealing crystals and stones carved into individual pendants. 'These are £15 each, but I can do a deal for you: three for £30.'

'Three for £30,' I repeated, looking into the box. The pendants were indeed beautiful, but none of them seemed to include the stones I had picked out.

'What are they?' I asked. Immediately he flicked out his wrist and pointed to each in turn.

'Amethyst, for astral travel like the ametrine. Rose quartz for opening the heart and developing self-love. Moonstone for calming anxieties. Lapis lazuli to bring out the energies inside you. Turquoise, for luck. Black obsidian for protection. And green aventurine to help make decisions.'

He held the box out for my inspection, and I found myself drawn to the set. I didn't have enough money to buy all of them, even just three would be a stretch. But a few of the pendants were calling to me in a way the tarot cards at my reading never did. And (I couldn't tell if it was down to my imagination running wild or the stall owner's wanton excitement), I felt an energy within me. It was as if my eyes were focusing in on particular stones just like they do in films. Maybe it was your standard retail therapy excitement, or perhaps these crystals were calling to me as conduits for my journey as this guy was suggesting.

'If I buy three pendants, could I have the tiger's eye stone as well? I'm a Leo, you see. It seems fated that I chose that one out all of the rest.'

I smiled sweetly, hoping he'd be swayed by my enthusiasm. He pursed his lips and made a 'hmm' sound in consideration. I was never one for haggling with stall owners. I never understood it. Mum always said that if you wanted something badly enough you should be prepared to walk away, but I just saw that as the opposite of what you should do. I always thought that if you want something you should get it, and if you don't, then you should walk away. If you like something enough why would you walk away?

'Three pendants and the tiger's eye for £30,' the stall owner repeated to me, and I nodded with the biggest beam of a smile I could manage. This £30 was more than I intended to spend today, and this originally included lunch, but as I saw the end of the stall owner's lip twitch I held my ground.

'Fine. I accept your deal.'

He put the box down and offered me his hand to shake. I did so, and then chose the three stones that I wanted and handed over my bank card and used the small amount of money I had in my account to claim them for myself.

'You bought what?' Paige said, as I held up my new pendant necklace, with its three gleaming crystal charms, for her inspection.

Paige had returned to the flat just after 3 pm with nothing to suggest where she had been all day. It was a long time for her to be out just wandering about by herself, and it seemed unlikely that she was shopping or she would be surrounded by a load of goodie bags not looking like she was – as if she had just got back from the gym.

She wasn't wearing any make-up, her hair was a in a loose pineapple bun and she was wearing trainers that she only ever wore to take out the bins. This was lazy-day Paige, not out for-the-better-part-of-the-day Paige.

'They're crystal pendants!' I said, ignoring my need to know what she'd been doing all day in favour of showing off my new purchases. 'Each of them has an astrological meaning that will supposedly help me get my life back on track. According to the stall owner over at the market, that is.'

'Crystals? You've got into bloody crystals now as well?' Paige said, shaking her head at me like a disgruntled mother picking up a dirty child from school.

'Yeah.'

She crossed her arms. 'And how did you pay for these life-changing crystals?'

'With the money I got from my last job,' I told her, rolling my eyes as I lowered the pendant from her gaze. 'Don't you want to know what each of them means?' I said, trying to shift her away from being annoyed with me to interested in my latest undertaking. I had just separated the turquoise stone from the moonstone when she threw her arms up in the air.

'Paige?' I asked, as she stormed into her kitchen, straight to the fridge to get a drink.

'I can't believe you right now,' she said, avoiding my gaze.

'Can't believe what?' I asked, a nervous laugh escaping my throat. What had I done to make Paige angry with me?

'I just can't . . .' she stopped to crack the can lip of her fizzy drink. 'Do you know how much money you've given me towards food and drink since you moved in?'

'Well, I haven't moved in . . .' I started to point out, although as soon as the words were out of my mouth I regretted. The day I split with David was approaching two months ago now. 'I made dinner last night.'

'Oh, wow!' Paige said, sarcastically. '*One* dinner. What a great contribution,' she scoffed and started for her bedroom.

'Okay, calm your roll. What's going on with you?'

'Nothing's going on with me actually. I've not had a chance to do much lately but look after you.'

'That's not fair.' I tried to laugh to make the moment lighter. 'It's not like I haven't given you space.'

'You're *in* my space,' she said. 'Every day. With your astrology, your birth charts and now your crystals. What's next, a spirit animal?'

I sighed. I didn't deign to answer her as I moved back to my safe space of the sofa. The fact that I considered it 'my safe space' was probably an indication that she wasn't out of order for getting annoyed at me about my ongoing stay.

'I didn't realise you wanted me to contribute more. If you want me to give you something towards the rent, I don't mind.'

Paige closed her eyes for a second and shuffled on her feet. For someone with a fair amount of money she was awfully awkward about discussing it sometimes.

'I'm not trying to pinch your pennies, I just . . . I just don't want you to fall down an astrological black hole thinking that it's going to solve all your problems.'

'I'm not,' I laughed. 'Planets and crystals won't do anything *for* me, it's just a way for me to concentrate on getting my life back together. They're just conduits for me to use. Like a plan or a to-do list.'

Paige said nothing but rocked from side to side slightly and sipped at a beer which bubbled noisily in the can.

'Fine,' she said, resigned, but not altogether happy either. 'Maybe you should just stop buying some of these crystals until you see this new flat at least. You don't know what kinds of shit you'll find in the hoarder's belongings.'

'Yeah,' I laughed, having not thought about my new flat. 'I'll be out of your hair soon,' I told her in, I hoped, a comforting way. But Paige said nothing as she turned towards her bedroom and shut the door behind her. I fell onto the sofa, deflated.

The stones were all strung onto one pendant chain that I had decided to wear daily. I held it above my face, letting it drift from side to side. Inhaling and exhaling, I focused on each of the stones patterns in turn and reminded myself of what they meant. I was glad I had chosen the moonstone alongside the turquoise and rose quartz, as my anxiety (which would usually be through the roof after any sort of conflict) was non-apparent. For just £30, I thought that it was a pretty good deal.

14

Leo: See the beauty around you and hold it in your heart ...
the Sun enters Aquarius.

When Clare text me to say that she was coming back to London two weeks after we'd met, I couldn't stop buzzing. The excitement was similar to how I had felt the night before Mum and I went to Disneyland for my tenth birthday. All my wishes were finally coming true.

Ever since Paige and I had had our little argument about the flat and needing space, she and I had been on our best behaviour around each other, and it didn't feel right.

It's true what they say, you never know what someone is like until you live with them. Paige was particular, loved routine and liked things done her way all the time, whereas I, it turned out, was a bit of a free spirit when I let myself go and didn't follow the rules. It wasn't proving to be the best combination.

Tina started to come over more often than usual after work to act as our intermediary, carrying conversations between the three of us rather than leaving me and Paige to come up with something to say to one another. I'd always wondered what it would be like not to have to be the intermediary between Tina and Paige, but this was not the dynamic I had been hoping for.

Dinners became more communal, and I had even ordered Paige a Tesco food shop delivery as a surprise, to make up for my lack of 'contribution' over the last two months. Admittedly, I was in the wrong about it, and I knew this well enough to try to fix it.

I didn't tell her or Tina that I was going to meet Clare in Kentish Town, which seemed strange. I was going on a date or meeting a potential employer for an interview I would usually text them about all of the details, down to the route I was planning on taking there and the precise time that they might need to phone the police to alert them that I had gone missing if I hadn't made it home.

My horoscope told me to focus on acceptance on the morning of the viewing, which I translated to mean accepting the generous offer that Clare had made.

The trip to Kentish Town from Dalston was uneventful and relatively calm for a London weekend, and Clare was texting me non-stop to say that she had arrived and couldn't wait to meet up. From her countless emoji usage you'd think we were old friends catching up for the first time in years. Not serendipitous acquaintances about to make a real estate deal.

As I approached the street that Google Maps wanted me to take to get to the property, I spotted her leaning against a street sign, a takeaway coffee in one hand and a phone in the other.

'Clare!' I shouted from the other side of the street, before wandering over.

'Aha!' she screamed in delight and pulled me into her for a big hug, which I reciprocated; it was just too genuine and warm to deny. 'I'm so glad you decided to come,' she squealed in my face. 'I was for sure certain that you were going to change your mind.'

I shook my head. 'Not at all. I'm excited,' I told her, looking down the street.

'Come on. It's this way. It's in a *mews*,' she said 'mews' like Miranda Hart says *Tuesday* in her titular TV show.

I thoughts that mews were for rich people and *Love, Actually* characters, not for the likes of elderly hoarders or, indeed, myself. Apparently I was wrong.

'The flat's a maisonette, technically, so it's all on one floor, and there's a flat above with a different entrance. It's got one bed, one bath, one kitchen and a glorious little garden. Although it's a bit overgrown.'

'A garden?' I repeated. Already I was plotting how to get my mum down to London to work her garden centre knowledge on weeds and inevitable overgrowth. Or, at the very least, get me a discount on some pruning shears and gardening gloves.

'It's the third one from the bottom,' Clare said, as we entered the cobblestoned mews. It was gorgeous. All the houses were lined up like Barbie dreamhouses, all whitewashed with flower boxes along the windowsills. The entrance was just off a residential road, but the street was ridiculously peaceful. We were less than a mile away from Camden and its raucous market, which made the place even more of a dream.

'Wow,' I said, looking around me at my potential neighbours' well-kept front doors and welcome mats flanked by pots of areca palms and buddleia trees. 'I feel like a Sloane Ranger.'

'Yes,' Clare said, slightly hesitantly. 'It's gorgeous out here. I'm a little concerned about the inside though. I really hadn't expected it to be in the state that it was.' She turned to face me, playing with a set of house keys in her hands. 'Don't think you're under any obligation to take this place, you know. I honestly wouldn't mind at all if you turned and ran in the other direction.'

How bad was it?

'I mean, with a little work it will be lovely but over the last few years . . .' She looked over her shoulder again and bit her lip. 'I'd better just show you,' her smile returned, however forced, and she headed for a yellow front door with number 13 on the front. Was 13 lucky or unlucky in these situations, I wondered?

As soon as Clare pushed open the door, being careful to remain on the doorstep as she did so, an almighty racket of tumbling newspapers echoed throughout the hallway.

'That will be the newspapers,' she laughed gently. 'I don't think she ever threw one out.' With a hesitant shuffle, Clare entered the flat and I followed obediently.

The smell that first hit me was of warm dust. Newspapers, takeaway menus and pamphlets carpeted the entranceway with towers of defunct magazines, and *Evening Standard* built up like curtain walls on either side. I twisted to get past, noting that the first things I would have to clear would be those towers. Otherwise, I ran the risk of a gust of wind from the door knocking them over and barricading me in my new flat, leaving me to wait for Alsatians to find my rotting corpse months later like a *Bridget Jones* cliché.

'My friend's nephew is coming over to help with the initial clean up. He has a van and can take most of the junk away to the tip, or recycling plants or wherever you're supposed to take things in London. Does London even have tips?' Clare rambled, as I continued to inspect my potential living quarters.

Underneath the hoarded ephemera, the walls were typical rental beige. 'Boob lights' (as I affectionately thought of them, since they were domed to the ceiling with a point that looked like a nipple) illuminated the room in a tinny yellow glow and the furniture that was visible was covered in a coat of dust as thick as a slice of bread.

'This is the living room,' Clare said, directing me out of the hallway. This must have been where her nan spent most of her time as there was a little floor space visible, as well as a continuation of towers around the room. In here, they were made up of books and cardboard boxes labelled 'bakeware', 'Christmas' and 'utensils'.

'Golly,' Clare said, stepping to one side so that I could edge around her into the limited space for inspection. 'How I'm ever going to find Grandma's tea set in this mess I'll never know.' I think she meant to say, 'How *you're* ever going to find', since I was the one potentially living here from now on.

Could I live here?

It was beyond a mess. I've been to landfills with more cleanliness than this place, and at least they're organised into sections. This house was just a grenade of leftovers waiting to collapse and take whoever was inside with them.

Everywhere I looked I saw a potential death trap. Death by doily suffocation, by an unstable curtain rail javelined to the heart, crushed by defunct takeaway voucher stacks, poisoned by old lady perfume.

I exhaled loudly, and turned on the spot to look around, like a dog chasing its tail in an attempt to quieten my over-active imagination.

'It's a lot,' Clare said, her voice lowering in concern. 'If I had known ...' she trailed off, as guilty grandchildren are wont to do after the loss of a grandparent.

I nodded, sympathetically. 'And all of it can just be thrown away?'

'Oh yes,' Clare nodded frantically. 'Obviously, things like jewellery and china and possibly furniture should be kept aside until I'm next down, so I can sort it all out for my mum. But otherwise, I say all of it needs to go.'

'And what about decorating?' I asked, reviewing the walls again. Underneath all the rubbish – and potential death-causing tower of boxes– the flat did look like it had good bones. There were exposed beams on either side of a boxed-over fireplace, and an archway that led to a 1950s' time-warp kitchen. With a lick of paint and maybe some garish banana leaf wallpaper I could bring the flat into the twenty-first century.

'Oh, anything goes,' Clare said. 'You can paint, put holes in the walls . . . go crazy. This place is trashed – you couldn't do anything worse to it.'

I laughed, not disagreeing with her. Trashed was polite; this was the Chernobyl of bed-sits.

'It's a big ask,' Clare said. 'I'm not even sure this place is *legally* habitable.'

'I'm sure it's fine,' I said quickly, not wanting Clare to suddenly change her mind about renting it out. One more week living at Paige's while walking on eggshells and I thought I might get a splinter from our friendship that I'd never be able to get out. 'The structure looks stable, it's just messy.'

Clare made a 'hmm' sound again and then sighed. 'Well, if you're sure and you're happy, like I said, I'd be *grateful* for someone to help me with the clear-out. Obviously, I don't think of you as just the person to *clear it out*. I'd put together some contract with the lawyers so that you'd live here rent-free for a time and then at a highly discounted rate. You know, he was saying I could charge someone over £1500 a month to live here.'

I gulped at that amount. That was more than David and I had ever paid together, let alone just me as a solo renter on a freelancer's rate.

'But I'm just not into real estate. It's too much bother and so far away from home. I'd just sell it the second it was clear. Although, if you cleared it, I would let you rent it until you wanted to move out. You could stay as long as you wanted on the discounted rate and I wouldn't increase it, either. And I really am happy to put it all in writing.' Clearly Clare *really* didn't want anything to do with real estate if she was giving away a potential mint. This place could fund her entire retirement, yet she seemed desperate to get it off her hands.

And I'm a charitable sort.

'I think I can do this,' I said to Clare with a smile. 'I work from home as a freelancer so I could clear bits out throughout the day, and I'm not too bad at DIY. At least, there's nothing I can't pick up on YouTube.'

'Are you sure?' Clare continued to press.

I took one more glance around, forcing myself to look past my potential death certificate and imagine myself as a pretentious Camden resident with her own mews flat, like a modern-day Princess Di. 'Yes,' I said definitively, offering out my hand.

She looked at it briefly. 'You should check out the bathroom first. It's avocado green.'

'Perfect,' I said. Avocado was a staple of my generation. 'So long as the plumbing works, I'm good with avocado.'

Clare beamed at me and once again looked at my hand before shaking it vigorously.

I'd either just made the best deal of my life or got myself into the biggest pile of shit. Figuratively and literally.

15

*Leo: Work towards maintaining peace by exposing truth . . .
there is a New Moon tonight.*

'I did it!' I ran, screaming into Paige's flat, one arm waving in
the air and the other holding the fish and chips takeaway I'd
picked up on the way back from Clare's grandma's flat.

Tina and Paige were sat together on the sofa.

'Jeez!' Paige said, her hand over her heart. 'You scared me.'

'Sorry,' I sang, skipping in. 'Hey Tina. You back already?'

She had only just been here last night for drinks after work.
It was Saturday, early afternoon – normally she'd still be in
bed, eating a bowl of dry Shreddie's and WhatsApping the
Chamber of Secrets group about the TV show she had
decided to binge-watch that day. Saturday daytime was her
chance to cleanse herself from work; Saturday evening was
usually the earliest I'd expect to see her.

She shrugged at me and began playing with her ponytail.

'What did you do?' Paige asked, walking around the coffee
table to get some plates out for the celebratory takeaway I
had just brought home.

'I went and saw the flat with Clare.'

'The woman you met on the tube?' Tina confirmed.

I nodded with a huge smile. 'She wasn't lying – she honestly
does have a flat and it *does* definitely need a clear-out, but she
agreed to let me live there rent-free. And, best of all, she said
afterwards that I could live there at a discounted rate which
is fixed until I want to move. Unless, of course, I meet

someone and they move in with me, in which case, she'll revaluate. But, of course, I laughed off that suggestion!'

If I was going to clear out and decorate a flat, it was going to be to my tastes and for my relaxation. I had never been able to do that with David, not least because of so many stupid contractual rules about making a flat liveable:

You can't paint. You can't hang pictures up. You can't burn candles. You can't have a life or good taste.

But now I had every opportunity to make a flat a home. And at an impossible-to-get-in-London price. If that didn't prove that following my horoscope and listening to my stars was working in my favour, I didn't know what would.

'I genuinely think my luck has changed. The place is a shithole, right now. But once I'm done with it, it is going to be spectacular. I just know it.'

All the time I was speaking, I was unpacking the greasy brown packaging of the fish and chips onto the breakfast bar, but Paige and Tina remained silent.

Paige was sorting the plates at a snail's pace, purposely quietly, while Tina just looked flushed.

'What's going on with you guys?' I asked.

'What?' they both said in unison, their heads turning towards me at once.

'We're just processing.' Tina laughed, awkwardly. 'It's kind of an unexpected piece of news.'

I scoffed, 'Not really. I've told you about all this.'

'Yeah, but we'd didn't actually think it was going to be pulled off,' Paige said. 'Living rent-free, in *London*?'

I shrugged. 'The planets are clearly aligned in my favour.' They bloody should be after all of the rules I was following with my daily horoscope, dos and don'ts and plotting my birth chart.

Paige turned away but I heard the 'oh God' muttered under her breath irritably; I chose to ignore it. She wasn't going to ruin my mood or good fortune.

'We're happy for you,' Tina said, smiling and forcing herself up from the sofa. 'We really are. And if you need any help—'

I saw Paige's head swivel to Tina with what was undoubtedly a scowl at Tina proffering help from both of them, but I shook my head.

'I think I'll be okay. Clare's got her friend's nephew, or someone, coming over to help me with the initial clear-out and then the rest is really just hoovering and dusting. It will be good to have a project.'

Tina leant on the breakfast bar and grinned at me. 'You do love a project,' she said, stealing a chip from the packaging that I had just opened.

'I do!' I agreed, joining her in eating some chips from the greasy wrapper, ignoring the plates Paige had laid out.

* * *

The following day I was up before the Sun. What little belongings I had at Paige's I packed into carrier bags (I'm so classy), ready to take with me to the flat in Kentish Town. Clare was going to meet me to hand over the keys, and to introduce me to the man she had somehow convinced to help with the initial clear-out. It would be a few days before the contract was ready to sign, but all of that could be done via email, and I trusted Clare to keep to her word.

Sure, I would have to pay the bills and all of the design costs for materials like paint and screwdrivers. But honestly, compared to paying regular London rent by myself it was an absolute steal. Even my mum thought so!

I called her the night before to fill her in on the details. Grandad was out with Rita at a local art fair to show off his latest sewing creations, and Mum was lazily tucking into a ready-meal roast dinner and watching *Strictly Come Dancing*.

'Whatever you're doing to appease the stars, keep doing it,' Mum said, her smile apparent even through the phone.

'Will do, Mum,' I said, before we returned to discussing the underlying sexual tension between judges Craig and Bruno on *Strictly*.

'Are you packed to go already?' Paige asked, as she appeared from her bedroom in her stylish Oliver Bonas pyjamas. She headed straight to the kettle to make a cup of coffee, and I noticed she didn't offer to make me one.

'Yep! I couldn't sleep.'

She nodded. 'How are you getting there?'

'Taxi. I'll order one in a minute. Don't want to get there too early in case Clare isn't there yet.'

'Can't you just text her to say you're on your way?'

I shrugged. 'It's only a half-hour drive, and I don't know where she's staying.'

'If she were sensible, she'd probably stay nearby.'

I got the passive aggressive edge of the word 'sensible' in Paige's voice but chose not to comment on it. I didn't want to leave the flat with an argument.

'You know you've been a lifesaver the last few months, right?'

Paige shrugged as she poured water into her mug.

'I mean it. You didn't have to let me stay here, or eat all your food. Or use your bathroom!'

'Well, I wasn't going to make you pee in the corner like a cat,' she smirked.

'I was actually referring to your amazing shower.'

She nodded. 'It is pretty amazing.'

'It's a miracle to find a good shower in a rental in London.'

'I know!' she said throwing up her hands in the air. 'In half the flats I've lived in, I've felt cleaner before showering than after.'

And just like that, we were back to the chilled-out mates that we were supposed to be.

'The whole flat's amazing. And I think I've finally broken in your sofa.'

She laughed.

'Honestly! I have the back blisters to prove it.'

'I'm gonna miss you,' she said, leaning against the breakfast bar as elegantly as Audrey Hepburn with her famous cigarette in *Breakfast at Tiffany's*.

'I'll miss you too. But now, you can come and visit me and stay over. Well . . . maybe leave it a few weeks. I don't think there's even a bed for me yet, let alone a sofa for you.'

Paige nodded. 'I'm looking forward to it. It'll be nice to have a change of scenery for once. I can't exactly depend on Tina for that, not with those irritating housemates.'

I nodded at that. The fact that they were all teachers made them rowdy as hell at weekends and tetchy as live grenades on weekdays.

My phone buzzed and I looked down to see a message from Clare.

'Aha, Clare's heading over to the flat now,' I said, smiling at Paige, who adjusted her footing and sighed.

'Better order that taxi,' I said.

'Yeah,' said Paige, somewhat sadly. 'I'd better get you a suitcase.'

'I'm fine with the bags,' I tried to argue, but she lifted her hand to silence me.

'Darling, you look like a homeless drag queen. No.'

Wow. I'd need some Sudocrem for that burn.

* * *

'I'm so excited!' Clare shouted in my face as she opened the door to the flat and pulled me and the suitcase inside. Immediately, her typical rambling began. 'I've got a train to catch so I'm a bit all over the place. But I spoke to the lawyer last night and everything is totally fine and on track – I mean, I think they think I'm crazy, but I'm used to that. Also, I booked a plumber to sort out that leaky sink in the kitchen and they're going to do a check of the pipes for me.'

Thank God. It would be typically Krystal if I moved into a new place only to have a pipe to burst on me, *again*. And you'd think it would be more likely in an older build like this, than the newly renovated flat David and I had previously lived in.

'I'll pay that all off. It seems unfair to make you pay for appliances. Also, I checked, and the fridge is clean. Thank God my grandma lived off tinned pear and condensed milk. Can you imagine if she ate fresh fruit or drank regular milk? We'd find a new disease growing in that fridge now!' Clare's laugh echoed around the room, threatening to cause an avalanche, but I was happy that she was happy.

I left my belongings in the centre of the living room and immediately began plotting my day's activities. Firstly, I needed to clear the entrance way and then I could start on finding space to lay down the sleeping bag I had ordered from Amazon to be delivered later on that day. There was no way I was sleeping on a dead woman's mattress, so until I could afford a new one, I would be sleeping on the floor. Thankfully, Paige's sofa had prepared me for that.

From outside, a car horn began to hoot.

'He's here!' Clare called out. I assume she meant the friend's nephew. 'He'd better stop honking that horn, though, or he'll wake the whole neighbourhood. And it's a Sunday!' Clare gasped in exaggerated horror and rushed out of the living room to the front door. I lingered a moment longer, smiling to myself as I processed that this was my new home.

I got my phone to quickly text the girls, taking the most close-up of selfies in front of the mantelpiece to avoid capturing some of the disastrous hoarding around me.

Kris: *I'm in the flat! And it's all mine.* 😬 *I can't wait to get*
you girls round here to show off my buried-deep-beneath-
shit new home.

I heard Clare's footsteps returning and pocketed the phone
to hide my selfie-shame. 'Mind your step,' she was saying to
the man.

'And this is Krystal, the new tenant and all-round lifesaver. You'll love her!' Clare said to the man, who began grinning the instant I turned around.

'Leo!' he said.

'Oh, fuck.'

16

*Leo: Don't make a move without evaluating things . . . Jupiter
and Saturn have nestled into Aquarius.*

'I didn't know you knew each other?' Clare was whispering
to me – although her whispers were more like husky shouts.

'We don't,' I groaned, lifting a load of papers into the back
of *Ryan's* van. 'We've met though.'

Clare had decided to stick around a little longer and help
with the initial clearing of the newspapers, mostly because
she wanted the gossip as to my less-than-happy greeting at
the sight of Ryan.

'I've known him since he was a lad. He used to come and
stay with his Aunt Aoife, during the holidays when she lived
in Liverpool. She and I were neighbours, before she moved
down to London. The amount of times he'd come knocking
on my door because he'd kicked his football into my back
garden. Eventually, I just left the door open for him.'

'I know Aoife, too,' I said, laughing unbelievably at the
shared connection. This was getting stupidly unlikely now,
especially for London. Not only had a total stranger given
me a rent-free flat, but now she knew my astrology teacher
and her arsehole of a nephew who I happened to have some
– potentially sexual – tension with? Had I fallen into a
Hallmark romance? Was I living in a *Truman Show*? What
was going on?!

'What are the odds that you know the only people I know
in London!' Clare said, as she piled some newspapers in next

to mine. She placed her hands on her hips. 'This whole thing has just been fated, hasn't it? If you believe in fate, that is.' Clare laughed.

'Oh, I'm coming around to it,' I chuckled darkly, heading around the side of the van to collect another set of newspapers. Ryan was just exiting the flat, his arms laden with cardboard boxes full of rubbish that clinked and clanked together. Immediately my smile vanished into a scowl, but his ever-amused grin remained in place.

'Nice place you got here,' he teased, as I grazed past him.

'Thanks,' I said bitterly in return.

'Oh, is that the time?' Clare said.

I turned to see her checking her watch.

'I really do have to go, otherwise I'll miss the train. Are you two going to be okay?' she asked, looking between me and Ryan.

'Yeah, o'course,' he said. 'You go on.'

Clare looked from him to me, her eyebrows raised. I sighed. He was only here to clear out some of the mess, then he'd be out of my life again. Until the next chance meeting anyway. I'm blaming Venus for this issue – she had clearly got her knickers in a twist when it came to Ryan and his stupid Irish accent.

'I'm good,' I promised Clare.

She offered out her arms for a hug and I embraced her quickly. 'Any issues, just let me know,' she said into my hair.

'Will do,' I said, squeezing her gently. No matter the unfortunate appearance of Ryan, I was still so grateful to Clare for giving me a new beginning.

'Bye love,' she said, releasing me and walking away. She patted Ryan on the shoulder and then she was gone. Out of the mews and out of the city.

'Right then,' Ryan said, standing up and shutting the van doors. 'What's next?'

Without replying, I turned on my heel and re-entered the flat. What was next? We'd cleared the majority of newspaper and pamphlet build-up from the hallway, so we could now at least enter the flat forwards and not sideways.

Next up was the living room. I stood in its centre, revolving on the spot trying to figure out which tower of belongings seemed the least perilous to move. All of them seemed to be piled on top of one another in the world's most spherical version of household Jenga.

With a sigh, I approached a tower of boxes labelled FRAGILE. Tiptoeing, I tried to get a grip on the top box.

'I wouldn't do that one first,' Ryan said easily from the doorway. He was resting with his arms crossed, observing me but not helping.

'And you're such an expert?'

'Well, I'm taller than you for one. I'd suggest leaving that whole wall of boxes to me, is all.'

'I'm fine,' I said, straining to get my fingertips around the box. So long as I could pull it forward a little way first, I would be able to grab it properly.

'Uh-huh,' Ryan said, aggravatingly.

I inhaled deeply and put my plan in motion, tugging gently at the boxes to pull the pile forwards, but as I did so I lost my footing and couldn't grab it in time. Falling backwards, I twisted my ankle beneath me and fell onto my tailbone, just as the box toppled.

Thankfully, the box was mislabelled. This box appeared to contain a multitude of not-so-fragile heavy moth-eaten knitted blankets.

Why was it that everytime I saw Ryan recently I was buried beneath some sort of fabric? The wool was heavy, but not sound-muffling; I could hear his laughter as I pushed myself back up with a groan. He had at least walked over and removed the box and started to take some of the blankets off me.

'Good attempt,' he smirked. 'That's one way to get a box down.' My face was burning, as was my backside, as I pummelled the blankets back into the box.

'It wasn't on purpose,' I told him.

'I know, I'm just teasing you.'

'I thought you were here to help me?' I reminded him.

He nodded. 'That I am. As a favour to Clare.'

'Then help me, don't laugh at me. You don't even need to speak to me. In fact, I think I'd prefer that.' With that scalding request I stood up, denying the urge to rub my back where it was throbbing from the pain of the fall.

Ryan said nothing, as per my request, but continued to smile. I'd never met a more smiley person in my life. He knew it pissed me off. It was a ploy to annoy me.

'And quit smiling,' I told him, as I attempted to take a step forwards only to remember that my ankle was properly twisted and I needed to rest a moment.

'You alright there?' he asked, lifting the box of blankets off the floor.

'I'm fine. And I told you not to talk.'

He shrugged and turned, taking the box with him without another word. The second he was gone I pulled a face and reached down to rub my ankle. This was not going to impact my day at all, I told myself. I was not a weakling, and I was not about to behave like Kate Winslet in *Sense and Sensibility* because of a stupid twisted ankle. I hobbled to the doorway and rested against it.

As soon as Ryan was back, I pointed to another box.

'I hurt my ankle, so you can do the heavy lifting. But I'll tell you what needs to go where.'

Ryan shrugged, still not saying a word. It was heavenly.

'You can take that one next.' I pointed to a box labelled 'Christmas' which was sat on top of several others by the closed-off fireplace.

Ryan walked over to where I suggested but hesitated. He turned and lifted his hand. 'Permission to speak.'

I rolled my eyes. 'What?'

'It would be better if I cleared this side first,' he said, pointing to the boxes under the arch. 'They're all balanced on top of one other. It would be better to take each of the boxes out from end to end, like a snake. You're less likely to cause avalanches then.'

I looked around the room and realised he was right. The boxes had a beginning and end, like the snake on an old Nokia phone. The sides didn't meet, and that was why there was space in the middle of the room. If we disrupted any of the boxes from the inside first, then we would likely lose the floorspace to fallen items. And since this was where I was planning to sleep, I couldn't have that.

'Fine. Do what you want,' I said, leaning against the wall with my arms crossed as my ankle continued to throb.

Ryan shrugged and started to work. He didn't say anything else for the next hour as he cleaned out box after box. Not once did he question my ability to carry anything, or moan about the fact that I was sat on the floor on my phone checking my horoscope most of the time.

Ironically, the prediction for the day was: *Life will throw you some surprises.* No shit. It had delivered on that at least – twice over. Ryan *and* a box of blankets!

The do's of the day included tea, messiness and music. And the don'ts included charged silence, blame game and below the belt.

Sometimes the planets really sucked.

As soon as I realised silence was something to be avoided today, I sucked my teeth and told Ryan that he was welcome to chat if he wanted to.

'Not really,' he said, a little breathless and sweaty. 'I could do with a cuppa though.'

'I don't have a kettle yet,' I told him. 'And I don't think you'll want a cup of tea from the one currently in the kitchen.'

'Why?' he asked inquisitively, leaning against the mantelpiece of the fireplace.

'Well, when Clare opened it up she discovered that a family of spiders had decided to move in for free as well.'

'Oh,' he said, nodding and shuddering.

'You don't like spiders?' I asked, smiling at having found a weak point of his.

'Can't stand the things. Big ones or little ones. It's the scuttling. Anything that scuttles should be stomped on.'

'They're not that bad,' I teased. 'They're really useful for minor pest control around the house. You never get flies if you have a spider.'

'You never get flies if you keep your house clean either,' Ryan suggested. 'I'm surprised *you're* not complaining about the spiders, though.'

I lifted my hands in my air to remind him of the room we were standing in. 'Do you really think I have the luxury of caring about spiders in a place like this?' That gave him pause.

'Ah,' he said.

'Yeah,' I laughed. 'We'll be lucky if there isn't a spider in every corner right now.'

'Don't say that!' he said, really shuddering this time.

'You're such a wuss,' I told him as I pushed myself off the floor. My foot was feeling a lot better now, stiff in places but fine enough to walk on and get back to light lifting at least. 'I thought it was supposed to be the other way around, that women were terrified of spiders and men had to get rid of them for them.'

'That's stereotypically sexist. I'm perfectly happy for a woman to get rid of my spiders for me.' He lifted a box into his arms and offered it to me. 'Can you carry this?'

I peered inside. It was just a box of tinsel with a brassy Christmas star on top.

'Sure, I think I can manage,' I said, taking it from him.

'The van's almost full, but just shove it in wherever you can,' he said as he followed me out of the flat and back into the mews. 'What do you want to sort out next?'

'Well, if I can't clear it then I'll just leave it I suppose,' I shrugged awkwardly with the tinsel sashaying in the box. 'Are you only helping out today?'

'No. Clare said this wasn't a one-day kind of job. And looking at the place I'm not sure it's even a one-week one either.'

I placed the box I was holding at the very edge of his van. It really was filled from floor to ceiling with boxes and rubbish bags of utter crap. To look in the living room you'd think we'd hardly moved anything – or Ryan hadn't.

I sighed heavily.

'Look,' Ryan began, placing his box beside mine. 'I don't mind coming back to help. It looks like you need it—' I instantly turned to glare at him. I didn't like the idea of him thinking that I needed help. It made me feel pitiful. 'I don't mean like that, I just mean you need a van. Do you drive?'

Exhaling through my nose shortly I shook my head. He had got me there.

'Well then, I can help.'

'But what about work?' I asked. I didn't even know what he did. 'And money?'

He shrugged and pushed his box into a spare nook and cranny he managed to find in the back of the van. 'I'm a photographer,' he said. 'I mostly do school pictures and it's only for a few hours here or there. I've got plenty of free time. What about you? Are you just a weekend home DIY-er?'

'No,' I said, attempting to push my box into the van as well. 'I'm a writer. Freelancing at the minute, so I'll be home all the time.'

'Right then. Well, how about when I'm not working and I don't need the van for storing my kit, I come over and help.'

Pausing at my failed attempt to get the tinsel into the van, I turned to look at him.

'I can't pay you, you know? I'm not just moving in and clearing out the flat because I feel like it or because I'm doing Clare a favour.'

Ryan shrugged. 'I know,' he said, smiling once more.

Something dawned on me. 'Why didn't she offer you the flat? I mean, if you don't know already, I'm living here rent-free. Surely, being a family friend, she'd want you to have the place over some stranger.'

Ryan nodded still smiling effervescently. 'Yeah, you'd think so, but I've got a place.'

'But you must be paying rent?' Why would he want to help me, when I could have just stolen a perfect financial situation from under him. He didn't know me or owe me anything. I didn't even like him.

'I live with Aoife,' he said. 'Rent's not really massive for me either.'

'But you could have your own place?'

'But I don't want my own place.'

My box was still perched on the edge of the van precariously. If I let it go, even for a second, it was going to spill tacky Christmas decor across the courtyard. Not something I thought would fit with its current aesthetic.

'I don't get you,' I said, without even thinking. My cheeks blushed, but Ryan continued to smile.

'Do you need a hand with that?' he asked, glancing to the box I was still holding up awkwardly.

'Sure,' I said, letting him move me out of the way and force the box into a space I hadn't seen. 'I don't think we'll fit anymore in there,' I told him, and he agreed, slamming the doors closed and clapping his hands together.

'Want to get some lunch?' he asked. 'I know a burger place around the corner. My treat.'

'Shouldn't it be *my* treat, since you're helping me and not the other way around?' I pointed out.

'If you insist.' I thought of the £12.60 remaining in my overdraft.

'No!'

He jumped and I cleared my throat.

'No, I wouldn't want to deprive you of an opportunity to be nice.'

Without giving him a second glance I went to lock up the flat. Looking up at the sky as I turned the key, I pictured Venus sitting smugly in the galaxy and muttered to myself: *I'm going to get you for this.*

17

Leo: Information exchange is a key part of bringing people and ideas together in a constructive manner ... Venus moves into Capricorn.

The burger place was a lot classier than I was expecting. Ryan gave across a bit of a skater-boy vibe, but really he was more indie chic when it came to taste.

The café was small, with about ten tables that sat two people each, surrounded by reclaimed wood decor and industrial lighting. The host sat us at the back, near a bar, and gave us the tiny menu, which included three choices: burger, steak or meatballs.

'I'll have the meatballs,' I said to the waiter.

'And I'll have the burger please,' Ryan said. 'Can we have water for the table as well?'

'You don't want a proper drink?' I asked.

'Can't, I'm driving,' he reminded me.

'Oh yeah,' I flushed. 'Just water for me as well, then. Thanks.'

The waiter hurried off with our order and suddenly I realised I was sat opposite Ryan and would need to make some sort of small talk to pass the time. For some reason, when I thought about us getting lunch I seemed to have forgotten this requirement.

'So . . .' Ryan said, resting his chin in hands.

'So?' I repeated, ever the cliché. Why did this feel like a

date? It most certainly was *not* a date. I didn't even have my rose quartz pendant with me. It was lunch after work. Nothing more, I reminded myself. But then I mentally smacked myself for needing this reminder in the first place.

'You said you were a writer,' he said, and I nodded. 'What do you write about?'

'Anything,' I said, smiling. 'Everything. I don't have a niche. It's not really possible when you're just trying to pay the bills.'

'But if you could write about anything, what would it be?'

'Erm . . .' I thought for a moment. 'Maybe tech,' I told him.

'Tech?' he seemed surprised.

'What? Did you think I was going to say fashion and cosmetics or something?'

'No, not necessarily, but maybe . . . celebrity interviews or opinion pieces.'

I scoffed. 'Celebrity interviews aren't all they're cracked up to be. Half the time you're left waiting around in hotel rooms with a load of strangers, and you get all of five minutes with some stroppy person who's hungover or jetlagged. They've probably been asked the same questions for the last two hours and don't know if they're coming or going. And opinion pieces are just so . . . personal,' I finished lamely. 'I'm not sure I want people to know *me* when they're reading my writing. I want to educate them, not give them my own thoughts and feelings.'

'Why not?' he asked, lifting his head off his hands for a moment.

'They might change,' I said quickly. 'An opinion I had in my 20s might not be an opinion I have in my thirties. I might suddenly be all about polyamory in my thirties when in my twenties I was very firmly monogamous.'

'That would be a very startling change of opinion,' Ryan laughed, and I realised I might have said too much.

'I mean, I'm not polyamorous, and I'm pretty certain I never will be.'

David might have wanted to force polyamory on me, but that was a decision that I knew I would never make. Or, at least, I thought I would never make. 'But, at the same time . . .' I held my hands up in defence.

He nodded. 'I know what you mean. Sharing an opinion for the world to read and process is very personal. It's the same with art, actually, to some degree.'

'Art? I thought you were a photographer?'

'Well, photography is a form of art isn't it?' he said, leaning back in his chair.

'Yes, it is, I suppose. But I'm not sure – and this isn't meant to be insulting – but I'm not sure if school photographs are what I would call art? At least, not according to my school photographs, which would look better in flames than they do in frames.'

Ryan laughed heartily. His chuckle was throaty and deep and seemed to go on for a long while. Long enough that even I began to laugh with him against my better instincts.

'Yeah, you're right, school photos aren't exactly going to land me in a gallery anytime soon. But I do it to pay the bills, not because I love it.'

'Good thing, too,' I said, 'I think *loving* taking school photos shows a lack of ambition, which is a complete turn-off.' I gulped. Why did I mention turn-offs? Once again, I found myself reminding my conscious that *this was not a date!* Ryan smiled again.

'You smile a lot. Has anyone ever told you that?' I said quickly, to change the subject.

He shrugged, still smiling characteristically. 'You smile, too' he remarked.

'Not as often,' I said, although I felt my lips twitch as I said it, and he caught it.

'You should. Or you will, after you spend some time with me.'

I scoffed, just as our waiter arrived with our jug of water and glasses. Ryan made a big gentlemanly fuss of thanking him and pouring us both a glass.

'You're also very cocky, on top of being very smiley.'

'Trust me, Irishness is catching. You'll see what I mean over time.'

'Sure I will,' I said sarcastically, sipping my water. 'I think the only Irishness I share with you is the fact that we both drive on the same side of the road, speak the same language and have joint custody of Graham Norton.'

'Cheers to that,' he said, clinking his glass against my own.

My smile escaped my tightly pressed lips before I could even think to subdue it. Damn it.

'So, what kind of tech?'

'What?' I asked, confused.

'What kind of tech would you write about? You said that would be your niche if you could write about anything.'

'Oh.' I'd already forgotten we'd discussed that. 'I like CMS. Content management systems like WordPress and such. I'd probably write a lot about the importance of owning your own website and keeping it up to date and not just leaving it as some ancient landing page like we're still in 2010.'

'Wow,' Ryan said, nodding in genuine interest. 'Do you build those systems then?'

'I can do,' I told him, with a hint of pride. 'I built my own website.'

'Really? You have a website?'

'Yes. I do,' I said pointedly, just realising I had walked into a honey trap in which he could tease me mercilessly. If he knew I wrote a blog about astrology and my cause to learn more about the planets' effects on my life, he would run with it like Usain Bolt and never fucking stop.

'Could you build one for me?'

You what?

'A website?' I confirmed. That wasn't where I was expecting this conversation to go.

'Well, more like, show me the basics.'

I sat back and held my glass of water to my chest. 'What do you want a website for?'

'Pornographic art,' he said, straight-faced. I lifted my eyebrows in my best attempt at some haughty school mistress of the 1960s.

'And really?'

He laughed. 'I want somewhere I can showcase my art. My *actual* photos, not my school photos – or pornography, just to be clear.'

'Good thing, too,' I smiled. 'I could build you a website. It would be a lot easier than just telling you how.'

'Yeah, but I can't . . .' he trailed off, clearly about to say he couldn't afford it. Not that I would charge megabucks anyway. I was being honest when I said I would write about tech because I enjoyed it. I really did have a passion for building websites and managing content systems. It was part of the reason I got hired at *Craze*, as I would have – had I not been made redundant – been responsible for posting most of the articles on the digital site.

'I wouldn't ask you to pay,' I told him, as if this was obvious. 'You're helping me clear out my flat. I mean, the hire cost alone of a van would bankrupt me right now, so you're doing *me* a favour. The least I could do is return it in some way.'

For the first time since we'd met Ryan was quiet. His lips didn't curve up in amusement and there was no teasing to be heard. I couldn't tell if it was shock that silenced him, or a genuine mind-blank of not knowing what to say. He just stared at me.

'Besides,' I said, to fill the silence, which I tend to hate. 'If I'm building you a website, then you can do all of the heavy lifting. Really, it's a win-win-win for me, and a win for you.'

'What's the third win?' he asked.

'Well, you're helping me,' I told him, as if it was obvious.

'Yeah, I'm helping you, and this would get you out of heavy lifting – don't think I missed that comment – so what's the third win?'

What is the third win? I wondered to myself. I hadn't considered it, I had just said it.

'I like CMS systems,' I said lamely, after a moment of consideration.

If Ryan didn't believe me or thought I was hiding some-thing – which I wasn't sure about myself – he didn't get a chance to say. Thankfully, our food arrived then, and we had an excuse to change the subject from our new business deal, to a discussion about my odd preference for pepper over salt on my chips.

'That's just odd, even for a Leo, he teased.

'I like things hot. Sue me.'

That shut him up quickly enough.

18

Leo: Going with the flow may be an easier route to follow ...
The Sun resides in Capricorn and your 6th house.

Sleeping in a hoarder's old house, surrounded by their furnishings and belongings, was strange to say the least. Curled up on the floor in the cheapest sleeping bag I could find online – which was definitely a stupid buy, since it was made of the thinnest material and practically letting the cold in and not out – my mind wouldn't let me relax long enough to drift off.

What if those spiders you talked about crawl over you in your sleep?

What if you over-stretch in the night and cause an avalanche of doilies to topple and suffocate you?

What if you forgot to lock the front door? Or you did, but the mechanism is so ancient that a light tap might let someone in?

What if that whooshing sound you keep hearing isn't the wind outside but something more Edgar Allan Poe-ish? What if there is a heart beneath floorboards?

There weren't even any floorboards! My mind was just intent on making sure I got no rest. After two hours of useless breathing and counting exercises, I gave up. Turning on the overhead light, I re-examined my life choices.

Three months ago, I thought I had *the* life. Then, I had this one, and it was exactly as it looked, overly messy and impossible to sort out. There wasn't even any Wi-Fi installed yet, which at least would have made it possible to watch re-runs of Marie Kondo's *Tidying Up* show to boost my confidence in my abilities to sort it all out. Nothing here brings me joy. '*Chuck the lot of it,*' I heard her sweet little voice say.

But even worse than that, there was no one to talk to about it at 1 am.

I realised, my heart sinking in my chest, that this was the first time I was truly on my own since I was ... never. Growing up, Mum was always there. Then university, where I shared a dorm room and later a house with six others. I moved straight to London with Tina, and then found David 18 months later. We lived in ratty flat-shares and overpriced studios until we moved into our own proper flat together. And then I lived with Paige.

This was the first time I was entirely on my own.

While I thought that this would be amazing, the rose-tinted idealism of having my own space had quickly faded and reminded me that I was on my own.

Just as Violet had said on Cecil Street: there was a big difference between being lonely and being alone. And right now, I was experiencing both.

My phone pinged, a notification that my latest horoscope had arrived in my account. I rushed to open it, my knuckles cracking as I moved my fingers in the cold.

Today you have opportunities to be creative. This could be a genuine lucky break achieved by being in the right place at the right time. You will probably take advantage of it, because right now, you're full of inspiration. Keep track of your ideas, write them down.

All it needed was a *You got this!* line at the end and it would have been like a life coach telling me to stop moaning and get on with it.

'Shit,' I said aloud, forcing my legs out of the sleeping bag – which was really useless for anything other than being a dust sheet – and got up.

Hoisting on a pair of joggers over my pyjamas bottoms and grabbing a thick cardigan, I got to work.

Sure, I couldn't do heavy lifting or chucking out hefty things without Ryan here to help. But I could sort things out in my own way and start making this place more habitable. I only had a suitcase worth of belongings, but there would be space enough in a wardrobe to hang up my clothes, or a shelf I could clear to line up the astrology books from the library.

I decided to ignore my self-pitying thoughts and got to clearing things into piles. Turning on a 'moving house' themed Spotify playlist and getting to work, I soon had a shelf cleared for my books. But then my new neighbour above me began shouting about the noise – clearly not an Ed Sheeran fan – and I thought I'd give the whole sleep thing another go.

★ ★ ★

Three days later, with the internet installed by a very confused engineer from Virgin and an impressive amount of space cleared for me in the living room, I started to give myself props for being so self-sufficient.

A very timely invoice had been paid into my account, giving me the chance to thrift some new homeware items. While all my instincts told me to go to TK Maxx and just go ahead and buy throw cushions and macrame wall hangings, I resisted.

Instead, I turned to online marketplaces and charity stores, seeking out all of the items that I needed at inexpensive prices.

My best bargain – although I was sure Paige would be horrified – was finding a barely used mattress on Facebook marketplace for only 75p. Delivery not included of course, but I knew I could ask Ryan to collect and haul it over for me in the next few days. I had texted him – yes, we had exchanged numbers – to ask his permission and he replied with a thumbs up emoji. (Although later he replied with actual words to point out that my mattress had cost less than two Creme Eggs and asked if he should fumigate it before he put it in his van. I ignored him).

I was surprised by the quality of the items I managed to find in nearby charities shops. I wasn't averse to them before I moved into my own space, but with two incomes and an overly active desire to impress, I think I avoided them and opted instead for more well-known brands in an attempt to fulfil an Instagram fantasy.

At a car boot sale in Hackney, that I dragged a hungover Tina too one Saturday, I found a pink tasselled pendant light I was determined to hang in the living room in place of the ugly boob light. And when I went to meet Paige for a morning coffee in Dalston, I couldn't help but stop in a vintage store that was selling a collection of depressed glasses marked up at half price in the window display. I couldn't wait to spread them around the flat holding little collections of crystals, loose change and stud earrings. There were also gold-tarnished candlesticks that would look gorgeous on the mantelpiece, not to mention a five-tiered bookshelf for only £10, which I had the bravery to carry to the flat on my own. Thankfully, the shop was only a couple of minutes away, otherwise I think my lungs might have exploded with the effort. Not to mention my arms – which hadn't had any weight training, apart from lugging boxes of old shoes and handbags to thrift stores down the road.

It wasn't only charity shop and online finds that I found a use for. Some of Clare's grandmother's belongings were not as terrible as I expected on first inspection. Yes, the creepy nativity scene – she owned a lot of Christmas stuff! – had to go, as did the countless shoes and dictionaries she owned. But the standing lamp with a tarnished monkey around its base that was hidden in a wardrobe of all places, along with her pretty art deco vases, were lovely finds. I checked with Clare whenever I found a new piece that was useable or maybe worth something, and every time she told me I could keep it or chuck it. I was surprised by how much I decided to keep, as was Ryan, when he showed up with my mattress a few days later.

'I have to hand it to you, Leo, this thing is spotless. Where do you want this?' he asked, dragging the mattress into the hallway.

'In the living room.'

'On the floor?'

'Yep,' I nodded, boiling the kettle – I had bought a new one for his sake. 'Until I clear the bedroom, the living room is my lot.'

'I suppose it's bigger than some flats I've seen,' he teased, as he pulled the mattress in and dropped it to the floor, heavily. 'Have you got sheets?' he asked.

I rolled my eyes and brought him the freshly brewed cup of tea.

'Of course,' I said. Although, I'd actually completely forgotten. Oh well, something else to add to my ever-growing shopping list. My horoscope was right again; I definitely needed a list.

'Wow,' Ryan said, taking the mug and looking around him. 'You've made some headway.'

'Ahh, I see you made the fatal mistake of doubting me.'

'I didn't doubt you, I just . . . didn't think it would happen so quickly.'

I shrugged and sat back down. Using copious amounts of precariously balanced cushions and a lap tray, I had created a little office nook for me to get some work done when I wasn't cleaning or re-decorating the flat.

'I'm a very impatient woman,' I told him, refreshing my work page and continuing on with adding the finishing touches to my latest blog post.

At my last astrology class with Aoife, who was aware that Ryan was helping me move into her old friend's grandma's house (say that three times quickly), we had been discussing the social planets: Jupiter and Saturn.

I was fascinated by anything to do with Saturn, as everything that was going on with my life was to do with my Saturn Return. While Jupiter was all about morals and idealism, Saturn focused more on boundaries and societal structures.

Looking over my birth chart, I had discovered that Jupiter's position when I was born meant that I was very into setting goals, while also finding success through introspection. That explained why I talked to myself so much. For a social planet, it ironically wanted me to be introverted, it seemed. Whereas Saturn's position at my birth apparently gave me a superiority complex and difficulties with romance.

Kris: *Do you guys think I have a superiority complex?*
Paige: *Not saying anything.*

That answered that, then.

I was having a whale of a time transcribing these new revelations into blog post about clearing out the flat and being single again.

The fact that my birth chart only seemed to become relevant in the last three months seemed fated to me. If I had read it prior to my Saturn Return destroying my life, it would have seemed completely wrong, but just then it was spot-on in every degree.

'What's this about?' Ryan said, crouching behind me to peer over my screen. I went to shut it and then thought: *No. This is my safe space, and why shouldn't he know that I wrote about my astrological experiences online?*

'You'll think it's mumbo jumbo,' I told him, continuing to type with his prying eyes peering over my shoulder.

'I think everything that isn't fact is mumbo jumbo. Certainly made me unpopular at Catholic school.'

I stifled a laugh and he got up again with a sigh, making no further comment which I appreciated.

'Right, where do you need me?' he asked, rubbing his hands together and walking over to a collection of bin bags I had prepared for him to take to the tip.

'Actually,' I said, leaning over my laptop screen before he could run away. 'I'd like to chat with you about your website.'

'Oh,' he said, his eyebrows a little screwed up as if he had expected to renege on my offer to create one for him.

'If I'm going to design a website for you, I need to know more about your art and what you want to showcase. Do you want an 'about me' page? Or a shop, a downloadable portfolio? Do you have JPEGs of your work?'

'Well, they're photographs, so yes I have JPEG's,' he teased.

'Oh, hardy ha, just come and . . .' I trailed off and patted the floor beside me. 'I've been working on a rough plan.'

With a little jolt and a small 'hmm', Ryan moved over and sat cross-legged on the floor next to me. I tilted my screen and showed him a rough outline of the page I had designed so far.

'This is only a basic guide. Until I know what you want, I can't populate it or build anything in.' I observed him take it all in, his lips twitching upwards slightly. Always a good sign. 'What are your priorities? What do you want people to see when they land on the page?'

'Is it stupid to say I hadn't really thought about it in those terms? I just wanted a place to showcase my art, so that people could find me and not the other way around. I didn't realise how difficult it would be to find work in London, I thought the whole Dick Whittington story of finding your fortune still applied.'

I rolled my eyes. Bless the naïve folk who came to London to live a better life. It was one of the most expensive cities to live in and everyone was here to work or to party. No one moved to London from another country because London had the best schools or reputation for good wellbeing and residential communities. People moved *out* of London for that. It was just a city-wide competition zone. A war-ground of business, built on the bones of others. Gentrification was purely that. Making a brand-new business from scratch in London was like trying to hook a duck from the river using a paper string.

'That's very sweet, but it's not going to get you far,' I told him, honestly.

'Aww, you think I'm sweet.'

I scoffed. 'It's my polite way of saying naïve.'

Ryan shrugged, content to think that I thought him sweet.

'I don't even know you,' I told him. My horoscope had told me that today was not a day for beating around the bush. 'I mean, I know you're Aoife's nephew, that you're a photographer and that you're from Ireland. I also know that you're incredibly opinionated and frustrating.'

'I think that's the nicest thing you've ever said to me, Leo,' he leant back on his arms, smirking in my general direction. With a loud exhalation, I turned to face him with my laptop perched squarely on my legs.

'Seriously. If I'm going to build this website for you, I need to know something about you. Your tastes, your preferences for design, even just your favourite colour.'

'Navy,' he said simply.

'Navy is your favourite colour?'

He nodded. And I opened a fresh Word doc on my computer.

'Navy,' I repeated.

'What's yours?' he asked me.

'My what?'

'Your favourite colour?'

'Why do you want to know my favourite colour?' I laughed. He wasn't building *me* a website, what did it matter?

'Because one-sided questions feel weird.'

'But I need to know them for your website, you just want to know . . .'

'For nefarious purposes,' he rolled his eyes. 'Yes, the untold damage I could do with the knowledge of your favourite colour. My master plans begin—'

'*Green!* My favourite colour is green. Now shut up,' I shouted and he laughed, resting back on his hands. I sighed. 'Do you have any other favourites?'

'Want to be more precise?' he asked.

'No, quite frankly. Because you'll just turn it around on me.'

He chuckled and looked up at the ceiling in consideration, then slowly began to list them all. 'I enjoy abstracts, particularly with metallics. I studied art at college and got a merit in the end, mostly because I was always hungover. My favourite beer is Guinness – don't judge me for being a cliché. I even had the harp tattooed on my shoulder.' He tapped the space behind his shoulder to clarify. 'I enjoy classical music, surprisingly. It's good for when I'm editing and getting out of my head. Erm, what else . . .'

'What about your photos? I've never seen any, so what do you take photos of?'

'Anything and everything,' he nodded. 'I'm not a massive fan of portrait photos, which I know is bad luck given my day job. Getting someone to hold a position you want to capture is almost impossible. Every good picture is candid which means you're constantly having to search for a moment and hope it happens on the day you have a camera with you. Whereas with landscapes and scenes, you can plan ahead. If you know you want to capture a sunset, you can look up the time and go set up. If you want to photograph a scene then you just need to position it and it will stay exactly where you place it. It's control.'

'So, you're very controlled then?' I pointed out, feeling almost like a therapist as I wrote mental notes about Ryan and his perception of his work.

He shrugged absently. 'That's one way to look at it. I think it's more a preference of reliability. I have no time for flakiness or wishful thinking.'

'Then why did you come to London? Everything about starting a business or a career in London is about flakiness and wishful thinking. There is barely any control, here. I mean, I know that better than anyone as a freelancer.'

'Aoife needed me,' he said simply. There was no hesitation in his voice, it was just a fact for him.

'Oh,' I said, suddenly realising what he had meant a few days ago when he was explaining that he lived with Aoife and didn't need a flat of his own. It wasn't so much that he didn't need or want one, it was that he was in London for a reason, and that reason was Aoife, not him.

'She's never told you about her muscle weakness, has she?' he said, sitting forward again.

'No, she hasn't. We've all seen it, the girls and I, at the classes, but we never wanted to be rude and ask what was wrong.'

'She has muscular dystrophy. It's a degenerative muscle disease, which means that over time her muscles just waste away and it's, unfortunately, very painful. But she won't let it stop her.'

A different smile to his usual one appeared on his face, a smile of pride. I used to consider this sort of look a sad one, the kind of smile my grandad gave me whenever he talked about his wedding day to my nan.

'I'm so sorry,' I said, feeling for Aoife (and also Ryan, surprisingly). 'That can't be fun.'

'It is definitely not fun,' Ryan said, his smile reverting back to his usual teasing version. 'But it is what it is and I'm happy to help. I love Aoife, I'm very close to her.'

'What about your family?'

He shrugged again. 'I'm the middle child of five, with divorced parents. Unlike my siblings I didn't choose to stay with either one of them full-time, and ferried myself between them growing up. Which means that I have quite a disconnect with them all. Poor me,' he scoffed. 'Also, just because they're family, doesn't mean you have to get on with them. Aoife was really the only constant for me. It's why I lived with her during the holidays. What about you?'

I could tell he wanted to move on from the topic of his family pretty sharpish and I took the bait, still feeling slightly odd about the revelation regarding Aoife and his choice to come and stay with her in a new city, with what seemed like little to no connections to anyone else.

'Well, I had a good childhood.'

'Oh, rub it in.'

'I didn't mean . . .' I began, only to realise he was laughing at me. I sighed. 'I grew up with my mum and my grandad. My dad and mum were separated well before I was born and he's alright, but I had a great time growing up with my mum. I'm very much like Rory in *Gilmore Girls*, minus the weird boyfriend-habits.' Well . . . urgh. Maybe I was more like Rory than I thought . . .

'Nice. What's your mum like?'

'She dances to her own tune most of the time. I mean, she

named me Krystal,' I said, as if this wasn't an obviously odd choice. It wouldn't exactly be my first choice of name, I saw myself more as Katie or a Charlotte. Not bloody Krystal Baker.

'Is she into all of this hooey as well?' Ryan smirked.

'Sort off. But I'm not named after healing crystals, exactly. I'm Krystal with a K.' He gave out an *ooh*. 'Just to be different. It was the 90s after all; my mother wasn't going to conform.' I held up the peace sign with my fingers, just to encapsulate more of my mum's 'third-wave feminist with an unhealthy opinion of society' personality. I let out a light laugh. 'My grandad is amazing. He's sort of addicted to being as many versions of himself as he possibly can be.'

'All of this make it sound like you had an eventful upbringing,' Ryan continued. I could tell he was a little surprised to hear that I didn't grow up in a perfect picket-fenced neighbourhood, complete with cute dog and perfect nuclear family. But who does these days?

'When did you leave home?'

'I thought I was meant to be getting to know *you*?' I asked.

'Doesn't it work both ways? It's like a game of 20 questions.'

'This is not that.'

He smirked. 'Go on, Leo. Humour me.'

I sighed, trying not to stare at his sweet smile as he leant on his hands on the table. He was just so easy to talk too, even when he was taking the piss out of me and calling me Leo. I hadn't felt this at ease with a stranger since I'd first met Tina.

'I went to university, where I studied Communications.'

'Bet you got a first.'

'I did, actually.' I stressed the *actually*, as I was very proud of my first. He gave me a mini round of applause and I denied the urge to shove him. 'Then I moved to London with my friend Tina and I did some work experience and graduate schemes, all that fun stuff. Before I met David.'

I laughed flatly at the mention of David. Ryan's forehead creased a little in confusion. Of course, he would have no idea who David was. My saying *David* was like saying *alcohol* or *university*: I had come of age and he had just appeared.

'My ex,' I explained dolefully, trying to keep it light-hearted.

'Ahh,' Ryan said, scratching his forehead. 'I feel like I may have just walked into some recent drama.'

'More like bulldozed in with all of your pestering questions.'

He shrugged. 'What was *David* like? I've got to admit, I'm imagining a khaki-wearing hipster with a man bun, covered in ironic tattoos.'

I scoffed at that. 'Hardly. He was a bloody accountant. Suit and tie for work, gym at weekends and every Clive Cussler book ever written on the shelf. We used to go to the driving range together, eat at one of the same three restaurants whenever we had a 'date night' and made Netflix and chill a literal way of living.'

'Sounds . . .' Ryan shook his head, and I could tell he was trying to stifle a laugh.

'What? Dull?' I said, laughing, although I didn't know why. It was as if I suddenly had to justify my comfortable vanilla life, even though it was already over. 'It all ended up falling completely to bits,' I began, without realising it. 'It turns out he didn't want a monogamous relationship and while I thought we were each other's "lobsters", it turns out I was one of many. *Many*, many, in fact.'

'Oh, fuck.' Ryan inhaled through his teeth. 'Well, he sounds like an absolute idiot.' His Irish accent added a gorgeous flair to the word 'idiot', which I consciously had to remind myself to ignore. Down girl!

'I apologise to all of the hipsters I previously insulted. That there is the worst of mankind, and, as a fellow member of the male species, I can only apologise.'

He placed his hand on his heart and leant forwards in subjugation, and I shoved him playfully.

'Anyway, enough about me,' I told him sternly, while referring back to my notes on him in the Word doc. 'I think I have enough here to get on with, but I could do with getting some photographs from you as soon as possible. So that I can come up with a really strong design concept.'

He nodded, accepting that there was nothing else I wanted to say on the matter of David, which he seemed to respect. He reached for his phone in his back pocket. 'Okay. I'll set myself a reminder. Anything else you need?'

'A bio, your best contact details . . . The basics of any business really.'

'Where are you doing all of this?' he asked suddenly, putting his phone down and looking around the room.

'What do you mean? I'm doing it on my computer?' I gestured lamely to the MacBook sitting in my lap.

'No, I mean, where's your desk or your office setup?'

With a flamboyant gesture I referred him to the throw cushions and the lap tray.

'You're looking at it.'

'Here?' he pointed to the floor. 'You're doing all of this on the floor?'

'Well, I haven't exactly got the budget to buy a desk yet. Can I refer you back to my 75p mattress?' We both laughed.

'I see your point,' he said. With a groan unbefitting a guy his age he stood up. 'Right, let's get some more space cleared, then. Can't have you working on my unmissable website with only this mess for inspiration.'

'You're such a charitable gentleman,' I said sarcastically, returning to my comfortable spot leaning against the cushions, and started to work on the next aspects of his website.

* * *

The following day, I was in the supermarket, pushing a trolley filled to the brim with Tesco Basics and reduced priced items. At this rate, my meals would mostly consist of beans and rice, orange squash and Tesco Value breakfast bars. I was looking longingly at my favourite brand of instant coffee when my phone buzzed, and I saw I had a message from Ryan.

Ryan: *You weren't in, but I've left something that you needed on your doorstep.*

What? I hadn't asked for anything, and I was pretty sure I *needed* a lot of things. But what had Ryan got me?

Feeling a desire to know what it was, I rushed through the check-out to get home.

As I came into the mews, my arms laden with heavy tote bags, I saw what Ryan had left me.

It was a simple white-washed desk, with navy stars and crescent moons painted along its sides. And stuck to the surface of the little drawer on its front was a post-it saying *Open me*. I did as it said, and inside was a folded note.

Leo, if you're going to create a half-decent website, you need a half-decent desk to work from. I hope you like it.

I scoffed in disbelief, the tote bags falling from my arms. 'What?!' I had no idea that Ryan was an artist in upcycling, but recognising his handywork and his trademark RM signature in one of the painted moons. I was grinning from ear to ear. I loved it.

19

*Leo: You should find that it's easier to be yourself in a part-
nership . . . there's a full Moon in Aries.*

October seemed to fly by. Tina and Paige came over to the
flat the first Saturday of the month, both prepared to see my
stunning new home in a mews, only to be greeted with bin
bags full of rubbish in the hallway and two floor cushions in
the living room that cast dust in the air when you sat on them.

It was Paige who suggested we go out for lunch rather than
order in, and Tina was the first to grab her coat without even
the briefest of arguments. I knew then how badly they thought
of the flat, but I didn't realise how much it would hurt.

Ryan and I had been working really hard to clear the place
of the hoarder's mess. He had already taken five van loads of
rubbish down to the tip and the floor was clear of all clutter,
except some boxes of items for Clare and a few remaining
bin bags from clearing the bathroom. Clare's grandmother
had never thrown away a bottle of Pantene in her life. The
bathroom was practically a homage to the brand.

After Tina and Paige's somewhat disappointing visit, I
decided to keep myself to myself for a little bit.

I hardly saw anyone, except Ryan and the girls at the
astrology class, as I only left the flat to get food, to go to class
or to do a charity shop run. It felt as if my leg hair was getting
long enough to plait because I didn't feel the need to shave
anymore. And I was sleeping for hours on end on my surprisingly comfortable mattress.

With Ryan's help I managed to clear out the dumping ground that was the bedroom and make myself a proper bed from a cheap bamboo frame from Amazon.

The living room was becoming more spacious by the day. While I still had no sofa, or any kind of seating, beyond a cheap office chair at my desk, it still felt cosy to me. The little touches of gold from the candlesticks and some old frames I'd found on a vintage stall in Brick Lane made me feel decadent among my cheap belongings. The kitchen, however, was revealing itself as more of a time warp each and every day, as the yellow cabinets cried out for a paint job and Ryan spent his days on his knees tightening up screws in shelves or freaking out whenever he spotted a cobweb.

We split the days he came around to help with clearing out the last of the unwanted housewares into runs to the tip, washing surfaces and basic DIY before we spent time discussing the website, which was coming together nicely.

Ryan sent his photos over one evening as I was tucked up in bed watching *The Queens Gambit* for the millionth time on my phone, and I was mesmerised. I immediately understood what he meant by capturing a moment that you could cast and control.

His photos were a combination of standard scenic photos that were used as desktop backgrounds and lifestyle stock images to images that would fit in a gallery on The King's Road. He shot products, scenic moments and the occasional lifestyle snap of London's busy high streets or candid moments featuring people.

My favourite shot was an image of a simple silver necklace hanging from a wooden mirror along with a piece of sage burning beneath it, slightly blurred. The rising smoke of the sage, the way the light reflected off the mirror and through the crystal pendant, it all made the image seem active.

It captured a moment that was beautiful in its simplicity, and it was what I ended up basing the entire design of the website's landing page on. I even used his photos for my vision board for ZodiActually and wondered daily about finding some vintage photo frames to turn them into a gallery wall in my flat. Another thing to add to my list of *things to buy when I have money again*.

Ryan's new website was coming along nicely, but with my freelance jobs needing to take priority, it had taken a back seat for a little while.

'What are you doing for Halloween?' I asked him one day, as he knelt by the fireplace, painting the skirting boards white for me. This was above and beyond the *I have a van* agreement that he had made with Clare, but he made it quite clear that he wasn't letting me ruin all his hard work of clearing out the flat just to give it a shoddy paint job.

'Paint is sacred, Leo. Don't touch the paint,' he told me, hugging a can of Dulux to his chest like he was a pirate and this was his hoard. I didn't complain. If he wanted to stick it out and continue with the manual labour for free, then by all means he could.

He shrugged at my question, not looking up. 'I don't really do anything for Halloween.'

'You're not going to go trick or treating?' I teased, and he scoffed.

'I'm going clubbing with the girls,' I told him. It was a tradition of ours that couldn't be broken, even by my slight disappearing act of the last few weeks. Tina had messaged on the Chamber of Secrets demanding my presence.

Tina: *Turn your hocus focus, to hocus pocus! It's time for Halloween!!!*

Tina: *Either you're coming out with us, Krystal, or I'm going to flour-bomb your new flat.*

Tina: *Either way, I'll be living my best* Meet Me in St
    Louis *Halloween fantasy!*
Paige: *That reference is ...*
Tina: *GENIUS!*

I had to Google *Meet Me in St Louis* to see what she meant,
and then I fell down a Judy Garland hole which left me weep-
ing over Renée Zellweger's performance in *Judy*.

Krystal: *You had me at hocus focus!*

Plans had been made and costumes had been ordered –
thankfully mine was ridiculously simple and therefore incredibly affordable.

'What about going out with your mates?' I suggested.

'I'm not sure clubbing is within Aoife's muscle range right
now,' he joked.

'What about other friends though?'

He said nothing, and I realised what that silence meant.
No wonder he was so keen to help me out and kept coming
around to effectively be my personal *Queer Eye* Bobby Berk.

'Well, if you want to go out, you're very welcome to come
out with us,' I told him, thinking I should probably ask the
girls first, as it was traditionally a girls' night only. David
never came with us, and he always used to complain at
Halloween – at the beginning of our relationship anyway –
that we couldn't make a couples' costume and go as something like Morticia and Gomez or asalt and a pepper.

It was important to me to keep some of my girls' night
rituals sacred and to not become that woman who only ever
talks about her other half, or her plans for the future. The
irony of that now!

'I've never been clubbing in London,' Ryan remarked
casually.

'Never? Like, *ever* ever?'

'That is the definition of never. It's a bit depressing to go on your own, isn't it?'

I couldn't disagree with him there.

'I'm more of a pub bloke anyway. In Ireland, there aren't so many clubs as there are pub discos.'

'They're my favourite kind, actually,' I told him, thinking of my favourite London hotspots with the sticky square dance floor on one end and the shot girls handing out Club Tropicana with a complimentary pot of glitter at the other. 'The place we're going to is kind of in-between. It's called The Cheese Club.'

'The Cheese Club?' he repeated, looking at me in intrigue and horror.

'Yep. Tina, my friend, has this obsession with cheesy pop music. Honestly, it's the funniest thing you'll ever see. She'll full on clear the dancefloor and just go for it to whatever song is playing. She doesn't even need to be drunk – she'll do the Macarena, the worm, 'Oops Upside Your Head!' All of it!'

'I haven't seen someone do 'Oops Upside Your Head' outside of a wedding in years!'

'It's compulsory in Tina's book. I have the videos to prove it.'

'Well, she sounds grand,' he said, turning his attention back to the skirting board.

'You should come,' I told him, more assertively than I initially thought I would. 'It will be fun. Think of it as a night away from you being my house decorator. I'll even get the first round.'

'A whole round? Somebody saw good fortune in their latest horoscope . . .'

'Well, how expensive is Guinness anyway?' he laughed and nodded, keeping his eyes focused on the skirting board.

I quickly logged onto my horoscope account via my desk-top, wanting to check that I hadn't just made a wrong decision, but I was gratified to see that my dos of the day included extending a hand, hydration and permission. All of which I thought summed up my intentions for inviting him just perfectly.

* * *

A few days later, my horoscope encouraged me to *widen my health horizon by undertaking a new exercise*. As someone who was pretty much allergic to the gym – mostly due to its connotations with David – I thought yoga would be a much more practical exercise for me.

I signed up for a class that specifically focused on realigning your chakras, which seemed comfortably astrological and was held not too far away from the new flat, in a run-down hall behind a church in Camden.

The class was £15 an hour and was meant to be for beginners, but when I arrived, I found myself surrounded by men and women with six packs and their own yoga mats. I was one of two people who had to ask the instructor for a spare, and the other woman was loudly expressing that she'd only not brought her mat along because the one she'd ordered especially for the class, had to be sent back due to it arriving in mint and not duck egg blue.

I should have known then that this was likely not the class for me. But I persisted, as my horoscope instructed, and managed to get into butterfly position at the back of the class. My phone was naughtily lying beside me so that I could keep up with that evening's chatter on the Chamber of Secrets group.

Paige and Tina had become more vocal in the last few days as I started returning their messages more frequently. I hadn't realised how secluded I had become in my new flat until I realised I had three unread messages from Tina about her disastrous parents' evening. One of the parents had turned up drunk and thrown up all over a welcome sign that

Tina had spent a large portion of the day painting and adding glitter to. Bad Krystal, I berated myself, and promised to get back on track with my replies.

'And we're breathing,' the yoga instructor said, starting the class after a few minutes of idle chatting.

And we kept breathing . . . and we kept breathing . . . and breathing.

I've been breathing my whole life, so why this woman wants to charge me £15 an hour for the pleasure I don't understand.

Kris: *How is this classed as exercise?*

I sneakily texted the girls while everyone around me had their eyes shut, loudly blowing nose whistles.

I was all for realigning my chakras, but somehow the crystals around my neck seemed to be more actively helpful than my lungs right now.

Tina: *Wait until you get to dogging.*
Tina: *Downward dogging!*
Tina: *DAMMIT! Downward dog.*
Tina: *I hate autocorrect.*
Paige: *If that's your excuse . . .*

I bit my lip to avoid laughing out loud, fearing that that would disrupt the atmosphere in the room and we'd all have to start breathing all over again. Thankfully, though, I managed to hold it in. With a breathy sigh, the instructor encouraged us to get into cobra position.

'Keep your pelvis firmly to the floor,' she told us ethereally. I pulled my phone to the front so that I could watch Paige and Tina's sarcastic conversation continue.

#Krystal: *I'm cobra-ing.*

After a minute or two of holding the pose I got bored and looked down at the screen.

Paige: *The only yoga pose I'm ever going to do is decom-pose.*

I snorted, and quickly had to cover my nose and mouth *sorry, I sneezed* to the yogis beside me who were glaring.

Tina: *Classic.*
Tina: *I tried yoga once. And then I realised I could lie on my own floor for free.*
Tina: *Paying for yoga . . . it's a bit of stretch.*
Tina: *Ba dum dum tish.*

I chuckled under my breath, but she had a point. Why did I sign up and pay for a class? YouTube was free, and I was pretty sure I had some will in me to force myself to do it at home. And it wasn't like I would have to move any furniture out of the way. Ryan had seen to that for me.

Paige: *I think the only useful ability that comes from doing yoga is the ability to zip up your own dress when you're single.*

And this is why Paige and I were friends. She got me.

Paige: *Just come round and play Twister with us. You'll get the same effect.*
Kris: *I wish I could. But for £15 I'm going to get something out of this class.*

I replied just before the instructor asked everyone to get into lizard, which was really just a lunging position, so that made it much easier to text.

Krystal: *By the way, I hope it's okay, but I've invited Ryan
 to come with us to The Cheese Club on Halloween?*
Tina: *What!!!*
Krystal: *I know it's girls night, but he has no friends.*
Kris: *He's never even gone out in London before.*
Kris: *I felt bad for him.*
Paige: *Sucks for him, but it's girls night for a reason!*
Kris: *Yeah, but now we're all single, why not just have a
 singles night instead?*
Kris: *You'll like him.*
Tina: *I kind of want to meet him …*
Tina: *This gorgeous handyman of yours.*
Kris: *He's not my handyman.*
Tina: *So you admit he's gorgeous.*

I awkwardly flattened my front leg int front of me to get into
half pigeon. Honestly, whoever came up with the names of
these poses needed to be shot for the sake of humanity.

Kris: *Jesus no!*
Kris: *It's a miracle we're even civil with one another.*
Tina: *Dude, you just invited him out on girls night. You
 didn't even do that for he-who-must-not-be-named!*
Paige: *It's kind of more than civil …*

I rolled my eyes and returned to focusing on my pigeon
stance, which was actually quite painful, and I had a suspicion I was doing it wrong as the yogi next to me was smirking
at me like they knew a secret I didn't.

Tina: *How rude would it be to revoke your invitation?*
Paige: *Screw rudeness, just tell him plans have changed.*
Paige: *Girls night! Remember!!*

I sucked my lips. Normally, I'd be all for doing what the girls asked and just having fun as the three of us. But I couldn't shake the feeling that maybe I wanted him there. I think I even wanted to introduce him to the girls, and not just because he was lacking a friend in the city either.

Oh shit.

My outer leg collapsed beneath me and I fell in a heap on my mat. The instructor looked over at me, initially sympathetically, then spotted my phone with its notifications from the girls coming in and glared instead.

Kris: *Please can he come?*

I wrote back to them as I corrected my position just in time to be told to move back into butterfly.

Kris: *He's house-trained and he's Irish. I bet you he'll charm your socks off.*

Like he'd charmed me?

Tina: *He's Irish!!!!*

Tina: *Why didn't you say so?!*

And just like the munchkin at the gates to the Emerald City, over-excited by the mention of the wizard, the Irishman made his way into our group outing. Even Paige relented in her misgivings.

Paige: *It'll be a gas.*

20

Leo: The stakes are high today, and the slightest movement is magnified several times over ... the Sun and Saturn unite in your partnership zone.

Halloween arrived surprisingly quickly. With freelance projects needing a lot of focus, along with Ryan's website and the house clearance, time for myself and daylight hours seemed to dwindle very quickly.

Soon I was in a taxi on my way to The Cheese Club in South-east London, wearing nothing but a black trench coat and holding a golden bust of Venus, the signature Fleabag look.

Our theme for this year's Halloween outing was Phoebe Waller-Bridge's characters. Paige had selected it, as she pointed out that Sandra Oh's character in *Killing Eve* was one of the only characters she could authentically dress up as, not to mention Sandra Oh was her heroine in life generally. Tina, of course, dressed as Villanelle in her plumpest pink tulle dress. I spotted her before I'd even gotten out of the taxi as she was impossible to miss among the sexy witches and cute Wednesday Addams' of women in the queue.

'Hey!' she screamed at my arrival, extending her arms for a hug. 'It's been so long?!' she shouted into my hair, already drunk by the tone of her voice. Paige's arm was around her waist, no doubt trying to keep Tina steady so that they didn't lose their place in the queue.

'Where's the Irishman?' she asked me, as I gave her an awkward side-hug, so that Tina stayed upright.

'He's meeting us here. I'll just text him.'

I heard the ping of Ryan's phone from just behind me as I sent the text asking where he was.

'Found me,' he said, stepping to join us with his hands in his pockets. He was wearing navy jeans and a smart, plain dark grey shirt.

'Not into dressing up much?' I teased him, looking over his outfit. To be fair, I hadn't shared that Paige, Tina and I were group costuming for the outing as I just assumed that Ryan would want to do his own thing. He clearly didn't get that silent message.

'You are useless!' Paige shouted, before offering her hand to Ryan. 'I'm Paige, and this is Tina,' she said, letting go of his hand quickly to gesture to Tina who waved happily.

'Hiya!'

'Hi,' Ryan said, laughing.

'Here, grab her will you,' Paige said to me, pushing Tina towards me.

'Where are you going?' I asked her, wrapping my arm around Tina whose head fell into the crook of my shoulder.

'I need to sort the Irishman's costume. Give me two secs.' And with that she was gone.

Ryan looked at me and nodded. 'The Irishman?' he repeated.

'Well, it was that or the Cockwomble,' I told him, and Tina giggled.

'Cockwomble,' she repeated under her breath.

'That's ... uh, a new one. I suppose,' Ryan laughed.

I shrugged.

'Ooh!' Tina shouted directly into my eardrum suddenly. 'You know that conversation we were having the other day about blowjobs?'

I saw Ryan's eyebrows raise.

'Uh-huh,' I said, biting my lip.

'I was speaking to a girl at work . . .' she began.

'I really hope it was a teacher and not a student,' I said, remembering that she worked predominantly with eight-year-olds.

'Well, duh!' she spat, rolling her eyes impatiently. 'I asked the English teacher about the correct verb.'

'You didn't,' I said, an amused grin bursting across my face.

'Correct verb?' Ryan repeated, clearly wondering how verbs and blowjobs came together.

I looked at him and saw that he was desperately trying not to laugh at this ridiculous conversation. As much as it was an odd one to introduce him to the girls, I thought we were just going to have to go with it until Paige returned with whatever organisational magic she was working in order to find Ryan a costume.

'Yeah,' I began, 'We couldn't figure out the verb for a blow-job.' I explained, deadpan, although everything was telling me to laugh based on his expression.

'Is it . . .?' Tina began dramatically, using her hands to explain. "Blowing jobs' *or* 'blow jobbing'?'

The things that three women will come up with to discuss over drinks.

Ryan stood open-mouthed, silenced for the first time since I'd met him.

'And it *is* 'blowing jobs'! I was right,' Tina said, swinging her arms in the air victoriously, almost leading me to drop her.

'Here we go!' Paige shouted triumphantly as she returned to us in the queue. We all turned to see her brandishing a folded piece of paper and nothing more.

'What is that?' I asked, but before Paige explained, she pulled Ryan down to her level and folded the piece of paper under the collar of his t-shirt.

'Ohhh,' Tina sung out in a high-pitched voice. 'He's the priest!'

The hot priest from *Fleabag*. The character who my character falls in love with. Oh God. I was couples costuming with Ryan.

'There,' Paige said proudly, patting Ryan on the chest. 'Perfect. You look very handsome. And very authentic too.'

Ryan played with his shirt collar, smoothing it down with a little pride.

'The priest,' he stifled a laugh.

'Oh my God!' Tina shouted again, I was going to have a headache in the morning, regardless of whether or not I drank tonight. '*You* watched *Fleabag*.'

Ryan laughed. 'I'm sorry, did I give you the impression that I lived under a rock?'

'Oh, your accent.' Tina practically melted in my arms. She was making it very difficult for me to hold her upright. 'Say something else.'

'What?' Ryan asked, bemused but not wholly surprised by Tina's reaction to his Irishness.

'Anything. Flowers, beetroot, musk!'

Ryan repeated all three words for Tina, adding more huskiness to his voice each time until he sounded like he was wooing her. I needed Paige's help to keep Tina upright now, not to mention her hands to herself.

'Oh yes,' she moaned, and Ryan took a step back to properly laugh his head off. He patted his collar and turned to Paige, swiftly changing the subject once he had recovered himself.

'Thank you very much for this,' he said to Paige. 'It's very creative, I must say.'

'Well I'm very, *very* creative sometimes. Don't believe anything they tell you about lawyers,' she told him, returning to her spot in the queue and gripping Tina around the waist so that I could take a break from her flailing limbs.

'Oh, you're a lawyer,' Ryan smiled. 'Very impressive. But remind me to never get into an argument with you.'

'Arguing leads to wonderful things sometimes,' Paige replied in a somewhat flirty tone.

'Yes, divorce and dividends,' Ryan said flatly.

'But also, the most amazing make-up sex. Or break-up sex, whatever your preference.'

I felt like I was watching a Wimbledon match. The two of them were *flantering*, as Zelda from astrology class would say effortlessly, and it was sort of getting my blood boiling. Paige didn't even want Ryan to be here, and suddenly she was being flirty?

'Have we got tickets?' I asked, interrupting the flow of their conversation.

Paige nodded, still giggling a bit. 'Yeah, the bouncer said it would only be a few more minutes and we'll be in. Did you hear Idris Elba might be DJing tonight?'

'Oh my God! I *love* him. He should have been James Bond,' Tina began, collapsing into Paige's body in a hot mess. A fair reaction: who doesn't love Idris Elba?

'He would have made an awesome James Bond,' Ryan agreed.

'Oh my God, I love you too!' Tina shouted, grabbing his wrists and shaking them. I pried her loose from him and explained under my breath that Tina's favourite part of the night was pre-drinks, to which Ryan nodded profusely.

'Have you been pre-drinking?' he asked Paige, who gave a Princess Diana shrug and said 'maybe,' in a coy voice.

She was so flirty tonight, and I wanted her to stop. Ryan was my guest not hers. But that was all he was, *my guest*. He wasn't my date; he was barely my friend.

As people began filing inside, I quickly took out my phone to review my horoscope for the day. I had already checked to make sure it was okay for me to go out clubbing (after the disaster last time) and in my interpretation of the message, *Letting loose is good for the soul*, I thought it was fine. But as I went through the dos and don'ts of the day, I also looked at the current position of Venus in my chart. It was the sign I most often overlooked as I had no interest in romance right now, but it appeared that Venus had entered the 6th house, the house of healing. The horoscope read: *'Now is the time to embrace change in your love life.'*

As we entered the club, our hands stamped with orange pumpkins, seeing The Cheese Club's interior covered in neon paint, I realised something huge.

It was time for me to focus on the next element of my to-do list for life and get back out there. I needed to start dating again.

21

Leo: You know what you want; trust your intuition ... Venus is in the 5th house.

In the taxi home from the Halloween night-out, after leaving without Paige, Tina or Ryan in tow – Ryan had been a gentleman and piled a singing Paige and Tina into a separate Uber before heading off for the night bus since we were going in different directions – I had downloaded every dating app in the app-store onto my phone.

Hinge, Tinder, Bumble and Jigsaw, I decided in the days following, were apps of mental torture that were clearly invented by the KGB.

A whole week after I had created my profiles and started to *like* various men I found myself obsessively opening and closing the apps, going over the messages I had exchanged with countless men between 28- and 34-years-old.

Some of the messages were coy and sweet, but going nowhere. Others were demanding and so overtly sexual that they were a complete turn-off, and some were just like hitting my head against a brick wall.

No, I'm not interested in using you as a bloody gigolo. I have a vibrator that fulfils that need quicker and more hygienically than some strange man.

No, I'm not looking for a travel buddy or someone I can teach English to on a gap year.

No, I'm not into puppies or wanting to go for long strolls in Richmond Park.

No, *Netflix and chill* is not a sexy invite anymore.

No, I don't find it a turn-on when you're surprised to see that someone as hot as me is single.

No, I don't want a fucking dick pic.

So far, my dating dramas had led to nothing but a fear that every single man in London was nothing more than a dick stuck on a skeleton with some muscle as Blu-Tack.

I hadn't gone on so much as a date yet, as no one seemed interesting or compatible enough. I don't know what I was looking for in a man, but maybe that was the issue. I didn't want a one-night lay, nor did I want a man to settle down with. I was stuck in the in-between, unsure of how to just have fun, as Paige had instructed me.

Paige knew how to do this; she was so expertly aware of herself and her needs. Just take Ryan and her on Halloween. There was barely a moment when they weren't on the dancefloor together or grabbing a beer from the bar. I felt like I was babysitting Tina for most of the night, apologising on her behalf whenever she whacked someone over the head with a jacket she had found – or stolen, knowing Tina – or tried to lasso her way into the centre of the dancefloor. Or, the worst, when she started taking off her knickers to fling at Idris Elba. This was something I thought that only our mother's generation did to members of Take That, not people like us!

I managed to stop her once, but not the second time. She was so drunk that the knickers didn't even reach the stage, instead they landed on some poor girls ridiculously high ponytail and just sat there for ages.

I couldn't stop watching those knickers hovering around the dancefloor, and whenever I got close enough to tell her that she had my friends' thong in her hair I was pushed to the other side of the dancefloor or the girl would do a slut-drop and I'd lose her in the crowd. Eventually I just gave up. And instead turned my attention to trying to stop Tina from spinning on the dancefloor so that her dress wouldn't fly up.

It wasn't my favourite night out, and it was leading to some quite anxious Tindering, that had lasted a whole week. I grasped my turquoise pendant for luck around my neck and made a grumbly kind of prayer to the dating gods to help me out. When nothing happened, I did what I always seemed to do at this point. I turned to my horoscope.

Sports pave the way to success.

Oh, for fuck's sake. Even my horoscope was against me. How did sports pave the way to a love life? I'd need Wagatha Christie to unravel that mystery for me.

Sitting up in my bed in self-pity, pushing away the Mary Berry voice in my head telling me that I should do some work not just lounge on my bed, I decided to go out.

There was a sports bar in King Cross, and that was as close to sports as I was going to get. I needed a walk to clear my head, and a drink to cloud it up again. It seemed like the perfect solution to me.

★ ★ ★

The bar was mostly empty, although there was a football match playing on one of the big screen TVs. I went directly to the bar and leant over it, looking for the bartender. I had decided I was going to order a giant glass of Chardonnay for my sins. Screw day-drinking rules; my life was my own and I wanted one.

'Oi! Love. You're blocking the screen,' a voice suddenly shouted from nearby. I looked over my shoulder to see a group of three men huddled together staring at me.

'The screen's behind you,' one of them said, pointing at me. I looked back and saw what they meant.

'Why would you sit there?' I asked them, feeling braver out of annoyance. 'Why not over there?' I said, pointing to another empty table opposite the screen. 'Then you don't have to worry about people ordering drinks.'

'Not many people order drinks from the bar when it's table service only,' one man said with a smile – a blonde guy in a casual white button down and jeans.

I looked at the bar and saw a notice that read *Table service only.* With a QPR code to download for orders.

These modern bars, I thought, stepping back and looking over at the group of guys.

'Sorry,' I said, though I was very un-sorry. I moved to the back of the bar. I wanted to be as far away from people as possible. Clearly my staying in the flat was mutating into full on introversion and stranger danger vibes.

Leos were meant to be super confident and the life of the party, but at that moment I just wanted to be on my own. Maybe I was about to come on my period or something.

I got to work on downloading the app and ordering my drink.

'Can I join you?' a voice said, and I looked up. It was the blonde bloke.

'Don't you want to watch the game?' I asked.

He shook his head and sat down, without waiting for my invitation. He was pretty good looking, and something about his casual confidence made me at ease.

'I'm more of a rugby man,' he said. 'Football is a game for gentleman played by thugs and rugby . . .'

'Is a thug's game, played by gentleman,' I finished for him. 'I know the saying.'

'I'd like to think of myself as a gentleman. Mostly.'

I laughed just as a waitress appeared and placed a cool glass of wine on my table without so much as a nod. The blonde bloke looked at it.

'That kind of day?'

'That kind of year, actually,' I said, clinking my wine glass against his near empty pint. 'But honestly, I'm a bit into breaking rules right now, and day-drinking is one of them.'

'Amen,' he said, clinking his glass against my own again before we both took a gulp. 'I'm sorry if my friends were rude back there.'

I shrugged – what did it matter, really.

'I'd much prefer staring at you than watching the footie, but uh . . .' The cheeky flirt.

But I couldn't say I wasn't enjoying it.

I really needed to get better at believing in what the planetary movements had to say, rather than just going along with it. For the most part, my horoscope had been right about everything I had done. And since romance was supposedly on the horizon, why couldn't this be it? Even if just for one night (or day, as the case may be). I'd never had a one-night stand, not properly. At university, I tended to sleep with a select few people on-and-off over the three years of my course. So while I might have slept with them after a night out, I'd often then get lunch with them the next day, or end up discussing course notes or how drunk we both were, before the next time it happened.

This would be different. This would be with a complete stranger I had picked up in a bar, like some sort of Katherine Heigl movie opening. So long as I didn't get pregnant, what was the harm?

'What do you do?' I asked the bloke. 'And what's your name?'

'Connor,' he said, and he leant forward to whisper: 'And I don't think that you're interested in what I do. But I have finished work for the day if that's what you really want to know.'

It was.

22

*Leo: Tension could come to you from all angles ... the Sun
swings into a tangled angle with Saturn.*

I had never realised that a one-night stand could lead to a
glow-up. I felt like Bridget Jones crossing Tower Bridge after
shacking up with Daniel Cleaver. Connor had been gentle –
but ferocious when I asked him to be – and didn't give a
damn about my living situation. He didn't comment on
where I kept the condoms in my flat (in a draw along with my
shavers and tampons in the bathroom) or the fact that after
we'd finished our second go-around, I wanted him to leave,
because I wanted to make dinner and watch *Casualty*.

He left his number on the side and told me in no uncertain
terms:

*I'm not looking for a relationship, but this was fun. And if you
want to do it again sometime let me know.* 😊

I had no idea that all I needed to do to get out of my low
mood – which I hadn't even realised I had sunk into, that was
numbingly low it was – and back into productive Krystal-
mode was have a good shag. I felt like I had just turned my
life on and off again, and suddenly everything was fresh and
working at full speed.

The following day I bashed out several pitches to editors,
nearly all of which I was then asked to draft up – a miracle in
the freelancing industry – and two invoices were paid at once.

I had enough money to return to Brick Lane, to my new
favourite stall run by Andrik (whose name I had since

learned) to purchase more crystals. Without realising it, I had become slightly obsessed with growing my crystal collection, which sat in pride of place on my newly painted mantelpiece.

I went big this time on my purchases; I avoided the amethyst which still looked scarily like a weapon to me, opting instead for a mountain of selenite that I had to carry in a bundle onto the tube as if it were a baby. I also treated myself to some clear quartz, green aventurine and red jasper wands to hold when I needed clarity, stabilisation and spiritual healing. All of which I felt I was still lacking.

If Paige were with me, I knew she would remind me that I would be better off saving my money for a smart purchase like a new sofa or a better desk chair. But, I thought, when I needed those things it would become clear in my horoscope. Right now, there were no mentions of needing to focus on my physical comfort. Instead, my horoscope was telling me to focus on my spiritual growth and self-understanding.

In the first week of November, Paige and Tina had texted me a few times about going out for dinner or having a night in at Paige's, but I wasn't feeling it. I really wanted to have some alone time to get properly centred and figure out what I wanted out of life going forwards. I was finally digging myself out of the shithole that was my 29th birthday, but with my Saturn Return fast approaching I had to consider what I would do in the new period of my life. I couldn't just keep coasting as I was.

While it felt shit at first, when I was just trawling through social media and dating apps to try and find the new 'one', after Connor and my sexual release, I felt more in control.

Even Ryan noticed the difference in me when he came over. After Halloween he had been around less during the day as it was school photo season, but he still popped by in the evenings to finish off some electrical work for me.

My Dickensian way of living with just candles for light was starting to feel a bit hazardous what with all the loose pieces of newspaper still lying around the flat. Not to mention the effect it was having on my eyesight.

Ryan told me that I seemed brighter (got to love a pun), even commenting on the fact that I had started humming while I was making us scrambled on eggs on toast for dinner. The only dish I could cook well.

Everyone noticed the change in me. Mum told me over FaceTime that I was clearly living my best life, and even Grandad couldn't deny my change in spirit. Though he refused to agree that the change was due to me following the planets' instructions. And he scoffed, although he tried to hide it with a cough, when I showed off my crystal collection, but mum was very happy to *ooh* and *ahh* with me.

Grandad, it seemed, had moved on from stitching anti-quarian clothing with Rita, and was now playing around with collage with his new friend Beryl. Mum had been furious when she came home from work to discover her monthly subscription of *Good Housekeeping* had pages torn out of it, and been plastered along corkboards in Grandad's study. He had even started his own Instagram feed to showcase his later artworks, #NeverWentToCollage.

I was supportive of him and his flaky activities like this one, so I couldn't understand why he wouldn't be more supportive of mine.

'Have you heard from David at all?' Mum asked one evening, after a few minutes of light chatter about the latest series of *I'm a Celebrity*.

'No,' I said definitively. 'Why would I?'

I had deleted his number the moment I got in Paige's flat after the World of Pop incident, and I had sworn never to speak to him again. I had gone so far as to even do a ceremonial burning of a photo of him, using one of Paige's expensive candles, and under Tina's manic encouragement.

I was done with him completely.

'He messaged me on Facebook the other day,' Mum told me.

'He did what?'

'I was going to ignore him, but he was asking after you.'

I sat at my desk, mouth agape, holding my phone as far away from me as possible. 'You didn't reply, did you?'

'Well . . .' she began sheepishly.

'Mum!' I shouted, furious that she would reply and get herself embroiled in my relationships. She should have blocked him just as I had done. Why would she talk to him?

'It seemed like genuine concern, and I thought since you two were together for so long, the least I could do was tell him that you were doing well.'

'I am doing well! Because I don't talk to him, Mum. And neither should you,' I practically growled down the line. 'If he messages you again, just ignore him. Or better yet, block him. I've got to go.' With a sigh, I hung up on her, although she had opened her mouth to say something else.

I didn't want to talk about David. He was out of my life for good, as far as I was concerned. I slammed my phone onto my desk, annoyed that I still felt so passionately angry whenever he was mentioned and dropped my head into my hands.

Everything I was doing was to focus on the future, not the past. Having David brought back into my life by my own mother was not going to be in the cards for me. I refused to deal with that.

Huffing, annoyed that my mood had gone from such a wonderful high to such a low so quickly, I decided to call my drug of choice to get it back up again.

'Hey!' Connor said, as soon as he answered the phone. 'I didn't think it would take a week before I heard back from you.'

'Are you free tonight?' I asked him quickly.

'Yeah,' he said. 'Do you want me to come round?'

'Yes, I do.'

'Good,' he lowered his voice in a sexy way that sent tingles down my spine, where usually it would make me shiver in taboo-ish embarassement. Not this time. I was my own woman and I knew what I wanted, and what I wanted was to forget about David and have some fun.

* * *

Connor stayed over. It wasn't the plan, but we were both hungry for some human contact, and our session – for want of a better word – lasted longer than we anticipated. It seemed unfriendly, after everything he had just done for me, to kick him out now.

He was fine with staying, although he made it clear that he wasn't into cuddling. Unlike some friends with benefits romcom, I knew that he was being 100% honest when he said that this was nothing more than sex. I pulled the duvet off him without any guilt and wrapped myself in my signature cocoon, telling him that there was a spare blanket in the living room if he got cold.

My sleep was blissfully dreamless. It was the kind of sleep that you never want to end, full of warmth and utter cosiness. But, of course, that means it's the sleep that's most likely to be disturbed. In this case, with someone banging on my door.

I jolted awake, my insides travelling up to my throat in surprise. No one had knocked on my door before 11 am since I had moved in. Only a handful of people knew I lived here, and even the postman didn't arrive until around 2 pm.

I twisted over awkwardly in my cocoon and saw that Connor was still snoring face-down on his side of the bed. He had foregone a blanket and his baby-haired butt was face-up for the world to see. Not the view I wanted first thing in the morning, particularly after a surprising wake-up call.

I forced myself out of the cocoon and reached for my nearby dressing gown as the person at the door continued to knock.

'I'm coming!' I hissed as I headed down the corridor (not that I expected them to hear me). I hoped that they would catch my venom when I opened the door to give them a piece of my mind.

'What?!' I said, flinging the door open just as I buckled my dressing gown. 'David?'

'Sorry it's so early,' he said, looking sheepish as he folded his arms and looked me up and down. I stood stock still, too shocked to say anything. 'Nice place,' he said, rocking on his heels and looking me up and down.

'What . . . what are you doing here?' I mumbled, trying to take control of myself. I hoped he wouldn't spot my post-sex bed-head.

'I really want to talk,' he said, whining a little.

'So you decided to show up on my doorstep at . . .' I looked about me for a clock or a watch to tell me the time but there wasn't one. Something to add to my houseware wish list. He looked down at his Fitbit.

'10.30 am,' he said, and I bit my lip to stop myself saying thank you. 'You weren't answering my calls. It just went straight to voicemail.'

'That's what happens when you get blocked.'

'But you didn't listen to my voicemails?'

'I sent them straight to the bin,' I scoffed. Wasn't that obvious? 'If I wanted to talk to you, I wouldn't have blocked you.'

'Look, I'm sorry,' he said, holding his hands up in unusual defeat. 'I've never felt worse and I really want to talk things out with you.'

'It's been three months and you show up *now* to apologise?' I gripped my dressing gown around my body tightly and pulled the door towards me, desperately wanting to slam it in his face but stopped by an internal desire to hear him out.

'I know, I know,' he said, rocking back and forth more so and messing up his hair with his hand. 'I'm the world's greatest idiot, an absolute prick.'

'Carry on,' I said and he smiled, relaxing a little.

'I realise now that I ... I lost the best thing that ever happened to me.' My heart fell into my stomach. 'And it was all my fault. I was selfish and didn't communicate properly, and ...'

'You cheated and lied to me,' I finished for him.

'I was an absolute arsehole.'

'You *still* are.'

'I'm changing,' he said, and I rolled my eyes. How was my life turning into a *Love, Actually* sequel?

'You're not, though,' I said, shaking my head and feeling my cheeks burn. 'I saw you at World of Pop on *my* birthday. You were snogging some tart on the dance floor like nothing had ever happened. And only a week before that you had proposed to me!'

'I was upset, and ...'

'No!' I shouted in his face, gripping the door handle so hard my knuckles cracked. 'You don't get to be upset. I was the one who was betrayed and hurt and left with nothing. You were the one who was living your best life with no consideration for anyone else, particularly not the person you just said you couldn't live without.'

'You *are* the best thing that ever happened to me.'

'Why? Because I did your laundry, I paid half the rent, I made sure that our TV licence was sorted and I dealt with all the everyday shit you couldn't be bothered with?'

'No, because you make me laugh like no one else.'

'Mostly because you were laughing at me,' I snapped.

'No!' he shouted back, frustrated that I wouldn't let him finish what I was sure was some sort of prepared speech that was supposed to make me melt at the knees.

'How did you find out where I lived?' I bellowed, instantly regretting it in case any of my new neighbours heard the commotion and sneakily looked out of their windows at the new crazy lady at number 13.

'I messaged your mum and . . .'

'Mum told you?' I was going to kill her.

'She didn't want to, but I said I was going to write to you and then . . .'

'Oh, for God's sake.' My mother was a Jane Austen romantic at heart, she probably thought a letter was the most romantic form of apology and didn't realise that no one in my generation wrote letters unless we were in prison.

'I just wanted to see you and explain,' he said softly. 'I miss you.'

'Krystal, where d'you . . .' Connor was coming down the corridor and I stupidly turned around on instinct, opening the door so that David got full view of Connor in his boxers walking towards us groggily. 'Oh, sorry mate,' Connor said to David, waving a hand in semi-apology for his state of dress.

'Oh,' David said loudly, his eyes popping. 'So *you* can have sex then?'

'What?' I scoffed loudly.

'So I get it in the neck for sleeping with someone after we break up, yet you're doing the exact same thing.'

'Excuse me? What the – how does *this* even compare to *that*?' I shouted. 'It's been three months since we split up. What, did you think I was just lounging around waiting for you to come back? I broke up with you, goddammit!'

'Everything okay?' Connor asked from the living room doorway.

'This doesn't involve you,' David yelled.

'Calm down,' I said to David, wondering how the hell I had just ended up as piggy-in-the-bloody-middle with him and Connor. But Connor was the calmest of us all; he simply shrugged and went back up the corridor to the bedroom.

'And you went for someone like that twat?'

'You don't – he's said all of two words and you . . . what is this?' I scrambled for words to say, confused as to what the hell was going on and how I was meant to deal with this. This is the sort of thing you should learn how to deal with at school instead of taking pointless PSHE lessons. We should have had classes on how to do a tax return and deal with manic sex-obsessed exes. 'Can you just go, David?'

'Krystal?'

I looked to my left and saw that Ryan had just walked into the mews and spotted me in my ugly penguin dressing gown, standing in the doorway having a bloody argument.

'You okay?' He spoke to me but was looking at David.

'Oh!' David exclaimed, slapping the air. 'It's like a revolving door.'

I went to step out of the flat to wallop him, when Ryan stepped between us and said: 'I don't think you should be here.' My head collided with Ryan's back and I grabbed his arm for stability.

'Really, and you are?'

'I'm the decorator,' he said, swiftly.

'Right,' David returned lamely, clearly at a loss as to how to retort to that after his accusation. Suddenly there was a clearing of throat from behind me. Ryan and I both turned and saw Connor, holding his things but still just in his boxers smiling at us.

'Scuse me mate, I need to get out.'

Ryan stepped aside without a word, leaving Connor and David in a bit of a face-off, which only David was participating in. Connor walked past me and gave me the briefest nod.

'See ya Krystal,' he said and walked out. He didn't seem to give a damn that he was in a public street in only his boxers. I wished to God he would have just put some jeans on so he didn't look quite so much like a gigolo leaving my house.

I wanted to die at the thought of someone watching this scene – three men and me – and in various states of dress at 10.30 am.

'Oh, for fuck's sake,' I mumbled, looking from Connor to Ryan to gauge the latter's reaction. He was just staring at David, who was watching after Connor in a red mist of fury.

'David,' I began sharply. 'I really don't want to talk to you right now.'

David said nothing.

'I think you should leave, mate,' Ryan said to David, who began to glare at Ryan, now.

'I don't think you get a say in this, *decorator*.'

'No, but Krystal does, and she clearly wants you to go.'

David looked at me and I folded my arms.

'Get lost David,' I said.

There was a stand-off for a minute or so before David turned on his heel and stomped off in the opposite direction of Connor. I put my head into my hands and released a massive exhalation in fury. 'God!'

'I'll put the kettle on,' Ryan said, side-stepping me into the flat and closing the door behind him. All the while, he had his hand on my shoulder, squeezing it comfortingly.

23

Leo: There's an easiness to today that will create openings for exploring creative outlets ...Venus and Pluto collaborate in the 8th house.

'I'm going to kill my mother,' I said, into my steaming cup of coffee. After David left, I'd quickly gone to my bedroom to change into fur-lined leggings and an over-sized band t-shirt. I then stripped my bed sheets, trying to erase everything that had happened the night before.

'There was bound to be some sort of awkward stand-off at some point,' Ryan said to me, smiling, as he got to work on adding a new curtain rail above the window. 'There always is with exes with history. And from what you told me, you have a lot of history.'

I groaned in agreement as I sipped my over-creamed coffee. I could taste a hint of alcohol, as well; clearly this was an Irish coffee and I appreciated Ryan's subtle act of bucking me up.

'You'll get through this. And I stand by my previous opinion of David, he is an idiot.'

I laughed, but said, 'I don't want to talk about it anymore.' Slumped against the wall and looking around the now relatively empty living room, I wondered what to do next.

'Talk about what?' Ryan said, and I started to laugh.

'That was beyond cheesy.'

Ryan groaned in agreement. 'Yeah, it was.' But then we were both laughing, and I appreciated his attempt to cheer me up and be supportive. It was more than I deserved after what he had had to face that morning as well.

'Can I help?' I asked, putting my coffee down on my desk and walking over to him, stood on a step stool drilling into the wall. He looked down at me, his lips curling upwards and nodded.

'Alright. You can pass me that,' he gestured with his head to a drill bit balanced on the windowsill and I passed it up to him.

I made a fantastic DIY assistant, if I did say so myself. Sure, I was terrible when it came to things like accurately putting down painter's tape or using a spirit level correctly, but I could hand over tools and thread curtains through a rail very well.

By lunchtime we were sitting on the floor eating a greasy Chinese takeaway and I was regaling Ryan with upcycle projects I had decided to take on.

'So, you know I've really got into this crystal collecting,' I said, gesturing to the various crystals on the mantelpiece.

He bit his lip and said, 'Yes,' in a very telling way. He still thought it was all ridiculous, of course, but he was begrudgingly able to hold his opinions back now.

'Well, I saw some Pinterest boards on how to use crystals decoratively but also imbibe your home with all these good energies.'

'I think it's going to take more than some plastic junk from Urban Outfitters to imbibe this flat with good energy,' he laughed and I threw a chicken ball at his head. He caught it in his mouth and instantly began chewing it whole.

'That's disgusting,' I said, recoiling playfully.

It took a moment, but eventually he replied. 'That's a talent.'

'You just shoved a whole ball in your mouth. That's teabagging, not talent,' to which he threw some chow mein noodles at me.

'Oi! Not on the carpet.'

Our small food fight ended when a piece of prawn toast got stuck to the ceiling, clinging on in its greasiness. 'You're cleaning that up,' I teased. Thankfully, the flat was still in its early days so I didn't care too much about greasy marks here or there.

The afternoon, which seemed to fly by despite the morning's events, was filled with arts and crafts. To distract me from my idea of crystal decoration, I think, Ryan taught me how to create tassels to add to soft furnishings. It turned out he was very adept at arts and crafts.

'When you have an aunt like mine, you tend to do a lot of make and mend during the holidays,' he said, artfully creating some red and pink tassels for me to add to my new linen curtains.

'You know, you should add a shop to your website,' I told him, biting my tongue in concentration as I attempted to recreate his masterpieces. My tassels looked more like shaven barbie heads then tassels.

'And sell what? I'm hired as a photographer; I've never even sold my own artistic photos as I didn't have a platform from which to showcase them.'

'But now you do. And you could sell other things on it, too, like these?' I spun a tassel around on my finger and he smirked. 'Or, you know, you could do some upcycling of your own. You're clearly good at it.'

I gestured to the desk he had made me. 'Why not put those make and mend skills to good use and get a few extra bucks here and there?' I said.

He said nothing, but there was something in the silence and the way he held his smile that made me think he liked the idea.

'I'll get the coding in place,' I said, under my breath. 'Also,' I hadn't meant to ask him about this yet, but I had been playing around with an idea for a few weeks ever since an editor asked me to share some analytics about ZodiActually with her. It turned out I had quite a big following for someone who had only been writing for only a short period of time. 'I was wondering if I could hire you as a photographer for a project?'

'What kind of project?' he asked, clearly interested, his brow furrowed in surprise. My phone buzzed, and to keep him in suspense, I reached out and read the notification.

Tina: *Hey babe, I'm in the area. Can I pop round for a cuppa?*

I decided not to reply. I was having too much fun just hanging with Ryan to want Tina to come in with her Red Bull energy and take over.

Instead, I turned back to Ryan who was still tasselling away merrily. 'I want to add some photos of my crystal collection to my blog – not just standard iPhone photos, but proper product ones.'

'Why?' he asked.

'I've had a bit of interest from editors about turning it into a column for their website.'

He stopped tasselling to look at me and his face erupted into a beam of a smile. A smile so infectious that I found myself grinning.

'That's amazing!' he said, sounding genuinely happy for me.

'It's not a big deal.'

'No, that's a huge deal,' he said, shaking his head at me at my false modesty. 'And yeah, of course I will,' he shrugged, as if it was a given that he would take these photos for me.

'Even though crystals are a load of nonsense.'

He shrugged again. '*I* think so, but clearly there is a market for people wanting to learn more about them. And your blog's funny and relatable.'

I stopped tasselling at that point. 'You don't read my blog?'

'I might do,' he inhaled and cleared his throat. 'Whenever, you know, some kids are taking forever to line up quietly for their shoot or when there's traffic on the M20.'

'Oh my God, you read my blog,' I shook my head laughing. 'I would never have thought you'd do that. Ever!'

'I grew up with Aoife!' he remarked, playfully annoyed that I misjudged him. 'Just because I think it's a load of crap, doesn't mean I don't know anything about it.'

'You read my blog, you read my blog,' I sung at him in my most annoying childish tone. He rolled his eyes.

'When I take these photos, you need to make sure you credit me and my new website,' he said, trying to change the subject. I was still giggling, but I nodded.

'Of course I will,' I said, 'I want people to see the wonders that I can create too.'

'Show off,' he muttered. I threw a tassel at him and it landed on his ear, hanging off him like an earring. 'Fetching, but not my colour,' he laughed.

24

Leo: Be aware that there may be some intense opposition to your plans ... Mars and Jupiter align.

After days of forgetting to reply to various texts, I finally gave in to Paige and Tina's repeated requests to join for them dinner. I had money in my account, and they were right, it had been three weeks since we had hung out at Halloween. I needed to get out and, apparently, they wanted to talk about something.

I had already messaged them about the David–Connor–Ryan stand-off, and I was pretty sure it was going to be something to do with that. A mini-intervention of some kind, or a single girls' support group.

Reviewing my horoscope, it said: *Old is new again. Find a fun way to express yourself today.* Without a moment's hesitation, I got dressed up in a peplum dress from 2012, another one of my salvable garments from the flat, which still fit me, and wore some garish red lipstick that I probably should have thrown away three years ago.

The restaurant that Tina had chosen was in Soho and served tapas, my favourite kind of food, so I was looking forward to gorging on sharable plates.

On the tube, I texted both Ryan and Connor. Connor had been fine with the awkward morning, and when I messaged to apologise and say thank you for the evening before he acted as cool as he ever was.

Connor: *Not a problem. It happens.*

This was not anything more than sex; it also wasn't my fault and Connor didn't give a damn about being caught in the middle. All of which I was very grateful for, and selfishly, I thought that that meant he probably wouldn't turn down another invitation if I asked him to pop round tonight for a little re-boot session.

Ryan, who had taken the photos I'd requested and was working on the edits, was texting me back and forth about colourways to add, and ideas for things he could potentially upcycle for his new shop. Our new business ventures in writing and photography were filling us both with energy that could not be turned off.

I spoke to him nearly every day and saw him every other. When we weren't doing something more to the flat, which was above and beyond what Clare had initially asked him to do, we were working together on our new projects, fuelling each other's creativity.

It felt like a productive day couldn't begin without first checking in with Ryan to see what kind of strange new idea had popped into his head – like doing 3D panoramas of each of my crystals to capture every angle in the light; he was my new morning coffee to getting going.

When Paige and Tina had convinced me to leave the flat for an evening, I text Ryan to let him know and he immediately replied with well wishes for both of them.

I was still laughing at his latest text – apparently Aoife had put *Gogglebox* on and decided that Giles and Mary depicted the gulf between the male and female species – as I entered the restaurant, 15 minutes late.

Tina and Paige were already half a bottle of wine down.

'We've already ordered the share plates,' Paige said stand-offishly, as I sat down and apologised for being tardy.

'Oh, great!' I said, hoping that she had remembered to order my favourite, *chopitos*. 'Can't wait, I love this place.'

'We come here a lot,' Tina said, nodding and smiling in an odd way.

'We've only been once?' I pointed out, pouring myself a glass of wine.

'No, she meant *we*,' Paige said, pointing at herself and then Tina.

'Oh,' I said, pouring my wine over the top of my glass in surprise. I leant forward and began to suck it up, like I would the froth of a shaken Pepsi. Not my finest moment, particularly in public. 'I didn't realise you two . . .' I trailed off, forcing a smile.

So, they hung out without me now? Was I really that quiet these days? I thought that a few days without texting was totally fine when you were in your late 20s. I thought we had passed that point in our friendship years ago when we needed to talk to each other every day otherwise our friendship wasn't valid.

'We hang out a lot,' Tina said, her face flushing. Tina never blushed unless she was drinking too much. Sure, the bottle of wine was half empty, but their glasses were full and I doubted that even they would pre-drink before a big meal.

'I didn't know,' I said lamely, picking up my glass for a large gulp.

'There's a lot you don't know,' Paige said, her voice low yet high with meaning. Here we go, the intervention comes into play.

'What's that supposed to mean?' I tried to keep my voice airy and care-free and remind myself that whatever was to come was out of love.

'You've not been paying attention to much besides yourself lately.'

Excuse me? My eyebrows nearly hit the roof. I wasn't

expecting that level of harshness, particularly not from Tina. Even Paige was looking at her in surprise.

'Sorry?' I said to Tina, but glancing at Paige.

'It's not just the lack of texts or choosing not to hang out with us anymore, it's the general vibes we're getting from you,' Tina continued, staring at me straight in the eyes like I knew she would a student when she was giving them a bad report.

'What vibes? I'm not—' I began, but Tina held her hand up.

'No, for once *you* need to listen to us and not interrupt with excuses.'

'I don't know what you're talking about,' I said, gasping in surprise.

'Let me explain then,' Tina said, shuffling forwards in her seat and resting her arms on the table. God, this was serious. She was pissed off at me, and I didn't know why.

'When was the last time you asked either one of us,' she pointed between her and Paige. 'About our lives?'

I sighed and looked around, trying to think of when I *had* last asked them. I hadn't replied to many texts, but when I did, it was usually to say that I was busy or that Ryan and I were working on a project together. Or that I had a deadline to meet, or, more recently, that I'd had some drama with David. I suppose I hadn't been the most receptive of friends lately.

'I've been distracted,' I said. I went to apologise, realising that I was in the wrong, but Tina shook her head before I could get there.

'You've become obsessed with yourself and your bloody Saturn Return.'

'What, no I haven't—'

'We read your blog,' Paige said, in a pitying tone. 'You are obsessed. You write about it every day and we know you're going out because you share photos and stories about your classes with Aoife and your trips to Brick Lane. But you never want to come out with us anymore.'

'I've been busy, with work and the flat,' I pointed out.

'Yeah, but there's busy and then there's ignoring people,' Tina said. 'And I'm sick of being ignored by you.'

'We went out three weeks ago,' I reminded them, leaning back in my chair and crossing my arms defensively. Where the hell was this coming from? I still wasn't sure.

'Yeah, and you invited someone along,' Paige said.

'You *loved* Ryan,' I said, scoffing. 'You were bloody flirting with him all night.'

It was Paige's turn to scoff then, but before she or I could say anything Tina interrupted.

'And you were off sulking.'

'I was trying to stop *you* from embarrassing yourself.'

Tina rolled her eyes. 'For all of five minutes, and then you just left me. You don't think I don't know about my knickers being on someone's head.'

'You love dancing, and I was just letting you be you. And you were drunk as fuck! I could barely do anything to stop you from flinging off your knickers, so don't go blaming me for that.'

'Fine. I was drunk, but you're my mate and you're supposed to look after me. I couldn't find you for half the evening, and when I did you were either on your phone looking at Tinder or flirting with Ryan.'

Every time I so much as checked my phone, I'd look up and Tina would be gone. 'Jeez, you must have been drunk to think I was flirting.'

'*I* wasn't that drunk, and you were clearly flirting with him,' Paige said, picking up her glass of wine and drinking it coolly. 'You like him, you just won't admit it.'

'Is this what this is?' I asked, leaning forward and trying process everything they were saying. 'Are you giving me an intervention to make me realise I like Ryan?'

Tina's eye roll was so large, she looked like an extra out of

The Conjuring. She flung her hand up in the air and brought it down with a thwack on the table.

'I'm sorry, at what point in your astral adventure did you realise that the planets revolved around you?' Tina snapped, turning to Paige. 'She hasn't realised, has she?'

'Realised what?' I asked.

'You don't see beyond the end of your nose, anymore,' Tina's voice cracked in emotion.

'I'm really confused here,' I said, my insides churning at the sense of being attacked. My fight or flight mode was in motion and I was still trying to figure out what the hell was going on with the two of them. 'If this is about my relationship with Ryan then I don't know what you want me to do? I finally got back out there, like *you* suggested I did when I'd only just broken up with a long-term boyfriend, who also seems to have returned onto the scene uninvited thanks in part to my *mother!* Then I've got you two acting like I'm some sort of self-obsessed idiot. I don't – what is going on?'

'We're sick of being ignored,' Paige said, ever calmly, which was just infuriating to me.

'I'm *not* ignoring you,' I said, the volume of my voice rising. 'I don't know why you guys have ambushed me like this? What have I done?'

Paige licked her lips and lifted her hand onto the table. In doing so, I noticed that she was holding Tina's hand.

It was such a purposeful move that I ended up staring at their manicured fingernails, wondering what else I was supposed to be looking at here.

'Okay?' I mumbled, shaking my head. 'You're joining forces? You've glued your hands together? You lost a bet? What? What am I looking at here?'

'I've asked Tina to move in with me,' Paige said.

'Okay?' I repeated. 'She can have the sofa, I vacated it a few months ago now.'

'No, she's going to be in the bedroom. With me.'

'Roommates?' I said, in surprise. Why would Tina leave her house-share to become roommates with Paige – they barely got on as it was?

'We've been dating for three months,' Tina said, shaking her head unable to look at me.

'What?' I laughed, looking from one to the other, then at their adjoined hands on the table. 'But Paige, you were flirting with Ryan?'

'Uh no,' Paige laughed then. 'I was *talking* to Ryan. *You* were flirting with him.'

'No?!' I said, laughing at the ridiculousness of the idea of the two of them dating. 'You and Tina barely get on.'

'We get on just fine.' Tina said.

'Better than fine actually,' Paige sipped some more of her wine.

'Three months? I repeated. They had been dating for three months?

'Yep,' Tina nodded. 'Three months and counting.'

'So, you two got together after I broke up with David,' Tina's gymnastic eye-roll was back and she downed her glass of wine.

'We'd been flirting with each other on-and-off for years, but during those few weeks where we all practically lived together, we realised we liked each other more than just friends,' Paige said. 'It took us a while to get into the groove of it. I mean, why did you think I wanted you out the flat so badly?'

'You said it was because I wasn't pulling my weight,' I reminded her.

'Well, there was that, too. You weren't. And you weren't trying to get out of your slump either.'

'Well now I have. I moved out, I got my own flat and I'm fixing it up. Work is better than ever, and I've just been offered an interview at *Styler* magazine to start my own column, thanks to my blog that you say makes me an obsessive. If it wasn't for my blog and my interests, I wouldn't have a career.' My heart was beating through my neck, I was raging so much internally. 'Everything you're telling me that I'm doing wrong, like focusing on myself, is making my life better right now.'

'So, ignoring us is making your life better,' Paige said, whip-smart in her best lawyer-defence mode.

'Maybe it is,' I returned. 'Based on this ambush.'

'We're not ambushing you,' Tina said, her eyes beginning to lather over with tears. 'We miss you, the *old* you.'

'I don't know what version of me you miss, but this is *me* and this is how I'm staying.'

'Then maybe we shouldn't,' Paige quipped, finishing her glass of wine in one and standing from the table. 'We're not your babysitters and we shouldn't have to ask for attention from you. You should want to know about our lives and hang out with us, and not just use us an excuse for a night out with a guy you like or for a bedsit when life gets shit. We were there for you – the least you could do is return the favour now and then.'

Paige released Tina's hand and grabbed her bag from the floor, leaving without another word.

Tina was quick to stand and follow.

'We miss you. But we don't like this version of you.'

'This version of me is happy,' I pointed out, for what felt like the millionth time.

'Really? So you didn't check your horoscope this morning when I asked you to meet us?'

'And if I did? Who put me on the path of astrology and horoscopes, Tina? I thought you believed in all of this.'

'No,' she said, rubbing her hands together as if to ward off the cold. 'I was just trying to find an excuse for you to use because your life was falling to bits. It's what friends do, they help each other. Or, at least, most friends.'

She stopped rubbing her hands together and walked up to join Paige at the door. They left without a second glance, and seconds later the tapas arrived in small bowls.

The last item to arrive was an extra-large plate of *chopitos*.

25

Leo: Consider your heart as well as your head ... Mercury retrogrades in Aquarius.

That evening I couldn't fall asleep. I tossed and I turned for what felt like hours but was really little more than minutes.

My friends hated me. And my friends were dating! And I hadn't even realised. How could I not have realised? I lived with one of them for more than two months. And the other was my longest friend, who I thought told me everything? How could I not have known?

And how on earth was I going to fix whatever had happened between us?

Feeling full of energy, mostly from my over-active brain that would not shut up, I fell back on what I knew and phoned Connor. His phone rang out a few times and I checked my new bedside alarm clock. It was only just gone 11 pm and I doubted he would be in bed yet; at least, not asleep. I didn't want to be alone right now, and Connor was the only chance I had for company. I phoned him back and he picked up. The background was full of noise, the undeniable sounds of a pub on a Saturday night.

'Hey! You alright?' he said, shouting over the din of bad house music and chatter.

'Yeah, I'm good. I was wondering if you could come round?'

'Nah, I can't tonight,' he shouted back.

'Oh,' I replied, surprised at the answer. He had never turned down a booty call before. 'Another time then.'

'Actually . . .' he began. 'I won't be around at all. I'm seeing someone.'

Fuck.

'Oh! Great!' I said, soundingly overly chipper when really I was deflated at the news that I had suddenly lost my new favourite sex toy. Not to mention an anxiety-relieving drug in human form. 'Good for you.' My voice was rising in pitch just as my heart was plummeting. I was alone.

'Yeah,' he said in a way that suggested he was impatient for me to get off the phone. I was nothing more than a nuisance to him it seemed. Screwing my eyes shut, I hit myself on the forehead.

'I'll see you then.'

'Yeah, bye mate,' Connor finished and hung up.

Mate? Well, that was the end of that then. The final nail in the orgasm coffin. Brilliant timing, I thought, as I threw my phone on top of my bed sheets and groaned. What a shitshow that had turned out to be. Two dates – or sort of dates – and a Mexican stand-off ensues between him, my idiot arsehole of an ex and a very attractive Irishman. It sounded like the cast of a terrible dad joke set in a bar.

Now here I was, in desperate need of distraction, with nothing to clear my head or stop snippets of Paige and Tina's attack, not to mention their relationship revelation, from rolling over me like a film trailer.

I tried, once more, to force myself to sleep, but I couldn't. My brain was in overdrive and I was too wired to consider properly relaxing. I searched for my phone in the dark and lit up my room with its screen. There was always Ryan, but he wouldn't be awake after 11 pm. And even if he was, it wasn't fair to him to dump all my problems on him. That wasn't in his remit.

But I wanted to talk to him; the idea fluttered in my stomach like a feeling of relief. I wasn't completely alone, I had him, Aoife and the astrology girls to fall back on.

Our next class was only a few weeks away. Technically, it should have been our last, but with the amount of cancellations due to Aoife's health, the classes were running behind. Not that any of us minded; we wanted Aoife's health to be her top priority, and also enjoyed the classes too much to want them to end. The girls had started to bring in baked goods, to make up for Millie's biscuit mania. I might not get my hands on a malted milk anymore, but Zelda's chocolate ganache cake more than made up for it.

Without another moment's hesitation, I turned on my bedside lamp and got out of bed. I returned within minutes, holding a large array of astrology books I had yet to return to the library in Dalston – for which I was pretty sure I was going to get slapped with a massive fine. If I couldn't sleep, I was going to study.

Clearly the planets were trying to tell me something with the girls flip-out at me at the restaurant, and their unexpected relationship status updates. Surely there had been something in the horoscope that had tried to tell me about that? Had I just ignored it? Was I really as self-centred as they claimed? I was half-arsing this astrology road, and I needed to either throw myself headfirst to figure out these problems and get my life on track, or I needed to give it up and let my life return to becoming the ultimate shitshow that it was.

I cracked open a dusty book. Whenever I ignored my horoscope or forgot my crystals on a night out, bad things seemed to happen to me. That had to mean something. *Alright universe, you have my attention, now what are you trying to tell me?*

I sat there until 3 am reading over the various positions of the planets and their meanings, waking suddenly at 10 am after falling asleep on Mercury – admittedly quite a boring planet – with a fresh energy.

Using Blu-Tack and a sticky note, I posted a reminder on my front door never to leave without my pendants or my mini crystals, including my tiger's eye for self-confidence, and my jasper and obsidian to absorb bad energy. These were the basics I should always carry with me, I thought. My gold-stone anxiety thumb-stone was also a handy one to carry with me, but since I tended to walk around my flat casually rubbing it with my thumb, I knew I would lose it somewhere sooner or later. Better to embrace my sieve-like memory in advance then panic when I lost it.

In a burst of guilt, I decided to return my borrowed astrology books to Dalston library. After reading and re-reading them since I got them back in July, I thought it was time to branch out and head to a local astrology store in Camden. There, I planned to throw myself on the bookseller's mercy and restock my shelves with all of the books, incense and tarot cards I needed.

Needless to say, my replenishing of my astrology stocks led to some increasing worry about my finances. My bills were due and I had food to buy, but when I remembered this, I consulted my horoscope, which promised that my fortunes were on the rise.

Aoife was very impressed with my astrological reboot at our classes.

'You have a heliotic glow about you,' she said (Helios being the Greek god responsible for the Sun).

'I'm glad,' I told her, as I sat cross-legged in my chair while shading in my latest Moon chart. 'I think Jupiter is in the 9th house, so I'm feeling quite philosophical at the moment.'

'Or you've just had too much coffee, Leo,' Ryan teased from behind his aunt. He had started to appear at the classes more and more, since his art classes had finally come to an end. It seemed that his taking the art class was mostly so that he could keep an eye on Aoife as her health got worse. It had gotten so bad recently that he had begun to act as her chauffeur to and from her workshops, which meant that he simply hung around as an acting assistant, but I didn't mind his appearance in our sessions.

The girls enjoyed it very much. Jane had to positively wipe the dribble off Zelda's chin for her, and Millie even offered Ryan one of her precious biscuits.

'Aren't you a tiny bit interested in what your birth chart would say about you?' I asked him, smiling as I tentatively began to pull out the books to review it.

'Don't you dare,' he said.

'His birthday is 23rd March 1991,' Aoife said under her breath, winking at me. Instantly, I started plotting on one of her pre-printed charts.

'Right, 23rd March 1991,' I repeated. So he was thirty . . . interesting. 'At what time and where?'

'Auntie . . .' he began, but Aoife held up her hand to him.

'At 1.15 pm in Beaumont Hospital, Dublin.'

'Do you have to be that specific?' he groaned. 'Do you need my weight and labour time as well?'

'You were seven pounds on the dot, and you took eighteen hours to make your appearance. I should know, I was there for every second of it,' Aoife murmured sweetly, turning towards him to give him a gracious smile. He was blushing and I was living for it.

'Okay . . .' I began, as I plotted out his Sun sign, his ascendant and his Moon.

'Don't leave us in suspense, Leo, what does it say,' he smirked, giving in to our playtime. The girls all pulled their chairs in closer to me to observe my dextrous charting.

'Well, as you said a while back, you're definitely an Aries. That's your Sun sign.'

'And what does that say about me?' he folded his arms defiantly.

'Apparently, you're naturally competitive, fiercely independent and you need to learn to understand other people as complex wholes.'

'It does not say that,' he scoffed, but I lifted the book up and pointed to the description.

'It was in your ninth house when you were born, meaning that you distinguish yourself from others through education and politics.'

'I'm not so sure that's true,' he said, rubbing his forehead in consideration.

'What about his ascendent?' Jane asked nosily.

'Oh yes,' Zelda began. 'That's the most interesting, as it's the face that you show other people.'

'The face?' Ryan repeated.

'How others perceive you,' I clarified, as I charted the position. 'Well, if I'm right, then your ascendant is in Leo.'

I tried to conceal my smile by rolling my lips together, but it wasn't working.

'That's right,' Aoife confirmed. Of course she already knew the birth chart of her favourite nephew, but she wasn't going to spoil our fun in figuring it out for ourselves.

'We're not so different after all,' I said to Ryan, fluttering my eyelashes teasingly. He laughed. 'You come across as bright and good-natured, even a little magnetic.'

'Ooh,' the girls crooned, as if they were schoolgirls.

'Your energy makes you appear like a know-it-all – now that I can confirm,' I said under my breath.

'Okay, give it a rest,' Ryan said, uncrossing his arms awkwardly. Was he embarrassed by this? Was I really getting to the heart of his personality?

'Wait, there's your Moon sign as well,' Millie interrupted, forgoing her plate of biscuits to partake in our little game.

'Your Moon sign ...' I began, looking away from Ryan's reddening face to the chart. 'Is in Cancer. Your Moon rules your emotions and moods when you're alone or deeply comfortable. Your emotional side is sensitive and empathetic. You secretly fear being abandoned by those you love. It was in your 12th house when you were born, meaning you find security through privacy and introspection. And you're most compatible with – never mind.' I shut the book quickly after seeing 'Leo'.

The ladies around me all made *ooh* sounds, but I didn't join in. I was trying to hide my blush.

It sounded exactly like Ryan; the Ryan I knew outside of these classes who was quiet and kind. Who refused to talk about the family that he was never close to, and who always helped me before he helped himself.

'That's a lovely birth chart,' Jane commended Ryan, as if he had a choice in the matter. 'Mine just tells me I'm organised and bossy.'

'Typical Sagittarius,' Zelda muttered.

'I read Ryan's birth chart when he was just born,' Aoife said calmly, as if this was an everyday habit that most aunts did at the bedside of a newborn. 'He's a sweet soul.'

'You never told me that,' Ryan muttered, shaking off his awkwardness as he walked over to his Aunt.

'You never asked. And it's not like you ever wanted to know,' she remarked, honestly enough. 'Sometimes our futures aren't worth knowing in advance. You were always going to be better finding your own path. Others need a little guidance.'

I put it down to a trick of my peripheral vision, but I was pretty sure she glanced in my direction when she said that.

I glanced away, looking at the paperwork as if focusing on my task for the day which was listing the effects of each planet in the different house.

In fact, I was finishing off Ryan's birth chart. Or at least, one strand of his chart: the position of Venus at the time of his birth.

According to my calculations, Venus was in Taurus and the tenth house when Ryan was born. Looking through the book, this meant that Ryan oriented towards comfort and stability. He liked to move slowly in relationships, in a way that sometimes came off as timid or intimidating, but love for him was simple. Venus being in the tenth house meant that his love was often expressed through success and responsibility.

Kind of like starting a successful new company with a creative partner responsible for launching his website. My heart gave a little flutter again.

No, I shook my head. This couldn't be true. There was nothing in my latest tarot card reading – done online, rather than in person this time – that suggested romance was on my horizon. My horoscope never mentioned relationships after that time about sports paving the way. All it mentioned at this stage was focusing on my goals.

Just because Ryan's birth chart claimed that romance to him was goal-based and simple, it didn't mean that I was the romantic recipient at its heart. No birth chart can tell you that.

Wouldn't it be so much easier if it did?

Sadly, for me at least, romance with Ryan was not currently on the cards. And if, as I said, I was going to throw myself wholeheartedly into what the planets had to say, then I had to accept that Ryan and I were nothing more than friends. Even if something inside me fell away at the thought.

26

Leo: Take care of other people and their emotions ... There's a
full Moon in the 3rd house tonight.

It was about a week and a half after my meal with the girls
when my horoscope even vaguely suggested anything about
reconciliation.

On Tuesday morning I opened my eyes and instantly
reached for my horoscope.

Forgiveness is available to those who ask for it.

It felt a lot like Dumbledore sending a message to me through
my paperback editions of *Harry Potter*, but if that's what the
horoscope said then that's what the planets meant for me to do.

I texted Ryan, feeling I needed a little boost to my confidence before I actually went.

Kris: *I'm going to go see the girls today.*
Ryan: *Good! It's about time you got back on talking terms.*

Ryan had had to listen to me talking about what happened
with the girls whenever he came around after that dinner. No
matter what topic we were discussing, from the website to the
latest episode of the *Great British Bake Off*, I always managed
to bring up the girls in some way. Paige wouldn't agree with
Ryan not having a manifesto on his website, and Tina would
have loved that bread sculpture of a fountain – the theme was

a romantic picnic – that featured on that week's episode of *GBBO*.

Ryan was very good at never actually expressing an opinion in favour of either party. I knew before I even talked about it with him, that he'd likely find more sympathy with the girls than he would with me, what with his views on astrology. But he was too polite, as my friend, to say anything against my own beliefs.

'Feel like I should bring a peace offering …' I wrote back, considering what such an offering could be.

'They love food,' he reminded me. And sure enough, it was a great suggestion. The three of us did love our food, it was the only London stereotype we openly admitted to fitting, being out-of-city girls for most of our lives. We loved the variety of takeaways and restaurants in London town we could try. It was always fun spinning the wheel of the Just Eat app to see what we would land on that week.

'Still can't wrap my head around Paige and Tina being a couple,' I replied, as I went about scrolling the app for ideas.

'I thought it was pretty obvious at Halloween,' Ryan replied.

'The way Paige had her arm around Tina at the start of the night.'

I had just thought she was holding her up after pre-drinking heavily. No, she was just being a handsy girlfriend.

'Can't believe I was so blind to it.'

Every time I thought back to Tina and Paige together, something would suddenly click in my head to realise that yes, they had made it pretty obvious that they were a couple and I had just completely ignored it as if it was irrelevant, or nothing to do with me.

The time that Paige nearly jumped out of her skin when I burst into Paige's flat after visiting the mews with Clare. Or the fact that Tina was always at Paige's flat after work, when usually she only ever came over once a week. And how Paige smiled whenever Tina came on FaceTime, and the way that she used to leave without telling me where she was going, just in her laid-back everyday clothes.

It was so obvious, and I had missed it. My head spun at the realisation that I had truly been as self-obsessed as Tina and Paige called me out on. Had I been like this before? Or had I just been obsessed with keeping everyone happy when I was with David, like the people-pleaser I always thought I was?

'*I recommend getting them Tapas, since they missed out on it last time*,' Ryan replied, without calling me out on my blindness. He was sweet enough to want to help me fix things, not focus on my faults.

'*I appreciate you*,' I replied quickly, finding a nearby tapas restaurant that did takeaway and leaving my flat with haste – only just remembering to pick up my tiger's eye, obsidian and jasper on the way out.

* * *

I knocked on Paige's door twice. The first time it was so quiet even I couldn't tell if it had truly made a sound. The second time I whacked the door with the side of my fist, just to make sure.

Tina answered the door, looking flustered in a teddy fleece nightdress as if she had just been interrupted. Likely, I had just got her out of bed. It was a Sunday, after all.

Oh God, I thought, what if had just been having sex with Paige? I shook my head sharply. *Get your head out of the gutter.* There would have been no way that Tina would have answered the door if she had been having sex, mostly because she was unlikely to be able to hear it over all of her groaning. I had lived with her through university; I knew how loud she could get.

'I come in peace,' I said, holding up the bag of tapas takeaway in greeting. Not really the best way to say hello after a fight, I realised, when Tina folded her arms. She wasn't so easily swayed as that.

I felt my throat begin to close up with nerves – a first for me when it came to talking to Tina. She was a university sister; we had no qualms being around each other, even when we were frustrated by deadlines or cramping with period pains.

Never once in our ten-year relationship had I felt ashamed of myself in front of her. And I had done a lot of shameful things in my time.

'Hey,' I said, as a way to get my mouth back into my gear with my brain. 'You were right. I was a self-obsessed bitch.'

Still nothing. She didn't move an inch, nor did her frown.

'And I deserved the intervention. In fact, I think I need notes as I really had no clue you and Paige were together, and it was under my nose the entire time. I was just too fogged up with my own life.'

She twitched. Finally, the glass was breaking. With my free hand I began to twist the obsidian stone in my pocket, keeping away any negativity that might creep into my heart-to-heart with Tina.

'I'm sorry I hurt your feelings, yours *and* Paige's. You were there for me without question when I needed you most, but I never returned the favour. In fact, I pissed on it. And for that, I truly am super sorry. Can you forgive me?'

I tipped the bag of tapas forwards slightly, so that it was just under her nose. I had foregone the chopitos for a fried squid with extra chilli oil, and the smell was sinfully decadent.

'Stop ... trying ... to ... bribe ... me,' she said, through gritted teeth, never once looking away from me but her eyes were brightening as she said it.

'Can we just agree that I win worst friend of the year, and tuck in?' I suggested.

'You do look awfully pathetic on the doorstep,' she said, side-stepping to open the door for me. 'I've seen strays with more *come hither* power than you.'

'Thank God I didn't have more *come hither*, otherwise it would be me you were dating not Paige.'

'Ha!' Tina scoffed, 'One second in the door and she's already cracking lesbian jokes. You really have transformed.'

'Where is the other half? I need to apologise to both of you.'

'She . . .' Tina said, taking the tapas takeaway bag of my hands and heading towards the slightly messier than normal kitchen. 'Is getting us brunch.'

'Ah.' Great. Not the best way to win over Paige; to bring food with me when she had probably just got showered and dressed just to pop to the fancy bakery down the street for smoked salmon bagels. 'Should I run and hide?'

'Not if you're going to take the tapas. I could smell that chilli oil when you got off the tube.'

'It was to cover the sweat of nerves.'

'Oh babe,' Tina laughed, and had the good grace to lean over the breakfast bar to give me a hug. 'You needed calling out, but I hate it when we're not talking.'

'I did,' I agreed, relishing the idea of the moment we were back to our usual selves again. 'It sucked, but I get it. Real friends call each other out sometimes.'

'Sometimes? Have you met Paige?'

I sat at the breakfast bar, feeling exhausted with relief.

'I have indeed, but I've not exactly been paying attention lately.'

'Understatement of the year,' Tina muttered. She sighed and stopped unpacking the food for a moment. 'Look, I'm not going to apologise for the intervention. You were falling off into the deep end and kind of hurting our feelings as you did so.'

'I never meant to hurt you,' I promised, feeling my stomach dip again.

'We know, honestly we do. But no one likes to feel ignored and we wanted to be open with you, but at the same time we were nervous about how you'd feel about our relationship—'

'Oh, I think it's great! Odd, but great.'

'Odd?' Tina repeated, screwing up her face playfully. 'Odd was dating that bloke that was so tanned he looked like an Oompa Loompa.' (A university mistake of mine). 'Paige and are not odd, we're just . . . unexpected.'

'For you, or for me?' I asked, tentatively leaning across to pick up a piece of a prawn from the steaming seafood paella.

Tina shrugged and smacked my hand away. 'Mostly for Paige, I think. I'm not exactly the K-pop dreamboat she thought she'd end up with.'

'I saw her more with a silent-Richard type. You know the kind of standard-looking bloke who doesn't talk, except to say "yes", "no" or "beer" at dinner parties.'

'Silent Richard . . .' Tina repeated. 'Sounds like a font.'

We both began to laugh just as a key turned in the lock of the door.

'The stupid dick-faced waiter put two cream cheese and one . . .' She stopped at the sight of me. And likely the smell of greasy chorizo and onion omelettes Tina and I had just begun tucking into. 'What the flip are you doing here?'

'Down girl. She came to apologise,' Tina explained nonchalantly, helping herself to the fried squid without bothering with cutlery.

Paige's arms sagged with brown paper bags, and she looked at me expectantly.

'I'm sorry,' I said, feeling embarrassed at the lack of Richard Curtis oomph I could give to it. My gentle natter with Tina had expelled my energy for epic apologies.

There was a pregnant pause and then she shrugged.

'I don't care what you brought, if you want a bagel you need to chip in a fiver.' And just like that, forgiveness was handed over to me, as swiftly as a fork was placed into Tina's hand by Paige the moment she spotted her finger-licking actions.

The wonderful thing with Paige is that she spent her nine-to-five job arguing with people, so come the weekend she couldn't be bothered unless it was completely necessary.

We spent the remaining portion of the morning swapping between licking cream cheese off our top lips and fighting playfully over the last prawn in the seafood paella.

27

Leo: Leave the flower unpicked so that others who come after you can also enjoy its splendour ... Mars enter Aries.

Paige, Tina and I barely left each other's company after our reconciliation, except when the two of them went to work and I overslept. Some things never change.

I more than made up for my mini-disappearance by having them round the flat for dinner – cooked by Tina – and drinks – brought by Paige. I supplied the Netflix and company, for once.

'Did you hire an interior designer?' Paige asked one evening, pottering around the living room, nursing her wine. The open-plan kitchen and living room were almost completely decorated. After Ryan's handyman work and my charity shopping prowess, I only needed to find an affordable sofa to fill the space under the window and I'd have a complete lounge. Over the last few weeks of searching, I had found a few Facebook finds that I thought would work nicely, but Ryan refused to let me spend less than £100 on what he called 'fart cushions' and 'frames'. After all the money I'd saved buying third-hand goods from questionable eBay sellers and flea market stalls, the least I could do was treat myself to a half-decent couch. Particularly as I was very much a couch-potato at heart.

'Nope. Turns out Ryan and I make a pretty good team.'

'Ryan and Krystal sitting in a tree ...' Tina hummed under her breath.

'Stop teasing her,' Paige said. 'Or if you must, do something less juvenile.'

'I can't help it. I work with eight years old day in and day out,' she defended.

'Originality wouldn't go amiss,' I said, topping up my glass of rosé.

'It's just so sweet. You and this handyman who randomly pops by. Sounds like the beginning of a good porno doesn't it?' Tina looked at Paige quickly. 'Not that I watch porn anymore though, babe.'

'I do,' Paige said proudly.

Tina smiled and kicked her legs up as she lay back on the floor.

'What would you call the decor then?' I said to Paige. 'Shabby chic?'

'Boho bonkers?' Paige suggested.

'I'll take that,' I laughed. 'Better than bloody awful.'

'Well . . .' Paige began joining us cross-legged on the floor and Tina smacked her thigh. Paige placed her hand on Tina's back sweetly. 'I'm just kidding. It might not be to my taste but it's still a miraculous turnaround.'

'It's gorgeous. Very you,' Tina said supportively.

'Why thank you.'

I tapped my glass against her own just as there was a knock on the door.

'Who's that? I thought *we* were your only friends?' Paige asked, leaning back a bit.

'Oi! Harsh much,' I laughed, getting up to get the door. 'It'll be Ryan.'

'Of course that's who it is!' Tina exclaimed, clearly delighted. I wanted to tell her to calm down, but I couldn't without revealing my smile.

'Hey,' Ryan said, as I opened the door to him. It was raining and he was waiting patiently under a flowery umbrella.

'Aoife's umbrella?' I asked without returning his greeting.

He ignored me but laughed as he stepped inside and shut the umbrella down. 'Tea?'

'Love one.'

'The girls are inside.' Immediately there was a chorus of 'Heys' from the living room.

'You alright?' Ryan asked them as I headed for the kitchen to make his tea. 'Wine, already? It's not even six o'clock yet?' he teased.

'It gets dark at 3 pm now, so day-drinking rules no longer apply.' Tina remarked immediately.

'Fair enough,' Ryan laughed.

'Do you want a glass?' I shouted from the kitchen, straining my ears to make sure I heard everything the three of them said to each other, just in case Tina let one of her pre-drink slips happen.

'No, I'm good with tea, thanks. I barely had a chance to eat anything all day.'

'Why?' I shouted, just as Paige asked, 'What were you doing?'

'I had a LinkedIn shoot for a business in Vauxhall.'

'LinkedIn shoot?' Tina repeated, and I knew they were on a safe enough topic for me to fully concentrate on not doing something like putting milk in the kettle.

'Yeah, just boring old profile pictures for professional LinkedIn profiles. Some companies make it compulsory.'

'That must be good money,' Paige said.

'Not really,' Ryan said, and I heard the hesitancy in his voice. Paige would bash that out of him right away; we were never scared to talk about money in our group, none of us had time for modesty. 'It's about £5 a head when I do them in bulk, so . . .' he trailed off.

'Hold that thought,' I shouted from the kitchen, leaving the kettle to bubble noisily. 'I need to talk to you about your photos. I have some news.'

'Well, I was hoping you would, since that's why I came over.' Ryan smiled, leaning against the wall. He had even taken his shoes off so he could rest his foot on the wall without leaving a mark.

Earlier in the day I had excitedly, and somewhat mysteriously, texted Ryan, asking him to come over to talk about his photos on my website.

'Ooh! What's the gossip,' Tina asked me.

'You know those photos on my blog, the ones of the crystals and the tarot cards?' I said to the girls, both of whom nodded – even if Paige did follow hers up by rolling her eyes. 'Ryan took those for me.'

'They look bloody gorgeous!' Tina shouted, her voice rising an octave. I noticed her glass was empty, so that made sense.

'You're cut off,' Paige whispered, leaning forwards to take Tina's glass. Tina let out a cackle of a laugh that just screamed *try and stop me* before she grabbed for the glass again. Paige was too quick for her, though. 'Carry on,' Paige instructed.

'So, this curator got in touch with me from a gallery in Bloomsbury and she's doing a show called *Self and Stars*. She really wants to incorporate your photos in the exhibit.'

'What?' Ryan said.

'She wants to include your photos in the show. And sell them!' I shouted, jumping up and down on my feet.

How was he not running around the room like the floor was on fire and he was the only flame-retardant thing in the world right now? I was barely controlling my excitement, and I was hardly involved.

'Oh my God! That's fantastic,' Paige said, gasping and clapping loudly. Tina turned onto her back to look at Ryan, shaking herself all over like a cheerleaders pom pom.

'Smashed it!' she screamed.

'What?' Ryan repeated, and I rolled my eyes.

'You've been scouted. They want to showcase your art,' I said, wanting to rush over and shake him by the shoulders to get him to react. 'Now do you see why I wanted to tell you in person?' I stepped towards my desk to open the email on my laptop and turned it to face him. 'Take a look for yourself.'

Ryan jolted from the spot as if a wave of electricity had passed under his feet, and leant over the desk to read the screen.

'I checked it out and everything,' I told him as he read it. 'She and the show are legit. It's in December; tickets are already on sale.'

'It's real,' Ryan repeated, clearly having reached the bottom of the email. 'She wants ten photos, five from the website and five new ones,' he dictated from the screen, a smile trying to creep onto his face by the way his lips kept twitching up and down in disbelief.

'Yep. And she said they'll print them for the show, so no costs on your part.'

'How do you make money from it, though?' Paige asked curiously, still grinning from ear to ear as Tina got comfortable lying with her head in her lap.

'People buy the prints on the day,' I said. 'Or they order them, I think. On the gallery website it said that they'll have a photograph in the largest size on display and then if you like it you can order a print in an option of sizes.'

'For how much?' Paige continued, and I turned to give her daggers. She got the hint to stop pressing about costs and cash, holding her hands up in apology quickly while Ryan's back was still turned. Money wasn't what Ryan wanted to think about right now, I guessed. From the discussions we'd had about his art I knew that money and prestige were not what he wanted to showcase his art for, not initially at least. It was about pride and self belief.

As much as being hired to take photographs for schools and business was a form of confirmation that he was a photographer, until his work was exhibited, Ryan was never going to feel like an artist. It was his dream and it had finally happened, entirely by accident.

'Is this your first show?' Tina asked from the floor.

Ryan nodded. 'Yeah, I've never shown anything professionally before. I mean, the photos are on your blog of course . . .' he began to backtrack quickly, shaking his head and blushing as if he had just massively insulted me in some way. I held my hand up to him.

'It's fine, I know what you meant.'

'Not to say your blog isn't professional, just that I've never . . .'

'You've never featured in a gallery show. You're going to be a full-on artist.'

I smiled and suddenly a grin erupted on his face. He was laughing and running his hands through his hair, jumping from looking at me to looking back at the screen. I was grinning, too, Ryan's smile was too infectious not to be.

'When is the show?' Tina asked.

'December 15th is the opening. Just before Christmas,' I told them, as I doubted Ryan would have processed that part yet.

'Oh my God,' Ryan said, stepping back and placing both his hands on his hips. 'It's actually happening.'

I nodded. I stood up and Ryan flung his arms around my waist and started spinning me around the living room. Tina and Paige's laughter echoed in my eardrums, and I also heard Paige's sensible *don't drop her* calls.

I squealed as Ryan put me down, his hands still on my waist as he beamed at me, just inches from my face.

'December 15th,' he repeated to me, and I nodded.

'December 15th.'

'Can I bring a guest?' he asked, and I shrugged, still catching my breath from losing it in his tight grasp.

'I presume so. I doubt they'd tell you no.'

'Then you have to come with me,' he asked, and I felt heat on my cheeks. 'None of this would have happened without you,' so it was a thank you invitation. Of course it was, we were just friends I reminded myself. We hadn't even hugged before he just swung me around just then. In fact, I realised that that was our first physical contact since that time he placed his hand on my shoulder to steady me after David showed up out of the blue.

'Of course I'll come with you,' I said breathlessly, docking the date in my mind and hoping that my horoscope would be positive for the day, just as I would hope it wouldn't rain on a picnic.

'This is so exciting!' Tina shouted, reminding me that both she and Paige were still here. 'We need more wine.'

'No!' Paige and I both said, but Ryan shouted, 'Yes!' in agreement, which was all the encouragement Tina needed to get up and head for the kitchen for a fresh bottle of rosé. I looked over at Paige who was resting on her elbows. Her eyebrows raised a fraction as we locked eyes and I mouthed *what?*, before she shrugged and returned to berating Tina about her bad influence on innocent Ryan.

28

Leo: You may need to balance your cloudy head with stable roots ... Mars will clash with Jupiter in the 12th house.

Kris: *Hey ladies! What are your plans for the week?*
Paige: *Same as always: Work. Work. Work.*
Kris: *Well maybe I can treat us to a nice dinner or a movie? Because guess what?! My insurance pay-out just got confirmed. I'm finally getting my safety deposit and furniture refund back from the old flat.* 👗👗👗
Paige: *About bloody time!!*
Kris: *My horoscope said that a windfall was in the cards today, so if that's not a sign that the planets are finally moving in my direction then I don't know what is.*
Paige: *It's not a sign of the stars. I filed that insurance claim for you in July! It's now December! I should send them a calendar for Christmas.*
Kris: *Potato, po-ta-ta. My horoscope was still right.*
Paige: *...*
Tina: *Oh, let her have it, babe.*
Tina: *Do you want to come shopping with me after work? Spend some of that well-deserved moneyyyyyyy!*
Kris: *Let me see how the interview with* Styler *goes.*
Tina: *OMG! Is that today?!*
Kris: *Yep. On my way now.*
Tina: *Good luck – not that you need it, you're going to totally kill it.*
Paige: *You got this!*

Paige: *Remind me what the role is??*

Kris: *They want me to write a column for them, based on ZodiActually.*

Kris: *See, following the stars really can lead to windfalls …*

Paige: *…*

Tina: *WE support you entirely.*

Tina: *Don't we Paige.*

Paige: *Never in question. You're an amazing writer and you deserve this.*

Paige: *GOOD LUCK!!!!*

Tina: *That's my girl.*

Kris: *Vom, guys.* 🤮

Kris: 😂

Tina: 😸😸😸😸

Paige: 💿

⋆ ⋆ ⋆

My interview with *Styler* was to be held at the company's offices just off the Strand. For weeks I had been emailing back and forth with the editor, Cameron, about my website and a potential column idea. From sending across samplers to answering potential questions from readers, submitting my CV for the formal HR process and more. It felt like I had already been interviewed over every digital platform, and this was the last hurdle to pass before it became official.

I was going to be a professional columnist with a weekly column online and a monthly feature spread in *Styler* magazine!

It was even better than the job I had at *Craze*, and only three months had passed since that catastrophe. This was without a doubt due to the stars; everything I had been doing was because of my horoscope, my cards and my crystals. Without them I would never have started my website or been persistent with keeping Cameron up to date with all of my latest posts when she first started showing interest.

When Cameron offered me the interview, I had checked my stars and it said that Friday 10th December would be the best for communication, so of course I told her I was only available on that date and she had agreed. It was a week after the date she had initially wanted to interview me, but the week before was a bad week for communication according to my horoscope, and it was right.

Not only had my Wi-Fi connection been disconnected without reason, but the internet support team kept putting me on hold and then sending me to the wrong department when I did get through to them to report the issue. I spent the better part of the week chatting to various helplines, using up all of my data on my phone to send angry emails and tweets, only to be told that it was scheduled maintenance that had caused the issue. Why couldn't they have emailed me that beforehand and saved me time and misery?

The stars knew all along, though.

I didn't feel nervous about my interview as I got off the bus. It was a busy Friday morning commuter bus, and even though it was packed, and I was being jostled from side to side constantly as I held on for dear life via one of the overhead handles, I felt relaxed.

The stars were on my side, I was well prepared and I knew that this interview was merely a formality. The office was ridiculously easy to find – I didn't even have to refer to Google Maps (which I'm sure would have made Ryan very proud of me). It was just off the Strand in a boutique office building opposite a posh Indian restaurant that was wafting glorious scents from its open doors during its brunch hour. My mouth watered and I hopped across the street to view the menu, knowing I had arrived in good time for my interview and could spare a few minutes to explore the nearby surrounds.

The menu sounded delicious and I could practically envisage myself and the girls eating there, laughing and chinking our wine glasses in cheers to celebrate my new role at *Styler*.

I reached into my pocket to grab my phone to take a photo of the menu to send to them – a little pre-planning wouldn't go amiss – but I stopped when I didn't hear the familiar sounds of my crystals hitting my plastic phone case. I always kept my phone and crystal in the same pocket of my jacket out of habit and my routine never changed.

My stomach dropped. I hadn't picked them up. It was the last thing I always did as I left the house, and I hadn't done it today. I had completely forgotten.

Today, when I had an interview that was going to decide whether I had a full-time career that would replace my sporadic freelance life. My dream job, that had come up completely out of the blue and that was the epitome of a once in a lifetime shot. Today was the day that I had forgotten to bring with me my good luck charms and negative energy repellent.

'Oh shit,' my vision began to spin. I went to pocket my phone I dropped it and it landed on the sidewalk with a crash. The screen smashed to pieces before my eyes, flickering a little where the undercoat had been scratched. 'Fuck!' I yelled, reaching down to pick it up.

The maître d' of the restaurant appeared at the door and shushed me with a hiss.

'You can't sit there!' he shouted, obviously thinking that by crouching down to the ground I had claimed this as my spot for the day. Did he think I was homeless? He certainly recoiled a little when I turned to face him.

'But I . . .' I began lamely, my palms sweating as I turned my phone over in my hands. He closed the restaurant door without another comment, glaring at me through the glass until he disappeared out of view. Clearly something about me horrified him.

'Shit!' I exclaimed again, in a barely audible hiss this time.

My breath was catching in my throat and everything on me felt too tight. Why had I worn a thick coat and a jumper to an interview? Sure, it was December, but I was dressed like an Eskimo and then I could hardly breathe. Maybe I had put my crystals in my pocket after all and they were just trapped in the layers? I pointlessly began searching again, knowing in my heart that they weren't there.

I began pulling at my scarf, hoping to effortlessly tug it free from my neck to get some air, but it was caught on my hood. I jolted my neck side to side in the hopes of loosening it, but nothing worked. My phone fell from my hand again and bounced with another sickening crack against the gravel.

Great. I forgot my crystals and I smashed my phone, and I can't breathe and I'm about to miss my interview.

The scarf gave way with one bruise-inducing tug but then it was just hanging off my shoulder and I was still too hot despite the cold on my exposed neck. I began tugging at the buttons of my coat but they too were against me, slipping from my clammy fingertips as I tried to undo them.

My heart was pounding, and I could feel my pulse throbbing in my neck. Everyone who passed me on that street was staring at me as they walked, and nearly all of them then walked inside the office building that I was due to enter any minute.

I couldn't go in now; I was ridiculous. I couldn't do this on my own; I needed the crystals to stop Cameron realising I was actually a fake. That I was controlling, demanding and a drama queen. It wasn't even that I currently couldn't speak with the dry lump stuck in my throat making it almost impossible to gasp for air. Or that I was wearing a beige puffer jacket that made me look like a giant walking penis, I'd just realised, looking in the restaurant window.

It was because I was a fraud.

Leaning over to pick my phone up from the ground, I found I couldn't find the will to stand up again. I swung my legs around and sat on the edge of the curb, still trying to catch my breath, and also having to pull my scarf out of the puddle it had just fallen into.

With shaking fingers and lots of squinting to see through the shattered glass of my phone I managed to make it into my contacts list.

Hesitantly, I hovered over Paige and Tina's names, knowing full well that both of them were at work and I was just a nuisance to them. The two of them probably didn't even want to be friends with me anymore, not after the way I had been acting over the last few months. It was only through begging and bribery with alcohol and tapas that they tolerated me the other night, I thought.

I blinked away the tears that inevitably began to flow as I continued to try and catch my breath.

There was nothing else I could do. I needed someone to help me. And there was really only one choice based on experience.

I tapped on Tina's name.

The phone rang out five times before she answered breathlessly on the last ring.

'Did you butt dial me? I'm on playground duty,' Tina whispered down the phone quickly.

'Ti . . . Tina,' I said, gulping through the tears.

'Kris? Are you okay?' her voice lowered.

'I can't . . . I can't . . .' I couldn't speak – my eyes were blurry and everything around me was starting to a spin. I put my heads between my knees and tried to focus on my breathing.

'I can't do—' I managed to spit out, and then the words came out all at once in a barely coherent mess. 'What was I thinking? There's no way I could be a columnist at *Styler!* I'm a 29-year-old old failure with a one-page CV that is mostly about being a freelancer, which we all know just means 'unemployed'. I don't belong here. I can't walk into that office,' I began to hyperventilate, unable to say another word as it sank in.

'Oh God. Babe, where are you?' she paused. 'Never mind, I'll find you on Find My.'

'I can't . . . I can't breathe.'

'It's okay, hun. I got you,' her voice was distant, and I could hear her thudding fingertips as she pressed buttons on her screen.

'I'm so sorry,' I continued, still crying into my knee. What if someone saw me? What if Cameron was looking out of her office window and spotted me right now. 'I need to move.'

'No!' Tina said suddenly. 'No, just stay where you are. I'm sending an Uber to come and get you and take you home. Just hold on.'

'Tina . . .' I whined, the tears flowing thicker even as my breathing eased a little. 'I can't do this,' I said.

'It's okay. It's all going to be okay,' Tina said, 'I'm here babe. Me and Paige will sort this out.'

'I can't do anything right.'

'Yes, you can,' Tina said softly. I could hear another conversation happening in the background of her call. 'You can do anything, just hold on one second. My friend is having a panic attack—' she said to someone quickly, clearly attempting to hold the phone away from her.

Oh God, it wasn't only my life I was fucking up. I was ruining Tina's, too, on top of everything else. Why couldn't I do anything right?

29

Leo: Realize that to conquer new ground you may have to make some sacrifices ... the Moon resides in Cancer in the 4th house.

For days I stayed in bed barely looking at my phone. Tina and Paige popped by a few times, bringing me food, convincing me to jump in the shower and at least change my clothes. I could hardly find the energy to move I was so tired all the time, and yet sleep rarely came. Every time I thought about going outside or doing something around the house I couldn't find the will to move my muscles.

The girls were the only people I could face seeing me right now, and even when they did come over I barely spoke to them. I was just too tired.

Tina had been my saving grace the morning of the interview, in organising my Uber and keeping me on the phone until it arrived – even when I heard the headteacher of her school berating her for her lack of professionalism. She ended up having a disciplinary meeting about it and everything, which only led to my increased guilt. I had almost lost her her job because of my stupidity. I was the worst of friends.

Thankfully, they believed her story about helping me through a panic attack, but that didn't stop them from saying that her phone was no longer allowed on her during school hours.

Paige had taken charge of dealing with *Styler* to let Cameron know why I missed our scheduled interview.

Cameron had been accepting of the situation, though no mention was made of rescheduling at the time.

It didn't matter. I clearly wasn't worthy of a job at *Styler*. It was a fluke. I couldn't even remember to bring my crystals with me, so why should I be trusted with a weekly column in an international award-winning magazine? Whatever my horoscope had been trying to tell me, I'd clearly interpreted it wrong. It was all my fault.

Of course, I didn't share these thoughts with Tina or Paige, as I knew they would just try and convince me otherwise, and I knew that it was my own fault.

I became a hermit living – or barely living – in bed. Ryan tried to call me a few times and WhatsApped even more, but I never responded. I didn't have the energy to charge my phone most days. I even ignored Mum and Grandad's requests to FaceTime, and Mum's barrage of texts. Whatever had happened outside the offices of *Styler* had sapped me, and before I knew it, an hour became a day and a day became a week as I continued to ignore the messages– they all snowballed into a number to scary to confront.

The only app I opened daily was my horoscope app, and it seemed that the stars and I were once again fully aligned as they said I needed to take time for myself over the upcoming Christmas holiday.

Well, what's a better way of spending time with yourself than lying in bed watching old re-runs of *Tattoo Fixers* on Netflix and eating chilli-flavoured poppadoms for breakfast, lunch and dinner? I couldn't think of a better solution right then than that.

I was so dedicated to listening to my horoscope and not making my current situation worse that I even decided not to go to the final astrology class with Aoife and the girls. We were going to throw a full-on graduation style event complete with certificates, and we were also doing Secret Santa where we were all just going to give each other a load of biscuits as a joke. It was a shame, but I wasn't feeling up to it, and if anyone was going to understand listening to the stars, it would have been Aoife and the ladies.

Maybe part of me hoped that if I followed my horoscope religiously it might lighten up by the 15th December. When the clock ticked past midnight on the 14th I reached for my phone with energy I hadn't had in days and tapped on the app. *Take a deep breath and refocus your energies on yourself. A break is needed. So step back, relax and find yourself again.* That was positive. That was my first positive horoscope in days. So why did I feel so crushed? I brought up my chat with Ryan, who I'd last messaged the morning of the interview. His last text was from just a few hours earlier.

> Ryan: *I know you haven't been feeling great. Hope we're still on for tomorrow, would be great to hear from you.*

I wanted so badly to tell him that I was still coming, but I couldn't. Not now.

He was truly going to become the artist he always wanted to be, and I was happy for him. He deserved it and was so talented, but I needed to stay away for his sake. I could only make something bad happen if I disobeyed the stars.

> Kris: *I'm going to have to pull out of going to the opening tomorrow. I'm sorry to miss it, but I know you're going to smash it x*

Shortly afterwards I also text my mum.

> Kris: *I'm sorry, I won't be home for Christmas this year. I have a lot on and need to be in London. I'll come down in the New Year instead. Give my love to Grandad. Merry Christmas x*

With that done, I put my phone on charge and turned over in my bed. I'd had enough social interaction for one day, and probably too many poppadoms. It was time to sleep.

* * *

I was woken from my midday nap by a loud knocking on my front door. I knew it couldn't be Tina or Paige – they had a spare key, now that they were basically keeping me in supply of sustenance. And Paige refused to leave me alone unless she had permanent access to check up on me.

Thinking it was the postman, who would probably give up and leave, I turned back over in bed. But the knocking continued. And continued . . . in fact, it just got louder and more intense.

Growling a little, I fumbled out of my tangled bedsheets and headed for the door. I felt dizzy standing up after so many hours in bed, but after hovering against the doorframe for a second I righted myself.

'I'm coming!' I shouted at the door, my voice hoarse from disuse.

I opened the door.

'What is this?' Ryan said, standing in the doorway with his phone in the air. It was the text I had sent him earlier about not coming to his show. I crossed my arms defensively.

'I'm sorry, I can't make it.'

'Why? Are you ill?' he sounded angry. I knew that if he was really asking if I was ill, he would have used a softer tone. He knew it wasn't the case.

'No, I—'

'You know how important this show is to me,' he said, pocketing his phone. 'And how much it meant that you were going to be there with me.'

'You don't need me.'

'No, but I want you there with me,' he said, scoffing a little. 'Did you really think I was asking you to come as a thank you?' Before I could answer, he continued. 'I wanted you there because when something good happens in your life, you want to celebrate it with the people you care most about.'

'Ryan . . .' I began.

He held up his hand. 'It's not because you don't like me, is it?'

'I do like you,' I said, before he could continue. I wasn't going to let him think that I had suddenly gone off him, when the complete opposite was true. 'Do you want to come inside?' I asked, feeling it was a little odd to be having such a hostile conversation on my doorstep, both of us starting to shiver in the December cold. My neighbours must have been wondering how many conversations I had inappropriately dressed on my doorstep.

'No,' he said simply, his lips twitching a little and not in the smiley kind of way that I loved.

Where was the Ryan I knew? The Ryan who called me Leo and placed a steadying hand on my shoulder to make sure I was alright. 'When you went quiet on me a few days ago I thought, *I know how to find out why.* So I downloaded your horoscope.' He got his phone out again and hurriedly tapped on it. 'I know your birthday, since it's all over your blog so it was easy enough to work out.'

'Ryan . . .' I began, feeling my cheeks flush in embarrassment at what he was about to say.

He shook his head, and then started to read from his phone, picking up right where I'd left off this morning: *The Sun's moving into Cancer and a more sensitive zone of your chart. Take this time to reflect on your emotions and avoid social contact for true self reflection.*

He stopped reading, nodding bitterly.

'Ryan . . .' I said softly, not knowing what to say. It was true, the horoscope reading was the reason I was avoiding him and not going to the show. The main one, anyway. I was still feeling like I was getting over the flu; even making a cup of tea took effort that it never had done before.

I would have loved to have got out of the house and seen his artwork on display, and been there to support him through the first night, which I knew would be the most stressful for him. But I couldn't. The stars were clear: I shouldn't be spending time with others right now. And who knew what the consequences would be if I ignored that? At the very least, I'd probably spend the entire evening hovering in a corner too anxious and scared to move, which Ryan would pick up on, and it would ruin his whole evening. At most, he'd probably get annoyed with me for being such terrible company and making the night about me, and then he might never want to speak to me again.

My Saturn Return was less than two months away, and I couldn't risk putting my life in jeopardy by giving up all of the work I had done to follow the rules, not even for Ryan.

'Don't,' he said, his voice breaking a little as he returned his phone to his pocket. 'You know, I was really looking forward to the show. Not just because it's my first, but because I was going to share it with you.'

I bit my lip, not knowing what to say.

'You know, it's one thing to accept that a woman's not into you, but it's another to accept that the woman you're falling head over heels for is more into an app than she is into you.'

I felt like I had turned to stone on my doorstep. A lead weight sat in my stomach and my heart pulsed in my chest.

I closed my eyes. How many times had I daydreamed about him saying that he was falling for me? How many times had I imagined myself flying into his arms and kissing his smiling lips as he held me close to his ridiculously warm and comforting self/

This was a date, after all. He wanted me there not just as support, but as his date. Did that change anything? I hadn't even bothered to check to the romance page of my horoscope. Maybe that meant I could go, after all. But why would he want me now? And how would I stop myself from ruining it? And, besides, romance hadn't been on the cards for me for months. All of this was probably not even brought on by romance or attraction on his side, it was just from excitement about the show. Maybe he didn't really like me, he just thought he did.

'It really is a blow to my self-esteem.'

'Ryan, it's not that . . .'

'I don't want to talk about it right now,' he said abruptly, looking anywhere but at my face. 'I'm going to go. I need to clear my head.' He took a step back and quick breath. 'I think it's a good idea we don't see each other for a while.'

He turned and walked up the mews, pausing once to follow up with: 'And I made that decision without relying on an app to tell me what to do.'

30

I shuddered on my doorstep as a cool breeze flew into the mews as Ryan left, but realised it wasn't just from the cold; deep down it was the feelings of embarassement and guilt. It wasn't dissimilar to the initial feelings of my panic attack outside *Styler*, but this time it was weightier.

I slowly closed the door and leant my body weight against the wall. Ryan had just admitted he had feelings for me, after all this time, and I had just stood there and not said anything all because of an app, just like he said.

But it wasn't just an app, that's what he didn't realise, it was the movement of the planets and the stars. If my relationship with Ryan wasn't in the stars then maybe Ryan and I weren't meant to have anything more than what we had had over the last three months.

It had taken him this long to admit his feelings for me, and at no point had my Venus chart suggested that I was about to meet *the one*. Maybe our paths had crossed for a reason and that reason had passed. Sure, it sucked, and right then I really wanted to cry and call him and talk to him about it. But I couldn't. If it wasn't meant to be, then that was that. Going against the stars hadn't worked for me before, so why would it work this time?

No matter how much I really, really wanted it to.

I turned to walk to my bedroom. Tears prickled my eyes as I saw Ryan throughout the hall. There was the hole in the wall he had made bringing in the third-hand dresser, which he promised to fill for me. The dreamcatcher he hung above my bedroom door, the strip of ugly wallpaper he thought he should leave as a homage to Clare's grandmother.

But there was no Ryan, and there never would be again.

I returned to my bed and hid myself between the covers and let the tears silently fall until I eventually fell asleep.

* * *

I didn't tell Paige or Tina what had happened between me and Ryan. I was too afraid that the two of them would try and act as matchmakers, texting him on my behalf or stalking out Aoife's house to kidnap him and lock me in a room with him. That or they would agree with him and tell me I was stupid for choosing to follow my horoscope over choosing him.

After my week of self-enforced, self-focused isolation, my horoscope read: *After a long period of feeling like you have no control over you own schedule, today puts you back in charge of your time.* As such, I met up with the girls in a café in Euston for our annual Christmas present exchange and I made sure to put the onus of conversation on the two of them rather than on myself, for once.

I wanted to avoid all topic of myself and just focus on them, and I think they appreciated it, though it hardly scratched the surface of helping to alleviate my guilt at the way I had been behaving recently. Every now and then a thought would creep into my mind that maybe Ryan was right, I was more interested in an app than my friends now.

But every time some self-pitying thought tried to distract me, I'd quickly squash it by asking Paige and Tina question about their latest going-on.

Paige had recently put herself up for a promotion that would offer her a much better bonus and give her the opportunity to terrorise – I mean *work with* – a full team on upcoming cases. It would even give her the opportunity to work on enforcing environmental legislation into the business manifesto and travel to the US office, all the things that made her choose a career in law in the first place.

She continued to claim that she would rather be a lawyer for Jane Fonda than a corporate brand whenever she talked about the debilitating interview processes she was undergoing, but it was clear to me that she really wanted the job. The money, the better office, the travel opportunities and the additional support would be a cut-through to the big-time for Paige, and as much as she complained about her current job, she was shamelessly ambitious underneath it all. Not to mention extremely talented at it, too.

Tina was being extra supportive and doing most of the cooking and cleaning around the flat, since Paige's usual anal routine had been disrupted with all of the projects she was working on to prove her worth at the company. As such, most of Tina's conversation was about her new love of cleaning products, including her research into the best type of multi-purpose sprays for cleaning kitchen surfaces. It wasn't as boring as it sounds, or at least not when Tina talked about it; she could make the most boring conversation exciting with her Duracell Bunny energy.

Paige asked me how Ryan's show went, and I fabricated a lie that I hadn't been well – diarrhoea as a result of eating too many chilli poppadoms in bed – but that Ryan had text me to say it had gone well.

She didn't say anything else after that, and I changed the subject back to her pretty swiftly.

It was a fun evening. Sort of. I could have done without the constant feeling of shame pressing on my stomach or the voice in my head yelling at me for the way I had been behaving lately. It may have made it harder to digest my steak dinner, but at least I could still laugh with the girls about ridiculous memories, like the time Tina had turned up drunk to the Santa's grotto we were working at during Christmas break at university, when she tried to get off with Santa. And Paige's terrible attempts at present-giving for our Secret Santa – her latest was a t-shirt for a project manager which read: *I got this t-shirt because my Secret Santa knows nothing about me'* – at least it was accurately mean.

I went home buzzing from laughter and the effects of Pinot Grigio, the first time I had done so in weeks, until the moment I got home and saw Ryan's handiwork everywhere I looked. Before I knew it I was on the floor, barely able to keep it together long enough to lock the door.

He had been true to his promise and not messaged me once since he showed up on my doorstep. He wasn't even reading my apology texts, or the well wishes I sent on the day of his gallery opening. No read ticks appeared alongside them and I wondered if he had muted me, or even just blocked me. It wouldn't be a surprise, although just the thought of it hurt.

After having him in my life so constantly over the last five months, not hearing from him at all was jarring. Every time there was a knock at the door I raced to see if it was him, but usually it was just the Amazon delivery man dropping off another pre-Christmas present to myself. Or, once, a neighbour asking if I had taken their takeaway by mistake.

I was completely on my own now, since Tina and Paige had headed down to Brighton to spend Christmas with Tina's family. That would be an awakening for Paige, who was yet to meet Tina's mad family. If she thought Tina was unique, she had another thing coming.

One evening, just as I was preparing my out-of-office email, I got a text. I expected to see a message of 'HELP' from Paige, but it wasn't either of the girls. Or Ryan.

It was David.

David 🌑 🔔 : *Hey, I'm sorry for the out of the blue message
so close to Christmas but I would really love to meet up
and chat. Just the two of us. I promise it'll be civil, I don't
want to fight or upset you. I just really want a chance to
talk it out and put things behind us for good.*

'Oh, for fuck's sake,' I said out loud, banging my head against
the desk that Ryan had so wonderfully designed for me. It
still hurt to sit at it every day and attempt to work, but there
were only so many days I could work from bed in my pyjamas before I felt guilty for allowing the pyjama myth about
freelancers to be a reality.

My phone pinged and I looked up out of instinct. My
horoscope notification read: *Give someone a chance.* Give *me*
as chance, universe, and then we'll talk!

The phone pinged once more.

David: *After six years together, I think it would be good for
us. Merry Christmas.*

Taking a deep breath, I reread his message and began to type
a quick reply saying no, but then I stopped.

I couldn't be hasty about this, not when my horoscope *and*
David's message came through at the same time. Clearly the
universe was trying to tell me something, even if was something I really, *really* didn't want to hear.

I couldn't be hasty.

My inner voice screamed *no* at me as I closed WhatsApp
and opened the astrology app. Surely the stars would say that
talking to an ex was an unhealthy way to spend Christmas
Eve Eve – otherwise known as the 23rd of December.

*Neptune has entered the 7th house. Redemption within rela-
tionships is possible for those who communicate.*

Fuck.

My heart plummeted.

I placed my phone face down on the table and my head in my hands. My head was screaming at me to just ignore him and not meet up like he had asked, but then my subconscious was saying I didn't have a choice. If the stars had said redemption was available, then surely I had to listen.

I exhaled loudly and picked up my phone.

Kris: *Meet me at the mezzanine of Waterstones Piccadilly in two hours.*

If I was going to meet up with an ex, then I was going to do it while picking up some last-minute Christmas presents, at least.

* * *

The bookshop was heaving, as was to be expected on one of the last days before Christmas. But there were a ton of seats upstairs in the mezzanine since no one wanted to hang around in the crowds for long. I nabbed a table for two and opened a book to pass the time, knowing full well that David would be late. He was always late.

He arrived 20 minutes later and sat down with a heavy sigh as if he had just fought his way past a dragon to get to me.

'Hi,' he said. A strong start – you'd expect an 'on your knees with a Shakespearean monologue' to beg your ex to take you back after cheating on them for over than five years. David probably hadn't planned this far ahead. I put down my book on Neptune and the qualities of redemption – it seemed appropriate.

'Hi,' I returned. 'I don't have long.' This was a lie – I had all the time in the world since I wasn't going up to St Albans to see Mum and Grandad this Christmas.

'I won't take up your time, I just really wanted to talk to you. Just us, face to face.'

'What about?'

'Well, us,' he said, as if this was obvious.

'What, specifically, about us?'

'Look, I know that I was an arsehole. I'm not going to get back into it, because I can't change anything I've done, and I know you're right. But I really mean it when I say I miss you Krystal. And not just miss you because you work from home and can do the laundry or order in takeaway before I get home, but really miss *you*. I miss coming home *to* you and sleeping beside you. Waking up next to you. All of it. I miss spending time with you.'

I inhaled deeply. I would be lying if I said his declaration didn't make something inside me twitch and come to life; that an instinct to take his hand and lean into him to smell his familiar cologne wasn't pulsing inside me. The last few weeks had been the loneliest of my life and David was familiar; tied to many fond memories from what felt like a lifetime ago. But there also the ever-burning pit of anger that was sitting at my core, reminding me that he had never once put me first during our six-year relationship and this was all too little too late.

I had just got my life on a track that could lead somewhere better, even if right then it felt a little shitty. The flat was almost completely done up the way I wanted it to be. My freelancing career was healthy and my bank balance even more so. Sure, my love life wasn't amazing, but then where did it say in the rulebook of life that a woman needed romance to make her life complete?

'David, we split up for a reason, and I'm in a much better place than where I was when I was with you.'

'I get that, I really do,' he said, lifting his hands above the table and leaving them on the surface, almost as an invitation for me to reach out and touch him. 'I was indifferent and absent over the last few months we were together. Honestly, I was confused. I didn't know what I wanted, and I felt guilty for lying.' *Oh, just for the last few months and not the entire five years of cheating?*

'That doesn't excuse what I did . . .' he was speaking too quickly for me to interject. 'I'm not asking for forgiveness for what I did, that would be too much to ask for, I know. But I really want to be with you, Kris, and I'll do anything to get you back.'

I shook my head and looked out the floor to ceiling windows onto the street behind the bookstore. Cars raced up and down while shoppers laden with Abercrombie and Fitch bags and the like waddled along the paths.

'David . . .' I began, but I stopped not knowing what to say. Did I want to get back with him? Could we make it work?

My answer to both questions was a resounding no. I could hear my inner Mary Berry reminding me of all the bad things in mine and David's relationship: the complete imbalance we had together – from the way he was unreliable to his gaslighting me into thinking it was me who had put too much pressure on him. Or the times we would spend arguing over something seemingly trivial, like our doing something together as a couple, only for me to give up and just go to bed, or even sleep with him in an effort to make us both forget our problems.

None of this was conducive to a relationship. Really, our being together for so long was purely out of habit, and also down to my fear of being alone. But neither of those feelings had gone away since our break-up. I still felt something for David, maybe it was still habit, but it was there like a flickering candle. And I truly was scared of being alone. I was nearly

30, and while being 30 might seem like nothing to me when older, then, it felt like it was the beginning of the time when doors began to shut in my personal life. After all, it was hard to remind yourself that you don't need romance to be happy when the whole world was yelling at you that the ultimate happy ending was true love.

'How could I trust you again?' I asked him, unable to think of a better response to his revelation about getting back together.

'I don't want to lie to you, I really don't. I didn't think I was before, but I see now that I was hiding myself from you and that hurt you. I want to be honest, completely and 100% from now on.'

'What does that mean?' I said, leaning back and rubbing my hand against my temple where I could feel a pressure headache coming on. None of this made sense to me anymore.

'Look, my opinion of monogamy hasn't changed in the last five months. I just don't think it's possible or even healthy. Humans were never meant to be monogamous, it's not in our DNA. And it's possible to have a completely healthy and open relationship, like RuPaul from *Drag Race* has. I know how much you love him, and he and his husband aren't monogamous. I was reading up on it; he said that if you love someone you should never restrain that person. If something is going to make them happy then they should go for it.'

'Wait,' I held my hands up. 'So you want to get back together, but only if we can have an open relationship?'

'I want to be honest with you,' he said, as if that was an answer to my question.

When I read *Cosmopolitan* and *Glamour* as a teenager, at no point was there an article on how to deal with your boyfriend – sorry, *ex*-boyfriend – asking you to have an open relationship.

'But what if I don't want an open relationship?'

'If you don't want to have sex with multiple partners, that's absolutely fine. Open relationships aren't for everyone.'

'Oh, right. So if I don't want an open relationship then you would be willing to not cheat.'

His face screwed up in thought. 'No, what I meant is that not both partners have to have relations with others outside of their relationship. Sometimes it's only one partner that needs that. But the option would always be open to you, and I would totally understand.'

I closed my eyes trying to settle the growing eagerness inside of me to reach over and shake him.

'So basically, you want us to get back together, but by doing so, you want permission to continue having other sexual relationships outside of our relationship.'

'We would find a way to make it work. You could set ground rules if there were people you'd prefer me not to see; I could get tested to make sure that I'm not bringing anything home. I know other people who do it. We could make it work, I know we could.'

Oh he *knows* we could. What the actual fuck?

How had I been with this man for six years and not realised what a complete and utter imbecile he was?

'Why me?' I said, finally. 'Why can't you find someone else to have a long-term open relationship with? Someone who knows they're in one from the start, perhaps, who maybe even consented to it?'

'Because I love you, Kris. I love you so much that I was willing to marry you.'

'*Willing?*' I repeated venomously.

'Well, not many people in open relationships choose to get married. It's the nature of the situation.'

'I'm learning so much,' I said sarcastically. 'David, when did you ever think I would consider much less *want* an open relationship? Did I ever, in our six years together, suggest that that would be something I would want?'

'Look,' he held his hands up again and leant back in his chair. 'I know this is a lot to take on, and I don't want you to answer me right now. Think about it and let me know, maybe before New Year's Eve. We always loved spending New Year's together. Just the two of us with that expensive bottle of champagne we'd always get from Fortnum and Masons, the Chinese share platter and *Chitty Chitty Bang Bang* on in the background. Our little traditions.'

I returned to looking out of the window. None of this sounded like what I wanted.

But maybe it was what I needed? Neptune was in the seventh house, and redemption was on the cards. It seemed like the stars wanted us to get back together, that maybe something good could come of David and I being in a relationship.

How could the universe want that? The thought that David and I might be written in the stars made me feel physically sick, and I wasn't about to sacrifice Mum's Christmas gift for a carrier bag to vomit in.

I stood up. I couldn't decide right now. With any luck, maybe tomorrow's horoscope would clarify the situation and it would all be fine; I was just misinterpreting the signs.

'Let me think about it,' I said to him, somewhat bitterly, and he grinned. Bastard. He didn't get to be happy. Not after he made me so unhappy for so long.

31

Leo: Be careful with how you use your words ... Mars enters the 4th house.

I entered into a research frenzy when I got home, study-Krystal to the max. My horoscope was ironically clear for once that redemption was key this week. Did it have to be romantic redemption, though?

I moved away from looking over my horoscope to my trusty online tarot reading which only offered '*Enjoy the holi-days!*' – what use was that?! I even tried flicking through a palmistry book for answers, but what did a strong love line mean? Take him back? Chuck him? And how does one clear a blocked heart chakra? And would unblocking it definitively tell me whether or not I needed to take David back?

I picked up my phone to text the girls in our Chamber of Secrets chat, only to feel guilty at making their Christmas break together all about me. It could wait until they got back. But could *I*? I had nothing to distract me but Christmas movies on Netflix and Domino's takeaway.

There were only so many times I could shout, *Takeaways here!* to an empty room to convince the waiting delivery driver that the two large pizzas weren't just for me, without him getting suspicious.

After a restless night and an even more restless day I knew I only had one alternative in order to get out of my head. I jumped on the last train to St Albans.

* * *

'You could have told us you changed your mind,' Mum said for the fifth time that morning, topping up my barely touched cup of coffee with a fresh batch.

'If I had told you I changed my mind it wouldn't have been a surprise,' I told her, snuggling into my oversized dressing gown, which still hung on the back of my bedroom door waiting for me whenever I came home.

We, my mum, Grandad and I, were reclining in our designated spots at the kitchen table enjoying a somewhat leisurely Christmas breakfast.

I had arrived just after 10 pm the night before, when Mum was just turning off the lights to go to bed. There were tears, which I should have known would be inevitable when I decided to turn up on my mother's doorstep on Christmas Eve like a character out of some sickly-sweet John Lewis advert. If only my motives had been sweeter than they really were.

Thankfully, because it was Christmas Day, I had a legitimate excuse to hide behind that stopped my mum from interrogating me about my life and what was wrong. Grandad had been suspiciously quiet about asking why I had decided to come home. He was doing a good job of acting as if everything was fine, but I knew him better.

He came down that morning to find my suitcases in the living room, in place of a bag of gifts.

'It's the best present I could have wished for,' he told me when I came down a few hours later (after a long lie-in) and he met me on the stairs for a hug. His bushy moustache scratched my cheek where he kissed me, and I took my time inhaling his familiarly comforting wood and paint scent.

'I missed you, Grandad,' I told him, finally letting him go. He took some time to release me, and I knew just from that that he guessed something was up.

We were settled in the kitchen, tucking into our traditional Christmas morning breakfast of pancakes smothered in golden syrup – or Grandad was. He squeezed a lemon over his and tucked in straight away, while I focused more on nursing my coffee and looking at my phone.

'Are you hungover?' Mum asked, slightly offended that I'd have fun without her. I managed to convince her that I was just tired and took it as my cue to tuck into my pancakes one-handed, still scrolling on my phone with the other. In the cold light of morning, the reality of what I'd done hit me. I'd gone against my horoscope's suggestion of a quiet Christmas and I needed damage-control to salvage it.

Find your centre today. Selfishness and self care are indiffer-ent partners.

That was typically cryptic, and at the same time, easy to understand, like girl-code and Mum asking for the *whatsa-majiggy* when baking cookies.

After breakfast we reassigned ourselves to the living room for presents and gentle talk about the latest goings on in our lives. Deciding to find my centre by skirting around the edges, I completely removed David and Ryan from my time-line when talking about my life, focusing instead on sharing the news of Paige and Tina's new relationship.

'Oh, good for them,' Grandad said, smiling widely. 'That Tina's a lovely girl. Paige is very lucky to have her.'

Grandad had met Tina on the few times she had come to St Albans to visit them with me. Both Grandad and Tina loved bright colours and mad hobbies, so of course it was hard to separate them when they got together.

'Paige is the one you moved in with in the summer, isn't she?' Mum asked me and I nodded. 'I should have got her a present,' she began to berate herself.

'No, you shouldn't have, Mum, she's a friend. It's what friends do for one another.'

'But still, looking after my baby like that.' She leant over from her end of the sofa like a heavy cat after some love and snuggled into me. 'The least I could do was send her some chocolates or make her some of my blackberry jam. Speaking of, there's a jar with your name on it in the cupboard.'

'She's not lying,' Grandad said. 'She bought herself a label maker, so now there's no way I can mix up the salt and the sugar again.'

'It was happening too much old man,' Mum said, still leaning against my shoulder, making it ache. 'Honestly, I think he's starting to go a bit senile,' she said to me, not bothering to lower her voice.

'Do you have to?' I asked, rolling my eyes at the two of them and trying to gently signal for mum to get off me. I really wasn't in the mood for childish snuggles or watching the two of them have one of their traditional teasing matches, even if it was just family banter. I was sick to my back teeth of banter and bickering.

'Can we not have a quiet Christmas for once?'

Mum took the signal with a petty moan and sat back up again. Honestly, sometimes I had to remind myself who was the mother and who was the child in this relationship.

'If it's quiet you wanted you should have stayed in London, Krissy,' Grandad groaned as he forced himself to stand and make his way to the kitchen, undoubtedly for his fifth cup of tea that morning.

Mum looked from him to me. 'What was that about, Krystal?' she asked in a whisper. 'It's Christmas.'

'I know Mum, I know,' I said, rubbing my forehead where the pressure headache (I was hoping to alleviate by coming home) was starting to return. 'It's just been a crap couple of months. I really just need a little TLC.'

I got out my phone to see what my dos and don'ts of the days were. I was pretty sure snapping at family members was probably on there for festive reasons.

'Well, if you had come sooner you might have got some,' Mum barked, just as I opened it and realised my don'ts only included single-use plastics, podcasts and needles.

'Don't get in a strop,' I mumbled, immediately accepting that bickering was inevitable and throwing gas onto the flame.

'Excuse me, *miss*, but I'm your mother. You don't talk to me like that. Particularly on Christmas Day. Or do you want me to take your presents away from you?'

'Mum, I'm nearly 30,' I reminded her.

'I don't care if you're 950, if you come home and start biting my head off like you're a child, I'll treat you like one.' She slapped at the leather sofa loudly to mark that the conversation was over and went back to nursing the remainder of her tea.

As I returned to reading through my dos and don'ts, Mum began shuffling fractiously to get started with opening presents and shouting 'Dad!' at the top of her lungs. It echoed in my head and only served to make the pulsating headache worse. This was why my horoscope had told me not to come home, I thought to myself. I should have listened.

To refocus on getting into my centre, I inhaled deeply using the old technique of counting to ten before I responded to Mum's irritating behaviour. By the time I went to speak to her, she was walking to the kitchen, shouting at Grandad, making sure he wouldn't help himself to the trifle in the fridge.

There was tension in the air all day, despite the façade that we all put on trying to cover it up. We opened our presents with lacklustre croons, reminding each other who had bought what and who we needed to send thank you cards to in the new year.

Grandad was thrilled with the new watercolour paint set I bought him, along with a new toolbox, since I could never guess what his new hobby might be. Paints and tools seemed like a safe bet.

Mum loved the Len Goodman book I bought her, plus two tickets to the touring *Strictly* show the following year.

'Ooh, I think I'll take Juliet from next door with me,' she said, knowing full well that I had bought the two tickets in the hopes that she would take me. 'She'll love it. Thank you darling.'

I nodded and smiled, pretending I wasn't hurt, when I clearly knew that she was only acting off with me because I had hurt her by snapping earlier.

My Christmas presents were the traditional set of pyjamas and a Papier notebook from Mum, plus a new set of crystals.

'I got them from Amazon. You're supposed to put them around your flat and they'll get rid of bad energies. That, or spiders, I think,' she said. I looked at the toy version of the crystals she'd bought me, and attempted a crude smile.

'Thanks Mum,' I said, putting the box to one side without another glance. It's the thought that counts, I found my Mary Berry voice counselling me in my head, but honestly, Mum was treating my planetary journey like a joke if she thought I was going to use what looked like a handful of pebbles from a beach to ward off bad energies. They were nothing like the crystals I bought from Andrik in Brick Lane. He probably sourced those from reputable sellers in Norway or Iceland. I'd never thought to ask, actually.

'Here's Grandad's gift to you,' Mum said,, as she handed me a beautifully wrapped present from under the Christmas tree.

I opened it with a wide anticipatory smile, since Grandad always gave me the best presents, and this year was no different. It was a handmade waistcoat; sapphire blue with gold and silver stars sewn intricately all over it.

'I worked with Rita to make sure it would fit you. She made the pattern for me from photos online. I hope it fits,' he said, blushing a little, as if it wasn't a great gift.

'It's incredible. I love it,' I told him, pulling it out of the box. It was lovingly wrapped in pink and white tissue paper. 'Thank you,' I said, holding it over my chest and running my fingers across the patterns. 'I especially like the stars.'

'They're authentic constellations, I'll have you know,' he said wagging his finger and leaning forwards to point out his handiwork. 'If you look carefully, you'll find Leo, like you, and Gemini like your Mum. Aries for me and Virgo like your nan. Plus a few little extras like Orion's belt from when I was practising.'

Tears prickled behind my eyes. He had put so much thought into it, not to mention the time he had clearly spent working on it, even though he'd made it pretty clear he wasn't a fan of my astrological adventures. His belief and acceptance in me was worth more than any other present I had received, but I couldn't say as much in case I offended Mum, which only served to add to the irritation bubbling inside me.

'It's perfect,' I told him, placing it back in the box carefully. 'Thank you.'

I got up and went to his armchair to give him a hug, leaning on his shoulder as I did so. He patted my head, without saying another word, and Mum reached quickly for another present to open.

Christmas lunch and the afternoon seemed to fly by until suddenly it was time for the Queen's speech. Grandad was a stickler for watching it live – although really, it was recorded months prior – and having a glass of champagne ready to toast the Queen afterwards. Mum was out in the kitchen handwashing our lunch dishes while Grandad and I curled up in our seats to watch.

'What did I miss?' Mum said from the doorway, removing her pink marigolds which were dripping suds onto the carpet.

'Ssh!' Grandad said, listening intently to the Queen's words on family and tradition.

'Nothing par for the course,' I whispered back. She came and sat on the edge of the sofa, completely ignoring that I was resting my arm on the side where she had decided to sit. She rested her damp gloves on the coffee table and sighed noisily. I found myself counting to ten once again.

'I hope I'm as fashionable as her when I'm in my 90s,' she said to no one in particular, jolting me with her elbow to point at the Queen on the screen. 'She's so stylish and traditional. I respect that in a woman, particularly a queen. And she's a proper family woman, too, despite what *The Crown* shows. Did you watch the latest series? I thought they did her quite dirty, actually,' Mum continued, muttering the whole time so that I could barely hear what the Queen was saying.

I don't know why but my mum's constant nattering, and complete disregard for my own personal space as she continued to nudge me with her elbow, suddenly had my blood boiling.

I knew I was feeling fragile – or rather, like a grenade, a hair's inch away from having its pin pulled – but I didn't imagine it would be my mother's random mumbling that would set me off.

'Can you just *stop*?!' I shouted, slamming my hands into the leather sofa and making both my mum and grandad jump.

'Krystal!' Mum shouted back in surprise, clutching her shoulder like I had just dislocated it from her body. 'What's gotten into you?'

'Can you just stop talking? Sorry, but it's so annoying.'

'Krystal,' Grandad began, his voice deeper than Mum's, and more menacing despite still having the effect of being calming. 'That's enough.'

'Oh, come on Grandad, even you have to admit it was getting pretty hard to hear with Mum just chattering away like that.'

'Well, I'm sorry I was disturbing you,' Mum said, somewhat sarcastically. 'You could have just asked me to be quiet rather than shouting. Now we've missed the whole thing.'

'We missed it way before I shouted,' I told her. 'Do you really think I care about the Queen's fashion or whether or not *The Crown* did her dirty? Mum, I *don't care!*' I shouted.

'Krystal,' Grandad said, 'Enough.'

'I just wanted a quiet Christmas,' I told him, feeing a lump develop in the back of my throat. 'Is that really too much to ask? A quiet, peaceful, thought-free Christmas?'

I got up and rushed out of the room, heading up the stairs into my bedroom where I managed to control myself enough to not slam my door shut like a child.

I sat on the floor, resting against my childhood single bed with my head in the crevice of my knees. I hadn't meant to snap; it was the last thing I wanted, in fact. But something inside me needed to get out and Mum was just the unlucky recipient of it.

Instinctively, I reached into my pocket to look at my horoscope and see what it had to say about the position of Mars, the planet behind anger and emotions, but I realised I had left it downstairs on the sofa.

'Dammit,' I said, feeling my stomach lurch as I wondered what I should do.

Moments later, there was a knock on the door. I didn't say *come in*, as I knew my Grandad would open the door whether I asked him to or not.

'I fancy a walk,' Grandad said calmly from the doorway, already putting on a pair of gloves when I opened my eyes to look at him. 'Would you like to join me?' It was a command more than a question, so I nodded.

32

Leo: The more you look inwards, the more you're apt to find
   solutions to your outward questions . . . the full Moon rises
   in Mars tonight.

'I'm sorry I snapped at Mum,' I told him, as we were walking
across Verulamium Park. It was spacious and open, and many
other families clearly had the same idea as Grandad, deciding
to go for a leisurely stroll as the Sun began to set. 'I didn't
mean to. She was annoying me with her talking, but it wasn't
that that made me snap.'

'I could tell as much,' Grandad said, wheezing a little as we
walked up a particularly steep incline. Without asking I
wrapped his hand around my arm to help him. As much as
he seemed never to age in my eyes, I knew in my head that he
wasn't a spring chicken anymore. He walked with an elegantly
carved walking stick, of his own design, and wore about three
scarves to keep himself warm during winter. In the cold park
he looked like an old man. It was strange that when he was at
home, working on his projects or FaceTiming with Mum
over an iPad, he looked younger.

'I really am happy to be spending Christmas with you,' I
told him, snuggling up against his shoulder.

'Who knows how many I have left?' he said, and I groaned.

'Oh Grandad, don't start that,' I told him.

'No, listen to me. One day I won't be here for Christmas
and that's the way of it. I'm not afraid and neither should you
be.'

'I don't want to think about it *on* Christmas Day though, Grandad.'

'I understand,' he chuckled darkly. 'And I don't mean to be that old codger who guilt trips you into doing what he wants by reminding you that one day I won't be here. But if ever there was a time for it, I think it might be now.'

'So what you're saying is, you're about to guilt-trip me.'

'Quite possibly, yes,' he agreed and I smiled. How could I not adore this man who spoke so bluntly and sarcastically? He was the male version of me, or rather I was the female version of him. 'You know, when you were younger, you were a little obsessive.'

'Obsessive?' I repeated and he shushed me – clearly he had a tale to tell.

'One week, you would be obsessed with macramé, the next week you'd only want to do karate, and then after that it would be a book journal or some sort of techy game that I'd never understand.'

'Sounds a lot like you,' I said.

'In some ways, yes. I distract myself with activities for a couple of months and then move onto something else. I wouldn't call it an obsession in my case, it's very much a distraction, but I know why I do it and I recognise it for what it is.'

'And that is?'

'Why don't we sit on that bench?' Grandad said suddenly, using his walking stick to point to a nearby memorial bench. We hobbled over, allowing a family of five with an overly zealous dog to pass us by, before settling ourselves down.

'It's been nearly 30 years since I lost your nan,' he began, looking warmly across the open park. 'And I know it's a cliché, but I miss her. I still wake up every morning expecting her to be beside me, and I always get that little jolt in my heart when she's not there.'

'I'm sorry, Grandad,' I said, taking his hand in mine and squeezing it gently.

'Oh, don't be, Krissy,' he said smiling. 'Everyone ends up in a wooden onesie one day.'

I laughed, only my grandad would refer to something as dreary as a coffin as a 'wooden onesie'.

'Ever since she died, I've been filling my time with distractions. Not only because I miss her, but genuinely because I need something to do. Without an activity, what do I have to do but wait? I don't know about you, but I'd rather get the most out of this world before I move onto the next. Even if that is just a few waistcoats here and a couple of followers there.'

'You reached 15,000 on TikTok, Grandad,' I reminded him. 'The local news wanted to feature you on TV.'

He shrugged, and made a *pft* sound like it wasn't impressive or important. I smiled at his nonchalance.

'I don't care about any of that.' He looked at me then and I realised he was still yet to get to his point.

'What does this have to do with me being a little obsessive as a child?'

'A little?' he scoffed before taking a deep breath. 'You and David were together for how long?' he asked.

'Six years.'

'And how many of those were happy?'

'Well . . .' I began, thinking that the majority of them were happy. The first two years when we were both discovering the city together, forever partying and travelling the world like nomads, barely able to stay in one flat for too long without wanting to go on a new adventure together, had been the best time of my life. But when he got his first full-time job and I started to work freelance and spend my evenings in, it became less fun.

By our third year together we had a routine and life was standard. I had fun with the girls, and he had fun with his 'friends'. Of course, I hadn't realised who his friends really were at the time. For at least the last three years of our relationship together we were just a habit for one another, we weren't in love.

But I didn't know what happened after the love fizzled out. I had no parents to compare it to and no films to watch where I'd see what life was like after the initial happy ending. I thought what we had was normal and domestic. But really, it was unhealthy and dull.

'Two or three, maybe,' I said, honestly.

'So you stayed for six because . . .'

'It doesn't matter, it's over,' I said, although in my head I corrected myself with the stupidly dramatic: *Or is it?* Was I really considering getting back together with David because of the stars and the planetary movements, or was it because I was obsessed with the idea of David? Or being safe in a relationship? If the latter was true, I really was a bad feminist, as well as in need of some therapy.

'When did you get into astrology?'

'That's because of my Saturn Return,' I began, not wanting him to go in the direction I thought he was going in. 'When Saturn returns to the position it was in on the day I was born, the next portion of my life will begin. Kind of like a mid-life crisis, but a nicer term for it.'

'Krissy, I don't think Saturn has any say in when our lives end or start again, otherwise Saturn has moved into the same position three hundred times in my lifetime.'

'That's impossible,' I said, 'It only moves into the same position a max of four times in one lifetime. And that's if you live to a good age.'

'You know, my life changed when I first earnt a wage when I was 13. Then again when I met your nan when I was 15. At 18 when we were married, and then again at 20 when we had your mum. At 21 when we bought our first house. At 28 when I lost my job during the three-day week. Then 30 when my mum died. At 32 when my dad followed. One chapter ends and another begins whenever a big event in your life happens. And a big event can be anything from a break-up to a lost job, a new relationship or a burst pipe in your home.'

I sighed. 'So what you're trying to say is ignore the stars and planets, as they have nothing to do with my life.'

'I think things only have effect on your life when you believe they do. It's prophetical thinking, isn't it. By all means, if you love astrology and following your horoscope makes you happy, then carry on. But only do it if it makes you truly happy. Not because you feel you *have* to. Why do you think I change hobbies every couple of months or so?'

'I always thought you just got bored with them?'

'Not at all. I love all the hobbies I've undertaken – except maybe disco dancing, that one hurt my hips – I change because what I enjoy the most is learning new things and meeting new people. Sure, I started it up to distract myself from missing your nan. But I continue it because it keeps me active and social. Does astrology do that for you?'

I thought for a moment. 'It did, initially,' I said. 'I went to a class and met new people.'

'But the rest of the time?' he looked at me through his eyelashes. 'You consulted your horoscope about the number of Brussel sprouts you were going to eat,' he teased.

'I did not!' I said, laughing at the notion. 'I was checking to see what today's horoscope meant for me in terms of health, actually.'

'Because an app knows more about your health and body than you do?' he queried. I said nothing. 'And what does it say about romance?'

'You're starting to drift into Mum territory,' I warned him playfully.

'If it were up to me, you would remain single forever. I

don't like the idea of another man in your life, particularly not another David. I know I shouldn't say it, but he was never good enough for you.'

'Will anyone be good enough?' I asked, sitting back against the bench and smiling.

'There's a person out there for everyone, and I'll know your person when I see him. Or her. I'm very open-minded for someone in their 90s.'

He laughed and I laughed too, cuddling into him.

'Well if you see him – I'm afraid I'm boringly heteronormative Grandad – give him my number would you?'

He laughed and patted my arm. 'What about that Ryan fella you were always talking to your mum about?'

'There is no Ryan, not anymore.'

Grandad leant back against the bench and hooked his walking stick around the arm rest.

'Don't tell me – your astrological journey led you to a hole in the fabric of the space time continuum and he fell through it.'

I sighed, stifling a laugh at his sarcasm. 'You aren't funny,' I said, as he nudged me playfully in the ribs, a twinkle in his eye.

'Ryan still very much exists, just not near me. We had a falling out,' I began. 'Well, more of a . . . he told me he didn't want to speak to me right now.'

'Why?' Grandad said softly.

I sighed, realising how heavy the shame over how I treated Ryan truly was.

'I let him down. When he needed me most, I proved I wasn't there for him. Not even as a friend. I was just using him and being a bad friend.'

'That doesn't sound like you. Why didn't you support him?' he asked, turning to look at my quizzically.

'He had this show, it was a really important gallery opening, and he asked me to go with him as his guest. Actually, as his date. I said I would. and then at the last minute I told him I couldn't go. I didn't give him a proper reason or anything, I just told him no.'

I shook my head at my own stupidity. While I was glad that I didn't lie, I couldn't believe I said no because I thought the universe wanted me to. Like the universe cared if I went to an art gallery. If the universe wanted me to put what it said before someone who meant a lot to ... well, maybe the universe could do one.

'I didn't go because my horoscope told me that I needed to spend time on my own and I took it to heart. That's why I said I wasn't coming home for Christmas, too. I thought I had to follow my horoscope and if I didn't, that something bad would happen.'

'Did anything good happen?'

I shook my head, the lump in my throat widening painfully. 'Nope. Nothing good at all.'

'And if you had gone to the show, or if you had come home earlier for Christmas. Would things have been better then?'

'I wouldn't have ended up seeing David, that's for sure,' I said, without thinking. Grandad looked at me in confusion and I just shook my head and said, 'Long story.' I wasn't explaining that one to my grandad. 'I probably would have had a great time at the show – I may have even moved forward in my relationship with Ryan.' If he could come to my flat and tell me he had feelings for me when I had turned him down, I wondered what could have happened if I had been there to support him on the biggest day of his career so far. 'I wouldn't have been feeling so guilty or wound up, so I also wouldn't have gotten into a fight with mum over something so stupid. And I'd probably feel like I had bit more control over my life right now.'

'So basically, what you're saying is: following your horoscope over the last few months hasn't led to a wonderful, happy outcome.'

I shook my head bitterly, realising that the ache in my head that was growing worse and worse with each day was caused by my own stress-inducing choices. I had thrown myself into astrology and not looked back. I was responsible for every choice I had made, even the ones that led to good things, not an app, a crystal or a tarot card reading. And here was a very simple solution to fixing my problems and getting rid of the headache altogether.

I just wasn't sure I was strong enough to suddenly let go of everything I had focused on over the last five months. It would mean taking responsibility. It would mean taking control. It would mean not having something else to blame things on when things went wrong. It would be all on me.

'You know,' Grandad began, after our heavy silence of contemplation, wrapping his arm around my shoulders and bringing me into him for a comforting hug. 'We always say, *Don't worry, be happy* whenever we say goodbye. I was thinking we should change that.'

'What? Why?' I asked looking up at him – it had been a tradition since I was a toddler to say that to one another.

'Maybe we should go with something more relevant to now? Maybe something like: *Follow your heart, not your horoscope.*'

33

Leo: Things will fall into place as you need them ... Mercury enters the 11th house.

Grandad fully embraced his new role as my life counsellor, regaling me with his best advice, while getting me to help him with cutting up our Christmas copy of the *Radio Times* for a new collage he wanted to present to Beryl in the new year.

Mum continued to sulk until Boxing Day afternoon. As we shopped amongst the sales-mad housewives in the John Lewis in town she couldn't help but let her excitement at a pair of half-priced alpaca socks send her into a spirited rendition of 'Meet Me in St Louis' in the middle of the shop. Without embarrassment or shame I joined in, and the two of us whisked about the shop floor like two dancers in a Fred Astaire film, giggling at all the odd looks people made. It was a tried and tested technique to making our way past people, with crowds parting like the Red Sea before us as we came swinging around the corner bellowing, 'Meet me at the fair!' like drunk carol singers.

We snapped up several good bargains and spent the evening sitting on the living room floor, eating cold meats and mashed potato, and showing off our latest buys to Grandad who had the good grace to appear excited on our behalf.

I didn't once look at my horoscope over Betwixtmas, a term I had never heard of before, but Mum used every other sentence to describe these days between Christmas and New Year's Day.

Paige and Tina messaged me in the Chamber of Secrets to see how my alone time was going and delighted that I had decided to go home after all.

Tina: *Give Harold a big smooch from me!!!*
Paige: *And tell your mum I'd love some blackberry jam!*
Paige: *I'm also quite partial to gooseberry ...*

As New Year's Eve approached, and I was beckoned to Paige and Tina's flat for the London celebrations, I left Mum and Grandad with a heavy heart.

It was strange how much coming home could put me into some sort of time warp and reset my whole life. It did make me wonder why I had chosen to stick life out in London for so long without even considering a short break at home. Although Mum's parting gifts reminded me that molly-coddling wasn't always good for me: a packet of toilet roll and six jars of jam, my presents and the bargain purchases she had bought for me in town. I'd be starting my 'get fit' New Year's resolution early, lugging all of this back to London.

'Now,' Grandad said, as he let the taxi driver handle putting my new suitcase – my main Boxing Day purchase (since I didn't expect to get mine back from David, ever!) – into the car. 'Remember what I said.'

'I remember,' I told him, pulling him in for a hug. 'Follow my heart, not my horoscope.'

'That's my Krissy,' Grandad said into my ear, his moustache scratching my face comfortingly.

I looked over Grandad's shoulder at Mum, who was watching from the doorway in her raggedy old dressing gown, with a Cath Kidston mug of tea held closely to her chest to warm her. Her bottom lip was rolled over in a playful sulk that I was leaving and I winked at her. She returned it and shouted: 'I'll see you in March for *Strictly!*' Thankfully, our making up meant that I was back on her list as the chosen guest for the show.

'Love you!' I shouted back.

'Love you more!' she replied, as I let go of Grandad and headed for the taxi.

'Merry Christmas, my darling,' Grandad said, kissing his hand and blowing it to me.

'And have a good New Year's,' Mum said, afterwards.

'See you next year!' I shouted, opening the car door and sliding inside. For once, the magic of Christmas seemed to spread across me like a character out of a redemptive Disney movie. Everything felt new, and nothing felt impossible to deal with, regardless of what my horoscope or the stars said.

* * *

'You wouldn't name your right ear Phil and your left ear Bob, so why would you name your vagina Bertha?' Tina shouted at Paige. Both of them were rosy-cheeked and giggly as I stood in the kitchen pulling out the last tray of pigs in blankets from the oven and then emptying a Pringles tube into a serving dish.

'Would *Beatrice* have been a better choice?' Paige argued playfully, snorting as she did so.

It was New Year's Eve and our festivities had begun early with our traditional *Harry Potter and the Chamber of Secrets* drinking game, followed quickly by a game of Taboo and *Never Have I Ever*. The fireworks at midnight were fast approaching, but I knew that if either Paige or Tina were going to make it then I needed to get some food in them fast.

I wasn't in my usual New Year's Eve drinking mood, so I'd mostly stuck to Buck's Fizz all evening, tolerating Paige and Tina's juvenile *ooh*s at my apparent poshness while they drank Strongbow out of cans.

'Here we are, ladies,' I said, offering them the Pringles. They tucked in like ravenous lions over a piece of meat.

'Krystal . . .' Tina said, her mouth crusty with half chewed crisps. 'You tell her!' she pointed at Paige.

'Tell her what?' I asked, leaning across the coffee table for a crisp before they all disappeared.

'That it's stupid to name a piece of your body.'

'I didn't know that you had named a part of your body,' I said to Paige, who shrugged.

'Men name their penises,' she argued.

'But men are all cockwombles,' Tina rolled her eyes. Paige leant forward at that point and kissed her. Both of them recoiled as sharp-edged flakes of crisps pierced each other's lips.

'Remind me never to crisp with Pringles in my mouth,' Paige said to me, which set us all off

'I think you mean *kiss* with Pringles in your mouth,' I laughed,

'Crisp!' Paige repeated, clutching her stomach like it was the most hilarious thing she had ever accidentally said. After Christmas with Tina's family, she had really let go and seemed to be enjoying herself enormously. I would have thought that Tina's family's annual carol singing concert and mandatory ugly jumper fashion show would have led her to flee, but apparently not. She and Tina seemed closer than ever and were not afraid of displays of affection in front of me anymore.

As much as I was happy for the two of them, the warmth of spending Christmas with my family was fading with every second the clock clicked closer to New Year's Day. I was following Grandad's advice as closely as possible and completely ignoring my horoscope, although I hadn't quite got the nerve to delete it from my phone just yet. I'd turned off the notifications, though, which was a start. But my Saturn Return still lingered in my mind. Even if I'd come to terms with the fact that following an app or an online tarot card reading wasn't going to lead me to happiness, I couldn't deny that I still held a belief in my Saturn Return.

'What are you thinking about?' Tina asked, shaking me from my morose daze.

'Hmm? Oh, just thinking about next year,' I said, standing to retrieve the pigs in blankets. 'Do you want mustard with these?' I asked her, trying to change the subject, but she wasn't having it. She stood up, leaving Paige to drift sideways on the sofa with a giggle.

'No you're not. I can tell it's something else,' she said, sitting heavily at the breakfast bar. 'Is it Ryan?'

I had finally told the girls about what had happened between me and Ryan. I half expected them to flip their lid when I explained I had cancelled on him last minute because of my horoscope, but they only squeezed my hand harder in an effort to support me while I was down.

Instinctively, I went to tell that Tina no, that it wasn't Ryan, but that wasn't entirely true. I hadn't heard from him in over two weeks. That was the longest we had gone not speaking since I had moved into my new apartment.

In an effort to reach out to him, I had already contacted both Aoife and Clare, while also wishing them a Merry Christmas and a Happy New Year. But neither of them caught my sneaky hints about asking after Ryan. Clare had said she was coming down in the new year to collect the last of her Grandma's things and to see the flat. I knew it was about time I started paying rent, as promised, particularly since I was financially back on my feet, if not secure in a full-time job.

'I miss him,' I told Tina quietly, not wanting Paige to over-hear in her current state and end up DM'ing secret videos to him, berating him for not falling for me, or something else that was stupid but seemingly sensible when drunk.

Tina tilted her head to one side and smiled, clearly pleased that I had managed to admit it.

'Oh babe,' she said, 'You need to tell him that.'

'I've tried,' I moaned. 'He won't text me back or even answer my calls. That's how much I've tried – I *called* him! I haven't called anyone except my dentist in years.'

'Wow,' she said, impressed. 'What does your horoscope say?' she asked, and I shifted my weight on my feet.

'I've not looked.'

'What?!' Paige suddenly screamed from the sofa. 'After all these months of following nothing else you've not even checked to see if there is even a smidgeon of hope in the stars?' Given her drunkenness, I couldn't tell if she was being sarcastic or serious.

'I'm closing that chapter,' I said placatingly, picking up a hot, greasy pig in a blanket for something to do.

'Well, I'm not. Give it here.' Paige clambered up from her seat.

'Paige . . .' Tina said, warning her.

'Since when have our roles reversed?' Paige asked her in surprise, taking my phone off charge in the corner of the room and tapping in my passcode with ease.

'How did you . . .' I began.

'Darling, I know everything,' she said, without looking up. 'Right. Horoscope. Romance. Here we go, it says: *Neptune turns retrograde at the start of the new year. You might have some pretty major realisations, including that you've been misled by certain beliefs. Don't squander that knowledge.* Oh wait, that's the daily horoscope. Where's romance?'

'Give it here,' Tina said, reaching over to take the phone from Paige's grasp. Tina squinted at the screen.

Romance: a relationship may grow stronger if you can

communicate with honesty. Well, that sounds pretty doable,' she said, turning back to me.

'I told you, I'm not paying attention to my horoscope right now. I'm . . .'

'We know, we know . . .' Paige rolled her eyes and bit into a pig in a blanket. 'You're turning over a new page. *Boring!*' she paused and blinked. 'Paige. Page. Ha!'

'Don't be mean,' Tina chastised.

'Honestly, you two are like yin and yang when you're drunk,' I laughed, watching as Tina handed Paige a napkin to wipe the meat grease from her fingers.

'We are, aren't we,' Paige smiled. 'Now we just need to get your yin back. Or is he the yang?' She looked to Tina for clarification.

'I don't teach Chinese philosophy until the summer term,' she said, deadpan.

Paige rolled her eyes again with another large groan. 'Right, I'm calling it. We need to get out of the flat.'

'What?' I asked, 'The fireworks are in half an hour,' I pointed out.

'Yep, I know, and I know where we can watch them from.'

'I'm not going down to Embankment,' Tina snapped hastily. 'I made that mistake before, and I'm not pissing into a policeman's helmet again.'

'I thought you could only do that if you are pregnant?' I said, hurrying to fetch my coat since Paige was already calling an Uber from my phone, which she had reclaimed from Tina. I knew better than to try and change her mind when she was drunk.

'I stole a load of scarves and shoved them up my jumper,' Tina explained. 'I also stole the policeman's hat, actually . . . thank God I'm small and fast is all I can say.'

* * *

'Paige, where are we?' I asked, stepping out of the taxi into the cold night air and looking around the bleak street we had been dropped off on.

'Oh, come on, it's not been that long,' Paige scoffed, wrapping Tina's arm around her own and beginning to skip with her up the street.

'Since when?' I asked.

'You used to live here,' Paige groaned. 'Look,' she pointed upwards at what was my old flat building, where David and I had lived together last. We were around the back of the building, but a few steps – or drunken skips in the girls' case – around the corner led us to the fancy double doors that opened into the brightly lit foyer of the building.

'What are we doing here?' I whispered, feeling it was a little ridiculous to be back here less than ten minutes before midnight on New Year's Eve.

'Because it's cathartic. Now, tell me you still remember the emergency lock code.' Paige stopped outside the locked doors and pointed to the emergency hatch with the spare key hidden beneath a hanging basket.

'The landlady's probably changed it by now,' I said, but Tina scoffed. 'No landlady would bother, not with work going on and the amount of comings and goings. She'd have to change it every week. Have a go.'

I sighed and leant across the ivy bush in front of the entrance and tapped in 2-2-4-5. The lock clicked and the hatch opened, the spare key inside. Tina and Paige both squealed and I had to hush them quickly.

'Stop it!' I whispered. 'What are we going to do with this? It'll only get us in the foyer, it's not for any of the flats or anything.' Paige swiped the key from my fingers and unlocked the door.

'We're not going to your flat,' she said, 'We're going to the roof.'

Within minutes, the three of us were racing up the stairs in our massive coats (in Tina's case, her typically moulting, faux fur purple jacket) to the rooftop. The emergency exit was open, as always, and the superfluous block of concrete was calling our names as we cascaded out together.

'It's three minutes to midnight,' Tina said, checking her phone. 'Quick, we each have to make a wish.'

'I've never made a wish,' I laughed, as she dragged me over to the concrete block and sat me down on its corner. Tina and Paige huddled into each other to keep warm, and Tina kept hold of my hand as we sat facing the direction of the Thames and waited for the show to begin.

'Humour me,' Tina said with a huff.

'I wish,' Paige began. 'That I get this new promotion.'

'I wish,' Tina also began, 'That everyone is happy next year.'

'Aww, that's sweet babe,' Paige said before fake vomiting. Tina shoved her so hard she almost fell off the block, before breaking into a fit of giggles. 'What about you Kris?' she asked me.

'I wish . . .' I said, but I stopped not knowing what to say. I wish that next year is better than this one? That David finally gets the message and leaves me alone? That I can get a second opportunity at *Styler*? That Ryan will answer my texts and forgive me? 'I wish . . .'

'I want to change my wish,' Tina shouted suddenly, throwing her arms out in a West End flourish that almost knocked Paige over. 'There's only a minute left and I want to wish that next year Kris is happy. Everyone is all well and good, but I honestly only like two people in this world and they're both sat with me right now.'

'Don't you want me to have a happy year too?' Paige asked, playfully disgruntled.

'You will, you've got me,' Tina fluttered her eyelashes. 'But seriously,' she said, quickly turning back to me. 'I want you to be happy, properly happy. Happy like when we graduated university and didn't have a care in the world.'

'I want to change mine now, too,' Paige said, leaning over Tina.

'Well hurry up, we've only got 30 seconds.'

'Of course I'm going to get the promotion, I'm a fucking badass,' she began, which led Tina and I to cackle at her insane amount of confidence. 'But I agree with Tina. I want you to be happy and to realise how much you are loved. Even when you're utterly bonkers and trust an algorithmic app over your best friends' wizened advice.'

I laughed, a little tear escaping from the corner of my eye which I was quick to wipe away.

'No!' Tina said, quickly hugging me so tightly that I couldn't move my arms. 'Embrace the tears. Take in the love.'

Paige quickly followed suit, rushing to my other side to hug me so tightly I could hardly breathe.

'Can you feel it?' she whispered, somewhat menacingly in my ear. 'We love you.'

I was jolting up and down with laughter and the two of them and their drunken displays of affection, but I knew in my heart of hearts that even if they weren't drunk this would have likely still have happened.

'I feel it. And I love you too.'

'Aww babe, that's so unexpected,' Tina said, just as the fireworks kicked off and we all screamed in surprise.

'It's not like we didn't know it was coming,' I said, clutching my heart as the two of them awkwardly leant over my head to have a sickly-sweet New Year's Day kiss. Followed sharply by the two of them slobbering kisses on either one of my cheeks. 'You're worse than children,' I laughed. But my playful protests were deafened by the continuing fireworks and the girls' gasps of delight as we went back to huddling together on the concrete block.

'It's bloody gorgeous!' Paige shouted as loud as she could over the noise, and I didn't even try to stop her. Why bother, it was a new year and a new day. Let her have her fun and damn the consequences.

I began to whoop too, and suddenly Tina was howling like a dog and Paige was screeching out 'Auld Lang Syne'. It was mere seconds before she had the three of us all up and holding up hands, dancing around in a circle, singing the words we knew and mumbling the ones we didn't.

It was the perfect New Year's Eve and, as much as I knew I had things to sort out, I also knew that whatever came my way in the new year, a Saturn Return or the return of an ex, I could face it together with my girls and not my horoscope.

34

January is unfairly classed as the most depressing month of the year. The weather is supposedly terrible, everyone is broke and there's nothing good in the shops except the broken leftovers from bargain sales. Everyone's got a New Year's resolution not to drink or only eat vegan food this month, and it feels like you're forever stuck indoors. But for me, January has always been my favourite month of the year as it signals new beginnings.

Even when I didn't hold that much sway with New Year's Eve – it was just another day after all – I found that I often had a new source of energy in January. Not the kind of energy that got me to the gym for all of two weeks or had me trying a new fad diet, but the kind of energy that meant I could churn out 20 solid pitches in a day and write to-do lists with ideas for presents for all of my acquaintances throughout the year. I ate more healthily just because I wanted to, and I spent more time outdoors because I could.

This year was no different. With the girls' wishes supporting me, I found I had the strength to not only completely delete my horoscope app from my phone and finish my relationship with David with a simple text message ...

David, it's over. I don't want to be in a relationship with you. I wish you the best of luck going forwards, but you don't need me, and I don't want you. Krystal.

. . . But also to get back in touch with Cameron at *Styler* and reschedule our interview.

I explained, over a phone call, no less – I was getting better at those – that I had had a panic attack on the day of my initial interview. It was due to an anxiety issue that I was combatting after a break-up and being made redundant. Whether Cameron was also drinking from the 'new year, new start' fountain like I was, or she was simply an understanding and lovely person, she accepted my abject apologies with a brush of, *No worries*, and offered to reschedule the interview for the following week. It took all my resistance not to check my horoscope first, and just agree. But I did it.

The relief I felt – at getting a second chance simply by asking – was so great that I burst into happy tears in the middle of the café I was working from. The hostess brought me a cup of tea and a plate of macarons to cheer me up, on the house. A miracle which led me to cry even harder. What is it with baristas giving me hot beverages when I'm an emotional wreck?

I realised quite soon after New Year's Eve, with the help of Paige and Tina, that everything that had happened before and after my break-up with David had piled up on top of me at such a height that the cascade down was an avalanche of Mount Everest proportions.

Horoscopes were something I was clinging to in the hope that the result would be happiness (which of course begged the question of why happiness wasn't something I already had). At that realisation, I knew it was time to seek proper help for my issues.

It was post-Christmas, so there was obviously a lot of want

for mental health services in London, but after a brief phone call with my GP, I was told that one-on-one counselling wouldn't be available for eight weeks at the earliest. But, before the GP hung up for their next scheduled appointment, they shared some information about a local group counselling session that was being held weekly at a community centre in Camden.

It was run by students at the London City College training to become therapists, who volunteered their time for those in need in between Christmas and Valentine's Day.

At first, I didn't think I was in need of help so direly and thought that I shouldn't take up a place in the group. But my GP said that the fact I had called her to discuss my mental health made it pretty clear that I was worthy of a place.

With encouragement from Paige and Tina, and even my mother (who had accepted my turning away from appeasing the stars with a resigned 'well that's that then' kind of sigh), I decided to attend my first session.

The community centre was really just a back room in a church hall, not far from Camden market. When I entered the room I was met with a rush of comforting scents familiar to me from the astrology classes that Aoife had run. There were a ring of chairs and a group of people huddled together by a hot water machine, surrounded by packets of tea, sugar and sweeteners. Two women, younger than me and most likely the students running the group, were standing over a table organising pamphlets and homework sheets, muttering indecipherably to each other.

I took a deep breath and reached into my pocket for my phone. As much as I was turning my back on astrology, I still kept my tiger's eye in my pocket. Call it a crutch, or simply a tactile piece of rock, it was comforting to have something to fiddle with when I was feeling nervous.

I set a course for the hot water machine, thinking a cup

of coffee would be a good choice, before realising upon grazing the selection of tea bags that only herbal tea and decaffeinated coffee sachets were available, possibly for good reason.

'I recommend the Pukka tea,' a red-haired young woman with braces said to me. She was probably only in her mid-20s, wearing denim overalls splattered with paint– and her hair had a white braid in it that wouldn't look amiss on Captain Jack Sparrow, but she grinned warmly showing off the rail tracks across her teeth.

'These students always spring for the good stuff,' she said, winking at me before jolting her head to the two women at the desk. I smiled and took her advice, ripping open a packet of Sleepy Tea. 'This your first time?'

'Yes,' I said, my voice a little hoarse from my anxiety about attending. I felt like a fraud even then, although no one was staring at me, or asking me why I had thought I wouldn't be welcome.

'Don't be scared,' she said. 'It's just a big conversation. I've been coming for a few weeks now.'

'Really?' she seemed so put together, even if typically Camden-ish with her outfit choice and her wild hairstyle.

'Yeah. Christmas is a lonely time of year, and it's good to know that there's someplace you can go to talk and not feel like a burden on society.'

'I know what you mean,' I said, slipping off my coat and wrapping it over my arm just as the students at the table cleared their throats and asked everyone to take a seat.

'I'm Bernie,' the arty woman, said picking up her plastic cup and heading to a seat. She saved the one next to her for me, patting it gently to signal for me to sit down.

'I'm Krystal,' I told her, gratefully placing my tea on the floor and wrapping my coat around the chair.

After that first interaction, my nerves about group counselling dissipated like steam from my cup of tea. There were no rules, except to listen and not to interrupt, no one had to speak if they didn't want to, and for the most part it was just a general conversation with gentle laughter, the occasional story and anecdote about life.

Of course, some hard topics were hit upon. Bernie was attending the course as she had always struggled with Christmas because her parents were abusive. Never to her, by the sounds of her stories, but towards one another.

Others were there because of loss; anything from a pet they'd had since they were a child, to their parents or a close friend. One person was there because they had recently gone through a divorce and this was the first year that they'd spent without their children on Christmas Day. Another person was there due to work-related stress. Two people said they were lonely, and others were crippled by the sense of being a failure to their families due to unfair expectations.

I spoke a little, mostly offering humorous remarks to lighten the tone – a technique that was picked up on by one of the therapists later in the session. She didn't direct her comments at me, or indeed with any sense of chastisement, but what she said affected me.

'Comedy,' she began, 'is a technique that people often use to avert attention from themselves. It feels easier and better to make someone laugh then to tell someone that you're struggling, just like it's easier to say, 'I'm fine' when someone asks how you are.'

Her partner quickly picked up where she left off. 'I've found, just from talking to people, that it is often a distraction technique used by those who consider themselves people-pleasers or feel overly empathetic towards those around them. Has anyone ever felt that they need to make other people happy before they themselves can feel happy? Maybe at a party, or even at work?'

Hands arose around the circle and I found myself lifting

mine in the air. What the two of them were saying about over-empathising sounded a lot like what my initial birth chart had said about my personality.

I'm afraid of people knowing how hard I try. I'm a people pleaser; I tell people what I think they want to hear and I often struggle to admit my mistakes.

'When my boyfriend cheated on me last year,' I began, speaking before I realised I had even intended too. 'I was convinced that I was to blame. That I wasn't good enough in some way, because I didn't try hard enough. Then I lost my job and my flat all on the same day, for various reasons and again I took on the blame for these incidences. I began to wonder what was wrong with me. I turned to astrology and tarot card readings to explain to me why I was the way I was and why I attracted such bad luck.' I stopped and licked my lips, fearing that the others in the group would roll their eyes and think me silly for turning to something as prophetic as the stars to get to know myself. But no one did. Bernie leant forward a little as if to push me forward in telling my story.

I took a deep breath and continued. 'In trying to change my life, in a really unexpected way, I ended up pushing people away. At the time, I thought I was setting myself on a new path and being really clever, but actually, I ignored my family, my friends and even someone who I think meant more to me than a friend. I was selfish, but not in a way that was beneficial to me, it wasn't self care in any way. I took this feeling that I was to blame, and I interpreted my *research*,' I bent my fingers in air quotes. 'So that everything continued to be my fault and my responsibility to change. It's taken me nearly half a year to realise that I was alienating myself from everyone and I didn't realise, until now – just from talking to you guys – how lonely I've been.' I cleared my throat.

'I didn't let anyone help me – not properly anyway. And when I did ask for help, I thought I was a nuisance and undeserving. That I brought everything on myself because I didn't follow my horoscope one day or because I *did* follow my horoscope another. Whatever happened, it was my fault and I didn't know how break out of that way of thinking.'

I stopped, not really sure if I was getting my point across but knowing that something inside my brain had just clicked into place as I let a truth out that had been eating its way up inside of me. I was afraid of being happy in case I lost it, so I blamed myself and made myself believe I was undeserving of ever being truly happy.

Horoscopes became my crutch; making decisions on my behalf when I was too scared to make them myself due to a fear of the consequences. Since I had finally been able to accept that that way of thinking was unhealthy for me, or obsessive, as Grandad put it so plainly.

Did I really think that my Saturn Return would come along and I would lay all this to rest? That I would finally be happy? No stars or crystals could ever force happiness into a person's life.

'I feel like that as well sometimes,' Bernie said beside me. 'Like, if I ask my parents to help me out by giving me lift then I feel like I'm using up currency with them, and that eventually it will run out. That I need to prove to them that I'm worth the effort and that I am lovable.'

'Same here,' said the recently divorced man. 'Particularly with my kids.'

'And me,' said one of the ladies, who had previously stated that she was never lonelier than when she was in a room full of people.

'I'm a people-pleaser to the extreme,' I told the two therapy students who were smiling softly as they looked around the group.

'The first step to breaking this cycle of self-blame, is to set yourself a task that is entirely doable and write down, before-hand, what you're most afraid of,' said one of the students. The other one picked up a few sheets and a couple of pencils and began to hand them around the room.

'Using this worksheet, we recommend that you each write down something you fear doing; be it organising something that your wife previously looked after . . .' she said to the divorced man. 'Or calling your mother for a chat,' she said to Bernie. 'And then see what happens. Enter your discomfort zone, and instead of predicting the results and then avoiding them, see what actually happens when you undertake an activity you would usually avoid. It might break a cycle in your head that you didn't know about, whereby you're setting yourself up to believe some things that simply aren't true. It's a technique you can do for anything, from choosing a differ-ent carriage to sit in if you're on the tube or going to a differ-ent shop to pay your gas bill.'

'And if something does go wrong, write it down and then break it down.' Said the other therapist, looking towards me now. 'Really look to see where the issues arise, as I expect it will likely have nothing to do with what you were initially afraid of.'

The other student passed a sheet to me and placed a hand on my shoulder as she walked by.

The sheet was simple, and the activity even more so, but I felt the weight of its effects on me like receiving an A+ on a school exam. This was something that would benefit me in the long run. It wasn't theoretical or open to interpretation. This was a healthy and legitimate course of action that I could do to make myself feel better. And I was determined to feel better. And maybe not get obsessive about feeling better this time.

35

Leo: If you're being true to yourself, you should not have trouble overcoming any obstacle . . . the Moon opposes Mercury.

'Well? How did it go?' Paige asked me via FaceTime. Tina was also on the call, currently locked in the teachers' bathroom and whispering into her headphones so that no one could hear us.

'I got the job!' I told them, promenading down the Strand like I was walking on a cloud. The two of them squealed down the phone (or more like squeaked, in Tina's case).

'That's so exciting!' she whispered. 'Well done.'

'I'm glad it went well,' Paige said, beaming at me.

'She was so lovely about the previous interview's no-show,' I explained, already envisioning myself changing my LinkedIn profile to read: *Columnist at Styler.* 'And she was totally okay with the direction I wanted to take the column in.'

'So no more astrology?' Paige asked, teasing out the word astrology a little longer than she needed too.

'Yes and no. The column is going to cover all manner of topics from the increase in popularity for astrology in the twenty-first century, to the fact that the cast of *Harry Potter* are old enough to have children. Plus, what to do if you have a panic attack on the way to an interview – the latter being my first piece.'

'Good for you!' Tina said, tapping two of her fingers together in the quietest round of applause she could muster from her hiding place.

'Yeah, I think it will be quite cathartic.'

'And did it measure up with your predictions?' Paige asked.

Of course, as soon as I had had my first group therapy session I had met up with the girls for cocktail hour in Shoreditch. We ended up going to a cat café. It was Tina's idea, but Paige was so enamoured with the kittens that the two of them were looking at flats together where they could responsibly rehome a cat. I was going to be a Cauntie, pronounced *carn-tee*, in Tina's language. I had spared no details of my therapy with the two of them, and we soon got about plotting my activities together. I had three 'uncomfortable' situations I had to get through that I had negative predictions about.

The first, was my interview with *Styler*. I was terrified that after speaking to Cameron about wanting to write about more than just astrology, she wouldn't want to hire me anymore. But that proved to be false.

As much as she wanted me to keep some elements of astrology in the occasional column, what she mostly enjoyed about my writing on ZodiActually was the way I wrote about how I was changing my life by trying new things and following new rules. We had brainstormed ideas for 30-day challenges that I could undertake, an idea that sparked from telling her about my grandad's habits of changing hobbies every season. The choices were endless: 30 days of trying out a new cuisine across the city – charged to the *Styler* credit card! – 30 days of journaling and 30 days of honestly Instagramming my life, to name a few. After the formal part of the interview, Cameron said she could see the column being more than a short-time assignment for me.

I was thrilled and absolutely buzzing after leaving the building. The feelings of fear that arose (around the magazine suddenly going into liquidation, or Cameron being killed in a hit-and-run before she could draft up my contract) were completely silenced by my ability to cross off my initial fear that she would not want me to work with her anymore. If that fear didn't come true, why would the others?

'I have so many ideas, I can't wait to write them all down.'

'Then go do it!' Paige said supportively. 'Go and find a café, treat yourself to an enormous piece of cake and go crazy.'

'I can't, I have to go and meet Clare.'

'Is that your landlady?' Tina asked, hesitantly checking the door handle of the school bathroom she was crouching in. Honestly, the things my friends did for me made them deserving of damehoods from the Queen.

'Yeah, we're finalising the contract for the flat today, now that I can officially afford to pay rent.'

Paige did a little happy dance on screen for me – I noticed that her assistant came into frame, saw her dancing and immediately left again. 'I'm so excited for you!'

'Calm down Pointer Sisters. One down, two to go.'

Not only did I have to conquer my fears regarding the job at *Styler*, I also had to face Ryan – in whatever capacity I could get him to talk to me – and then I had to handle my Saturn Return in February, despite no longer following my horoscope. All of that hard work had been for nothing, and I was afraid of the consequences I might reap as a result, despite how hard I tried to mimic Paige's cynical attitude towards all of it. After five months of pretty much non-stop obsession, it was hard to relinquish everything I thought I knew and pretend like everything would be fine and dandy.

'Nothing bad is going to happen. I promise,' Paige said, leaning forwards to grin toothily into the camera.

'And if it does – which it won't – we'll never desert you,' Tina said awkwardly.

'We're like your Rick Astley duo,' Paige began, pausing

just so she and Tina could unitedly begin singing 'Never Gonna Give You Up'. Thank God for headphones and the mute button was all I could say.

* * *

'This place is a revelation!' Clare was standing in the middle of the living room and twirling on the spot. She had already inspected the kitchen, filled to the brim with an array of copper-tone and rose gold utensils I had found across Camden market and in various charity shops. She'd laughed at the avocado green bathroom which now had slightly mad flamingo pink wallpaper on one side and a neon light flickering *Get naked* on the other.

The garden still needed to be done, but I figured that it might be better to tackle when the ground wasn't frozen.

My bedroom was fairly neutral, with its sage green walls and white linens, Keith the bonsai sitting healthily on the third-hand dresser Ryan had fixed up for me. Throw cushions were scattered everywhere, as I had since realised the true lesson of my break-up with David: you can never have too many scatter cushions to hand. You never knew when you'd have to chuck them at a cheating boyfriend's head.

'I'm stunned,' Clare said, still spinning. I was worried she was going to make herself dizzy. I came in from the kitchen carrying two matching mugs of tea.

'I'm sorry there's no sofa. That's the one thing I've yet to sort out.'

Using my foot, I pulled out my office chair for her and took up my place on one of the floor cushions. I felt a little like a schoolgirl kneeling at a teacher's feet for story time, but Clare didn't seem to mind.

'I hardly recognise the place. I didn't even know that there was so much space in here. And you've kept it so clean.' As soon as her backside hit the chair she was up again, walking over to my mantelpiece and admiring my knick-knacks, most especially my crystals which I had still yet to get rid of. They had been too much of an expense for me to simply throw away, and too pretty just to give up to charity. I knew I would have to make a decision about them at some point, but for now they were just pretty ornaments.

'The last of your grandma's things are in the box in the hall. I wrapped the tea set in some of the tea towels you said your mum wanted. Plus, her old jewellery box, just in case. Didn't want anything to get damaged.'

'Oh, you are a sweetheart,' she said, returning to focus on me once more. 'And a miracle worker, honestly. I'm so impressed.' She beamed with delight as she took her seat again and sighed. 'It feels like I should be paying you and not sorting out a contract for the other way around.'

I scoffed. 'No, it's fine. It feels about the right time I stopped relying on charity and paid my own way.'

'Well, I'm knocking off £50 a month,' I went to protest but she held up her hand. 'Consider it a repayment for all your hard work. I just know that if the realtor saw this place now, he'd add a whole other zero to the price tag.' That made my stomach clutch. 'Not that I have any intention of selling until you're wanting to move,' she confirmed. 'I keep my word.'

'I trust you,' I told her. 'And I'm really grateful.'

'Decorating this place must have cost you so much. Did you hire a painter and decorator?'

I looked towards my feet, feeling the heat rush to my face as I lifted my tea to drink.

'No,' I told her. 'Ryan helped me with everything. He did most of the painting and built a few bits and pieces here and there. Turns out he's pretty decent at electrics too.'

'Ryan did all this?' she asked, her eyebrows raising above her forehead. She smiled too, knowingly.

'Yeah. He's been a saint.'

'Oh, bless him. He really is a good boy.'

'To be honest, I'd be better off paying him back with that £50 a month. Not that it would cover the labour costs,' I laughed privately. 'I think he's spent as much time in the flat as I have done.'

It did feel as if he had become a part of the furniture, the way he would just appear after a long day at work for a natter and a cup of tea. Which was usually followed closely by a takeaway and some Netflix on my computer screen, not that we ever watched it. We were always too busy talking, working or teasing each other mercilessly.

'Shame he's not around today,' Clare said, practically beaming with matchmaker's delight. 'I would have liked to see him.'

'He hasn't come by in a while,' I told her, drinking some more of my tea as her smile began to fall. 'We had a bit of a falling out.'

'Oh no. I'm sorry to hear that. Still nothing that I'm sure couldn't be fixed over a cuppa. This is lovely by the way.' She lifted her tea mug in the air and quickly began to gulp it down, ignoring the fact it had only just been boiled and was probably scalding.

'I hope so,' I said quietly. 'Have you heard from Aoife at all?' Since I wasn't speaking to Ryan, and my astrology classes had finished before Christmas, I had lost my connection to checking in on Aoife and her condition.

Clare smiled sweetly, but with some sadness around the edges. 'A bit here and there. She's getting by, bless her. But every day is a challenge. It's such a shame as she used to be so active, always training for a half marathon or some obscure sport, our Aoife. Put me quite to shame. I think the only thing I ever trained myself in was to not eat the whole packet of biscuits when I bought them from the shop.' She forced herself to laugh and I smiled with her, thinking that that was actually quite a feat.

'Ryan takes good care of her,' I told her comfortingly. 'And Aoife adores him. I love seeing the two of them together.'

'Oh, isn't it sweet? She always said she would have been a rubbish mother but to that boy she's as good as. Darlings, the both of them.' Clare swallowed the remaining part of her tea and slapped her leg. 'Right, sweetheart, I need to head over to see the lawyers for that meeting to draw up that contract. Consider this my first, and probably last, inspection. I trust you implicitly.'

She stood up and held her arms out for me as I awkwardly pushed myself up from my floor cushion. I really needed to prioritise getting a sofa. 'If you need anything at all, if anything house-y breaks let me know. I'll sort it out.'

'Thanks Clare,' I said, stepping into her overly tight hug.

'And don't you worry about Ryan,' she said, as soon as she had me in her impossible-to-break grasp. 'You two will fix whatever went wrong. I'm sure of it. He may be stubborn but he's a teddy bear, really.'

'A teddy bear.' I laughed – never had I heard Ryan described as something as frivolous and soft as a teddy. 'I'll have to tell him you said that.'

'By all means,' she said, loosening her grip now she had managed to slip in her meddlesome, if well-meant, commentary. 'He's too soft to ever complain to me. And if he did, he knows what kind of response he'll get.'

I didn't even need to imagine with Clare; it probably would have been a short death stare and then death by a thousand hugs. If Ryan was a teddy bear at heart, then Clare was made wholly of fleece and candy floss.

'Thanks Clare.'

'I knew there was something special about you when I met you that day on the tube. I tell everyone at work that it was fate that led me to you, even though I'd never believed in it until then.'

I smiled knowingly, taking her cup from her.

You should take a leaf out of her book, my Mary Berry voice said as I walked Clare to the door and watched her walk out of the mews.

36

Leo: There's an airy, uplifting feeling to the day that you should enjoy ... just before midnight the Moon will trine Mars.

6th February 2022

The dreaded date of my Saturn Return had arrived with what felt like remarkable speed, despite the ups and downs of the last six months.

Since it was part of my behavioural therapy to face the day and then review the consequences later (instead of wallowing at home sitting in the overgrown grass of my neglected back garden staring up at the stars) I found myself in Paige and Tina's flat surrounded by cardboard boxes containing all of their belongings. They were preparing for the epic task of moving into their new joint flat.

'When you said you were looking for a place, I didn't think you meant you *found* one,' I told them, as I helped Paige fold copious amounts of t-shirts and blouses into a box. Tina was unhelpfully sat at the breakfast bar eating peanut butter out of the jar, having one of her many breaks.

'Paige is the most efficient person you've ever met,' Tina pointed out. 'Did you really think that finding a flat was going to be a year-long task with her on the case?'

'Well, with me *and* my team on the case,' Paige said delightedly. She had got her promotion, as we all expected her too. And apparently her first action hadn't been to introduce the new team to each other over doughnuts and Starbucks coffee, but to get them on the trail of hunting for a spacious one-bedroom apartment in Greenwich that allowed for pets.

Paige was paying most of the rent, but what Tina couldn't contribute to financially she was making up for in possessions.

'How did all of this fit in your tiny flatshare?' I asked her, looking over the mountain of boxes which made Clare's grandma appear like a substandard hoarder in comparison.

Paige, with her collection of K-pop band t-shirts from the 90s and tote bags full of Chanel products, was a minimalist compared to Tina with her suitcases of chicken feather jumpers, *Funko Pop!* collection and countless pocket nail kits. Clearly, she had never thrown away or donated a single possession in her life. She shrugged nonchalantly.

'It's surprising what you can fit into a 9 x 10 room when you use every inch of wall space for storage. That's where renters go wrong – they only ever use the floorspace. Amateurs.' Paige and I exchanged amused looks as we finished packing the last item into the box. 'Anyway, how are you feeling. Has Saturn hit its apex yet?' Tina asked, while I handed Paige the duct tape and scissors for the box. I shrugged again.

'Not yet,' I told her. 'I checked and it hits at approximately 4 pm.'

'Still got a couple of hours,' Paige said, encouragingly. I smiled at her and she nodded. There was an unspoken agreement between us not to talk about astrology like it was important anymore, not that Tina had got or would even have listened to that subtle memo.

'It's so exciting!' she beamed, spinning on the bar chair with her peanut butter. 'The next portion of your life is about to begin.'

'So is yours,' I pointed out. 'You two are moving in together.'

'And buying a new sofa,' Paige groaned under her breath. 'Apparently mine doesn't pass muster.'

'It is bloody hard,' Tina said.

'Only when you sleep on it,' I teased, unable to even see the sofa under all of Tina's boxes atop of it.

'I know,' Tina said.

'When do you sleep on the sofa?' I asked.

'When I'm in the dog-house,' Tina joked.

'Tina!' Paige shouted, 'When she *naps!*' she said to me before looking back to her partner of choice. 'Don't make me sound like some tyrannical patriarch.'

'I'm not. More like a tyrannical matriarch. My mum always made my dad sleep on the sofa when he annoyed her. But I think it's mostly because he snored,' Tina laughed, giving a grunt as an example.

'Well, the acorn doesn't fall far from the tree,' Paige mumbled.

'I don't snore,' Tina laughed. But when neither Paige nor I said anything she flushed. 'Do I?'

'Why do you think we're moving?' Paige teased. 'The neighbours complained.'

We all started laughing, and through our laughter and Tina's *I do not!* screams, we nearly missed the knock at the door.

'Did you order takeaway?' I asked Paige, seeing as she would usually be the most organised of the three of us and might have pre-empted our packing with a Just Eat order. She shook her head, avoiding my eyes as she walked to answer the door.

'Come in,' she said, and I leant forwards across the table trying to see who the mysterious guest was who was currently hidden behind all of Tina's packaged belongings.

'It's for you,' Paige said, a little sheepishly, as she appeared, closely followed by Ryan.

He avoided my gaze initially, staying silent. When he finally looked up, the two of us locked eyes for the first time in weeks.

'Ryan,' I said, finally letting go of the inhalation I had taken upon seeing him.

'Leo,' his lip twitched, playfully.

'Tina,' Paige said, clapping her hands together and rocking on her heels. 'I think we should go to the restaurant and put our order in, in person.'

'Why?' Tina said, putting her used spoon in her peanut butter jar as if nothing was at all amiss, although you could cut the air in the room with one of her many nail scissors. 'They already know our order off by heart, we get it often enough.'

'Well, I want to make some changes to my side of the pizza.'

'Why don't you just get your own pizza, for once?' Tina said, grumbling like a teenager being dragged to the supermarket as she hunted for her jacket underneath one of the boxes. 'True love is understanding that you don't want to share,' she whined.

'I wished you'd told me that before I signed the lease on the new flat,' Paige muttered under her breath as she jumped from glaring at Tina with hardly subtle looks to flicking her eyes over to me apologetically. All the while Ryan just stood there, trying not to smile at the stupidity of the scene going on between the two of them. 'Just come on.'

'That's a valuable love lesson, that is,' Tina said, with a sigh. 'You two should take note.' She pointed between me and Ryan as she passed, winking at me as Paige pummelled her out of the flat.

'We'll knock when we're back,' she said to me in a hushed tone before closing the door behind her. Instantly we heard the two shouting at one another down the stairs.

'I *was* subtle!' Was all I heard from Tina before the two of them got into the lift and their voices dissipated.

'Oscar-worthy performance, that,' I said, closing my eyes and shaking my head.

'To be honest, I was expecting Paige to behave more smoothly than she did.'

'It's Tina's effect on Paige,' I said, sighing and opening my eyes to look at him again; he was smiling freely now. 'Ever since the two of them got together she's all lovelorn and sappy. No more Olivia Colman in *Broadchurch*, now, she's much more Olivia Colman in *Hot Fuzz*.'

'Never seen it,' Ryan remarked, folding his arms.

'Which one?'

'Neither. I don't want much telly.'

'You did with me,' I said, moving to the other side of the breakfast bar in the pretence of washing my hands after packing. Duct tape residue still lingered on my fingers and I was picking at it aimlessly, suddenly self-conscious of my hands as Ryan just stood there.

After weeks of waiting for him to call or to text, suddenly he was here, and I didn't know what to say.

'How did the show go?' I asked him, lowering my head a little as the sharp stab of guilt quickened in my chest.

'It went really well,' he said, shrugging and loosening up a little as he came towards the breakfast bar, carefully manoeuvring himself around some boxes. 'Sold a few pieces and got some good reviews. Even got a commission from a gallery in Euston. Not quite Mayfair, I grant, but it was only my first exhibition.'

Instinctively, I wanted to look at him, to show him the beam of pride that had stretched across my face but at the same time something inside me resisted. I was so happy for his success, but so ashamed of the way I behaved that I was afraid to meet his eye, let alone tell him how pleased I was.

He cleared his throat. 'Paige said she was moving.'

'Did she message you?' I asked, now intrigued enough to turn my head a little and turn off the tap that I was running my hands under.

'Yeah. On Facebook.'

'She never told me.'

'I expect that's because I didn't reply to her for a while.'

'Ooh,' I said, cringing at the thought of what Paige must have been like when he finally had. The word 'explosive' came to mind. Paige was not a woman you wanted to ignore, and I know because I had done it accidentally and she had been icy as hell. 'Glad to see you survived.'

Ryan laughed, bucking a little as he leant on the bar, seemingly as chill as anything.

'Yeah. It was a little scary, I've got to admit. And I'm not afraid of much.'

'Except spiders,' I teased.

'Yes, except for spiders. Quite frankly, after the bollocking she gave me, I think I'd have preferred a jar of spiders to be dumped all over my head.'

He chuckled gently to himself. 'I remembered that today was your dreaded Saturn Return.'

I groaned and let my head fall into my arms on the table.

'God,' I mumbled incoherently, feeling myself overheat with embarassement.

'You said that that was the reason why you were doing all this astrology stuff. I asked Aoife about it and she explained some things to me, about how it's the beginning of a new chapter and it can cause your life to up-end itself, if you believe in all of that, anyway.'

I said nothing, just shook my head in my arms.

'I asked Paige what you were doing, and she said she had summoned you over as a distraction. I wanted to pop by, make sure that you were okay. I knew what today meant for you. If it didn't mean so much then maybe you wouldn't have done things the way you did.'

Wincing at his words I finally gave into myself and looked up at him. He was pale and a little gaunt around the eyes, like he hadn't been sleeping very well. I'd hadn't noticed before that he had soft smile lines just starting to appear around his lips and when he was tense his shoulders rose about his ears.

'I'm really sorry,' I said to him.

He shrugged. 'Same. I was a little harsh.'

'And I was a more than a little idiotic,' I argued quickly. 'I didn't mean to get so wrapped in all of this. It was just supposed to be an experiment, a distraction, and it turned into an obsession.'

He shrugged again and stood up straight. 'Still, I should have recognised that and not just cut you off.'

'I'm glad you did,' I said without thinking. 'If you hadn't, I might have just carried on with it all. You were the one who made me realise all the mistakes I was making.'

He pressed his lips together. 'I should have said something earlier or made it clearer how much I wanted you to come to the show.'

My pulse beat heavily against my neck as I forced myself not to childishly start grinning at being desired.

'It was all on me, no one else. It turns out I have a bit of a compulsive, all-in attitude. I have done since I was a child.'

'All-in? Like supreme stubbornness?'

I scoffed. 'Yes, if you want to call it that. *Supreme stubbornness.* That will be the name of my autobiography, or my superhero identity. One of the two.'

'I think mine would be *The Idiot.*'

'I'm afraid Fyodor Dostoyevsky fans might claim that's already taken,' I teased.

'Not the Irish version it's not.'

'Would every chapter have to start with: *what's the craic?*'

'No, probably: *It was a gas.* Particularly when writing the chapters about you.'

I blushed. 'I really hope that my Irish translation is right and *gas* means funny and not funky, because I am a lady I'll have you know.'

He snorted so hard he nearly hit his chin on the bar, and I couldn't help but respond with a similar reaction. The two of us leant over the bar like misbehaving children, cackling so hard it echoed between the boxes and Paige's high ceilings.

This was what it was like with Ryan, easy and fun. Yes, we teased and bickered, but no more so than I did at home with Mum and Grandad. To me, it was almost like being with family – but my extended family, not the kind of family that makes a family tree look like a wreath.

'I've really missed hanging out with you,' I said, rubbing tears of laughter from my eyelids.

'Same. I didn't mean to stay away for so long. But then it was Christmas, then New Year's Eve, plus Aoife's not been well.'

'Oh God, is she okay?' I asked, reaching out and placing a hand on his arm.

'Yeah, she's good now. She just got a really bad cold over Christmas which turned into a chest infection. Add that in with the whole degenerative muscles and basically I was her personal slave for a few weeks.'

'Gosh, if I'd have known I would have come and helped.'

Ryan smiled and placed his own hand over mine on his arm. 'It hardly seemed like the right time, after telling you I needed space, to suddenly text and say can you come over and make dinner for my aunt?'

'You've had my cooking,' I scoffed. 'It's a good thing you didn't, otherwise it might have finished her off.'

'It's not that bad,' he said supportively.

'David used to say I could burn water.' I rolled my eyes.

'David was an idiot, an even bigger one than me. In fact, I might even go so far as to say he was an arse.'

'He *was* an arse,' I agreed.

'I quite enjoyed your scrambled eggs on toast.'

'I add a spoonful of mustard to the mix,' I said proudly, although I knew it was a comment that had the ability to misfire quite quickly. Ryan nodded.

'Secret ingredient.'

'Yep. Adds to the colour as well.' We both laughed again. 'You know, you and I have a remarkable habit of going very off topic very quickly.'

He nodded and stretched out his back, finally releasing my hand and I did the same.

'That we do,' he said. 'And Paige only promised me ten minutes of alone time before she'd be back.'

'How very Arnold Schwarzenegger of her.'

'I trust that she'll keep to her word and be back at ten minutes on the dot.'

'Most likely. And then she'll draft you into the packing process, regardless of your plans for the day.'

'I have no plans,' he said quickly. 'After I told Aoife I was coming here she asked one of the neighbours around for a tea and cake and told me I wasn't allowed home until after they'd had their natter about the latest goings on at the church and the bloody parish council. That could take hours. For an astrological soul she sure does care about her Catholic upbringing. I might have to sleep under a bridge tonight.'

I slapped his arm playfully. 'I would say you could come and sleep at mine, but that seems a bit presumptuous of me.'

'I'm a gent – I'd take the sofa.'

'I still don't have one,' I pointed out.

'Still? What, could you not find a service to help you lift it?' he bantered, lowering his head in his hands. 'That's all I'm good for, for you isn't it. Hard labour.'

'No!' I said quickly, standing next to him against the bar so that the sides of our bodies were touching. 'You mean much more to me than just that.'

'*Just that*,' he repeated, and I elbowed him in the ribs.

'You're one of my best friends, practically a piece of the furniture in the flat. It felt very weird not having you there for a couple of weeks. Plus, not being able to talk to you and share your successes.'

'And vice versa,' he said softly. 'Paige may have filled me in on *Styler* by the way.' I flushed. 'Congratulations. I mean it. You've worked hard for it.'

'Thanks,' I muttered, conscious that I wasn't great at taking compliments and would need to work on that going forward. 'Actually, I was hoping I'd be able to commission you for some work. But obviously, we weren't . . .'

'Whatever you need, Leo,' he said as quick as a hiccup. 'I'm yours.'

We stood there for a moment, our bodies touching so much so that I could feel his ribcage expand with every breath and his muscles tense when he leant over slightly. Without hesitating or making light of the situation like I was wont to do, I allowed him to lean over and kiss me.

It was brief and sweet, nothing like a Regency romance, bodice-ripping kiss that causes fireworks to explode in the background and declarations to run forth like Niagara Falls after a storm. But it was perfectly lovely. Warm, comforting and just what I would have expected from Ryan, the quiet romantic.

'I should have asked before I did that,' he whispered, as he stood up straight again, unable to straighten the smile on his lips. I tilted my head to one side and rolled my lips together, tasting him on me for the first time.

'I wouldn't have said no,' I told him.

He was nodding but not relaxing away from me. There was a current in the air that I was suddenly fluent in translating, which made me aware that he wanted to kiss me again. But I turned on the spot and placed my hands on either one of his shoulders.

'I want to be honest with you. 100%,' I said, and I saw as his face fell. 'I really like you. Like *so* much. And I'm really happy you're back in my life and don't you dare leave me again,' I playfully slapped his shoulder which made him laugh. 'But I just figured out how to be single and happy, and as much as I want this ...' I flourished a hand between the two of us and he caught it and held it against him after a moment. 'I need some time.'

He nodded, biting his lip and continuing to hold my hand to his chest while my other rested on his shoulder like we were attempted the first statuesque waltz. It would be all the craze on the next season of *Strictly*.

'I understand,' he said quietly, and leant forward to kiss my forehead. Just as a wrap of knuckles on the door indicated that Paige and Tina had arrived home.

'Ten minutes,' I said, exhaling loudly as Ryan released my hand after one final squeeze and looked towards the door.

'You've got to admire her punctuality,' he joked. 'Do you think the world would start spinning off its axis if she was even a minute late?'

'I dare you to ask her,' I said winking at him as I went to answer the door. Paige and Tina bustled in, apparently in a heated discussion about the difference between mozzarella and gorgonzola on a cheese base.

'This may be the most important conversation we have ever had in our relationship!' Tina was screaming as if she hadn't just walked into a scene. Paige's eyes were darting from me to Ryan as she laid out three pizza boxes in a cardboard stack.

'What'd you get?' I asked with a cheery grin, my muscles as loose as a ragdolls as I went to help.

'Pizza!' Tina screeched from the kitchen where she was collecting plates, as if she hadn't made that quite clear already.

Paige wrapped an arm around my shoulder and pulled me into her.

'I love pizza,' Ryan said, clapping his hands together and heading behind the bar to help Tina.

'Thank you,' I whispered to Paige as I rested my head on her shoulder momentarily.

'Men . . .' she sighed. 'Better late than pregnant, ay,' she said, patting me once on the shoulder before releasing me and quickly opening the boxes to dish out our takeaways. 'I've got garlic dip!'

37

Leo: A burst of inspiration can lead to a rewarding journey . . .
Mars resides in your 12th house.

'So this commission . . .?' Ryan said, standing in my garden lifting a hefty sledgehammer onto his shoulder. He looked at me questioningly.

'It's a surprise,' I said, walking out from the kitchen with a covered tray and placing it on the overgrown grass. The interior of the house might have been finished but there was still the garden to tackle come spring. 'I'm writing my final blog post on ZodiActually and I would like to have a few before and after photos to showcase.'

'And the before and after involves a sledgehammer?' he swung the heavy hammer down and it nearly landed on his foot.

'Careful,' I jumped, almost falling into him. He caught me and I stumbled backwards. I may have said I needed time, but that didn't mean our gentle breakthrough with regards to physical contact had needed a break too. We were now more comfortable in each other's presence than ever before. So much so that he had fallen asleep on my sofa – or Paige's old one – when I was making us dinner one night, so I left him there with a blanket and a glass of water and texted Aoife to say he was with me.

The emoji reply I got back from his aunt was highly unexpected – taco and aubergines had been involved although I expect innocently since the message was simply: 'He must have really enjoyed the dinner you made him'. It did make me giggle.

'I have to do my reveal,' I said to him, getting an edge of the towel covering the tray and starting a countdown. He patted his thighs in a drumroll as I pulled it back with a flourish and shouted: 'Voila!'

'It's your crystals?' he said, looking down at my collection of selenite, tiger's eye, rose quartz and turquoise. Everything I had ever bought from Andrik was on the tray ready for him to smash to smithereens – excluding my thumbstone, which was my equivalent to a fidget spinner. 'Really?' he said as I told him his task.

'Yep. I want all of them smashed into tiny little pieces.'

'Why?' his eyebrows rose.

'Because when they're all tiny, we're going to use them in some upcycle projects.' I returned to the kitchen doorway with a turn of heel and reappeared with a bundle of wooden frames, a bamboo mirror and a suede lampshade. 'I want to take the crystals and use them for decor.'

'Aha, so this is another one of your hot glue projects.'

'And yours,' I reminded him. 'Since we added those tassels to your website shop, they've been going out of stock quicker than we can keep up making them.'

'Still seems weird to be a serious artist who sells tassels,' Ryan said, provocatively.

'It's not just tassels though. Soon you can add your other upcycle projects too. Like those art prints from your classes that you said you were going to let me have to make into notecards and prints, not to mention the stickers we can make with your star and Moon designs from my desk.'

'This is all theoretical,' he reminded me, leaning on the sledgehammer. What was it with men and tools, and always having to lean on them like they're so tough? I scoffed and took it from him, surprised by the weight of it in my hands.

'It's a secondary income to support you if you ever have a dry spell. As a freelancer, I know the benefits of having multiple income streams. This will be good for you.' I wagged my finger at him, and he batted it away playfully, knowing full well that I was right.

'Come on then,' he said, finally. 'How are we going to do this?' he tilted his head towards the crystals and reached over to the tray where two pairs of safety goggles were waiting.

'Safety first,' I handed him his goggles and slipped mine on over my head.

'Very fetching.'

'Shut up,' I blushed, as I walked over to the tray, picked up one of the bigger crystals and placed it on a piece of tarpaulin that I had already prepared further up the garden.

'Be careful,' Ryan said, following me closely.

'I think this is going to be quite liberating,' I said, preparing to lift the sledgehammer up to my shoulder and back down again in order to smash them to bits. 'Like one of those rage rooms where you get to destroy things for fun. Or a driving range.'

'Hitting balls is a pastime for you?' Ryan's voice went a little high-pitched and I ignored the innuendo.

The sledgehammer really was quite heavy, and it took a lot of effort to bring it down effectively to even chip at the crystal. After a few goes I got the hang of it and even managed to miss bringing it down on my foot or between my legs. The selenite I had chosen splintered off into pieces across the tarpaulin.

'Your turn,' I told Ryan after a few swings, feeling breathless and expecting I looked rather like Bridget Jones after she puts her blusher on in the dark taxi.

'Bring it on,' Ryan said with glee, taking the sledgehammer

and barely leaving me time to get to a safe distance away before he brought it down so hard on the crystal that pieces flew off in every direction.

'Careful!' I shouted, and he just laughed. Boys and their toys.

* * *

After a purifying afternoon of destroying crystals and then collecting all of the pieces into buckets, we returned to the living room to get to work on our projects.

Ryan's eye was particularly useful when it came to decorating the frames, and I spent the majority of the afternoon making us tea and refilling a bowl of crisps with Doritos as he hot-glued away merrily. While he did the hard labour, as ever, I added more to his website which was live and already getting tons of traffic as a result of his exhibition.

The reviews of his photographs had been better than he'd made out. *Time Out* called his pictures: *Captivatingly modern, without a hint of insincerity.* The *Evening Standard* referred to him as the best up-and-coming artist in years, and even artists like Damien Hirst had left one-word reviews like *Exquisite* and *Dominating.*

Of course, as soon as I found these reviews, I plastered them onto nearly every page of his website until Ryan told me that his humility was now in jeopardy. Every artist needed an ego, I just happened to be his and he happened to be mine.

When my first column about mental health and astrology was printed in *Styler*, Ryan not only asked me to sign the magazine for his own personal use but he secretly added a page to his website – likely with Paige or Tina's help as, God knows, he's hopeless at technology – just to share a link to ZodiActually and my own profile. If his website was getting traffic, he said, then he was going to use it just as much to share my work as his own.

'First one's done,' he said to me, as I typed up my draft of my next digital column. He had used the selenite and turquoise in conjunction with one another, plus little snippets of glass, to create a gorgeous A4 photo frame.

'Perfect!' I said, reaching for my phone to take a quick snap to share on Instagram and to send to the girls.

Paige: *STUNNING!*
Tina: *I'll have one in green please.*
Paige: *Green? Where would we put that? It would not match the decor.*
Tina: *Since when do things need to match?*
Tina: *LOOK AT US!*
Paige: *Tina 1. Paige 0.*

'What are you going to put in it, do you think?' Ryan asked, laying the frame down carefully as he got back to work gluing the rest of them.

'I was thinking my university certificate or my first published article. An achievement of some kind.'

'Not a photo?' he laughed.

'Most of my photos are on here,' I said, holding up my phone. Like most of my generation, Facebook was my photo album, and Instagram was where I put my photo frames. 'I do have one that I want to hang up, though. Hold on.'

I got up from Paige's old sofa, smothered in scattered cushions to make it remotely comfortable, and headed to my bedroom. On top of my dresser with Keith the bonsai was a polaroid photo strip. I picked it up and returned to the living room. 'This one I want framed.'

I handed it down to Ryan who's face lit up upon recognition of the strip.

It was us on Halloween. The first two photos included the four of us trying desperately to shove ourselves into a booth with Tina's gargantuan pink tulle dress, plus the wine bottle she had stolen from the bar, and the third was of Paige kicking Tina out while Ryan and I laughed manically in the background.

The last photo was just of Ryan and I, in our couples-costume of Phoebe Waller-Bridge's character in *Fleabag* and the hot priest, staring at each in absolute fits. It was the most joyous photo I owned of myself.

'Yeah,' Ryan said, grinning so widely his laugh lines increased in size. 'That deserves framing.'

He handed it back to me and I placed it carefully on the desk that he had made for me, smoothing it out before I returned to lounging on the sofa with my laptop on top of a cushion and he sat with his back resting at the other end gluing crystals into the frames.

Styler had its own horoscope page. Today's said I should be prepared to weather romantic storms, but I didn't think I had much to worry about.

It wasn't a day of perfect happiness like I'd hoped to find after my Saturn Return – but it was perfect for me.

EPILOGUE

When I started this blog, I was in a dire place. Not physically, as I was in my best friend's flat and her interior design skills put even *Queer Eye*'s Bobby Berk to shame, but emotionally and mentally.

As I sat moping around, bloated from drowning myself in Merlot and chips, still crying about my ex-fiancé's wayward ways, I turned to the internet as most millennials do. My Google search bar was filled with the typical information requests:

List of movies to watch post-break-up
List of movies to watch post-break-up that don't feature Katherine Heigl
Where to buy revenge glitter kits
Destination holidays for horse riding escape trips
Peng break-up haircuts
Where is the nearest nunnery?

Your typical 20-something year old's over-dramatic search bar. I also added in a search for: *When is my Saturn Return*.

My friend had mentioned the astrological phrase the night before, after the initial break-up, and follow-up fiascos. To say it intrigued me would be an understatement. In need of information about this astrological phenomenon that I decided was responsible for my sucky life at this point, I ravaged the local library for books on the subject and hauled Google until the 108th results page in pursuit of answers, looking anywhere but at my own life and choices.

As dedicated readers of ZodiActually will know, your Saturn Return happens approximately every 29.5 years and signals the beginning of the next stage of your life. If astrology isn't your thing then you could break it into three easy segments: your quarter-life crisis, your mid-life crisis and end of life crisis. And, if you reach the ripe old age of 118: the epiphany!

My Saturn Return was in February, a few weeks ago now, and was remarkably uneventful.

The months beforehand were full of your typical peaks and pitfalls, as much as any other eventful portion of my life thus far. But at the time, I was convinced that everything was to do with the stars and my dedication to following them was crucial. I took inspiration from slaves of the Greek Gods, disciples and divinities, and threw myself at the stars' mercies.

I've since relinquished my horoscope's power over me and gone back to the more traditional ways of following my stars: theoretically and not astrologically, which is why my posting on ZodiActually has dropped drastically since the New Year.

In my last post, I shared in-depth details about my experience of preparing for my Saturn Return, complete with details of tarot cards readings, my now dismantled – or should I say destroyed – crystal collection, and more. The response was astronomical – if you can forgive the pun. Many of you were surprised that after such a dedicated run of following my horoscope and being so astrologically minded that I would be so willing to leave behind my astrological life.

I recently delved back into the books about Saturn Return – with the help of the super talented astrologer Aoife McQueen, who has become something of a part-time spiritual guide for me – for an article I wrote for *Styler* about my experiences. The research revealed that Saturn might be a social planet, but it is also known as the Great Malefic. Its transits across the galaxy are often met with a foreboding sense of dread, due to the change it brings about in a person's life.

We are creatures of habits who don't take lightly to realisations that our lives need to change, even when it's for the better, and our Saturn Return is supposed to trigger just such a realisation. Whether you want to believe in it or not, it *was* around the time of my Saturn Return that I realised that I needed to reassess my life. Although, the cynic in me – slowly coming back out of its shell post-Return – reminds me that my break-up, redundancy and homelessness came months before my Saturn Return was supposed to hit.

Honestly, dear star siblings, I don't know what to believe anymore. A part of me wants to wipe everything I learned about astrology, birth charts, Saturn Returns and crystals under the metaphorical carpet. But another part of me wants to hold on to some elements, finding comfort in the idea of a higher power that isn't a divinity or some dictatorial presence determining our lives.

What I have decided, though, is that this will be my last post on ZodiActually.

A wise man – no, not a mystic man or a psychic – once told me that I should follow my heart and not my horoscope, and he was right. Of course, he was right, he's my grandad.

If something is truly in the stars, then surely it will be in my heart, too, mistake or otherwise.

Maybe one day I'll return to sharing some new adventures or learnings about astrology – I'll admit to still having one foot in the door a little.

But with my new job at *Styler* and the extra-curriculars I find myself partaking in – I've started a side hustle designing websites, my best friends have me decorating their flat with/for them, and I've signed up to a digital art class – ZodiActually has reached its apex for now.

My crystal collection is now spread about my flat in the

wonderful format of a gallery wall, my tarot card collections have been used to make a stunning coaster collection – available to purchase at *Ryan McQueen Photography and Art*, if you're interested – and the horoscope app has been deleted from my phone.

Although ... I did manage to sneak one last look at my horoscope today in honour of ending my journey at ZodiActually.

It said: *Love and romance will begin going well for you this month.*

I know a certain someone who might be pleased to hear that. And my mother will be delighted!

Until we meet again, star siblings, in this life or another. May your chakras be aligned, your crystals never crack and your planets ... do whatever the hell planets do.

THE END

ACKNOWLEDGEMENTS

Firstly, thank you for reading this book. As someone who works in the book industry, I know that it is no mean feat to grab a reader's attention enough for them to finish a story. I'm overwhelmed, therefore, that you chose to read mine.

Endless thanks to my agent, Hannah Weatherill. I'm so glad we met at that party, and that you still remembered me six months later when I awkwardly landed in your inbox. Also, special thanks to the Northbank team for being so bloomin' lovely: Lorna, Sophie, Diane and James.

To my creative partner-in-crime and editor extraordinaire, Bea Fitzgerald. Thank you for nurturing this book with your cool wit and stunning one-liners. Not to mention your acting props – the sales video is everything!

To the wider Hodder Studio team, thank you for being a part of Team Planet:

- Marketing: Callie Robertson
- Publicity: Niamh Anderson
- Production: Claudette Morris
- Copy-editor: Christina Webb
- Proofreader: Aruna Vasudevan
- Designer: Kate Brunt
- Cover Designer: Holly Ovenden
- Audio editor: Ellie Wheeldon

And to the wonderful sales teams, booksellers, reviewers and readers who helped people to hear about this book. I'm beyond grateful. In fact, I'm *super-utterly-immeasurably* grateful!

To my family – particularly my beyond-supportive and brilliant parents – thanks for putting up with my constant 'I need a writing weekend' declarations and 'I'll be upstairs if you need me … so don't need me' sass while writing this book in lockdown. Not only did you accept my pretentious 'I'm a writer' exclamations, you also kept me in ready supply of coffee, biscuits and anecdotes for me to use in my stories. I love you loads.

To my best friend, Freyja. You're the manager of a cat café and I'm an author! See, dreams really do come true. Thanks for being my dynamite cheerleader throughout it all. And to Nini, my little sister from another mister.

To my mentors and inspirations across the years: Phoebe Morgan, Francesca Riccardi and Christine Alison – and my wider Bybrook fam. Thank you for raising me from my bubbly 'calm-down-love' depths and always offering me wisdom and advice.

And finally, to the Books before Boys club – Holly Domney, Siân Heap and Clare Holloway. Thank you for letting me rant, rave and pilfer bits of our WhatsApp conversations. I could never have done this without you guys.

ABOUT THE AUTHOR

Ellie Pilcher is based in London and works as a marketing manager in the publishing industry. She is also a journalist, blogger and public speaker. She writes and speaks about a variety of topics including careers, lifestyle and zero waste activism, and has previously written for *Glamour*, *The Telegraph*, *Huffington Post*, among others.

Find out more about Ellie at www.ellesbellesnotebook.co.uk